TRIPLE JEOPARDY

TRIPLE JEOPARDY

RICHARD MASON

BWM Books Pty Ltd

Edited by Peggy Shaw and Ruth Silver

1

Terror

Tripoli, Libya, Oct. 14, 2011, 9 p. m.

A shrill, penetrating sound rattled windows and elicited screams from several women as a whistling mortar shell dropped toward the compound. There was a moment of panic, as the occupants of the room huddled against an interior wall an instant before the rebel mortar shell exploded in the courtyard. It hit only a few feet from the building's north wall, and a blinding blast, then a wave of destruction, sent a hail of metal and fire toward the compound, shaking the walls, and spewing shrapnel that shattered windows and sent raw steel slashing into the room. One jagged piece of shrapnel ripped into a guard cowering near a window, and sent him staggering across the room, blood gushing from his abdomen.

A piercing scream echoed throughout the room as the young man grabbed his midsection and staggered toward the doorway, only to collapse on the threshold where blood quickly pooled around his dying body. A gray fog of acrid smoke from the explosion drifted into the room contributing to the chaotic scene. A wail of despair reverberated from the assemblage of family members and remaining government ministers, who huddled together against the protected inside wall. It was a scene reminiscent of Dante's hellish prose and seemed to suspend reality as if the room were floating in space. Fear swept through the room like a tidal wave of misery, punctuated by the grisly horror of a surreal catastrophe.

The scene had changed dramatically during the past two weeks from cheering crowds in Green Square to a huddled group of Gaddafi loyalists who were now trapped in the President's compound as the rebels slowly tightened their noose around the remaining loyal defenders of the regime. A deathlike gloom hung over the compound.

Gen. Yusif Gaddafi, who had been pacing back and forth, braced himself against an interior wall as soon as he heard a whistling motor shell dropping toward the compound. And although he gripped a marble pillar partially supporting a massive door frame, he still staggered from the reverberating shock. He managed to steady himself, and, surveying the scene, he realized the seriousness of the matter. It was the beginning of what Gaddafi knew was the end of resistance in Tripoli. He steadied himself, brushed fragments of shattered glass from his uniform, and rushed into the next room where his father lay sprawled on a reclining couch, oblivious to the mortar.

Yusif's eyes were flashing and his hands trembled. His face mirrored desperation. It was long past time to leave this country and live in luxury with the money his family had put away safely in Luxembourg. He had begged his father to leave weeks ago, but the old man was delusional and refused to leave. Now it was too late—much too late. His mind flashed; *I must start the alternative plan—yes; I have no choice. I must do what is necessary.*

The women in the room were huddled together, sobbing, and a medic was trying to minister to the dying guard lying in the doorway. Yusif knelt by his father, and tried to make himself heard above the chaotic clamor of the sobbing women and the dying screams of the guard.

"Father, it's time; we must leave Tripoli, or we'll all be captured or killed before morning!" Yusif's body was trembling, but there was no response from his father, who ignored the pleas from his son. Yusif shook his head in frustration, knowing the old man's drug-abused mind couldn't comprehend the seriousness of the situation.

Yusif pulled on his father's arm, and tried to rouse him from a dazed stupor, but his father continued to ignore him. Gen. Muammar Gaddafi merely glanced up. A glassy-eyed stare from under the brim of his cap was his only answer. Gaddafi was dressed in a full, five-star general's uniform, but even in a resplendent regalia, he looked disheveled and disoriented. Saliva ran down a scraggly mass of a scratchy, patchy beard. Both shoes were untied and his tie was merely draped around his neck. The General's hat was pulled down over his eyes, and he seemed to be either in a mild coma, stupor, or drug-induced haze. Yusif tugged at his father's arm trying desperately to rouse him.

Finally, a frustrated Yusif managed to get his father's attention. Gen. Gaddafi raised his head slightly, seemed to recognize his son, and nodded, "What is it, Yusif? I am very tired, and I was trying to get a bit of sleep."

Yusif took a deep breath, and, in obvious frustration, shouted at his father.

"The rebels will be at the compound in less than an hour! They will kill us all or they will take us prisoner! You have heard how they have tortured some of our loyal soldiers! We should have fled to Niger last week, or at least gone to Sirte. If we don't leave Tripoli within the hour, our family will be killed—Father, get up!"

Yusif pulled his father into a sitting position, moved his face until he was only inches away from his father's ear, and continued to plead with the General.

"Father, please *listen* to me! We cannot stay here. Only a few loyal soldiers are left here in the compound, and the rebel scum are coming with thousands! Don't you realize what is about to happen? We have lost the war, and those rebel beasts from Benghazi will kill all of us when they arrive. The devils have arrived, and you know how they hate our tribe. They have wanted to kill us for years, and now they are—at this very minute—less than an hour from the compound!"

When Yusif mentioned Benghazi, Gaddafi seemed to comprehend at least some of his son's last statement as he heaved himself to a sitting position, shoved his hat back from over his eyes, and shook his fist. His eyes were bloodshot from drugs and lack of sleep. He slurred his answer, but shouted it as if he were speaking to a crowd in Green Square.

"Yusif, my son—the true Libyan people of Tripoli will never let the scum from Benghazi touch me! Stop this talk about leaving! Go get General Mohammad, the head of security. He will tell you how thousands are, at this very minute, coming from Green Square to protect us. We will be fine. Do not worry. My people love me, and they will lie in the streets to keep the rebel bitch dogs from harming me. If you do not believe me, go ask General Mohammad. He will tell you we are safe."

Yusif realized the futility of trying to reason with the man and then hurried off to find Gen. Mohammad el-Hisami. He rushed into the compound's courtyard where he found Gen. el-Hisami trying to organize the few remaining loyal Libyan soldiers into a defensive force. They were a pitiful group, and as the General exhorted them, Yusif spotted several soldiers slipping out the compound gate—dropping their weapons and discarding their uniforms as they ran. It was a depressing sight.

"General, can we hold the compound?"

"No, Yusif—look at these soldiers. Most of them have never been in combat, and they are melting away—throwing off their uniforms and running when they see the rebel dogs approaching—look there is another one leaving us!"

"Then we must at least go to Sirte, General."

"Yes, I know, and I've told your father, but he refuses. I've assembled eight cars and trucks, and if your father agrees we will head there now. But we must hurry. The rebels are within mortar range, and I expect to see some of their trucks with .50-caliber machine guns approaching the compound within the hour. Those trucks the filthy rebels have may not look like much, but a .50-mm machine gun is a very serious weapon, no matter now it is used. They may attack the compound with as many as a dozen trucks, and they will overwhelm our troops in just a matter of hours."

"That is exactly what my sources say—Follow me, General; we must make my father leave immediately."

Yusif hurried across the compound yard with Gen. el-Hisami following him. As they turned their backs to the few soldiers remaining there, Yusif glanced over his shoulder and was astonished to see most of the remaining troops rushing through the main gate, discarding their uniforms and tossing their weapons aside.Seconds later, Yusif rushed into the inner family residence with an obviously distraught Gen. el-Hisami following him.

Gaddafi struggled to his feet and walked over to meet his security chief, who—before even acknowledging Gen. Gaddafi—blurted out, "My General, we must leave immediately! The filthy rebels from Benghazi are even now in Green Square! They are destroying our last checkpoint on the road to the compound as I speak. We must go to Sirte where the By-Rania-El -Gamal tribe—your tribe—can protect you! It is the only way to assure your safety, and the safety of those of us who are loyal to you!"

Gaddafi slowly comprehended the seriousness of the situation, but in a drug-induced fog tried to dismiss the threat. He grabbed Gen. el-Hisami by the shoulders, tried to collect his thoughts, and slurred, "But where are the thousands from Green Square that just a few days ago swore they would protect me with their lives? You told me a hundred thousand men were there chanting their loyalty to me. Surely, that many men will stop the rebel scum from coming into my compound!"

"They have vanished, my General, and thousands of our soldiers have thrown their uniforms away to keep from being killed. The last of our loyal troops were chased out of the Square yesterday afternoon, and tonight the rebel bitch dogs are in Green Square. Our spies have told me dozens of trucks with .50-caliber machine guns mounted on the back, will be coming to attack the compound in only a few hours. We cannot stay here. I can count on only a few dozen men to defend the compound. We cannot possibly hold out for more than a few hours. We must leave immediately!"

"I cannot believe this, but I must trust you."

"Come, General, I have already loaded our staff and your closest associates into several cars and trucks. We will leave the compound in less than ten minutes. I've contacted our commander in Sirte. He assures me that we are in full control there, and he can repulse any attack. You have many friends in Sirte. It is our only hope."

Gaddafi dropped his hands to his side, realizing the gravity of the situation as Gen. el-Hisami took him by the arm, and started for the waiting covey with the last contingent of loyalists, Yusif moved alongside his father and whispered in his ear. It was the plan. The message seemed to resonate, and the General, who, seconds before, had seemed defeated, suddenly seemed to emanate a burst of energy. And just before he left the room, Gaddafi straightened up, stopped in the doorway, and defiantly yelled, "I will slap their faces with a blow they will never forget! From Sirte, we will deliver hell! Something that will shake the world, and scatter the Benghazi scum and the bitch dogs of NATO!"

Astonishment was on the faces of everyone in the compound. but Yusif's. *Yes, the plan! When everything else fails the plan will save me!* As the last group of assorted soldiers, ministers, and family members rushed out to waiting trucks and cars, Yusif stopped, pulled out his Blackberry, and sent a quick text: **Leaving for Sirte—make plans to intercept when we head south.** Yusif smiled grimly as he watched dozens of crying women and panicked men trying to board the few cars and trucks available. He had just initiated the plan.

The scene turned into a panicked rush to board the various cars and trucks, reminiscent of the last helicopter flight from Saigon. Gen. Yusif made sure he was not in the lead vehicle, knowing NATO planes usually took out the first two or three units. His father was placed in a BMW near the middle of the eight-car convey, and Yusif followed Gen. el-Hisami to the waiting car behind the BMW. As the convoy drove out of the compound dozens of screaming men and women chased after the caravan. Trucks and cars headed east, down the coast, and Yusif asked the General about the security situation in the city

"Mohammad, do we control this part of the city?"

"No, Yusif; the rebel scum from several neighborhoods have taken up arms that were smuggled in, and we're nearly sure to encounter some resistance. However, by traveling at night, and with hooded lights, we will have a much better chance of getting out of Tripoli. The rebels are very disorganized, and I have four of my best men on motorcycles riding ahead of us. They will destroy any checkpoints manned by the rebels before we get to them. I just hope we don't encounter any of the Benghazi rebels patrolling neighborhoods that we'll be passing through. They will be in trucks with fifty-caliber machine guns mounted in the back. Their guns would rip this convoy to pieces."

"What about the road to Sirte?" asked Gen. Yusif.

"We control the road and, of course, Sirte. However, we will not be able to evade the French warplanes that patrol the airspace. The American AWAC's will pick up the convoy as it leaves Tripoli and pass the word on to the French. I have instructed all of our drivers to fly the Red Crescent from their cars and hang rebel flags on the trucks. That worked last month, but the rebel scum have told NATO that we are using their flags and the Red Crescent to ward off attacks. We'll be very lucky if all our vehicles reach the safety of Sirte."

In a few minutes, the convoy was speeding through dark streets littered with burned-out military trucks. Yusif had just begun to lean back in his seat and relax when he heard automatic weapon fire coming from behind the convoy. Gen. el-Hasime's walkie-talkie lit up and a frantic soldier screamed, "General, we are under attack! Two trucks—fifty-caliber machine guns! *Ahaaaaaaaaa!...*"

Yusif looked behind them in time to see two rebel trucks, with .50-caliber machine guns mounted in the back, roar out of a side street with guns blazing. The gunners had turned their weapons on the truck bringing up the rear, and in seconds, a hail of bullets ripped through the windshield sending the truck, loaded with Gaddafi's security detail, crashing into a light pole. Then it turned over, blocking the narrow street.

Injured soldiers crawled out of the overturned truck, trying to surrender, but in seconds the two rebel trucks' machine-gunners turned their weapons on the survivors of the ambush and sent an unrelenting carnage of lead at the wounded. It was all over in seconds. The rest of the convoy never slowed, and as the burning truck blocked the street, the rest of the fleeing Gaddafi family entourage left the city, heading east along the coast road.

2

Execution

NATO Patrol, AWAC Tail 343, monitoring Tripoli airspace

"Central Command, this is AWAC 343, do you read me?…over."

"Loud and clear, 343. What have you got?…over."

"A convoy of seven trucks and cars has just turned onto the coast road in the direction of Sirte. Revolutionary fighters knocked off one of the trucks before it left the city. The trucks are flying Red Crescents and have rebel flags, and several cars in the middle look like government cars. I've contacted rebel command, and they assured me, this is not one of their convoys …over."

"Got it, 343. Will alert HQ and see if they want to knock it out. Could be some of Gaddafi's ministers, or, hell, maybe even the old son-of-a-bitch himself…over and out. "

***

Libyan Governmnet Covoy near Sirte, Libya

As they approached the outskirts of Sirte, Gen. Yusif began to relax, knowing that if the convoy made it into the city, NATO planes, fearful of inflicting civilian causalities, would not attack it.

"I've never been so glad to see Sirte, Mohammad," said Yusif.

But Gen. el-Hissim looked worried. "I think I heard the sound of a jet. We may not be safe yet."

"But we're nearly behind the old city walls. Surely the French Mirage jets won't attack when we are this close to town."

"You never know, Yusif. We have seen them attack when the AWAC's tell them no civilians have been spotted in the vicinity, and since it's well after midnight, we are by ourselves on this road. Don't relax just yet."

Yusif shook his head, thinking Gen. el-Hissami was being overly cautious, but just as he leaned back, thinking about the coming days and his plans, there was an explosion, and then the roar of a jet as a plane went over. The convoy came to a halt and Yusif jumped out to check the damage. The lead truck in the convoy had suffered a direct hit and was burning in the ditch. There are no survivors.

"Don't stop! Drive around the truck, and do not stop until we reach the villa! And drive as fast as you can!" screamed Yusif to the soldier who was now lead driver—a man still sitting in shock from the bomb explosion that narrowly missed his own truck. The convoy began to move again, and two additional explosions from French Mirage jet fighters announced that they were not through with the convoy. Yusif looked back to see the two trucks bringing up the rear turn into a flaming mass of fire and steel.

The remaining three trucks and two cars finally roared into Sirte, and in a few minutes they had reached the relative safety of the inner city.

It was well past midnight when the convoy arrived at Gaddafi's lavish villa, located near the center of the city. After the trucks and cars were unloaded, Gen. Yusif motioned for Gen. el-Hassaime to follow him into a private room.

"Mohammad, we need to check the security in the city. In the last few days, our supposedly loyal troops have suddenly vanished. I want to make sure we have the fighters available to repel any attack by the rebel scum."

Gen. el-Hassaime waved a driver over and they began to drive around the outskirts of Sirte to see the condition of the pro-Gaddafi fighters who were manning checkpoints on the edge of the city. As Mohammad's driver wove in and out of the narrow streets, Yusif was shocked at the few remnants of pro-Gadafi loyalists who were still manning their posts. Only around the harbor and on the coast road did he find adequate security.

Yes, the coast road is still in our hands. We can easily move the material into the city and then south, Yusif thought. But the city will fall in days. I must hurry and get everything done.

Yusif returned to the villa at 3 a.m. and fell across the bed exhausted. However, before he dropped off to sleep he told his aide to wake him at 6. *I can't waste any time. The material must be loaded today, and the earlier we start, the better it will be.*

At 6 the next morning, Gen. Yusif struggled to his feet, wiping the sleep from his eyes, and hurriedly dressed. He was rounding up a security detail in minutes, and soon his driver was proceeding through the empty streets followed by a bevy of heavily armed soldiers in three trucks.

"Take the coast road and watch for a side road that leads toward the cliff," Yusif instructed the driver. "I'll tell you where to turn." In less than 35 minutes, after leaving the edge of Sirte, Yusif spotted at heavily wired compound with a large metal gate heavily guarded by soldiers with automatic AK .47s. Two bunkers with anti-tank weapons were positioned on either side of the gate.

As they pulled up to the gate, Gen. Yusif waved his photo pass at the nearest soldier, who buzzed for the gate to be opened. Yusif directed his driver to stop at a door that had been cut into the side of the cliff. As soon as Yusif entered the room, Colonel Hasid Segundo, who was in charge of the facility, came out to greet him.

"General Yusif, I thought you were still in Tripoli. What are you doing here so early in the morning?"

"Colonel, the situation has gotten much worse in Tripoli, and my father decided it is time to use all the weapons that we hid from the NATO inspectors in order to suppress the rebellion."

"You mean the radioactive material we have in the cave?"

"Yes, and also the biomaterial."

"General, as you know, this material could cause a tremendous number of casualties if it is used in a population center."

"Yes, we know, and that's why we have decided to move it to the central part of the desert where we can demonstrate to the

NATO dogs that they must stop the bombing where we can destroy the rebels. After we explode a small nuclear bomb, they will stop the bombing of our troops and come to the negotiating table.

Of course, we will threaten to use one of the SCUD missiles we acquired from Iran to launch toward a Western city. It is the only way for us to stop the rebel dogs from taking our country. But we would never launch the missile."

"Yes, that's a good plan, General. I was very worried that the biomaterials would be used on the NATO cities, where it would kill hundreds of thousands of people."

"Don't worry, Colonel. My father would never harm innocent people. Have you arranged for the material to be moved?"

"Yes, General. Just as you ordered. We have it loaded on two specially equipped trucks, double-encased in lead. Two other identical trucks will go along as decoys. The biomaterial is loaded on another smaller truck. We have painted Red Crescents on all the trucks, but that may not stop the NATO dogs from bombing them. The Red Crescent worked when we first started doing it, but the rebels have alerted NATO about using it on troop trucks."

"Very good, Colonel. It sounds as if everything is just as I instructed. Have your drivers standing by. We may have to move the material on very short notice. I am going back to Sirte now, and after I assess the situation, I will instruct you."

"General, I will be awaiting your orders."

As Yusif drove back into Sirte, he inspected the loyal soldiers posted on the entry points into town, especially those on the main road from Tripoli. What he saw discouraged him. The regular Libyan army troops had almost disappeared, replaced by a rag-tag group of fighters who were concerned more with protecting Sirte from rebel looters than they were in protecting Gaddafi.

Yusif inspected the men's weapons and was dismayed at the lack of any heavy firepower. These men could make it difficult for the rebels to occupy the center of town, but a concentrated rebel attack, with truck-mounted, .50-caliber machine guns on the various checkpoints would destroy the greatly outgunned, remaining pro-Gaddafi troops and militia fighters.

When Gen. Yusif returned to the compound, he gave orders to General el-Hassaime to deploy his men in a tight ring around the city center as a final line of defense. This would undoubtedly be needed when the rebels pushed through the checkpoints.

"They may drive and fight their way through the outskirts of Sirte, General, but when they get to the center of town we will slaughter them. They will not take the city without a bloody fight."

"General Yusif, my officers are about to give a security briefing. Let's hear what they say about our defenses before we pull back to the center of town."

"Very well, General, but I've just checked on several entry points, and I found the security lacking."

For the next 45 minutes, Yusif and Gen. el-Hassaime listened to a security briefing from several officers. They told the generals that their defenses could repel any attack by rebel forces. Yusif, however, knew better, and when they described the rebel troop movements, they told of disorganized, poorly armed militia with only a few hundred soldiers in position to attack Sirte. They simply dismissed any threat by the rebels to take the city.

Yusif knew the security men were only telling General el-Hassaime what he wanted to hear, and from bits and pieces of information that they mentioned, he was able to discern that the town would fall in less than 48 hours. Thousands of rebels were pushing south from Tripoli, and within 24 hours they would be massing at the main gateways to Sirte. The push into the center of the city would take place shortly after that. *Yes, it is time to move forward with the plan,* was all he could think about.

It was time to text Colonel Segundo. Move convoy with all material to Liimi Square with heavy security. Have some women and children available to ride in the open canopy trucks. Tell them we are taking them to safety in refugee camps. Be sure they are visible from the air.

3

The Flight to Juba

Oct. 16, 2011, Sirte, Libya

Yusif went into the compound's family quarters looking for his father, but before he entered the inner area where General Gaddafi was staying he stopped and sent another text.

Convoy will leave Sirte at dawn tomorrow. Be ready to intercept.

He strapped his Blackberry to his hip and walked into his father's bedroom. Gen. Gaddafi was leaning back on a sofa drinking his morning chai (tea) when Yusif entered the room.

"Yusif, my son, I think these people who are telling me we must be ready to leave Sirte are lying to me! Tell me the truth!"

Yusif sat down beside Gen. Gaddafi and said, "The situation is very serious. I have examined the forces that are holding the city, and each day they dwindle away as more and more of the scum arrive from Benghazi and Tripoli. We must put the plan into effect. Remember? The Plan—the Plan with the materials that we can use to stop the NATO bitch dogs from helping the rebel scum."

There was a puzzled look from Gaddafi until Yusif said to him, "Remember the Plan to scatter the NATO dogs?"

A nod, and then a shout. "Yes, yes, I remember! We will slap their faces and take back our country!"

"Father, I have instructed Colonel Secundo to bring the trucks with all the material into the Square today, and be ready to leave with a heavy security guard at daylight tomorrow. We cannot wait any longer; more of the rebels are arriving every day. Your plan to humiliate the NATO dogs by setting off a nuclear explosion in the desert is brilliant, but we must hurry and leave or we will not be able to get the trucks through the rebel lines."

"Yusif, I don't remember everything. Tell me the plan again."

Yusif smiled as he thought, Of course, you don't remember. It's my plan.

"Father, the American and NATO inspectors came to be sure we had destroyed or turned over all of our nuclear and biomaterial."

"Yes, now I remember."

"And, I found some old Italian fortifications cut into the cliff just north of Sirte."

"Yes, yes, now it is coming to me."

"Father, you instructed me to hide some of our enriched uranium and biological weapons in the cave. Now, is the time for us to use them. Our plan is to set off a nuclear bomb in the desert to get the attention of the whole world. Then we will demand the NATO dogs stop helping the rebel scum, or we will launch a SCUD with a bomb attached."

"Yes, yes, I remember now. Is everything ready?"

"Yes, Father; the convoy with all the material is moving toward Sirte as we speak. At daylight tomorrow, we will let our fighters break through the rebel line on the south route, and then we will head into the desert toward Juba. We have many supporters in Juba, of course, the Tuareg desert fighters will help us any way they can."

***

French NATO Command Center, Le Alisha, Italy

Captain Roger Blister was reviewing intelligence chatter that had been picked up over the last 24 hours when he turned to a coded message. The code was a simple one, and NATO transcribers had broken it almost immediately earlier in the year, when they began picking up messages from Gaddafi loyalists.

"Colonel Norwood, take a look at this message sent from Yusif, one of Gaddafi's sons. It sounds as if they may make a run for it tomorrow."

The Colonel glanced at the message and nodded.

"You're right. Relay details to the Fighter Command Center and tell them to watch for a convoy leaving Sirte at daylight. I'd be willing to bet Gaddafi is trying to get out of town. They can't possibly hold out more than a couple of days. The only forces that are still loyal to Gaddafi are near Juba in Southern Libya, and I would imagine that's where they are headed. Those Mirage Jets'll be ready when they head out. I would hate to be in that convoy."

***

Sirte, Libya, Oct. 20, 5 a. m.

It was a little after 4:30 a m when Gen. Gaddafi and his entourage arrived in the Square to join the convoy of eight heavy trucks. Yusif met with Colonel Hussiane and went over plans for the drive south.

"General Yusif, I could only find twelve women and four children to ride in the trucks. Where do you want me to put them?"

"Put half of them in the open canopy truck I am riding in, and the rest in the truck behind me carrying the material."

"What about your father's truck?"

"He spoke to me earlier and said he did not want to be protected by women and children. Have the truck carrying the General in the last position, and fly a white flag from the antenna."

In less than 20 minutes, the line of trucks was ready to pull out, but before they pulled out, Gen. Yusif talked with the head of security, about the difficulty of breaking through rebel lines.

"General Yusif my best intelligence tells me that the south road toward Juba is very lightly guarded. I will send a contingent of my best men forward to clear out the few rebels that are manning the checkpoint. Then I will notify you when the checkpoint is destroyed so you can to move forward with the convoy."

"Very good, General. Tell your men to kill every one of the checkpoint rebels. We don't want anyone telling the rebel command that we have left the city."

"I will do it, General. As soon as I get the all clear, I will text you and you can move forward. I must caution you though, have your drivers to go at top speed and don't stop for anything. It will be impossible to travel across the open desert without being spotted by the surveillance planes. Don't even slow down when we come under attack. The women and children should keep the French planes from attacking some of the convoy."

"We won't slow down."

It was nearly 5:30 when the platoon of pro-Gaddafi soldiers directed by Gen. al-Hassime attacked the small contingent of rebels manning the south road checkpoint. After an unusually fierce firefight, the rebels tried to surrender, but were cut down by pro-Gaddafi troops. A few minutes later, a text message lit up Yusif's Blackberry: **All clear—proceed.**

4

Strike

"AWAC's are reporting a large convoy leaving Sirte, heading south—more info to follow shortly—HQ has a standing order to destroy any Gaddafi military—note surveillance indicates at least two trucks transporting visible women and children."

Sgt. Pierre Aground quickly routed the message to squadron leader La Fosse Capering, who roused his crews out of quarters. In less than 20 minutes, four Mirage F-15 fighter jets were airborne and heading for Libya.

Aboard AWAC Tail 342, Sgt. Bill Stafford studied his enhanced computer screen shots of the convoy as it pulled out of town.

"Damn, Red Crescents, white flags, and women and kids trying to dodge those French jets. That's not going to work."

"Commander La Fosse—AWAC 343—Do you read me?—over."

"Loud and clear, 343, continue—over."

"I am tracking a convoy of eight vehicles leaving Sirte, heading due south at high speed. In trucks number three and four I see visible women and children. Intelligence says this convoy could be transporting very high-level pro-Gaddafi people. I am relaying conformation from HQ to take out the convoy, but don't hit trucks three and four where the women and children are... over." are.—over."

"Read you loud and clear 342, will do. Over and out."

***

Convoy of Pro-Gaddafi trucks leaving Sirte

As the convoy crossed the main highway south, it turned out into the open desert. All of the trucks had desert tires and other equipment that would allow them to travel in the open desert without problems. The convoy was speeding along at more than 100 KPH when the first Mirage Fighter struck. Before Yusif even heard the plane, the lead truck in the convoy exploded. A 150-mm anti-tank shell blew the cab off the truck sending it spinning out of control and finally coming to a stop as it rolled over. The convoy never slowed down, but seconds later the second truck took a shell and careened over, disabled and burning.

"Keep driving—don't slow down! Faster!" yelled Yusif. He glanced back in time to see two more trucks in the rear of the convoy take direct hits and turn over. As trucks 3 and 4, with the women and children onboard, continued into the desert, General Gaddafi's truck, which hadn't been hit, suddenly turned around and headed back toward Sirte.

"Don't go back!" Yusif yelled into a walkie-talkie that was in direct contact with Gen. Gaddafi's truck.

"We must or we'll be killed!" came the reply.

Yusif looked back to see Gen. Gaddafi's truck, which was fleeing back toward Sirte, come under fire as a Mirage Jet bore down on it, spraying .50-caliber machine-gun bullets at the truck.

***

NATO Air Operations, Naples, Italy

"Captain, I've just received a confirmation that the convoy heading south from Sirte, has been intercepted and three trucks were destroyed. One truck turned around and headed back to Sirte where it was disabled. And get this, Revolutionary forces claim they have captured Gaddafi!"

"Did they capture him alive?"

"Yes, I think so, but I just got a second confirmation, and it was very vague about Gaddafi being alive."

"What do you mean?"

"I'm not sure. It seems Gaddafi was wounded, but from the first message the wounds didn't seen serious. The second message indicated the wounds were more serious. I suspect someone may have executed him."

"Well, it's probably just as well. With him dead, this war will wind down in a hurry."

"Captain, the commander of the Mirage Fighter group requests permission to take out the remaining trucks—the ones carrying the women and children. He said he suspects other high- level, pro-Gaddafi personnel are onboard."

"No, tell him to break off contact and return to base. I think, with Gaddafi out of the picture, this war will wind down in a hurry. There's no sense in killing more people if we don't have to."

***

Fifteen hours later—The central Libyan Desert, near Juba

Yusif received several text messages confirming the death of his father and other family members at the hands of Revolutionary Troops. They confirmed his family was executed by rebel soldiers when the French Mirage Jets took out the other five trucks of the convoy. He kept his drivers moving at top speeds across the desert until they reached Juba early the next day. Then, after releasing the women and children, he sent another text message: **Just arrived in Juba—Will rest today and deliver the material to you tomorrow.**

***

NATO Air Operations Headquarters

"Captain, AWAC #343 just passed on a message from Juba, Libya. It's from someone in the trucks that left Sirte yesterday."

"*Hummm*, deliver the material? What in the hell does that mean?"

"I don't know sir, but that's the third time we have picked up a message from the encrypted cell that mentioned some sort of material."

"Sergeant, I want you to go back over all the AWAC transmissions during the last two weeks and see if you find anything that might have something to do with these messages."

"Yes, sir, I'll get right on it. There's not very many so it shouldn't take but an hour or so."

An hour and a half later, Sgt. Tucker laid out a series of messages to Captain Peterson.

"Sir, the only thing new is a notation from AWAC Tail #234 about a weak radioactive signal. It was attributed to an oilfield tool used to measure rock formation in the wells that have been drilled in Libya."

"Have we picked up signals like that before?"

"Yes, sir, a number of times, especially south of Marsa Brega."

"Well, that's right in the heart of the Libyan oilfields so that figures. Are there any oil wells around Sirte? Or what about staging areas where these tools might be kept?"

"No sir. After the report was sent to staff, a check was made to see if any undisclosed radioactive material was in Sirte, and it came up negative."

"Have the AWAC's picked up any signals lately?"

"No, sir. No reports at all."

"Wait an minute! You're telling me that after the convoy left Sirte, the AWAC's stopped picking up signals?"

"That's right, sir."

"Tell me, Sergeant, how far do the AWAC's range from the coast?"

"Not far, sir. I would estimate a hundred miles, since all the action is near Benghazi and Tripoli."

"Oh, my god! We don't have any surveillance as far inland as Juba do we?"

"No sir, all the AWAC's are positioned near the coast."

"Sergeant, have the AWAC nearest Juba do a flyover around Juba immediately, and run an ultra-high detection for radioactive material. Report the results to me as soon as you receive them."

"Yes, sir, we'll get right on it."

Three hours later, Sgt. Peterson rushed into Captain Jones's office.

"Sir, I've just received a report from AWAC 234. It's very disturbing. They picked up that weak radioactive signal again, and, using the high-resolution detector and running the analysis through the discernment program, the program indicates possible enriched uranium, concealed in lead. And it could be a considerably quantity. They recommend immediately confiscation of the material."

"My god, Gaddafi must have had some stuff concealed and was trying to get it into the desert, but for what I don't know. Anything else, Sergeant?"

"Yes, sir. We have an asset on the ground at Sirte, and one of the Revolutionary commanders took him to a secret cave they found cut out into the cliff wall north of Sirte. He thinks it was used to conceal something. The also found gas masks and suits that could only be used when someone was handling either biomaterial or enriched uranium."

"Can we tell who received the text message from Yusif Gaddafi?"

"No, sir we can't. The only thing we can tell is that the person receiving the message is in Niger."

"We've got a message that calls for an intercept and a delivery of material, and we've located a truck in Juba that may have enriched uranium onboard. For god's sake, let's get this analysis to HQ as soon as possible."

After an hour meeting with the Central NATO Command, a unanimous decision was made to send a team of French Special Operation troops and American Seals to Juba to intercept the truck and confiscate any material, as well as apprehend or disable all personnel connected with the trucks.

5

The Delivery

Juba, 6:30 a. m. Oct. 22

Yusif considered his situation. He knew NATO planes never flew anywhere near Juba, and after he arrived he was met by a contingent of pro-Gaddafi soldiers who were still loyal to his father. He was getting ready to carry out the last part of his plan, and the extra security made him more confident about making the delivery.

He pulled out his Blackberry and tapped in a message. **Leaving Juba—I will meet you at our designated delivery point. Have half of the material.** *Half will be plenty,* he thought, *and I've got all the biomaterial in my truck. That should be enough for them to give the NATO dogs something to worry about, and enough money for my retirement.*

***

AWAC Tail 343 picked up the message and relayed it to NATO headquarters.

"Captain, a new message from one of our AWACS—Here."

The sergeant handed Captain Jones the translated text.

"My god, I hope we get there in time. Get HQ on the phone, Sergeant."

"Yes, sir, we have the latest from one of our AWACS. We can track the truck and coordinate the strike team. We should be able to intercept it before it gets to the meeting place. I have a feeling it will be somewhere near the Niger border. The only thing that concerns me is the number of fighters who will be with Yusif, and how many will be at the meeting place. I hope we have enough men to take them."

"We have twenty-four of the top men in the world, and unless they run into an overwhelming force that will be enough."

***

Yusif prepared to leave Juba with two trucks carrying the biomaterial and the enriched uranium. However, he was still concerned that there might be rebel or even NATO planes to contend with, so he had two open top trucks with Pro-Gaddafi troops armed with AK-47s and RPGs accompanying them. They left Juba at 8 a.m., driving across the open desert for the designated meeting place on the Niger border. It was about a two-hour drive, and Yusif was anxious to get the material delivered. He had contracted some local Tuareg tribesmen who were staunch supporters of Gaddafi, and they were going to assist him in leaving Libya and finding asylum in Niger or Mali.

As they pulled out of Juba, Yusif sent a text: Leaving Juba, will arrive in two hours. Have security and conveyance to meet me.

***

Central NATO Headquarters, Naples, Italy

"Captain, this message just came in from AWAC 343. A convoy of four trucks has just left Juba on a bearing vector that will take them to the Niger border in two hours. The intercepted message requests security and trucks to take material."

"Sergeant, have Air Command relay the details to both choppers, and notify AWAC 343 to get in direct contact with pilots on the choppers."

"Yes, sir."

"What's the ETA on the Black Hawks based on the latest AWAC info?"

"Three minutes ago it was one thirty-six."

"Damn, it's going to be touch and go. I just hope they catch the trucks before they hook up with their Niger fighters."

***

Black Hawk Helicopter Tail 444, Captain Robert Murphee pilot

"Captain, I just got a heads-up from our God in the Sky, AWAC 343. We should have a visual in fifteen minutes. I have weapons that will take out the truck. Are we cleared to destroy the trucks?"

"Negative. We are to disable the trucks, either kill or capture the occupants of all vehicles, and wait for a containment team to come and secure the cargo. Have a gunner in the door shoot the block of the lead truck, and we'll see if the whole convoy'll stop. If it doesn't, then keep shooting until all of the trucks have been rendered inoperative. Whatever you do, don't shoot in the cargo area of the trucks."

"Roger, will pass on the word to the door gunner—sighting! Dust! Looks like the convoy at two o'clock."

"Pull the door and get ready! We should be in range in thirty seconds!"

Seconds later, the Black Hawk turned and banked parallel to the lead truck in the convoy, and the door gunner sent a short blast into the engine block of the lead truck.

***

Gen Yusif Gaddafi's convoy 90 miles west of Juba

Yusif was leaning back against the passenger's side door when the .50-cal machine-gun rounds hit the engine of the truck. It was a jarring, ear-piercing blast of metal being shredded and the impact shook the truck. A roar of steam from the radiator and a ball of fire from the engine block signaled a successful strike. The lead truck coasted to a halt and the other three trucks stopped behind it.

Chaos erupted as the fighters jumped from their trucks. Yusif ran to get into one of the other trucks, but the Black Hawk turned and, seconds later, more machine-gunfire disabled the second truck. Yusif quickly stepped behind the truck and pulled out his Blackberry. He texted, **Under attack! Send fighters quickly, or we will lose the material!**

"Open fire at the helicopter!" Yusif shouted to the soldiers, who were milling around in confusion.

Soon there was a roar of automatic weapon going in all directions, some of which was actually directed at the Black Hawk that was turning to disable the remaining trucks.

★★★

Black Hawk Chopper, Tail 444

"We're taking incoming fire!" yelled Captain Murphree. "The main rotor blade just took a hit, and I've got to put this bird down! Hang on—rough landing in about three seconds! Be ready to receive incoming fire when you exit the chopper!"

There was a jarring thump and the Black Hawk hit the ground. The back cargo door dropped, and in seconds the 24 men scrambled out. Soon a major firefight erupted as the Special Operation Troops poured fire into the disorganized pro-Gaddafi troops. The Special Operation Soldiers, from an elevated position on a low ridge, were firing down on Yusif's security forces. They had no cover, and the crack Special Operations marksmen methodically shot them. It was all over in less than 10 minutes. As the firing stopped, Yusif waved a handkerchief from behind one of the trucks where he had been hiding during the firefight.

"Captain, one of the Libyans is still alive. He was hiding behind one of the trucks during the shooting."

"Bring the man over here, Sergeant, and search his pockets for any information."

Two of the Special Operation troops ran up to Yusif, handcuffed him, and quickly emptied his pockets. They were back to the captain in less than five minutes.

"Here you go, Captain. It's his passport."

Captain Murphree looked at Yusif and smiled. "Well, so you are Yusif Gaddafi. Boys, we caught a big fish today."

The team gathered around and as they got the word, there were hollers and slaps on the back.

"Sergeant, contact AWAC 343 and confirm we have the material, and we also have Yusif Gaddafi. Tell them to send the backup Black Hawk. we've got a damaged rotor and can't use this one."

"Yes, sir."

In a few minutes, Sgt. Pierson hurried back, waving a transmission from the AWAC.

"Captain an urgent message from 343!" yelled the Sergeant.

"A very large group of unidentified fighters are approaching your position. They're in trucks and indications are that they'll flank you on both sides. Estimate at least 175 armed men—backup chopper is in route, but will be 40 minutes before arrival. The fighters are coming from inside Niger, and will be at your position in 12 minutes. Recommend you deploy 500 meters north to a more defensible position. Chopper can pick you up behind the ridge."

"Sergeant, pass the word to move and take up defensive positions behind that ridge to the north," the captain replied. "We can't defend this position. Ask for air support."

In seconds, the Special Operation troops were moving toward the low ridge north of them, taking Yusif Gaddafi with them. In about 10 minutes, they could see clouds of dust from the approaching trucks. As the trucks carrying mounted machine guns came in range, the SF soldiers begin to fire. Soon, as the rest of the fighters arrived, a major firefight was under way. After being flanked, Captain Murphree moved his men farther down the ridge to prevent the fighters from circling behind them. Several SF men had been wounded, and they were carried along with those retreating.

"Captain, look! They're driving off in the two undamaged trucks!"

"We can't stop them, Sergeant. It'd be suicide to leave our position. The backup chopper will be here in ten minutes. Maybe with the firepower on that Black Hawk, we can stop them before they get to the Niger border."

Soon the two trucks were out of sight and the remaining fighters suddenly left the fight to follow them in other trucks. Five minutes later, the Black Hawk chopper dropped down and the SF team scrambled aboard.

"Sergeant, we've got to stop two trucks that are heading for the Niger border! Are your guns live?"

"Yes, sir."

"Okay, go due west toward that dust cloud, and I'll spot the target for you."

Ten minutes later the Black Hawk approached the end of the line of trucks that had just left the firefight.

"Should I take them out?"

"No, about a mile ahead are the trucks we have to stop. Ignore these. They're just the security."

Six minutes later, Captain Murphree pointed to a cloud of dust, and as the chopper approached the dust from the vehicles, he spotted the two trucks.

"Disable those two trucks leading the convoy, Sergeant."

"Just a minute, Captain. I've got an emergency radio call from one of our AWAC's."

"Sergeant, this is AWAC 343. Hold up! You are approaching the Niger Border, or have just crossed it. I must get permission for you to cross an international border and take action."

"What?" yelled Captain Murphree. The chopper pulled back and waited for orders from HQ.

"Damn, if we don't get the okay to fire in the next five minutes, we're going to lose them," groused Murphree. He slapped the side of the chopper as he watched the trucks disappear in the distance.

It was nearly 10 minutes before the radio flashed.

"Sergeant, permission is denied. Turn around, you're a hundred yards inside the border, and you will create an international incident if you destroy those trucks."

"Oh, shit!" yelled Murphree. The chopper pilot was turning the craft around when Murphree shouted back, "Sergeant, this is a matter of national security. I'm countermanding that order."

"What? That order came from the NATO commanding general. Captain, I want to take out those trucks as bad as you do, but I'm not about to follow your orders over a general's. Sorry, but I'm pulling back across the border."

6

Surprise

Former SF Sergeant Josh Martin and his new bride, Nafisa, had only been back from their harrowing experience in Cordoba for a few months. Nafisa had fully recovered, but she was still waking up screaming for Josh as she remembered being tied to a chair for days in the old section of Cordoba.

Josh had recovered from his wounds inflicted by the assassin, Patto, but because of the fall from the second floor onto the cobblestone courtyard, he suffered injuries that forced his retirement from Special Forces.

The two had bought a house in Savannah, Ga., in order to be close to Josh's training facility, Camp Thunder, and it seemed as if they would have an opportunity to settle into a quiet married life away from the threat of terrorism. When Josh retired from active duty, he'd promised Nafisa that he would strictly be a Special Forces trainer, and would not take on any more missions.

It was hard for Josh to forget the recent struggle just to survive, when he fought the assassin and finally prevailed—killing Patto with his own knife. However, as he trained units at Camp Thunder, the young man was comforted by the thought that with his training and his gleaning of intelligence, he had been able to inflict a severe wound on al-Qaida's Central Command. A Combat Divers strike force team had eliminated the Middle East al-Qaida leadership council by attacking their meeting place in Lebanon. And Rangers and Special Operation troops had destroyed a new training camp at the Selma Oasis in North Sudan.

After that, Josh considered al-Qaida mortally wounded. He believed he and Nafisa would settle into a married life free from the pressures and fights that Josh had been a part of as a Special Forces soldier.

A vibration from his cellphone interrupted Josh's thoughts. He glanced at his phone and for moment felt a wave of apprehension wash over him. Not many people had Josh's private cell number, and when it did ring, it was usually a crisis. For a second he stared at the caller and then gasped, "General Davis, oh, my god! What now?" It gradually sank in that Gen. Davis—the head of the Interdiction Strike Force Team—was calling from his private number. He would have to answer this call.

"Yes, sir! General Davis. What can I do for you sir?"

Gen. Davis, as always, spoke clearly, distinctly, and bluntly.

"Josh, I want you to come to Washington as soon as possible. I know you're not active anymore, but we need your expertise to help us with a very serious problem that has come up. I want you at Jacksonville Air Force Base immediately. We have a plane waiting to fly you directly the Washington, D.C."

"I understand, General, but can you tell me anything else before I fly to Washington?"

"Josh it's very urgent problem, or I wouldn't be telling you to fly directly up here. When you get here, come to my office immediately. Something has come up that's critical to national security. Your job in Afghanistan was so remarkable that our team would like for you to take a look at this project and give us your input."

"I appreciate that General, but I'm just getting settled here in Savannah with my wife."

"Josh, you can bring your wife to Washington. I'm sure she'd enjoy seeing some of the sites in D. C. after all you went through when you were in Cordova. We need you, and she deserves a little vacation."

"Yes, sir, we'll be in Washington as soon as possible."

Josh was home in minutes, and when he told Nafisa about having to fly to Washington immediately, she was at first delighted, but then a worried look crept over her face.

"Josh, is the General calling you to Washington to send you on another mission? I don't think I could stand it if you went back to Afghanistan."

"I don't think so, Nafisa. General Davis told me it was just to consult with his team on how to solve a serious problem that has to do with national security."

But Josh had only said that to keep Nafisa from worrying. He knew Gen. Davis would never have sent for him just for Josh's input on an operation. *Why on earth does General Davis have a military jet waiting to pick me up at the Jacksonville Airport? It must be extremely urgent, and important.*

Two hours later, the jet touched down at Reagan International, and Sgt. Wilson Humphrey ushered Josh and his Nafisa into a waiting limo.

"Mr. Martin, I have instructions to drop you off at the Pentagon and take Mrs. Martin to the the Willard Hotel and check her in. Is that satisfactory with you?"

"Yes, Sergeant, just make sure Mrs. Martin gets registered properly and shown to her room."

Gen. Davis, who had been informed of Josh's arrival, was waiting in his outer office when the young man walked in.

Josh, it's good to see you again. I haven't seen you since the Cordoba incident. My god, you and your wife were lucky to come out of that alive."

"We weren't lucky, General. It was SF training."

"Well, I'm glad you're here. Come into my office. We need to talk."

Gen. Davis was his usual blunt, self-assured self, but Josh instinctively knew he was very anxious about something

"Josh, what I'm going to tell you is extremely confidential; it is top secret, and you're to tell no one anything about it. However, considering your recent circumstances, you may confide what I'm about to tell you to your wife."

Gen. Davis opened a briefing file and began to thumb through it.

"Evidently, our problem started after we knocked off the Leadership Council and hit the new al-Qaida training camp at Selma Oasis. From the chatter we've picked up, al-Qaida, instead of floundering and dissolving, has multiplied and expanded. And not only have they grown, they're mad as hell and are determined to get revenge. From our intelligence, they say it will dwarf 9/11.

"Let me start back to early last year," Davis said. "Actually, the plot we uncovered was hatched about six months ago. It started when the revolution in Libya was in full swing and Colonel Gaddafi was trying to salvage his position as a dictator. He fled to his hometown of Sirte, and many people thought he was just going to make a last stand there. And it certainly looked that way as things played out.

"However, making a kind of "Custer's Last Stand" in his hometown wasn't his plan. After Gaddafi supposedly got rid of his weapons of mass destruction, we stopped worrying about him. However, the sneaky bastard didn't really get rid of all that stuff. We had no idea, but Gaddafi secreted away enough highly enriched uranium to make at least three nuclear bombs. We have confirmed—from confessions within his closest associates—that when he fled to Sirte, he planned to take one of the enriched uranium bombs, hook it to a Scud Missile, and threaten to destroy one of the major cities in the region if NATO did not stop the bombing.

"If that wasn't enough, he had some god-awful biological stuff he was going to use on his own people in order to stay in power. He was going to use some of the nuclear material to create an explosion in the desert to show the world he had the capability. It was his last hope to stay in power.

"However, things went to hell a lot quicker than he expected, and he had barely arrived in Sirte and started to remove the enriched uranium that was stored in a cave, when things begin to disintegrate all round him," Davis explained. "As chaos issued, someone, probably Gaddafi, ordered the enriched uranium and the biological material to be loaded on several trucks and hauled south.

"Now, let me tell you something that we found out late lately. It turns out that the middle son who followed him to Sirte was an al-Qaida plant. Salem al "General" Yusif was recruited a few years ago by al-Qaida, and he was instrumental in moving the enriched uranium. Of course, it wouldn't surprise me to find out he had cut a deal to sell the stuff to al-Qaida.

"After the rebels moved into Sirte, Gaddafi loaded the uranium and bio stuff into two special desert-equipped trucks. His plan was to head south and try to connect with some pro-Gaddafi tribes near the Chad border. However, things went extremely bad for Gaddafi. He was captured, and, as you know, killed.

"But his son, General Yusif, managed to escape with a group of men, the enriched uranium and bio stuff, and they headed south to rendezvous point—not with the pro-Gaddafi tribes, but with al-Qaida. Our AWAC's picked up his conversations with the al-Qaida cells south of Niger and Nigeria, and we were shocked at what they heard."

General Davis paused, and walked over to a wall map that covered the north half of Africa.

"General Yusif was going to deliver the enriched uranium and bio stuff to al-Qaida," Davis explained. "There was never a plan to set off a nuclear bomb in the desert. After they left Sirte, the CIA was brought in and they picked up the trail, and with our AWAC planes, managed to track the radioactive material as the truck headed south—Note the highlighted route on the map.

"The CIA sent a team of Special Forces and Seals to capture the truck. They intersected the convoy near the Niger border, and after a fierce firefight, they did manage to capture Gen. Yusif Gaddafi. They turned him over to the revolutionary troops that were trailing him. But during the firefight with the loyal Gaddafi troops, the truck, with the radioactive material and bio stuff, managed to cross into Niger and meet up with the al-Qaida forces.

"Before the SF's and Seals could pursue and stop the truck from being carried deeper into Niger, a large al-Qaida force appeared and managed to hold off our men," he continued. "They left the area with all the enriched uranium and biomaterial. HQ in charge of the pursuit wouldn't let our SFs and Seals cross the Niger boarder, which was a stupid-ass mistake." Davis paused, in thought.

"When they got away from the border, the men put the radioactive material in some new impervious lead containers to prevent the AWAC planes from trailing it. However, we have satellite pictures showing the truck and its guards heading across Niger and into northeast Nigeria. The truck was last seen disappearing down a rough; hard to see from the air, jungle trail into the tropical forest that covers the region. From what we have picked up on our chatter from our surveillance AWAC's, we believe that the truck and a large al-Qaida force is somewhere in eastern Nigeria. Shit, you could hide an aircraft carrier in that jungle."

Josh walked over to the wall map to see the details of the route the trucks took as Gen. Davis posted a couple of high-resolution aerial photos.

"Yes, General, I see what you mean. Do we have any on-the-ground backup?"

"Yeah, but they are just on the edge of the jungle, collecting info from the natives that they send in. We've got to have a team on the ground that can go into the bush and inpoint the camp location. We can't send in a strike team until we know exactly where the bastards are located."

"But there's a lot more to the story," said Davis. "From what we learned from intercepting the chatter, and from information we got from Libyan authorities interrogating some of the captured al-Qaida fighters, al-Qaida has plans to use the radioactive material to make three dirty bombs that they'll place the three Western cities. The only thing they didn't have to make these bombs operational was the capability to make the trigger mechanism that would detonate the bombs. We captured and destroyed the truck carrying the detonating devices."

For the first time, Davis showed a hint of a satisfied smile.

"Al Qaida has been working desperately to obtain the trigger mechanism expertise," he went on. "About a week ago, after they had tried to get the Iranian government to furnish them with the information, al-Qaida operatives assassinated one of the top scientists in the Iranian nuclear industry. Of course, the press blamed the Israelis, but the Iranians knew better. Shortly after that, we picked up messages threatening the Iranian government. I know it's hard to believe, but al-Qaida said they would continue to assassinate Iranian atomic officials until Iran allowed someone to come and construct triggers for the three nuclear weapons.

"We found out that within the past couple of days the Iranian official who's in charge of the inner workings of their nuclear atomic system has flown to Niamey, Niger, and left the city driving east toward Nigeria. He was under surveillance by AWAC planes, but when he entered the heavy tropical forest, he disappeared from surveillance.

"Josh, you know this is a very serious matter, and we've got to do everything we can to stop it. The reason I called you to Washington is to inform you that after your successful intelligence strikes against al-Qaida in Beirut and Selima Oasis, the Joint Chiefs of Staff believe you are the one man who might be able to track down these catastrophic weapons, and get them destroyed. We do understand the dangers involved and the complexity of the situation, and we have implanted four deep-cover agents in Nigeria. One of those is a female—and she's damed good. She is posing as a Baptist missionary in a small town in the west central part of the Nigerian Republic."

Josh, who had been listening intently, and solemnly, leaned forward in his chair. "General, after Nafisa went through that horrible kidnapping—which nearly killed her—I promised her I'd resign from active duty, and that she would never have to worry about me being in danger again. Of course, since I've had some medical problems as a result of my encounter with the assassin, being an active SF soldier was really not an option."

"Josh, I have your latest medical report…"

"What?"

"Yes, Sergeant. You should know by now that anything to do with National Security is never off-limits to our group. And, certainly, I'm not telling you something you don't already know. Your doctor reports: "Mr. Martin is in excellent health, and shows no debilitating effects from his recent attack.""

Josh smiled, and nodded.

"So let's don't talk about not being fit. To get right to the point—will you take this assignment?"

"General, I can't give you an answer right now. I have to talk with Nafisa. It wouldn't be fair to her after all she's been through."

"I understand, Josh, but things are so critical that I can't give more than twelve hours. Go talk to your wife, and come back here first thing in the morning. I have to move on this ASAP. And this is very irregular, but, again, I'm giving you permission to tell Nafisa about the assignment."

"Thank you, General Davis. I'll be here at nine o'clock."

"Make that seven, Josh."

Josh nodded, the General dismissed him, and Josh hurried out of the office and walked briskly to the Willard.

Nafisa jumped up from the chair where she'd been reading a magazine, and yanked open the door as Josh inserted his key card.

"What is it, Josh? Why did General Davis fly you to Washington?"

"Sit down, Honey. This is going to take more than a few minutes."

Josh took a deep breath, and slowly told Nafisa the details of the mission Gen. Davis wanted him to take. As he talked, he watched Nafisa's demeanor change until he could tell by her body language that she was furious. *Well, she really doesn't want me to do this,* Josh thought. He finished and waited for Nafisa to tearfully beg him to not accept the assignment.

Nafisa jumped to her feet, cursed loudly in in the Iranian language called Pashto, (her former tribal language) and begin to yell at her startled husband.

"Those scum! Plotting to kill thousands of innocent people! Josh get back down to the General's office, and tell him you'll take the assignment! You could never live with yourself if you didn't and something horrible happened!"

"I'm supposed to let him know first thing in the morning. You really think I should take the assignment?"

"In the morning? Josh, this is too important to wait another twelve hours! Go! Don't wait another minute!" As Nafisa finished the sentence, she shoved Josh toward the door. Twenty minutes later, Josh was in the General's outer office waiting to see him.

A surprised Gen. Davis looked out, beckoned him in, and pointed to the chair in front of his desk.

"Back here in less than an hour?—Not going to take it huh? When my secretary buzzed me that you were back, that's what I figured."

"No, General, just the opposite. I'm at you disposal."

"I have a feeling I don't know the whole story. How did your wife react?"

"She pushed me out the door. I've never been so surprised."

"Smart woman! Well, Josh we can't waste any time. We're behind the eight ball as it is. I want you on a flight to Niamey, Niger, later today, and I'll have someone escort your wife back to Savannah. Don't worry about packing. Everything you will need, we will have waiting for you."

"That'll be fine, General. Nafisa will be more than cooperative after what she was put through. She a Pashto and she wants revenge."

"Fine Josh. Now, I am going to send you over to Bill Paxton's office. I'm sure you remember Bill, the CIA liaison from your last mission."

"Yes, General. It'll be great to work with him again."

"Missy, get Bill Paxton on the phone, and tell him I'm sending Josh Martin over for a briefing—code **Triple Jeopardy**."

Minutes later, Josh was ushered into Paxton's office. He was expecting a friendly, low-keyed briefing from someone he knew. However, he was surprised to see six agents in one room, a Smart Board for a PowerPoint presentation, and an inch-thick briefing manual on the chair where he was to be seated. Paxton walked out from behind his desk to welcome him, and immediately began to introduce him to a group of men and women who made up the leaders of the various CIA sectors.

"Josh, I want to make you aware of how serious this situation has become. We have some recent hard evidence that a target date has been set for two weeks from today. All we know is that a major Western city is targeted. We don't know if we're dealing with a nuclear weapon or bio. Most of us suspect it's a bio, but that's just a hunch, since Hassan el-Kohannie, the Iranian nuclear scientist, has been in Nigeria only a few days. We think it'll take him at least a week to prepare the three weapons and a lot longer than that to move them.

"Before we start the briefing, I have a couple of other items I want to mention. You are not to take notes, or write anything down later that was said in this meeting. However, you must memorize virtually everything that *is* said, including the names and passwords of every agent involved. In addition, before you leave this room, you are to read the briefing notes that are on your chair, and, naturally, you must commit them to memory. You are to leave this room with absolutely nothing except what you have memorized.

"Now, I recommend you refresh yourself with some of your early training in ************** (classified). Josh, this is not my idea, but my superiors requested you be tested after this information is given to you to be sure you've retained it. After all even though you completely recovered from the injuries from your last mission, we want to be sure your ability to memorize and react hasn't hasn't been impaired."

As Josh listened to Paxton, he quickly recalled the grueling, repetitious drilling that required exact memorization. He nodded to Paxton, and readied his mind to absorb every detail, every word said. Josh thought, *So, no mission if I don't pass the memory test.*

"Agent 643 will start by giving you local background about where you will be located."

It was three hours later when the last agent finished her presentation. Names and passwords were repeated only once, and Josh was not allowed any pauses between presenting agents.

"Okay, Josh, you have thirty minutes to read and memorize the briefing manual you received when you arrived—You may start now."

Josh quickly opened the inch-thick, single-spaced briefing manual and scanned the first page. The he zeroed in on the salient sentences and committed them to memory. Page 2, then 3 and on and on, page 135…

"Josh you have five minutes."

Josh glanced up a few minutes later to see Paxton raising his hand. He knew that meant one minute left. He take one last look at the final page and flipped the briefing manual over.

Paxton pulled open his folder and addressed Josh. "Tell recognition and answer for Agent Y47."

"Recognition, bird; answer, cat."

"And Agent L27."

"Recognition, snake, answer fang."

"Code words for emergency."

"Delta red."

"Agent U23 capabilities."

Josh hesitated, "Not in the briefing material."

Paxton closed his file 15 minutes later, and looked over the assembled briefing team. "I believe we can consider Josh Martin cleared to proceed. Any discussion?—All right, you may return to you assignments."

As the room emptied, Paxton walked over to where Josh was sitting.

"Josh there's a car waiting to take you to Reagan International where you will board a private jet. Everything you need is aboard the plane. When you reach your destination, Agent L27 will contact you with further instructions. The only additional information I can give you now concerns your backup. You have automatic clearance to use at least two SF Teams and a Seal team if needed. And just in case things really get out of hand, several squads of Rangers are standing by in Djibouti."

"My god, Bill, I've never seen anything so rushed. Are things that serious?"

"Josh, on a need-to-know basis, I can only tell you that you wouldn't be flying on a military jet to Niamey, Niger if they weren't. One more thing; you have the authorization to use any means to accomplish your mission. That includes a direct clearance from the President to use lethal force anytime and against any individual. At your discretion, you may use any amount of force or any other procedure to accomplish this mission. Nothing—absolutely nothing, is off-limits. Remember that—nothing is off-limits—nothing. Of course, you have unlimited funds available to use if money will help your mission succeed.

Don't even return to the hotel. Give Nafisa a call from your car, and from what I understood from General Davis, she will just wish you well. One more thing, Josh: If you're successful, this mission could save several hundred thousand lives."

"I'll do my best, Bill."

"I hope that's good enough."

7

Niamey

Corporal Ben Macklin escorted Josh to a waiting car, and soon they were speeding toward Reagan International. As soon as Josh settled into the 34-minute ride, he tapped Nafisa's number on his cell.

"Nafisa?"

"Yes, Josh, where are you?"

"I am being driven to the airport to catch a plane. You should have let me wait until tomorrow. I can't tell you anything else, or where I am flying. All I can say is this is a critical mission and the time frame is extremely tight. One way or the other I should be back in less than two weeks."

"Josh, you are doing the right thing, and I'm sure you are the person to handle this mission. I have had a peace come over me since you left. This is the right thing to do."

"I hope you're right, Nafisa, because I'm in too deep to back out now. I see the airport ahead; I love you. I'll call as soon as I can, but don't expect any word for a week or so."

"I love you too, Josh. Seek out those who nearly killed us and give us revenge. After the horrible five days strapped to that chair in Cordoba, I have thought of nothing else. This is our opportunity to eliminate another nest of rats!"

"Well, maybe, but as you know, we cleaned out the bunch that did that to you."

"Al-Qaida is evil, Josh, and I believe God has given you the strength to destroy these evil ones. Goodbye, Josh. And when you shoot one of the bastards, think of me."

"Bye, Nafisa." My god, she is one tough women, he thought.

Josh was escorted to a waiting car, rushed out to a taxiway, and, 11 minutes later, he had boarded and the jet was cleared for takeoff. As the jet reached cruising altitude, Todd Pearson, the co-pilot, came back and handed Josh an envelope and a thick belt.

"I'm supposed to give you this stuff once we're airborne. Here you go."

"Thanks, Todd." Josh put the package and belt beside him and waited for Pearson to return to the cockpit.

"I know the routine. You won't open the package until I'm back in the cockpit. Right?"

Josh smiled. The pilot had obviously been on numerous flights of this nature.

"Yeah, sorry."

"Oh, don't sweat it. This old bird has been early everywhere in the world, and we've hauled some of the tightest lipped people I have ever seen. But I'll say one thing: I don't think we've ever flown into Niamey, Niger."

"Well, I sure like going first class. No lines, security, or holding on the runway," quipped Josh.

"Yeah, that suits us, too. Heck, old Uncle can really throw his weight around when he wants to. By the way, you won't have to clear anything in Niamey either. We've been instructed to land and stop at the end of the runway, and wait for someone to come pick you up. We got a direct call from an agent on the ground."

"That's great service, but I think it'll go downhill from then on," said Josh.

"Really?"

"Yes."

After a few seconds of silence, Pearson nodded and headed back to the cockpit.

"I understand, and good luck on whatever you'll be doing."

"From what I can tell, I'm going to need more than luck," cracked Josh. *God, I wish I hadn't said that*, Josh thought. *He didn't need to know.*

Pearson started for the cockpit, but just has he was about to close the door, he looked back and said, "Oh, yeah, when you finish reading whatever is in the package, just stick it in the electronic shredder right behind you. Won't be nothing but dust left in twelve seconds."

"You bet."

Pearson turned back to the cockpit, closed the door, and locked it. Josh glanced in the belt—noted the money—and then ripped open the envelope. It was a continuation of the earlier briefing, but it also included details of the on-the-ground agents as well as various meeting points in the country. Josh studied it for 16 minutes, memorizing everything, and then—before leaning back to get a little sleep—he shredded everything, including the envelope.

As he drifted off to sleep, his thoughts were on the mission. *Tropical rain forest—like Southeast Asia—*crossed his mind as he recalled several missions that took him deep into the rain forests. *I'll need some good on-the-ground intelligence—plus AWAC's—maybe the agents on the ground will have something….*

Josh, benefiting from numerous overseas flights, had trained his body to almost immediately fall asleep when flying long distances. Twelve hours later, he heard a beep and the co-pilots voice announced they were making their final approach into Niamey, Niger.

"Be ready to hop off as soon as you hear me kill the engines," barked Dawson. "Someone will be waiting to pick you up."

Seconds later, the jet's wheels touched down, the pilot reversed the engines, and the plane came to a stop near the end of the short runway. Josh glanced out the window toward the terminal and watched as a pickup truck pulled out, circled a fuel delivery truck, and headed for the jet.

That's rather strange, crossed his mind.

"Have a nice trip. We'll be back to pick you up when you're done."

"Thanks, Todd. I'll look forward to the trip home."

Pearson opened the side door of the jet and flipped down the retractable stairs, and then Josh scampered down the stairs just as the pickup truck pulled up beside the plane.

"Cat," said Josh as he opened the passenger's door of the truck.

"Bird—get in! We need to get off this runway ASAP!"

Josh hit the seat, slammed the door, and the truck roared off across a grassy strip beside the runway heading for a four-foot perimeter fence that circled the airport.

"Hold on, this might get a little rough!" the driver yelled. She hit the fence going at least 40 mph, and Josh gripped the armrest wondering what the hell was going on. The truck never slowed down and soon the driver took another sharp turn, crossed a second grassy medium, and sped down a gravel road that led into a residential neighborhood. After another couple of turns, she slowed down and eased the truck into a stream of heavy traffic.

"What was that all about?" snapped Josh.

"Well, you have complete clearance from the Niger government, but the locals wanted to get a look at you. Shit, your picture would be all over the internet if we had gone though the terminal. Oh, by the way, I'm Gloria, and I assume you're Josh Martin." She gave Josh a little smirk, and continued, "Gonna show us how to do it, huh?"

"Yeah, I'm Josh, Gloria, and I'm SF not CIA. And another thing, I don't do any solo work. It's always team. I'm a team member just like you. That's the way I work, and that's the way it's going to be here. The only reason General Davis put me in charge was because I have experience in direct action with known terrorists, and I've had some success."

"I was just kidding, Josh, but your resume has preceded you, so naturally we're looking for Mr. Superman to save the world, or I should say 'Mr. Super SF.'"

Josh spent a few seconds sizing up Gloria. The CIA briefing had skipped over her slightly caustic demeanor, but Josh found the little jabs—given with a smile—amusing and even positive. He'd been surprised to find out that one of the CIA on-the-ground agents was a female, but after the airport pickup, the ride, and Gloria's attitude, he put his reservations behind him.

Gloria looked to be about 5-foot-10, slim, but with a physique that he categorized as extremely fit. Her forearms tensed as she jerked the pickup truck through traffic, and she spoke with a slightly British clip in her voice. Her salty red hair was cut short, her skin was well tanned, and she didn't have a scrap of makeup on. She was wearing a very conservative, almost nun-like dress. Even so, she was an attractive woman.

"Josh, listen up. I've got new identification papers for you in this pouch. While you are in Niger and Nigeria, you are officially Reverend Theodore Perkins from Starkville, Mississippi. Your home church is First Baptist, Caledonia, Mississippi, and you're on a vacation assignment to work in a mission that the church established a few years back. I'm your assistant."

"A minister? You've got to be kidding."

"No, I'm not Josh. The other choice was for you to be a doctor and work in the hospital where one of our other agents is working as a nurse. I didn't think you could fake being a doctor, but since you're from the South, preaching should come easy. In case you need refreshing, I've got some tracts you can review before your first sermon."

"Okay. I can handle that. Where are we going now?"

"Our mission is in northwest Nigeria, but we've got a safe house just this side of the border in Niger. The other members of your team will meet us there to go over what info we've gathered. After that, we'll drive into Nigeria via a non-border check road, and by late tonight, we'll be at our outpost mission. The village is about as close as we can get to what everyone thinks will be the focus of our search."

Josh leaned back and looked for a seat belt, but after not finding one, he slouched against the the pickup door and made small talk with Gloria. He estimated she was around 40 years old. Her drab, conservative clothing gave her a missionary look that belayed her attractive features.

Gloria looked nothing like a seasoned CIA Agent. However, as she whipped the truck through traffic, she fed Josh bits of info she had gained though the use of natives on the ground. And gradually, Josh began to respect the abilities of this Agent.

As they neared the Nigerian border, Gloria turned down what looked like a trail to Josh. But after plowing through overgrown weeds and bushes for at least five miles, she pulled up to a low, thatched cabin that was almost hidden in the underbrush and shielded from view by dense foliage.

"Josh this is where we meet and receive items that we need for our mission. Over to your left, note the small clearing. That's where the Black Hawks land and drop off equipment. Last night your requested weapons arrived, and we have them hidden in a secure cache. You have enough stuff in there to start a war. Before we leave the meeting tonight, you can take what you need, and hand out any other weapons that our team might need. The Black Hawk chopper will drop down at ten tonight with the rest of the stuff you ordered."

"My god, you have everything, but the kitchen sink coming," Gloria quipped.

"Gloria, when you're facing a completely unknown situation, as we are here, you can't scrimp. I know some of that stuff I ordered looks like things we'll never use, but I want to be prepared."

"Okay, whatever you say. Stay in the truck until I get a positive ID."

Gloria punched her satellite cellphone, and then quickly added a 10-digit number. Seconds later a beep indicated a text message had been received and acknowledged. Gloria nodded.

"Come on, Josh."

Josh and Gloria left the truck and walked up the front steps of a darkened, run-down frame building. Gloria opened the door and pulled Josh in behind her.

"Josh, close the door," she said emphatically.

As the door shut, the room lit up with LED-focused lights. The first thing Josh saw was a man standing beside the door holding a flip-back Russian Wasp, an automatic .09-caliber automatic weapon. His finger was on the trigger.

"Guys, this is Josh Martin SF—donkey."

"Burro," said the agent holding the Russian Wasp. He lowered his weapon and stepped forward.

"I'm Bob Gibson, Josh. Great to have you aboard." Gibson was a rather plain, soft-spoken young man and his dusty, black skin obviously helped him fit into the population. He was wearing old, soiled jeans and a dirty, white shirt. Josh estimated that fewer than 130 pounds hung on his thin frame. He looked nothing like a CIA agent.

"Damn, Bob, if you don't look local, I don't know who does."

"I am local, Josh. I lived in Heathcourt, Nigeria, until I was eight, and I'm fluent in three tribal languages. I've been in deep cover for two years working as a gardener in Niamey."

"That's great. Your background will be invaluable when we get into the tropical rain forest in western Nigeria."

Josh turned to meet the other two members of the team.

"Hi, Josh. I'm Phil Harris."

"Nice to meet you, Phil."

"Josh, from what I know about you, my specialty should fit you to a T. I'm the head of the regional takedown team. Well, we actually call it the Extreme Interdiction Team. I've got a list and photos of fourteen al-Qaida operatives that my team is authorized to take down. Six of those bastards are hiding out in the jungle with the stuff."

Phil looked about as mild-mannered as anyone could imagine. His hair was a soft blond and slightly disheveled, and his clothes looked as if he had been teaching school all his life.

"Great to be working with you Phil. I just hope you get to apply your expertise on this job."

"If you can pin 'em down, my men can take 'em out."

The last agent stepped forward to shake Josh's hand.

"I'm Sid Crawford. Just a regular, run-of-the-mill agent. Well, I've put together some good stuff durning my twenty years here in Africa—guess it wasn't good enough for General Davis—you bring your magic wand?"

It was more than just a good-natured bit of sarcasm. Josh quickly analyzed him. *Senior man in Africa—passed over for the job—he'll be a pain in the ass.*

"Mr. Crawford, you are dismissed from the team. Go outside and sit on the porch, and wait for the chopper to take you back."

"What? You can't dismiss me! I'm the senior CIA man on this continent!"

"Actually, I can. I have complete authority over every item in this assignment, and that includes personnel. Now get your ass out of the room. We've got work to do.—Gloria send in a dispatch saying Crawford was dismissed for insubordination, and ask that it be placed on his record."

There was a stunned silence as Crawford slowly left the room. When he closed the door behind him, Josh motioned for the other agents to gather around him. "I hated to do that, but this team must work together, and smoothly, for us to do this mission. We didn't need some pencil-pushing desk jockey with a chip on his shoulder dragging us down.

"Now, before we proceed are there any more comments or questions?"

"Yes, I have one," said Gloria.

"Go ahead," Josh said, expecting the defense of a fellow agent.

"Good move. You did the right thing. The guy should have retired years ago. He's been nothing but a prick to work for."

There were nods from the other team members.

"Well, let's put that behind us and get down to business."

Josh nodded in satisfaction, and walked over to a large, square table that had a half-dozen chairs around it. The small windows on the front and side of the house were blacked out. Josh immediately cut the small talk and got straight to the point.

"Let's don't waste any time. We've all been briefed, and we know exactly what our mission is. Update me with the latest info you've managed to pick up," Josh said. "Who's first?"

"Okay," said Bill Myers. "Josh, let me give you an overview of what it looks like in my sector. We've divided the area into five sectors...."

"I know that; continue."

"Well, my biggest problem concerns the locals. They're predominately Muslim, and any hint that we are hunting al-Qaida is met with a stone face, and I would bet a report goes straight back to the guys we're hunting..."

"Stop right there! Surely, we are not programming our mission to the locals. Are we?"

"Uh, well, how do you expect us to locate the bastards if we can't describe them?" asked Myers.

"Listen up and I'll tell you how. Tomorrow I want each of you to recruit five local men to go into the bush and report back to you. Tell the men you recruit that you are working for the Nigerian government undercover, and are looking for poachers. Give them several hundred dollars before they start to work, and tell them that for every poacher we catch they'll get five-hundred dollars. Of course, the 'poachers' will be anyone not native to the area.

"Now, let's go over the map of the area, and see if we can narrow down the search."

Myers pulled out a large roll map of the area, and for the next hour, every possible sighting was noted on the map. In addition, the AWAC's last coordinates were spotted and every road in the vicinity was highlighted on the map.

"It looks as if we can make a square like so," Josh said, taking a yellow highlighter and drawing a large box on the map. "Our target is somewhere within that thirty-square-miles. Do any of you think there's any possibility that the bad guys could be outside this box? Anybody think the box is too small?"

A shaking of heads "no," and Josh continued. "Okay, a couple of things we must do immediately. From your briefing material, you've been made aware that an Iranian nuclear scientist went into the jungle just a few days ago. We need to monitor the road back to Niger, where we can grab him when he heads back to the airport in Niamey. Myers, can you handle that?"

"Yeah, I've got some local assets that can set up a roadblock, and if he tries to pass we'll grab him."

"Good. Now, the second item of business is to set plastic demo charges on the support columns of every bridge in this Square. I will have the charges flown in by sometime tomorrow. We'll divide up the work and set the charges ourselves..."

"Wait a minute, Josh. If you blow all those bridges it'll create havoc..."

"Myers, don't you think a bomb in London's Victoria Station would create more havoc than blowing a half-dozen bridges in Nigeria? Okay, hear me out on this matter. We're not going to blow any bridges right now, but if we nab the Iranian, we'll know the bombs have been armed, and we can't afford to let them leave this area. When we capture the Iranian, we'll blow the bridges, and hopefully by then we'll have enough clues about where the sorry bastards are for us to call in some Seals and Rangers."

"Wait a minute, Josh. CIA methods aren't usually that in-your-face. Don't you think we should consider some other tactics?" Meyers asked.

"I have, and this is just a start of phase one of the operation. I'll keep you informed on a need-to-know basis as we proceed. Now, let me be very clear on one subject: The rules of engagement on this mission are not going to be decided by a majority vote. My direct instructions from General Davis put me in charge of all operations that are to be conducted. That was not my idea, it was General Davis's. So—bottom line. We need to address this mission with one thought: If we do not succeed, our lack of success might cause the death of hundreds of thousands of innocent people.

"With that thought in mind, I suggest we bond together as a team and resolve to do everything—and that means anything. There is nothing; absolutely nothing, that is off-limits. We are to use all our resources to stop what could be horrendous consequences if we fail. Are we in agreement?"

A nod of heads, and Josh went back to the map.

"Okay, let's spend some time and see if we can narrow the area down. I want each of you to take this yellow highlighter and put an arrow where you have credible information from one of your local assets. Bill, you go first."

For the next hour, the five CIA agents studied the map, sometimes drawing arrows in one direction or another. Finally, after the last agent finished, the team gathered around the map and Josh began to evaluate the intelligence.

"First, let's remove all the individual arrows that aren't in agreement with the majority of the data." Josh and the rest of the team began to scan the map, and point out arrows that conflicted with the majority. After another 30 minutes, the team stood and looked at the arrows that were left, and then Josh spoke.

"I think it is pretty obvious that somewhere in our large, overall area of interest we have a target, and it looks as if it will be on the eastern one-half of the quadrant. We have to make some educated guesses because of the tight time frame, so I want Bill and Troy to link their assets together and focus just on the ten-mile section in that eastern area. Naturally, I don't want to ignore the other areas, so the rest of us will employ the additional assets I mentioned earlier, and see if we can come up with anything. Anyone have any observations or comments?"

"Gloria, you look a little concerned. What's your problem?"

"Josh, I've been through most of the area we've highlighted, and it's the heart of the Nigerian Tropical Rain Forest. You could hide a battleship in there. Actually locating the camp will be worse than looking for a needle in a haystack."

"Yeah, I've gathered as much, just from looking at the topo map. Anyone else?—Go ahead Phil."

"Josh, as you know the northern part of Nigeria and Niger has the largest concentration of Muslims in the region. Al-Qaida has been very successful in recruiting, and that was the reason they were able to stop the Seals and Rangers from capturing the enriched uranium at the Niger border. When they entered the eastern Nigerian jungle, they had ninety-two fighters with them. Any direct action by Seals or Rangers in that jungle would be like fighting Vietnam all over again.

"Whatever we do must be with an overwhelming force, or we won't stand a chance. I think we should consider a joint operation with Rangers and Nigerian troops."

"Well, if you want to guarantee another mini-Vietnam, that would be the perfect way to do it. So we're not going to use a hammer to do the job. Sometimes a small, coordinated team can accomplish more than a whole company of Rangers. However, we do want to be flexible enough to call in a hundred Rangers or six Seals, if we have an exact location of the al-Qaida camp.

"And what we do every minute of the day must have one goal: to find the material and use any asset available to kill the men who are trying to move it into a Western, populated country. Got it? Now, let's go back over there maps have see if we've missed anything."

The team spent another two hours discussing contingincy plans until Josh signaled that the meeting was over.

"It's late and I think we've covered almost everything we can tonight. Make sure you remove anything that would signal this house is being used, and set two surveillance cameras and a parabolic listening device in the bushes near the front door. I'll give the AWAC's the password so they can monitor the cameras and listening devices. They will report to me if anyone approaches the house.

"We don't want to show up some night for a meeting and run into an ambush. The sorry sons-of-bitches know we're after their ass, and it would surprise me if they didn't try a preemptive strike. We should take every precaution to prevent a surprise attack.

"Tonight, I'm going to send headquarters an encoded text with our coordinates at this safe house and get some plastic explosives delivered sometime tomorrow night. Everyone should check your text messages tomorrow for the exact time. Be here to receive your demo charges, and take tomorrow night to put them in place on every bridge piling in this quadrant. The timers should be set so they can be activated by my cellphone—got it?"

Josh paused, eyeing the members of his team carefully.

"Okay, let's set the cameras and listening devices, so we can get out of here and get some sleep."

Another 17 minutes passed, and as each agent signaled completion of the security set-up, Josh called an end to the meeting.

"I'll see you tomorrow night—same time, unless you receive a coded text from me."

8

Stealth

Josh and Gloria left the safe house and drove east on a secluded, back-road trail into Nigeria, to avoid the official Nigerian border crossing. At 2:23, they arrived at Mamboddie, a small village at the end of the only road into the area. It was an assorted group of thatched huts, along with several unpainted wood-frame buildings.

"This is it, Josh. One-hundred and twelve natives live here. We're the only outsiders. The Southern Baptists started a mission here three years ago, but they didn't stay. I've been working here in deep cover for the last two years. The Baptists left about the time I arrived. I'm officially your assistant."

"Okay, I've got it. Let's get a little sleep."

As they got out of the Land Rover, Josh nodded to Gloria. "That was damn good driving when you picked me up at the airport."

"Thanks, Josh. Actually, as I said earlier, it was just to save a little red tape. The authorities knew you were arriving on a private jet, and the State Department had cleared you, but the locals still wanted to throw a little weight around and check you out. I took it into my own hands to not go back to the terminal and waste time, and have you photographed by the local police. Hell, they would have sold your picture straight to al-Qaida before dark."

"Good thinking, but where did you learn to drive like that?"

"My dad was a stock car driver, and I was racing with him by the time I was twelve. You'd be surprised at the amount of damage a pickup truck can take and still keep moving."

"I'm sure I would."

"Josh, this is my cabin and yours is next door. Everything, including your new clothes, are in there. Tomorrow morning, don't forget to put on the missionary clothes laid out on your bed. At eight in the morning, I'll come by and we'll walk over to the village chief's house for breakfast. After that, I'll show you the routine here in the village. I know this will be a little awkward for you, but you'll have to lead services and do some Bible teaching.

"I've have left a prep book on your bed. Be sure and review it before tomorrow—and be sure to carry the Bible on your bed everywhere you go—Got it?"

"Okay, I'll see you in the morning."

Josh stepped into his sparsely furnished room and looked things over. On his bed, which was covered with mosquito netting were the clerical clothing, a Bible, and a stack of tracts. He first took care of security by turning his cellphone on camera alert, using the CIA ******classified–app. Any movement of the door would trigger a signal, and give Josh time to pick up his Glock that he'd place on the bedside table.

He wedged the only chair in the room under the doorknob for a little extra safety, and then crawled under the mosquito netting and into bed. Before he dropped off to sleep, he sent an encrypted text message, requesting that the plastic demo charges be dropped off the next night at the safe house. That done, he slipped under the sheets, and was asleep in less than 10 minutes.

It only seemed as if only minutes had passed when a ring from his cell alarm told him it was 7 o'clock and time to get up. After a quick shower and a review of the religious tracts, Josh dressed in his missionary clothes and walked out of the cabin with the Bible tucked under his arm. Gloria was waiting for him.

"Am I late?" Josh questioned.

"No, not at all. I just need a few hours of sleep, so I'm always up early. I jogged for an hour before I showered and dressed."

Josh, was surprised at Gloria's fitness, but considering the seriousness of the mission, he wasn't surprised that she was selected to be the key member of his team. He was becoming more and more aware of her abilities. *She not here to fill out some quota for women in the CIA,* crossed his mind. Gloria interrupted Josh's thoughts.

"We're going to walk over to the village chief's house for a breakfast of fruit. He's a very religious Christian, and you will be expected to pray before we eat, so get ready. After breakfast, we'll tour the village and then go to our meeting place where you will teach a group of young kids in Bible School. If we're going to stay under deep cover, we must do these things.

"Later today—after lunch—I've set up some meetings with several young men. I think we can trust them, but I'm not sure, so carry your weapon under your shirt."

"Gloria, we need to have security on the east side of the village. That dim road leads directly into the jungle and intersects the west boarder of our quadrant in less than a half-mile. It seems to be the only road from the jungle that leads directly into the village. If the bad guys decide to come visit us, they will almost certainly approach the village from that direction. They know we're hunting them, and since they have a large group of fighters, I'd be surprised if they don't make a preemptive strike."

"You're probably right, Josh. I'll have two of my best locals watch the road, and notify me if they see anyone coming. By the way, telling them we are working with the government is a great idea. The tribesmen in the village hate the poachers, and for five-hundred dollars they'd sell their grandchildren and turn in their mothers."

"Good. I'll also put a surveillance camera on the road. Animals will probably trigger it, but it may help spot anyone trying to come in at night."

As the day passed, Josh went though the missionary paces with Gloria by his side, translating for him as he taught Bible School to a large group of village kids. Because of Josh's early childhood in southern Arkansas, where he had a perfect attendance in Sunday School, the Bible teaching was easy.

Almost all the work done by the missionary team, which consisted of just Gloria and Josh, was done in the morning. And after a lunch of roast chicken with chopped liver and sugared dates, he and Gloria met with the young men she had hired to work with them.

Josh, with Gloria translating, went into a long-winded explanation of how they were assisting the Nigerian Government in locating poachers who were killing off endangered species. When Josh mentioned the dollars they would receive if poachers were caught, there was almost a stampede to take the jobs offered. After making an initial payment of 25 percent of the funds offered, Gloria and Josh explained what each of the men would do.

"Miss Gloria will show you the route you will take into the jungle to hunt for the poachers. Be sure to stay exactly on your assigned route. She will give each of you a compass and show you how to use it. Your job is to report to Miss Gloria anyone you see that is not a member of a local tribe. Remember, we are trying to locate men who have come into the jungle from the north to hunt animals. If you see somebody who's not from this area, come back out of the jungle and go directly to Miss Gloria. Does everybody understand?"

Heads nodded.

"Very good. Every day you work, we'll pay you the agreed amount, but you are to tell no one you are working for us. If you tell anyone, we will not pay you."

Josh issued each of the young men a compass, and, after a few minutes, they had mastered how to take a bearing and figure out how far they were traveling into the jungle. The men were to make a report to Gloria every afternoon at 3 o'clock and describe everything they had seen on their trek into the jungle.

After dinner that night, and before Josh retired to his cabin, he gave Gloria instructions to meet him at 11 on the edge of the village in her Land Rover. While Josh was waiting, he plotted out distances from the village into the jungle and reviewed the most likely spots for the al-Qaida force to be hiding. He poured over Google's detail map of the area, and came away depressed at the thought of having to find the al-Qaida force in the dense rain forest.

For the last hour before he met Gloria, he circled the bridges in the 30-square-mile quad. Josh was convinced that one of the most positive things they could do would be to confine the al-Qaida fighters, the enriched uranium, and the biomaterial to a rain forest in central Africa, far away from any population center.

At 11, Josh and Gloria headed for the safe house, and 43 minutes later, they cleared code and walked into the house. The other three members of the team were waiting for them.

"I've got confirmation of a supply drop by chopper that will occur at 12:33. I want everyone to put their daily reports in the pouch, which will be taken back to headquarters," Josh ordered. He pulled out a three-page summary of his last 24 hours, and put it the CIA courier pouch.

"Your reports will go straight to General Davis's desk by jet courier, and every day of this mission you will do the same. Got it?"

A nod from everyone in the group and each member put a report in the pouch.

"All right let's review everything we set up today," Josh said as Bill Myers unrolled a topo map of the area.

"First, item: Did everyone hire their locals to scout your territory? Okay, how many men total do we have going into the jungle?"

An hour passed and every item and possible clue that pointed toward where the camp might be was analyzed in detail, and included in the overall report.

"Be sure everything—and I mean everything—is in your report, and if money will buy info, spread it around. Uncle has more money than god. All of the information we send in will be put into the most sophisticated computer program you can imagine, and the computer will send us a daily best guess of where the camp is located****" Josh was interrupted by a ding from his cell.

A glance: "ETA in 32 seconds. Let's get outside and make the swap. Chopper won't stay on ground over 5 minutes—orders from General Davis."

The team finished stuffing their reports into the CIA pouch, and then walked outside to wait on the chopper. It was descending before they heard it using silent ******classified—rotor blades and showing no lights. A soft thump in landing was all the noise it made. The door flipped open and a man in the chopper shoved a large package into the doorway.

"Hey, don't drop this mother, or you might blow us all to hell."

Josh shook his head. Hell, he thought, you couldn't make this stuff blow up if you hit it with a hammer. But you damn sure can with the proper detonator.

Myers tossed the CIA pouch into the chopper as the man inside pushed another package into the doorway.

"That's it, guys. We're out of here!" he yelled as he gave a thumbs-up to the pilot.

Josh and the others carried the packages back into the cabin as the chopper rose above the treetops.

"Okay, this box is the demo stuff. Each of you take what you need for the bridges you've been assigned. Let's go back inside and be sure we have all the bridges spotted. I've got them noted on my Google map.

The rest of the stuff is extra equipment I think we might need. During the next few days, if you think of anything that would help us do our job, let me know and I'll have it dropped in the next time the chopper comes. One other thing: There's a special mask and clip-on detector for each of you. It's the latest technology, and, according to the briefing I received, when your buzzer sounds, you had better get the mask on in seconds or you're dead meat. The detector will pick up both chemical and biomaterial. We probably won't need the protection, but if we run into something I want to be prepared. Remember, wear the detector and keep the mask hidden on your body at all times.

"One other thing: In your demo package you'll find a new technology—chest body armor. Put it on immediately and don't take it off, even to sleep. It's a new item that is supposed to stop anything south of a fifty-caliber slug. But it won't stop a shot to the head. SF research tells us that ninety-one percent of all al-Qaida wounds are to the upper torso. Hell, if this new armor is as good as they say it is, the U. S. casualties might really drop.

"Oh, just a reminder: We started trying to give the Afghans some of our old body armor, but as fast as we gave it to them, they sold it on the black market to the Taliban. So remember your training, and shoot for the head. I wouldn't be surprised if we run into some of that old body armor here. I had an SF in Indonesia panic, and he emptied his gun into the chest of a fighter who'd burst out of the undergrowth. But the fighter's momentum carried him forward, and I had to pull a machete out of the SF's stomach. That's why we're trained to take headshots."

For the next 45 minutes, the team separated out the demo charges they would need to blow the assigned bridges, and after Josh had double-checked the map to be sure he hadn't missed a bridge, everyone left. He and Gloria were driving back when she suddenly began to question the bridge demolition.

"Josh, if we blow every bridge you assigned, it will bring the Nigerian Army down on us. We can't possibly keep our cover."

"Don't worry about that, Gloria. State has already informed our ambassador that in order to intersect known terrorists we may have to destroy some bridges in the suspect area. I don't know how much American aid our ambassador promised. But Uncle can buy almost anything that is for sale, and the Nigerian army is for sale—it's just a matter of dollars. We won't be bothered, and if al-Qaida can't get the bombs and biomaterial out of the jungle, sooner or later we'll nail the bastards."

"I know that, Josh, but some of those bridges are the only lifeline for the natives living around here. It will cause a great hardship for them."

"It can't be helped, Gloria. If we let one of those bombs out of this jungle, it will be hell to pay. In one of the Libyan interrogations with a top Gaddafi loyalist, actually, one on the old bastard's sons, he mentioned London as a target. It was just something an al-Qaida contact mentioned, but I wouldn't be surprised if it is a target. I can't even imagine what would happen if those sorry mothers managed to sneak one of the bombs, or hell, the biomaterial into metropolitan London."

"I know, we have to do this, Josh. I just hope we can nail those guys quickly."

"It may not be quickly, but we'll get 'em."

***

For the next couple of days, Josh monitored the local assets who were venturing into the jungle on the compass vector lines he had set out. Almost immediately, he began to receive bits of information about unusual men who had been seen in the jungle. However, the sightings were always brief glimpse, and even with these sighting, they did not narrow the search for the al-Qaida camp. However, a series of transmissions from the Pentagon's computer program did begin to reduce the 30-mile-square Josh had outlined. He was confident that in another day or two he would be able to located the camp.

The men working for Josh and the other CIA agents had been searching the jungle for three days, when at 11:15 on the third day, one of Josh's men from the village rushed into the open pavilion where Josh was teaching Bible School and frantically motioned for him to come outside. Josh and Gloria followed the man to the back of the building, and he breathlessly told them.

"I saw two very unusual men in the jungle. Wearing cloths not like we wear here. They saw me, and I ran back here as fast as I could, but they followed me, and they are just a few hundred yards down the trail from the village."

"Sinndal, go to your hut and don't come out. We will take care of this matter. Do not mention this to anyone. We may be able to capture some of the poachers.—Gloria, follow me and hurry." Sinndal rushed out running for his house and Gloria followed Josh as he hurried toward the jungle trail that led to the village. As soon as they got a hundred yards from the village, Josh started looking for a place to ambush the fighters,

"Gloria crouch behind these bushes. If the men are armed, they are al-Qaida fighters. Get ready to shoot. Be sure to have your silencer on. We don't want to have the whole bunch come down on us, and upset everyone in the village."

In a few minutes, Josh spotted the two men following the trail heading toward the village, noting the trail would pass within 10 yards from where they were hiding. Josh nodded to Gloria and pointed to his eye. He pulled his Glock from under his blosey shirt and saw Gloria do the same. As the men approached, Josh saw they were dressed very much in the style of north Africans not sub-Saharan Africans, and they were armed, carrying AK .47s slung over their shoulders. They were less than 10 yards away when Josh punched Gloria, stood up and shot the nearest man in the head. A half second later, Gloria sent several slugs into the chest of the other man, who staggered back bleeding profusely. A second shot to the head from Josh dead checked him. The only sounds were several dull pops as the new ultra-silencers reduced the sound to a minimum.

"Damn it, Gloria! Don't ever shoot a person in the body! Always go for the head! How many times am I going to have to tell you?"

"I know, Josh, but I was so nervous. I've never shot anyone before."

"Come on, let's drag the poor bastards off the trail into the bush. We will come back and bury them tonight if some animal doesn't eat 'em. Search their pockets to see if they are carrying any identification."

In a few minutes, Josh and Gloria had hid the bodies in the brush near the trail, and Josh was thumbing through the papers the men were carrying.

"Look at this, Gloria. It is a Libyan driver's license, and here is more stuff from Tripoli and Sirte. These guys are some of the men who met with al-Qaida and transported the nuclear material out of Libya. Well, we know one thing for certain; the vector reading Sinndal took leads fairly close to the camp. We are narrowing the search. Tonight we will follow the vector I gave him, and see if we can spot the camp. Hell, we might get lucky. Oh, by the way, put one of your most trusted men down the trail about a half-mile from here. I have a feeling they may send some others to see what happened to the two we shot. Meet me behind my cabin at one seventeen tonight, take an automatic weapon, and wear NVG's. I'll bring some extra stuff in case we run into trouble."

***

Josh was behind his cabin that night by one twelve waiting on Gloria. He had a backpack carrying some additional items, and his Israeli Uzi was in his hand. Gloria stepped out from behind the cabin where she had been waiting for Josh to arrive. She was carrying a flip down automatic AK .47 with silencer.

"You don't think we'll actually need these automatic weapons tonight; do you?" Gloria asked.

"Well, you never know. Remember, our best intelligence says there are nine-two fighters in the camp. I would sure hate to stumble into that hornet's nest and not be well armed. Come on, get let's get moving, and watch out for any trip wires when we get a few miles into the jungle. I am certain they have some outlying security, and don't step on a snake."

"What? You're not worried about snakes, are you?" asked Gloria.

"Well, I wouldn't just tromp through the jungle. After all most snakes are nocturnal, and they may think this trail is easier to move down than the weeds and other stuff they run into out in the brush. Of course, a lot of the snakes in Nigeria are pit vipers, and you're dead meat if one of them sinks their fangs into your leg."

"Well, now you've got me worried. I'm not afraid of al-Qaida, but snakes damn sure give me the willies."

"Okay, I'll watch out for you. Come on we need to get moving."

Josh and Gloria moved down the trail at a steady pace and Josh watched his compass to be sure they were on the vector Sinndal had followed. The moon was out and the NVG's were doing a good job. *Just a little light makes all the difference,* mulled Josh as he welcomed the bright moonlight. The NVG's amplified the moonlight until it seemed as if it were daylight.

Another hour passed and Josh calculated they had walked nearly three miles down the game trail they were following.

"Gloria let's keep up the pace for another hour, and if we don't come across something, we'll head back to the village."

"Okay, Josh, just tell me when…"

"Stop!*** Don't move! I think we tripped an alarm!" Josh whispered. He raised his weapon to his shoulder, flipped off the safety, and gently squeezed the trigger.

A flash from the barrel of Josh's weapon sent a man, who had stepped out from behind a tree, spinning around. He fell in the trail about 10 yards ahead of Josh and Gloria.

"Outpost security… come on, let's get out of here. That wire will trigger the camp, and we'll have a dozen al-Qaida fighters on our ass in a few minutes."

Josh and Gloria hurried back up the trail, and after 100 yards, Josh stopped and dug something out of his rucksack.

"What are you doing, Josh?"

"Well, when they find the body of that guard, they'll be coming up the trail like a bunch of wild Indians. When they get to this Claymore anti-personal mine, it will slow them down. This is a Leaping Betsy. When they trip this trigger wire, the mine will go off, but not until it pops up about four feet in the air. Then it will explode and spray steel ball bearing out. If you're within ten yards of this baby, you are a dead man, or woman—Okay, let's get moving. I've got it set."

Josh and Gloria picked up their speed until they were moving at a slow jog, weaving up the trail toward the village. They had been jogging for about 10 minutes when a *boom* echoed through the jungle.

"A few less of the sorry bastards to worry about," quipped Josh.

"Look out! Snake!" yelled Josh. In one motion he yanked Gloria back, turned his Uiz down, and sent two slugs into the snake's head.

"Damn, that's a huge black mamba. That damn snake is one of the deadliest in the country."

"Josh, I'm walking behind you for the rest of the way back. I'll cover our backs if the al-Qaida fighters catch up with us."

"Okay. When we get back to the village, we will note the GPS location where we picked up security. That should put us one step closer to pinning down the location of the camp. I'll bet we were within a half-mile of the main camp. When we get back give the GPS coordinates to the AWAC command, and ask HQ to have a satellite infrared scan made of a five mile grid. Got it?"

"Yeah, I'll have it out in a few minutes."

"I'll bet we'll have a one kilometer probable location from the Pentagon computer as soon as it processes this GPS. We're a day away from closing the noose on them."

An hour later, Josh and Gloria jogged back into camp, and went to Josh's cabin where he pulled out the Google map with the vectors and sightings.

"Okay—hey take a look at this. I would be willing to bet that security guard was within a half-mile of the camp, and if he was, the camp is somewhere along the Occulate River. There is a faint trail of a road leading in that direction, and with the balloon desert tires, the trucks could drive on it. Get the AWAC's to focus on that area, and see if they can pick up anything. And I'll get Washington to do a new series of aerial shots from one of the satellites, and have it infra-red coded to see if we can see through the leaves. Hey, it's nearly five o'clock. Let's get a few hours of sleep. I don't think we can accomplish much more tonight."

***

The next day passed without any sightings from the men sent into the jungle on compass vectors. Josh had decided not to send anyone back on the vector where Sinndel spotted the two fighters. He was almost sure, from the GPS readings and the other sightings that he had narrowed the area down to a minimum of a five-mile square, and the Pentagon computer program had it down to a square mile.

The AWAC's were picking up a variety of signals from the general area, but they could not pinpoint it much better than what Josh had already discerned. The satellite pictures and the infra-red gave some addition hints and allowed him to eliminate several areas around the suspected site. Josh thought about what he needed to do before he called in Seal teams or any other Special Operation soldiers. He would have to personally confirm the exact location of the camp, and take out the primiter guards.

9

Hasanni el-Kohimine

Josh was taking a short break from his Bible teaching when he felt his cellphone vibrate. He quickly glanced at it, punched the decode icon, and gasped as he read the message.

"Have the Iranian scientist! Please advise." He punched in the answer.

"Take him to the saft house, strap him to a chair, and inform team to assemble there: ASAP."

Josh strolled over to where Gloria was teaching a large class of young girls how to prepare a nutritious meal and signaled her to join him. Gloria quickly told the class to take a water and bathroom break, and walked over to where Josh was standing.

"We have the Iranian," he whispered. "I've told the team to meet at the safe house as soon as possible. This means the Iranian has given them information to arm the bombs, or he may have actually armed them himself. This is a critical moment, and we don't have a moment to lose."

"Okay, I'll tell the village chief we have some medical problem, and we'll have to return to Niger to have it seen about."

"Good, now I need to detonate the charges we placed on all the bridges." He pulled out his cell and began to punch in the code number that would set off the demo charges wired to all the bridges in the marked off quadrangle.

"Oh my god, Josh, do you have to blow the bridges?"

"Yeah, I do, Gloria. The sorry bastards are not going to sit around with three armed nuclear bombs. They are going to move them as soon as possible, and we have got to confine them to this area. Hell, with all the trails and roads in the area we could never set up enough checkpoints."

Josh finished punching in the 10-digit code and hit send. Seconds later, a series of thundering rumbles could be heard in the distance.

"Well, Gloria, in a few minutes the al-Qaida boys are going to know we've blown the bridges, and that will set off a desperate search to find a way to move the material. Blowing those bridges may keep the material in the jungle, but it will also force their hand. We need to be ready. We've passed the point of no return—let's head for the safe house. We have an intensive interrogation to do on the Iranian, and what he tells us may help immensely in our hunt for the camp."

As they drove toward the safe house, Josh handed his phone to Gloria. "Send Bob Myers this additional text. **"Tie the Iranian to a chair with arms and strap his arms to the chair's arms with his palms down."**

"Josh, what are you going to do with that man? Aren't we going to turn him over to our security for them to interrogate?"

"No, it would take three days for security to pick him up, interrogate, and get the info back to us. We're going to do the interrogating ourselves. And since he knows that our government wouldn't do much more than question him, our guys probably wouldn't get much out of him. We'll use a little more pressure. And if it takes it to make him talk—a lot more pressure."

"Isn't that against protocol?"

"Fuck, protocol!—We're going to squeeze every drop of info out of that asshole, no matter what it takes. General Davis told me to use all means in order to accomplish this mission, and that's exactly what I'm going to do."

"You're going to use extreme means to get him to talk?"

"I'm going to torture the hell out of him, if that's what "extreme" means, and do it as rough as necessary. He *is* going to tell us everything he knows, or he'll regret it. I'll use a little technique I picked up in Afghanistan. I'm sure it'll work on someone like the Iranians, but not the hardened al-Qaida fighters. It won't be anywhere near as rough as what our friends in Egypt put al-Qaida fighters through."

That ended the conversation, and they drove along in silence for the rest of the trip. Thirty-three minutes later, Josh and Gloria pulled up in front of the safe house. They could hear the Iranian yelling before they opened the door.

"Well, it sounds like he speaks English. That will help, but I do know Farsi, which is the most common of the languages spoken in Iran."

As soon as Josh opened the door, the Iranian yelled to him, "I insist you release me! I'm an Iranian diplomat, and I demand you take me to the Iranian embassy in Niamey!"

Josh walked over and looked at the Iranian, who had made a clumsy attempt to disguise himself, and shook his head. The man was obviously a person of some means, sporting a diamond Rolex and manicured nails. He ignored the man's demands, and handed Gloria his rucksack.

"Gloria, there's a kit inside that says "interrogation aids." Hand me the elastic wrapping strap and hook the monitor cord into the connector. Bill, when I start the interrogation, write down every question and answer and the redline reading from Gloria. We will establish a baseline first, and then we'll get to the pertinent questions. Got it?"

Bill nodded and pulled out a pencil and pad as Josh pulled his knife and cut the Iranian's coat and shirtsleeve off, exposing his bare arm.

"What are you doing? I'll have you charged with assault, if you so much as touch me!" he yelled.

Josh and Gloria ignored him as Josh wrapped the Iranian's upper arm with the elastic wrapping.

"Okay, Gloria, see of you're getting a reading. I'll ask him some questions."

"Sir, if you cooperate, this interrogation will be over in a few minutes, but if you don't it may take much longer."

"You have no right to interrogate me! I've got diplomatic immunity! I demand you release me, and take me to my embassy in Niamey!"

Josh grabbed the Iranian by the throat and squeezed until the man was nearly unconscious.

"Now, since I have your attention, let's proceed with this interrogation," Josh snapped to the gasping man.

"I'm looking at your passport. Is your name, Hasanni el-Kohiminne?'

"Yes, it is, but you…"

"You are only to answer the question," said Josh. "Any further comments and I will strangle you again. Do I make myself clear?"

That stopped the conversation and Josh continued to ask the man questions derived directly from his passport. After another five questions, Josh looked over at Gloria. "Do you have a baseline?"

"Yes, it's very even," she replied.

Josh nodded, and took a step closer to the Iranian. "Sir, what was your mission in the Nigerian jungle?"

"I was conducting an assessment of humanitarian needs."

Josh glanced at Gloria.

"He's lying."

"Are you an Iranian nuclear scientist?"

"No, I swear. I'm a diplomat on a humanitarian mission."

"He's lying."

Josh continued to question the man intensely, and to every question that had anything to do with al-Qaida or nuclear weapons, the lie detector indicated he was lying.

After the Iranian denied even knowing the presence of the al-Qaida fighters, Josh addressed him: "Okay, I understand. You are not going to willingly give us any correct information about you actual mission or why you were meeting with al-Qaida operatives. Is that right?"

The man was silent. Josh pulled out his Glock .9 mm, gripped the barrel, and motioned to Myers, "Bill, hold his hand still and separate out his little finger."

"What are you doing?" the Iranian screamed, realizing Josh was serious about using force.

"Now, one more question, and I strongly suggest you give me the correct answer. Did you meet with al-Qaida operatives?"

"No, I did not."

"Lying," said Gloria.

"Hold his finger still, Bill."

Josh smashed the butt of the Glock's handle down on the Iranian's little fingernail with so much force that it nearly turned the chair over. It was a crushing blow that broke the nail and nearly flattened the end of the man's finger, splattering blood across the room.

"*Ahaaaaaa!*" More screaming, cursing, and yelling, and then the Iranian stopped, took a deep breath, and yelled, "You will pay dearly for attacking me!"

"Move the knuckle up a bit," Josh said to Myers, as he ignored the man's desperate protests. "Don't touch me again! I'm warning you. If you do, it will cause a severe diplomatic incident!"

"Okay, I won't touch you again—if you answer the questions. Did you meet with al-Qaida fighters or operatives?"

"No, I only met with local farmers and others to see if the aid package we sent was being distributed properly."

Josh glanced at Gloria.

"He's lying."

Josh nodded to Myers who shoved the Iranian's hand toward the end of the chair arm.

"No! Stop! I am telling the truth!"

"He's lying, Josh," said Gloria quietly.

The butt of Josh's Glock came down on the man's knuckle, flattening it. There was more screaming and yelling, which Josh ignored. The Iranian slumped over, holding his head down and moaning, as Josh stepped in front of him. He grabbed the man's hair and yanked him so that he was sitting straight up in the chair.

"Now, Mr. al-Kohiminne, I am going to ask you another question, and if you lie to me, I'll smash another finger. You have nine left plus ten toes and then your penis. So before you lie to me again, consider the consequences. Did you meet with al-Qaida operatives?"

There was a long pause, and then the Iranian spoke, "No, I did not! I'm an Iranian diplomat, and I demand…"

A quick look to Gloria.

"He is lying, Josh," she said.

"Hold his hand down, Bill."

"No, don't! Don't!*** *Ahaaaa!* Oh, no! No!"

"Move the knuckle down a bit, Bill."

"*Ahaaaaaa!* Please stop! Oh, my hand!"

"Bill, move to the next finger down."

"Wait! Stop! Please, no more. I will not lie again! I promise."

Josh put his Glock back in his shoulder holster and crouched down to be right in the Iranian's face.

"Listen to me!" Josh yelled. "If I hear the lady say you're lying one more time I will smash the other three fingers on your right hand. Do you understand me?"

There was a nod, and Josh began to ask questions again, glancing over at Gloria after each question. She was nodding "yes" every time, until Josh zeroed in on the actual arming of nuclear weapons.

"Did you configure the trigger mechanism for the bombs, and are the bombs operational?"

There was a pause, and then the Iranian said, "No, I only delivered some information to the leaders of the camp."

"He's lying on the first part of the question, Josh," Gloria noted.

"By god, I warned you!" Josh yelled. "You're not going to have any fingers left, if you keep lying to me!"

Josh pulled his gun and flipped it over to hold the barrel as the Iranian began to recant his story, "Wait! Wait!—Yes! I did connect the trigger mechanism, but I did not attach it to the bombs—Please don't hurt me! I promise I won't lie again!"

Josh slipped his weapon back into his holster and continued the questioning.

An hour later, Josh motioned for the team to assemble near the back of the room. "Can anyone think of anything else we can ask this piece of trash?"

"No, I can't, but what're we going to do with him?" asked Myers.

"We're going to shoot him and bury him in the bushes beside the road, when we finish the interrogation," replied Josh.

"What? Josh, we cannot execute an unarmed man tied to a chair! You know that!"

"The hell we can't, Bill. Listen up and I will tell you why we have to kill him. First of all, he's a known terrorist who has just armed three weapons of mass destruction. Secondly, we can't get security in here until tomorrow night, and just by having him, it will hold up any action we might contemplate taking. And the last point: A dead Iranian nuclear scientist will certainly be appreciated by the State Department. A live Iranian scientist would be an unbelievably hot potato. They wouldn't know what in the hell to do with him. We're going to shoot the bastard, and I'll do it, since you guys obviously don't want the job…"

Josh was interrupted by a pop from a .9 mm Beretta revolver with silencer. The team turned around to see Gloria calmly slip her weapon back in its holster. She had just shot the Iranian in the temple.

"Damn, Gloria, I was going to take him outside to keep from messing up the floor," said Josh. But he was obviously pleased by Gloria's action. *My god, she's got more balls than the rest of these guys combined,* he thought.

"Okay, let's get him in the bushes and bury him. We've got a lot to do."

10

The Quest

After burying the Iranian, Josh and the rest of the team spent several hours reviewing a topo map trying to pinpoint the exact location of the camp. They were sure it was within the five-mile square Josh had drawn on the map after he and Gloria returned from their late-night trek into the jungle. However, even though the Pentagon computer had narrowed it down even further, Josh knew he could not call in an air strike or even get on-the-ground strike forces without a positive exact location. After pouring over the map for another hour, he informed the team of a decision he had made earlier in the evening.

"All right, I think everyone understands exactly our situation. We are very close to pinpointing the al-Qaida camp, but we must have an exact location before we call in Seals and Rangers. Since I've had jungle training in Malaysia, I'm the logical one to spot the exact location of the camp. I'll go tomorrow night."

The team was shocked, but after Josh explained why the camp must be exactly located, they stopped questioning him.

Josh drove back to the village in silence, thinking about what he would be doing tomorrow night. He knew the camp would have extra sentries posted anywhere from a half-mile to a mile away from the center of the camp. This time he would have locate them undetected, take them out, and lock in an exact GPS coordinates on the center of the camp. Gloria broke the silence.

"Josh, you shouldn't go by yourself. Why don't you let me go with you and provide extra security?"

"Gloria, I appreciate your willingness to go on this mission, but I think it's a one- person job. Back when I was a boy, growing up in

South Arkansas, I was a crack squirrel hunter. I became a good hunter by being able to move through the woods without making a sound. I had a couple of months of jungle infiltration training in Malaysia a few years back, too, so I'm the logical one to search out the camp. I noted on the resumes that your CIA team members are all from big cities, and none of you has had any training experience of this nature. Besides, it will be harder for two individuals to go undetected rather than one. By now, they know we've destroyed the bridges. We can expect extra security around the camp, and they may be panicked into doing something desperate."

Gloria understood, and for the rest of the trip she leaned back in the seat and tried to sleep.

"Wake up, Gloria. The village is just around the next curve."

Gloria sat up and stretched as Josh drove into the center of the village and pulled up in front of their cabins. *Sure seems quiet,* he thought. *The place looks deserted.* Josh turned to Gloria with some last-minute instructions.

"Tomorrow, we'll just go through our normal routine, and if anyone asks about the bridges, we'll profess ignorance." Josh opened the Land Rover door and started to step out when the detector on his belt let out a loud beep.

"Don't get out! Put on your mask! Hurry!" Josh yelled.

Josh jumped back in the car, slammed the door, and, in seconds, they had their gas masks on. After Josh and Gloria has secured and adjusted their masks, Josh nodded. "Come on, Gloria. Let's check things out. Be ready to shoot," Josh commanded. He opened the Land Rover door and cautiously moved away from the vehicle, holding his Glock out in front of him. Not a sound came from the village, and as Josh moved along beside the cabins and huts, he became aware that there were no signs of life. Soon they saw the work of a powerful hydrogen sulfide biochemical gas—a gas that can kill a human being after one breath. Josh spotted an exploded canister in the center of the village. It was obvious that al-Qaida operatives had exploded it to try and kill any American CIA agents who were in the village, and in doing so they killed every person in the village.

"Gloria, they must have followed the trail from where I killed the sentry to this village, and assumed we were staying here. God, I hate that these innocent villagers were killed, but there's nothing we can do for them now. The gas they used is so deadly that one whiff is fatal.

"We can't stay here. We must go back to the safe house in Niger. The militants are getting desperate. They know we're closing in on them, and they are doing everything they can to stop us. If we don't zero in on the location of the camp within the next 24 hours, I'm afraid they'll find a way to break out of the area, and take some of the nuclear and biomaterial with them. We can't let that happen. If they get out there is no telling where they'll go or what they'll do."

"But what are we going to do about all these dead villagers?"

"What can we do, Gloria? If we call the authorities, they will at the very least haul us in for questions. We can't let anything impede our search for the camp."

"You're right, Josh, but it's so hard for me to just ignore all the bodies. I've worked for months with some of these people and it pains me to see them scattered around on the ground. They are all dead because of al-Qaida's hatred of us."

"I hate it too, Gloria, but it would be even worse if we don't eliminate this nest of rats and recover the material."

"I know, Josh, but it so hard to just walk away from this tragedy."

"Well, let's get back to the safe house in Niger. We have a lot of planning to do." Josh and Gloria quickly packed up and in a few minutes, they were on their way back to their safe house in Niger.

Gloria was still distraught about the deaths of the people she had worked very closely with over the past several months.

"Josh, I've never seen anything so horrible. It's hard to just drive off and leave all those bodies. Many of them were my friends. Did we have to leave them just scattered on the ground like so many dead animals? What is going to happen to them?"

"Someone will come by the village in the morning, and they will call the authorities. We can't hang around and answer questions. Besides, what could our presence do for them now? What we have to do is prevent those bastards that killed the villagers from killing more innocent people."

"What about the hydrogen sulfide gas? Won't it be dangerous to whoever comes into the village?"

"No, it will completely dissipate in a few more hours. It was just barely dangerous when we arrived. When we get to the house in Niger, I will send an encrypted e-mail to the CIA and give them a heads-up. The local authorities won't have a clue what killed all those villagers. It will take a few days for them to figure out everything, and our guys can get them to keep the lid on this while we try to pin down the camp location."

"Josh, I think this is getting to be more than we can handle. Don't you think we should call for some additional help?"

"I've been considering that option ever since I saw all those bodies, but instead of more personnel on the ground, I'm going to reduce our footprint."

"What?"

"Yes, I think we should, as the Mafia boys would say, 'hit the mattresses.' E-mail the other team members to meet us at the safe house in Niger, and disband all of our watchers. We need to keep a low profile while I pin down the exact location of the al-Qaida camp. There is an old motor bike at the safe house. I'll take it and ride as far as the trail into the jungle from the village, and at eleven tomorrow night I will go into the jungle and determine the exact location of the camp.

"We need to have the Seals and Rangers ready to hit the al-Qaida camp at daylight. When everyone is at the safe house, we'll get the exact drop off point for the strike force. Notify the rest of our team to come immediately to the safe house. The situation has become increasing dangerous, and we must coordinate a strike within the next twenty-four hours or risk another horrible situation like the one at the village.

"I hadn't planned to attack the camp this quickly, but when I saw the bodies of those innocent people in the village, I knew we had to act immediately. Instead of just spotting the al-Qaida camp, I am going to eliminate all the sentries so we can do a surprise attack at daylight tomorrow. We can't wait any longer."

"Josh, don't you think you might be rushing it? After all, you only know the camp is within a five-mile grid. What if you can't find the camp?"

"Then we'll just hold everyone at the staging point until I do. But I think my chances are very good since I know exactly where the first sentry was located. I'll take his replacement out first and that should let me follow the trail he left back to the main al-Qaida camp."

"Josh, you said the camp probable has extra sentries now that we are closing in on them. How are you going to eliminated all of them without being spotted?"

"I've got some new extra sensitive NVG's so I'll have a big advantage. When I get my camouflage suit on they won't recognize me, especially in the dark. I plan to cut the throats of all the sentries. The pop of a silencer would be too loud to risk."

"Josh, that's the most dangerous thing I have ever heard of. Are you trying to commit suicide?"

"Gloria, my training takes the risk out of the operation. This type of mission is considered routine by SFs."

That concluded the conversation, and they drove back toward the safe house in silence for the rest of the journey. As he drove along, Josh's mind was swirling with questions and plans. When they arrived, Josh immediately began to pore over the topo map, and when the rest of the team arrived, Gloria briefed them about the hydrogen sulfide gas attack on the village.

"My God, Josh; al-Qaida has killed something like a hundred villagers, we've blown up every bridge within a thirty-mile radius of the probable camp location, and we have nothing to show for it. Don't you think we need some backup before we go forward?" asked Myers.

"Backup for what? Just by having a couple of Seal units or more CIA folks won't solve anything. What we need is the exact location of the camp, then we can call in hell on the slimy bastards. Now, I'm as pissed off as anybody in this room because it is my fault the villagers were killed. But we can't let a tragedy like that stop us from completing our mission. Let's go over to the table and look at the topo map one more time. I have a plan that will allow us to take out that nest of snakes."

A somber group of agents gathered around the table to hear Josh's plan.

"First off, we must admit we have failed on part of our assignment, but we must do everything we can to make sure what happened at the village is our only failure."

Bob Myers spoke up again, "Josh that was something out of our control. We can't be blamed for a vicious attack by al-Qaida."

"Bob, the strength of any team depends on recognizing failure, and coming back into the fray with determination to do better the next time. I should have realized, that after killing the two scouts they sent to check out the village, and then after I killed the picket guard, that they would know some of the people who were trying to attack them were staying in the village. However, our big mistake was not to a set up a guarded perimeter after we blew the bridges. When we destroyed the only way out of the jungle with the loaded trucks, the al-Qaida fighters became desperate to strike at something or somebody. The village attack was only their first blow. We must strike them within the next twenty-four hours, or face the possibility that they will manage to slip the material out of the jungle camp, or wipe out another nearby village.

"This is what I'm going to set up with the approval of General Davis. First, since we do not know the exact location of the al-Qaida camp, I will have to reconnoiter the area and pinpoint the exact location of the camp. However, unless we want a jungle fight that could go on for days and result in heavy causalities, we must have a surprise attack. I have, after looking over the topo maps, decided that a minimum of four outpost guards are on duty at all times, and they will be wearing NVG's at night. They probably will change guards at somewhere around one o'clock. I will be in position where I can eliminate the guards after the change. I will have to do it silently, and I can't even risk a headshot with a silencer. However, they will only have second grade NVG's while I will be wearing the new extra-sensitive ones that have just become operational. That is a big advantage."

"My god, Josh, are you telling us you are going to knife at least four al-Qaida fighters—slip up on them and kill them without being detected?"

"Yeah, Bob, that's the only way we can bring in the Seals and Ranger to surprise the main camp, but there's more to the plan. I will ask for a Marine sniper team that I will deploy around the camp prior to the attack by Seals and Ranger. They can eliminate at least twenty percent of the fighters before being noticed. I will spot them in the upper canopy of four of the biggest trees that surround the camp and they can pick off the camp early risers as they leave their tents. Since they will be so far away, and of course they will use silencers, we could get lucky and nail several dozen before they figure out they are under attack.

"The last part of the plan is to split the Ranger battalion into several units and block the exits from the camp. I will have them spotted well before daylight, and we will attack with all combat personnel wearing NVG's and the attack will start before it gets fully light. Standing by will be a special containment team. You will position yourselves with them and at my signal, bring them to the camp zeroing in on my GPS signal. If everything goes according to plan, we can accomplish our mission within the next twelve hours and get the hell out of here.

"There are many details that we don't need to go over right now, but after I get the authorization from General Davis and we are sure the requested Seals and Ranger are on the way, we will coordinate the positioning of the various teams. Right now I need to e-mail the General an overview of the operation and get his approval."

11

Preparation

Josh waited until the report detailing out the hydrogen sulfide attack on the village, and the interrogation and execution of the Iranian nuclear scientist, had been received by the CIA, and enough time had elapsed for them to notify Gen. Davis. He took a deep breath and punched in the call on his satellite cell with encryption.

Gen. Davis answered on the first ring.

"For god's sake, Josh! Surely you didn't execute one of Iran's top nuclear scientists?"

"Yes, sir, I did. I was responding to executive order two two three."

"What? He wasn't a terrorist! The man was a principal scientist in the Iranian nuclear program!"

"Yes, sir, he was a terrorist. Eight hours before our team executed him, he armed three al-Qaida nuclear weapons. I believe that makes him a terrorist, and under order two two three all CIA and Special Operation Forces have the authority to kill known terrorists. If a man who arms a nuclear weapon that is intended to kill thousands of innocent civilians, isn't a terrorist, who is? I believe it was an act of terrorism to arm those weapons and that makes him a terrorist."

There was a long pause, and Josh waited for the General's response. If Gen. Davis and the CIA did not agree with him, he could face courtmartial and possibly be charged with murder. Finally, after another agonizing few seconds General spoke.

"Josh, you continue to amaze me. I guess that's the bottom line. You are on this mission for exactly that reason. Yes, as usual, you are right in executing the guy. By the way, did you do it?"

"No, sir, I was going to take him outside and do it, but Gloria Sanders, a CIA agent, shot him seconds after I authorized it."

"Damn, is that the CIA woman, who is posing as a missionary?"

"Yes, sir, General; she's tough as nails."

"My god, the longer I stay in this job the more I'm amazed at the people we have working for us. Okay, now since that's behind us, update me on your status—by the way, I think blowing all the bridges was a damn good piece of work."

"Thank, you, General. That should keep them cooped up at least until we know exactly where the al-Qaida camp is located. In about six hours I am going into the jungle to get an exact location of the camp and take out the four perimeter guards..."

"Are you going in by yourself?"

"Yes, sir; I've trained Malaysia Special Forces along the Bolognas River in jungle very similar to this stuff in eastern Nigeria. None of the CIA people have any stealth training. I am confident I can take out the perimeter guards and get an exact location of the camp."

"What are the details of your plan to take out the camp and secure the enriched uranium and all that other shit?"

"I'll set a GPS locater in a clearing I have located approximately a mile from the camp as a staging point, and by four tomorrow morning I want the following assets to meet me at that location. I need the top four marine snipers you have available. Be sure they all have the new double SS silencers for their weapons. I also want two, twelve-man Seal combat divers and seventy Rangers. Have them at the checkpoint, and I'll place them in assault positions."

"What are you going to do with the snipers?"

"I am going to place them in the canopy of four of the largest trees adjacent to the camp,

and let them pick off al-Qaida fighters as they exit their tents."

"I trained some of those guys. They are excellent at concealment, and they can light a match at a hundred yards. We may be able to inflict a significant amount of damage before the camp is alerted that they are under attack."

"How are you going to use the Rangers and the Seals?"

"I'm pretty sure the camp boarders a large river so I am going to split the teams and

Rangers up into three attack squads. As soon as the camp is alerted by someone, who discerns the camp is under fire, I will give the order to attack with a three prong assault. That way our firepower will be directed toward the river, and they will be hemmed in against the river. By the way that's the way Hannibal slaughtered the Roman 10th and 11th Legions at Atticism."

"That's a good plan, Josh. I'll clear it with the Joint Chiefs, and get the men moving toward the rendezvous point within the next couple of hours."

"That's great, General. You contact person will be Gloria, L-seventeen, and she will give

the okay to deploy as soon as I take out the perimeter guards."

"Good luck, Josh."

"Thank you, General, but as you know, SFs don't believe in luck—only training, skill, and courage."

12

Stalk

Josh took a few minutes to detail out the request he had just made to the General before he briefed the CIA team. As he walked back in the room, and looked at the faces of his team, he knew there was a lot of concern that the mission had taken an unexpected twist, and failure was in their eyes. Josh felt the pressure very much as they did, but his training pushed him on. As an SF soldier, he was conditioned to move forward on a mission even though the circumstances were grim. The most intense part of every SF soldier's training is to respond with even greater intensity when under pressure. Josh was about to respond, but his team was wavering.

The gassing of over a hundred villagers and the interrogation and shooting of the Iranian nuclear scientist was clearly more than any of the CIA team members had ever experienced. Only Gloria seemed to have the resolve to continue without calling in reinforcements. Josh had been impressed with Gloria from the moment they met. First, it was the airport pickup and, of course, the assignation of the Iranian, but it was more than that. She was a person who could one minute teach a Bible class to African teens, and an hour late execute a terrorist. However, the rest of the team didn't have Gloria's determination. It was time to reassure them and move ahead with the mission instead of retreating and calling for help. Josh was convinced that the chances for mission success were weighted heavily in their favor if they could react to the circumstance instead of asking for help.

Josh motioned for the team to stand around the table with the topo map as he addressed them.

"Okay, listen up; I'm going to repeat this once: I don't have to tell you we have a dangerous enemy out there in the jungle, and since we blew the bridges and killed several of their fighters, they are like a caged lion. We can expect the worst they can lash out, and if we do nothing, we will almost guarantee another strike with either biomaterial or heaven forbid, nuclear weapons. Therefore, it is imperative that we act immediately and go on the offense. For the moment we have them pinned in, but that may not last very long."

"Wait a minute, Josh. We're outnumbered and at their mercy. We can't order a strike because we don't know exactly where the camp is, and we risk having hundreds of more civilians killed if we don't get help…"

"Hold it right there, Bob. Our new plan of action is going to take the fight to them, and if it is successful we can knock them out and secure the material. I've already briefed Gloria, but let me give you an overview of what is coming up next. Tonight, I'll go into the jungle and locate the camp. Of course, I will have to silently take out what I believe to be four perimeter guards. Gloria will be my coordinating contact, and she will direct the on-the-ground action from the GPS rendezvous point."

Josh went on to describe the details of the mission to the team and then asked if there were any questions.

"Josh, your plan of action goes against every CIA directive I have ever read. You are the key to this mission, and if you have a problem then the mission is doomed. We'll have boots on the ground without any place to send them, and al-Qaida will have either killed or captured you. We need another plan."

"Bob, in every plan of action, there are risks. I've accessed the risk, and I believe the risks are acceptable. We must attack the camp from a position of strength combined with the element of surprise. The only way we can do this is to determine the exact location of the camp, and silently take out the perimeter guards. I am confident, with my training, I am equipped to do the job. If I don't return or contact

Gloria by four a.m., the attack will be canceled and the assault teams will be sent back to the carrier.

"This team doesn't act in a democratic manner. You may send HQ your reservations, but as the team leader, I am making the decision on matters such as this. I'm going to get a few hours of sleep before I head into the jungle. Wake me at eight tonight. The meeting's over—Gloria stay here a few minutes, and let me give you the exact details of the rendezvous point and the vectors in which to send the Seals and Rangers. "Josh spent another 20 minutes giving Gloria the details of the coordinated Seal–Ranger attack that was to strike the camp. It all depended on Josh getting an exact GPS location and taking out the sentries. It was time to sleep for a few hours.

***

A beep from Josh's cellphone announced that his allotted time for sleep was over. He quickly dressed in the latest jungle dress made up of tangled reeds, leaves, and pieces of limbs, strapped on his new super NVG's, which were a distinct improvement over the old ones, and prepared his primary weapon—an 8-inch double cutting assault knife. Josh assumed the perimeter guards would be wearing NVG's, but having to procure them on the Black Market assured him they would have only the oldest NVG's, which were only slightly better than not having any vision help. That would be the overriding advantage Josh would have in completing his mission.

After painting his face, it would be impossible for someone to recognize him in the jungle, even from as close as 10 feet away. The last thing he did was to strap on leather leggings to protect his legs from snakebite. His breath quicken as he stood up and motioned to Gloria.

"Let's go, Gloria. Set the GPS on the rendezvous coordinates. We're going to take the Land Rover instead of me riding the motor bike. You need to be on the ground to coordinate the strike team."

An hour later, Josh eased the Land Rover up a clearing in the jungle that he had spotted from his surveillance photos. He was at the rendezvous point. It was 10 P. M.

"Gloria, you should be receiving transit information from HQ's command post within the next hour. The full complement of Seals and Rangers will arrive via Black Hawks. You will coordinate the landing. Once they are on the ground here, contact Colonel Ted Dowson and tell him to have his teams ready to move out on short notice. I will return at approximately three-thirty to lead the teams to the al-Qaida camp, and spot the Marine snipers in the canopy around the camp. Have the containment-quarantine group stand by until we signal the camp is under our control. Got it?"

"Yes."

"Okay, now let's drive down to where the trail enters the jungle. You can let me out and then return to the rendezvous point and stand by for my signal."

Thirty minutes later they arrived at the trail leading out of the village into the jungle. Josh got out, tucked his Glock with silencer in his shoulder holster, put his knife and a bush machete in his belt holder, but instead of walking down the trail, he immediately stepped into the dense jungle growth. Josh smiled and nodded as he felt a light breeze. It was just enough to move the leaves on the trees, and that would make it much easier to move through the jungle.

Gloria was wearing NVG's, and she watched him carefully as he stepped into the jungle, but seconds later, he seemed to disappear into the underbrush. She listened, expecting to hear him walking through the ground cover, but it was as if Josh had become a part of the jungle. He was moving silently through the jungle using his GPS coordinates and vectors to direct him in the direction of the camp. He knew, as silently as he was moving, it would take at least an hour to reach the area where the first perimeter guard was posted. Josh felt relatively sure the new guard would be at almost the same place as the old one, and that there would be a trip wire somewhere along the trail. However, he was approaching the spot from the thick jungle growth, and not walking on the game trail. Suddenly, he felt something under his left foot, and he knew instantly he had stepped on a snake. The reptile quickly coiled around his foot, and as Josh looked down the Carpet Viper sank his fangs into Josh's leggings. Josh grabbed his bush machete, and as his foot held the snake down he made a slashing swing that cut the snake in half. *Damn, thank God for these leather leggings,* crossed his mind. He was still at least a half-mile from the first sentry post so his movement wouldn't be noted. Even so, he stood motionless for about five minutes to be sure the movement he made killing the snake, hadn't been seen. He began to slip silently through the dense foliage again, this time watching the ground more closely knowing the Carpet Vipers were never solitary creatures. Sure enough, he had only gone less than 10 yards when he detoured around another one.

Damn, snakes! Yeah, good name; they look just like the carpet of leaves on the ground, he whispered to himself.

Josh had been creeping through the jungle for nearly an hour, and was approaching the GPS reading he had noted when he and Gloria had spotted the first sentry. He stopped and stood motionless for 10 minutes, then, just as he was about to continue forward, he spotted movement off to the left of the direction he was traveling. He stood and watched intently at the spot where he saw movement, and a couple of minutes later there was another slight shake of a bush. Then, as he watched, the man lit a cigarette. *Yeah, that cigarette is going to kill you, but a lot quicker than you think,* Josh thought. The red glow from the tip of the cigarette stood out in the darkness, and as Josh got closer, he could see the man's hands moving to ward off mosquitoes. It was a simple matter to slip around to where he would approach the man from behind. Thirty minutes later, he reached out from behind a tree the man was leaning back against, grabbed his hair, and with a quick swish of his knife, cut his throat. It was a demonstration of how to silently kill a person without the person being able to make a sound. A knife to the heart would always result in at least one scream.

Josh quickly went through the man's pockets, and was shocked at what he came up with; it was a cutout of a topo map with the camp located and the guard posts noted and circled. He was astounded at his good luck, and considered returning to the rendezvous point and sending in the Seals and Ranger to attack assaulting from the point where he had killed the perimeter guard. But he knew their movement would be spotted by the other sentries and would result in a fierce firefight with Seal and Ranger causalities. It was not something he relished doing, but considering the importance of the mission, taking out the other guards was a way to assure its success and capture the enriched uranium and biomaterial.

With the map he had taken from the perimeter guard the stalk of guards number two and three went very quickly. However, the last guard was more difficult. As Josh approached his position, he spotted him immediately. Instead of standing still the guard was impatiently moving up and down a well marked trail. After observing his movement for almost 15 minutes, Josh decided how to approach him. Josh noted the guard always stopped just as he approached a large Banyan tree, hesitated a few seconds, and then slowly walked back down the path. Jose was on the edge of the trail when the guard passed, and as soon as his back was turned, Josh stepped into the center of the trail. It would be a frontal attack or a side attack at best. Josh anticipated the guard merely brushing by him, and he would grab the guard's hair and cut his throat.

Seconds passed and as Josh watched, the guard came to the tree, hesitated for a few seconds, and then slowly began to walk toward him. Josh had already raised his knife to shoulder height and was holding his breath as the man approached. As the guard approached the camouflaged SF soldier, he stopped; seemingly puzzled at something being in the trail. He was a few feet to far in front of Josh to be attacked. Josh didn't breath or make a move. After a second or two, the guard took a couple of steps toward Josh and reached out to push away the camouflage connected to and concealing Josh. For a mili-second Josh's eyes met the guards. The guard's mouth opened to yell, but the sound never got out of his mouth, as Josh's knife severed his windpipe, and with a slashing twist, cut his throat.

That was the last of the perimeter guards, but before he left the area, he circled the camp noting the best trees for the Marine snipers to be positioned in, and to make sure no other guards were posted in or around the camp. *Everything is ready for the assault. These bastards are going to have a shock when they get my wakeup call,* Josh thought. He checked his watch; he had taken longer than he anticipated to take out the last guard. It was almost three o'clock, and he had to get back to the rendezvous point by 3:45 at the latest. *Got to do a fast jog to make it,* crossed his mind, and he began to quickly head back up the game trail to meet Gloria. It was nearly three miles, and he jogged the last mile in under seven minutes to get there on time.

Four Black Hawk helicopters had just finished disgorging the Seals and Rangers as he trotted up. Josh, spotted the unit commander, Colonel Dowson and introduced himself.

"Colonel Dowson, I'm Josh Martin. I'm in charge of the CIA team that has located the al-Qaida camp. I've just taken out the perimeter sentries. The camp is ready to be assaulted. We need to get the assault teams together and head for the camp. We want to be in position before dawn."

"It's great to meet you, Josh. You're somewhat of a SF legend after what you did to knock out that group of regional al-Qaida bigwigs. Have you got us an exact location for the camp?"

"Yes, Colonel. Get your GPS, and I'll give you an exact fix. After I've spotted the Seals and Rangers in their forward positions that I've noted on this topo map, I will take the Marine snipers and show them their trees. They may be able to take out a good number of fighters before anyone in the camp knows they are under assault. I will be observing the camp, and as soon as they sound an alarm. I will alert you, and you will order the teams to attack.

We'll need to leave here in eighteen minutes, and we will have to march double-time to get to the camp area before dawn. Can your men do five miles in less than an hour?"

"Yes, they can, Josh. Give me the topo and the GPS coordinates, and we'll get underway."

Fifteen minutes later the assault teams formed up and Josh led them out at a slow jog. As they moved toward the trail into the camp

Josh checked his Breitling Oceania Chronograph II and picked up the pace. They were six minutes behind schedule. *Got to have those snipers located before dawn,* he thought. The last mile was almost a dead run, but as Josh pulled up, he nodded to the Colonel.

"We're okay. Split your team into three units and position them pointing at this X on the topo map. Don't get any closer than three-hundred and forty yards until I give you the signal. Then let the Rangers spearhead the assault from the front and have a Seal team on move on each flank. You will trap everyone in the camp against the bank of the river. If everything goes as planned, it should be a turkey shoot. Got it?"

"We'll be ready, Josh."

"Okay, I'm taking the snipers in tight to position them. They will take out anyone who sticks their head out, and will keep popping them until the fighters realize they are under attack. When I see them sound the alarm, I'll signal you and then send the assault teams in as quickly as you can."

The four Marine snipers had pulled out their guns, affixed to new ultra-silencers, and were standing at ready when Josh walked over.

"Does everybody have their climbing shoes on? Ropes? Extra ammo? Double check your partner, and we'll head into the jungle. I will be twenty-yards ahead of you just to be sure they haven't replaced any of the guards I took out earlier."

Josh and the four snipers moved out and soon they were slipping through the dense foliage. It was nearly five o'clock, about 45 minutes before sunrise, as they approached the camp. Josh had already picked out the trees and after a quick comment, he was ready to position them.

"Get in a very high and concealed position, and take out anyone who exits the tents. You know to go for headshots to start, but when a camp alarm is sounded, keep shooting and take any shot available. The Ranger and Seals will be on the way. Now let's start climbing. You need to be in position in the next seventeen minutes."

In the next few minutes, the Marine snipers climbed four of the tallest trees surrounding the camp. The snipers were in full jungle gear, and when they reached the canopy of the trees, they seemly disappeared and only a stub of a rifle barrel could be seen emerging from the mass of foliage.

The snipers were in position, and as Josh had planned, from their vantage point, they would be able to overlook the entire camp and anyone who stepped out of a tent would be a target. The new ultra-silencers they had fitted on their rifles were so good that only the impact of the bullet would be heard. If things went as Josh had planned, the snipers might be able to take out 10 to 15 fighters before someone sensed they were under attack. The headshots would stop the hit fighters from sounding the alarm.

Josh watched as the snipers positioned themselves, and then moved back into the underbrush near the edge of the camp and waited. He sent a quick text to Colonel Dowson; **Snipers in position—be ready to move.** It was 5:16 and it would be daylight in 31 minutes.

Josh felt his breath quicken, and he took a last look at the map before he slipped back in the jungle. Time seemed to drag as the minutes ticked away. A glance at his Breitling told Josh it was less than five minutes before sunrise, and as the light penetrated the dense jungle, he knew the camp would begin to come alive. He waited, scanning the camp to see if he could make out where the trucks carrying the biomaterial and the nuclear material had been hidden. He finally made out an unusually thick patch of underbrush, and as he looked through his binoculars, he spotted a truck tire that was only partly concealed. *Yeah, there are the trucks carrying the stuff behind the tents next to the river. No wonder we didn't see them with all the camouflage they have covering them.*

Josh had just put up his binoculars when someone opened the tent flap near the center of the camp. The fighter stretched and started walking toward the edge of the camp obviously going to urinate. He went less than 10 yards when a head shot dropped him. Josh heard the splat of the bullet as it hit the man, but there was no other sound. Minutes passed and then two other men stepped out from another tent. As they started across the open area in front of the tents, they saw the body of the first man, but before they could say anything, they jerked back as the four snipers sent a hail of bullets into their heads.

Several of the bullets passed through the men and hit a metal container behind the men, and the loud ring brought a stirring from several tents. Within a few seconds several men emerged from tents only to be hit by sniper fire, and then one individual, who realized what was happening, screamed in alarm. He had barely gotten the words out of his mouth when a bullet smacked him.

Josh immediately sent the signal to attack, knowing within a few minutes the whole camp would be aroused and the snipers could only take out a few of the hundred fighters. However, as the men rushed out of their tents, the hidden snipers moved from man to man, and as Josh watched, nearly a dozen more fighters fell. There was panicked firing in all directions by the al-Qaida fighters for a few minutes until the first squad of Rangers emerged from the jungle. Then there was a few shots fired in the direction of the Rangers and the remaining fighters ran, first to the left, where they were turned them back by one of the Seal teams, and then to the right where the same thing happened. Soon there was a rush toward the river, and a short firefight erupted as the al-Qaida fighters tried to make a stand. It was over in less than five minutes.

Josh quickly sent a text to Gloria, who was with the containment team.

Camp under our control—send containment team.

Colonel Dowson had just finished receiving the reports from his squad leaders when Josh walked up.

"Looks like our intelligence was a little off, Josh. We only counted forty-eight bodies. I was expecting over a hundred fighters based on our AWAC and CIA briefings."

"Only forty-eight? That's hard to believe. The Seal team was hit by over a hundred fighters when they tried to stop the trucks from leaving Libya," Josh said.

"Well, I guess some of them left after we blew the bridges, but I think we have what we came after. I spotted the trucks over there on the edge of the camp under all that camouflage."

"Great, the containment team will be here in a few minutes, and they can take care of the stuff. I won't let any of our men near the trucks until the team arrives."

"That's a good idea, Colonel. If our info is correct there are three armed nuclear weapons there along with some god-awful bio stuff."

In less than an hour, the containment team and the CIA agents arrived at the camp. Josh pointed out the concealed trucks and the team began to remove the camouflage and check the trucks for IED devices. The CIA agents finished collecting the data from the dead fighter's bodies and from the abandoned tents and in another hour, they were ready to leave.

"Let me check and see how long the containment team will be before they are ready to move the material in the trucks. We have a heavy lifting chopper standing by," said Josh.

Josh started for the area where the trucks were being unloaded when the major, who was heading up the containment team, walked out from behind of one of the trucks.

"Josh, we have a problem. We have some of the material we were after, but it's obvious there are some things missing."

"What?"

"Yes, I'm afraid one of the nuclear weapon devices is gone along with some of the enriched uranium material, and I can only guess, but I think several boxes containing biomaterial are also gone. One of our men noted a scraped off trail where something heavy had been dragged toward the river. In fact, you can see where it was loaded on a boat. I hate to say it, but we only have two of the three weapon devices, and none of the biomaterial. Evidently, the rest of it was loaded on a boat and has left the area. We can see the imprint of the boat against the bank and what looks like a sled tracks that were used to drag the material to the boat."

13

The Chase

Muhammad el-Habibe had been working for most of the day to secure the material onto the two boats that were sent by al-Qaida operatives in Chad. He was the camp commander who had been selected by the Leadership Council to meet the Libyan trucks, and to secure the material in a jungle camp where it could be concealed and later transported to other al-Qaida units closer to the intended target. He knew it had always been the plan to transfer the material to a boat from the camp, but the destruction of the bridges in the area had forced the Council to push forward with the plan, knowing the camp was in eminent danger of be located and attacked.

Now, as the slim, bearded fighter nervously smoked a cigarette he worried that an impending attack by U. S. Special Forces would occur before he could make the transfer. After two of his men turned up missing, and he presumed they had been killed or captured, he hoped the hydrogen sulfide gas attack on the village where CIA operatives were staying would disrupt the planned attack, and give him more time to make the transfer. Then when his sentry was killed and the bridges destroyed, he decided an attack on the camp was imminent. And not only did he need to transfer the material, but the Leadership Council alerted him that he must create a diversion to direct the hunt by the Americans away from the cargo that the primary boat was carrying. He had sent an emergency message to the Leadership Council detailing out what he was sure was an impending attack on the camp, and that morning he had received a troubling message.

Co-ordinate attack by U. S. Seals and Rangers and is planned within a week. Boats will arrive today. Load the critical material material as noted on boat F. A. 387, and one of the radioactive units on boat F. A. 998. Send boat F. A. 998 up the river to Lake Chad and rendezvous with boat 387 as planned. Expose material on boat 998.

El-Habibe had spent most of the day sorting out the critical material that was to be on boat 387, and as soon as it was loaded, he had his men place one of the nuclear devices on boat 998. And as the crew prepared to leave he ordered one of his men to remove the top lead shield from the container. It was a task he disliked; knowing he was putting the crew's life in jeopardy, but the Council had demanded it. The American surveillance planes would easily pick up the signal.

"Your orders are to proceed upriver to Lake Chad where you will meet reinforcement to help you carry out your mission," he instructed the captain, well aware, the by exposing the radioactive material, he was sentencing the boat's crew to a horrible death.

"Remember, if you are attacked, you must fight to the last man. Allah Akbar!"

Allah Akbar!" shouted the crew.

The boat slowly pulled out from the dock and a few minutes it was out of sight heading upstream toward Lake Chad. A few minutes later, the larger and faster boat, F. A. 387 pulled away from the dock heading downstream. The second boat, which was larger and was heading downstream, had taken about half of his men who would be dropped off at an al-Qaida camp near the coast. El-Habibe checked his watch. It was almost six o'clock in the afternoon, and too late for the remainder of his men to abandon the camp. He would wait until morning and cross the river taking the rest of the fighters with him. Even though he knew the camp was sure to come under attack within the week, he considered it almost impossible for the Americans to bring in sufficient forces to attack in the next few days.

He awoke the next morning to the sound of gunfire and as he ran toward the river hoping to escape, a Marine sniper took him down. The remaining fighters who had rushed out when the attack started were no match for the Rangers who cut them to pieces.

14

Shock

The shock that some of the most critical material had been spirited away by boat was a stunning blow to Josh. He was sure, since the material had been trucked in, that by blowing the bridges, all the material would be confined to a 30-square-mile stretch of jungle. He had completely overlooked the possibility that it could be transported out of the jungle by boat. It was another failure, and the CIA team he had assembled was sure to be shaken by this revelation. But the real fear Josh had was that the material was either rapidly heading down the river toward the open ocean where it would be a lot more difficult to find, or that it had already made it to the ocean, and it was heading for its European target.

It was a frantic couple of hours as the CIA team set up an operations base, and established a direct contact with the AWAC's that were attempting to track the boat carrying the enriched uranium and the biomaterial. Josh felt personally responsible for the missing material, and he was determined to track it down. An hour later, he received the first confirmation.

"Tail 924 to station L-7.—do you read me?"

"Loud and clear; got anything?"

"Yeah, strong signal. We should have a visual in a few minutes."

"Roger, can you give me any quadrants?"

"Yes, looks like the boat will be just entering Lake Chad, when we make a visual."

"My god; I thought they would surely make a run for the open ocean. I can't figure out going into the interior, but we're going to move our strike team in that direction. Get back to me when you have a visual."

"Roger, over and out."

Josh hurried to find Colonel Dowson, the Seal team commander.

"Colonel, AWAC 342 has picked up radioactive signal from the boat that carried away the missing material. Get your Seal Combat Divers loaded on that Black Hawk and head east on coordinate 61. Tail 342, the plane patrolling this area, will contact you direct and give you an exact reading. We should have a visual soon, so be prepared to disable the boat and have your team board. Subdue any crew members, but don't go below until we have the containment team check things out."

"You got it, Josh. I'll have the team airborne in a few minutes."

Five minutes later, Josh and the Seal team were heading east toward Lake Chad. The second Black Hawk with the backup Seal team was right behind them. A visual sighting from Tail 342 was reported 10 minutes later.

"AWAC 342, Josh, do you read me? ...over."

"Yeah, loud and clear, go ahead ...over."

"Josh, the boat is approximately thirty feet long sitting low in the water. I see two armed men on the deck... over."

"Colonel, I'm going to tell the pilot to come up from behind the boat. He'll drop in low, and when the chopper comes around to where your door gunner has a clean shot tell him to take out the two men on deck. Have one of you snipers put a slug in the motor to disable the boat, and alert the rest of your Combat Divers to prepare to assault the boat."

There was a nod of recognition and Josh passed the info on to the pilot. The chopper made a wide swing around behind the boat staying out of range of the fighters on deck, and then as the chopper put the boat between the fighters on deck and the chopper, the pilot dropped in low and seconds later the chopper came alongside the boat. A quick burst from the .50 cal door gun sent the first of the fighters spinning around and the second blast knocked the other fighter overboard. A Combat Diver stepped into the open door and with two quick shots brought a puff of black smoke from the motor. The boat glided to a stop as the Black Hawk dropped a hanging ladder down.

Josh signaled the pilot and the chopper dropped to within a few feet of the water. Six Seals were in the water in seconds and in less than a minute, they boarded the boat. Suddenly, a man with an AK .47 appeared in the door that led to the engine room. The chopper door gunner opened up and a quick burst knocked the man back into hole. The captain of the boat, who had remained concealed behind the bridge, jumped up and began firing with a semi-automatic weapon wounding one of the Combat Divers. Immediately he drew fire from two Seal team members, who disabled him. The Seal team leader peered into the open hole of the ship, and signaled that no one was there, only cargo.

"Okay, Colonel, let's get the containment team onboard. Maybe this will wrap up this mess."

The second Black Hawk dropped in close and two members of the containment team in protective gear dropped down the chopper's ladder, and soon they were inspecting the interior of the boat. One of the men quickly stuck his head out and yelled to Josh, "Get you team back in the chopper! There is a piece of live enriched uranium open to the air!"

As the team scrambled to leave the boat, Josh was wondering why the material wasn't encased in lead. An hour later the containment team, still dressed in there protective gear, scrambled aboard carrying a small lead lined container. Josh's fears were soon realized.

"This is it, Josh. It's a decoy. Nothing else is onboard. The crew was on a suicide mission. They have been exposed to a lethal dose of radiation from this small piece of enriched uranium. The rest of the uranium and the biomaterial is missing."

Josh could feel the pit of his stomach tighten as the words sunk in.

"My god, they sent those poor souls out to die just to get a few hours more head start. They must have gone west down the river in another boat!'

There was a hurried boarding of the Black Hawk, and as they headed back to the base camp. Josh was on the radio to the circling AWAC's as they approached the temporary base camp.

"Tail 342 this is station L-7—come in. Do you read me?"

"Roger, loud and clear. Go ahead."

"932 discontinue this mission, and head west. Follow the Occulate River and set your detectors on ultra-high and do a low altitude surveillance of the river. The boat we just assaulted was a decoy. The main items we are looking for are on a boat heading downstream to the Atlantic. We need to intercept before it reaches the open ocean.—over."

"Roger, will do. I'll give you a heads up as soon as we pick up a signal—over."

"If you don't pick up a signal, call for backup and set up a north-south grid up and down the coast for a hundred miles. Get back to me with any sightings… over and out."

"Roger, Josh, will do… over and out."

The failure to find the primary boat concerned Josh, knowing if the boat carrying the nuclear and biomaterial made it to the open ocean it would be extremely difficult to pick up a radioactive signal from enriched uranium if it was encased in lead, which it probably was. His worst fears were about to be realized.

"Tail 932 to Station L—7—come in—over."

"Roger, you're loud and clear. What have you got?"

"Nothing, we tracked from the initial GPS at the al-Qaida camp all the way down the river to where it flows into the ocean. We even did some low altitude passes over the fishing boats that were docked at the town of Sepetta. Now, we're circling fifty-miles out over the Atlantic, and we haven't gotten a bleep."

"Start flying your grid, and give me and hourly report, or a call if you make contact—over."

"Got it L-7, over and out."

It was six hours later when Josh made the call he dreaded—to Gen. Davis.

"…and the AWAC's are working a grid in the Atlantic."

"Damn! I can't believe they managed to slip out of the trap you set. You did everything right. They were just lucky—and smart to be able to pull off that decoy. Get a detailed report in the CIA pouch today. Keep you team intact and be ready to move and set up an intercept on short notice. I'll dispatch a couple of more AWAC's to join in the search, but it may be too late. If they are in a high speedboat, they could be a couple of hundred miles into the Atlantic, and if they have double lead encased container for the enriched uranium, we'll have to fly almost right over it in order to pick up any signal."

"General, it was my fault in not realizing the river was a potential route to move the material. I will note that on my report, as a failure directly attributed to my misjudging the situation."

"Nonsense, Josh. You single-handily took out the four sentries, set up a perfect trap, and coordinate an assault that resulted in the killing forty-eight al-Qaida, and capturing of a large part of the material. Hell, Josh; suck it up, and get after the rest of those bastards. You are the best man on the planet to accomplish this mission."

"Thank you, General. I won't disappoint you again."

Josh and General Davis continued to go over possible destinations for other 30 minutes.

"Josh, I'm still confident you can get those bastards. Keep me posted; and one more thing: Remember, you have full authority to use all means necessary to carry out your mission. Let me make myself very clear; do whatever necessary to stop what could be the worst act of terrorism we have ever seen. I've approved your execution of the Iranian scientist under the 9-11 policy of executing known terrorists when encountered and confirmed."

"Thank you, General. We'll update you daily." Josh quickly made a second call.

"Gloria, move your command post back to the safe house in Niger, and set up direct radio and electronic contacts with every CIA asset in Africa. We went after a decoy, and the boat carrying the material made it into the Atlantic. We will have three AWAC's girding three-hundred miles of open ocean, but we may not be able to locate the boat. If the boat docks anywhere in Africa we need to be able to converge on it immediately."

"I'll set up everything. How long will it be before you arrive?"

Josh moved over to where the Colonel was sitting, and apprised him of the situation.

"Colonel, after the containment team finishes, and my team of agents have collected the intelligence data, take chopper number one, return to your carrier base and await orders to deploy. We're doing everything we can to track down those bastards, but if the AWAC's can't pick up anything, it may be days or weeks before we locate them."

"Give me as much lead time as possible. We'll have significant air time, and to be fully operational will take a few hours."

"I'll do everything I can, but you know how these things go. I may have to go in alone if it's time critical. I'll be on the second chopper that will drop me off at the safe house, and I will direct that chopper as needed."

***

Two hour later Josh arrived back at the Niger safe house where Gloria was busy setting up a command post.

"Josh, we have an open, secure line to every CIA post on the continent. I've instructed them to do twenty-four hour monitoring of all known and suspected al-Qaida operatives."

"Good job, Gloria. Be sure to alert them to possible coded messages, and give me hardcopy readout of any suspicious messages."

"Will do, Josh. Where do you think they will try to bring the material shore?"

"My best guess is they will hookup with a strong al-Qaida support team, and take some time to plan a strike before they move the material. If I had to make a guess, I would circle Algeria, Morocco, and the Moroccan Western Sahara. I don't think they will try and go around the south tip of Africa through the Straits of the of Good Hope. That passageway is narrow and the AWAC's would pick them up. It may be a few days before we know anything. Let's sit down and plan our reaction and strike that we will initiate if we get a confirmed signal."

***

Josh managed to get a few hours of sleep before he started reviewing the AWAC's and CIA station reports. The AWACS had managed to pick up radio messages from two boats that were smuggling drugs and weapons into Nigeria. The Nigerian military was notified, and a surprise would be waiting for them when they arrived in the country. The CIA listening post's reports did have a small bit of pertinent information. A coded message had been intercepted from al-Qaida operatives in Algeria and Morocco. The CIA had quickly broken the code, and passed on the short message to Josh.

Corfirm—open seas—onboard.

"Damn, they could be anywhere in five-hundred miles of open ocean, with hundreds of other fishing boats," Josh muttered.

Josh assembled the team and as they focused on the large map on the table, he began to review the information he had received.

"Nothing from the AWAC's, but we do have something very interesting from two CIA listening posts. Listening Posts in Algeria and Morocco intercepted the same coded message. Of course, as you know al-Qaida codes are some of the easiest to break. That is why they make the messages so brief. They probably know we are going to pick them up and break the code. Well, that is beside the point. I think this message tells us several things. One, they have the material out of the country, they still have it on the boat, and the possible handoff to a new group of al-Qaida will be in the northwest part of Africa. I'm sorry I can't be more specific, but at least we can concentrate on this area of Africa and ignore South Africa."

"Josh should we move any of our assets into the area?" asked Gloria.

"Yes, contact Central Command HQ and ask them to move the carrier with the assault teams to position themselves in international water off the Western Sahara province of Morocco, and move the AWAC's grid north, but tell them to keep one plane monitoring the southern tip of Africa just in case we're wrong."

***

Two days passed before any other clues surfaced. The chatter was from an area noted to have several al-Qaida cells—Morocco. The Moroccan listening post in Rabat reported a number of suspected al-Qaida operatives were moving westward, and were seemingly waiting on orders. They had positioned themselves in western Morocco near the Western Sahara province border. It was the bit of information Josh had been waiting for. The dispatch only told the Moroccan group to be ready on short notice to move to another location. With that information, Josh called the team in, and as they poured over a more detailed map of the African countries bordering the western Atlantic Ocean, Josh summarized his thoughts.

"I didn't think they would risk going into the Mediterranean through the Straits of Gibraltar. It would be easy to spot them as they passed the British base at Gibraltar. I believe they are going to meet up with another al-Qaida group somewhere along the northwest coast of Africa, and probably transfer some or all of the material. At that point, we will be strictly guessing as to which route they might take to move the material. They sure aren't going to use it to kill people in Muslim Morocco. I think they are planning to take it overland by either plane or truck, and then transport it into Europe possibly by boat to the European mainland. But let's don't get ahead of ourselves. Our first point of intercept is on the upper African coast.

"The only problem with that is it's over three-hundred square miles, and evidently the boat carrying the material is well insulated. I've had the AWAC's working the area for the last twenty-four hours without picking up anything. I think we will have to rely on the northern African listening posts if we are to get any pertinent information that might help us pinpoint the northern African landing site.

"Bob, I want you to head to Rabat and coordinate with the Moroccan military. They have been brought along by the State Department, and just the idea al-Qaida might try to smuggle a nuclear weapon into the country has them very co-operative. If we get a confirmation that the material is being offloaded and moved across the Sahara, we will need Moroccan SFs and some of their other troops to act as blocking agents. You can coordinate that.

"Phil, you and Sid will stay here and keep this command post operative while Gloria and I set up a temporary, secondary post on the coast of Western Sahara. I have the carrier assault group moving toward the area. They should be in position within twenty-four hours. I have a feeling this thing is coming to a head, and we need to be ready. Gloria be ready to leave in thirty minutes. I'll have one of our assets meet us in Niamey with a private jet, and we'll hop over and land in Rabat, let Bob out, and then have a Black Hawk that can spot us somewhere along the coast. I think it is very possibly we'll have more exact coordinates within the next twelve hours."

The team hurried to begin the transition, when an emergency transmission came in over the radio. Gloria received the transmission.

"Josh, come here quick! The Moroccan western desert listening post picked up some low frequency transmissions. One of them mentioned the biomaterial and a transfer!"

Josh rushed over to the printer where the transmissions were being printed out. What he read made his plans became much more urgent.

Intercept—Wangoo Intercept—Wangoo (could not translate) at 1300.

"My god, that's less than four hours from now! No change in assignments—let's get moving." Gloria, Josh, and Bob hopped in the Land Rover, and with Gloria driving, headed for the airport.

"Gloria, State has cleared us so we don't need to drive through the fence and across the grass to meet the plane."

"Yeah, we do, Josh. If we don't the local officials will hold us up for hours, until they finally get a call from someone in the military."

"Now, come on, Gloria. You can't be serious. I think you just like to drive through chain link fences."

"Josh, I've been stationed in this part of the world for nearly eight years. I think I understand how things work a hell of a lot better than you."

"Well, maybe you do—*Damn, talk about an assertive woman*—Okay, do it your way. Anything we need to do?"

"No, just lay down some suppressing fire when they send the airport security to arrest us."

"Damn, Gloria is this really necessary? Those security guys aren't al-Qaida. If I kill one of them, it will be a nasty incident. Are you sure you know what you're doing? Running through fences, and then having me shoot the security guys, who will be heading out to check things out? Don't you think we can pull a little weight, and skip the customs and security?"

"No, I don't. Trust me on this one, Josh. Just have an exact—to the second—ETA from the pilot, and step out of the Land Rover ready to hold off the security guys. All you'll need to do is hit their motor with a few rounds, and then kick up some dirt in front of them. For god's sake don't pull off any of your headshots."

Josh nodded and slipped some rounds in his weapon. As they approached the airport, he made radio contact with then jet that was on its way to pick them up.

"L-7 here. Do you read me?"

"Loud and clear, L-7."

"Give me an exact ETA—to the second—this will be a non-conventional pickup. We'll transfer passengers at the end of the runway."

"Oh, is this a Gloria pickup?"

Josh laughed and answered in the affirmative.

"Hell, Josh, this isn't going to be a big deal. They probably haven't even fixed the fence," said Gloria.

The radio beeped and the pilot of the jet gave Josh the plane's ETA.

"One minute and twenty-three seconds, Gloria, and counting."

"Okay, we don't want to be early. I'm going to stop, and wait until we have six seconds till ETA, and then I'll turn the corner and head for the end of the runway."

Josh nodded and Gloria pulled over to wait.

"Twenty seconds and counting*** ten, nine, eight, seven, six—Go!" yelled Josh.

Gloria jammed the accelerator to the floor, whipped around the corner, and turned off on a grassy strip that bordered the airport.

"Shit! They fixed the fence!"

"Damn, Gloria, that's a six-foot chain link fence!"

"Uh huh, I'm going to pick up a little more speed—hold on!"

The Land Rover hit the fence, ripped out a 20-foot section, which wrapped around the front of the vehicle with two fence posts still attached. There was a yell from the other three in the Land Rover, but Gloria never slowed down and as the jet landed the Land Rover, still dragging the 20-section of fence, came to a stop about 20-yards from where the jet was taxing. Everyone jumped out and Josh stopped with his weapon ready, as several armed men ran out of the terminal and hopped into a waiting truck.

"Josh, take out the truck before it blocks the runway!" yelled Gloria.

"Okay." Josh quickly sent a volley into the trucks motor sending a puff of black smoke pouring from the hood. The men jumped out and one of them began to fire an AK .47 at them. The first few rounds pounded the Land Rover.

"Put him down, Josh!" yelled Gloria.

"Damn, Gloria I can't just kill a security guard for trying to do his job!"

"Well, shoot him in his fuckin' foot then!"

Josh lowered his sights and sent several shots that kicked up the gravel at the security guard's feet. One of the shots glanced off the pavement and into his leg. There was a yell and then he dropped his weapon and ran with the other guards back into the terminal. The side door of the jet popped open and the three team members scrambled in. Seconds later the jet flashed down the runway.

"Damn, Gloria, was that worth it?" asked Josh.

"Well, Josh, you said we're in a hurry, and less than a minute after we arrived at the airport, we're in the air. What do you think? 'Course we donated them another Land Rover, but hell, Uncle won't ever miss it."

Josh was a loss for words, but he managed a weak smile, as a thought crossed his mind, *Damn, that woman continues to amaze me. Too bad the rest of my team aren't that good.*

As they reached 10,000 feet, Gloria's encrypted cell vibrated flashing a red exclamation point. "Gloria here."

"Yeah, I'll put him on—Josh, I'm patching you in to HQ. They have some info about the Moroccan situation."

"Thanks, Gloria; I've got it."

"This is Josh Martin...camel....coat...code clear—Yes, we are moving in that direction, and should be there in less than two hours. I will set up a temporary post and have it manned by one of my men...Roger, give me the direct Moroccan military contact where I can coordinate any joint action...okay, I have it...yes, Colonel Hassem...how many fighters do you estimate?***got it. Anything else?***no, goodbye."

"Bob, our local assets have already contacted the Moroccan Military, and they will help anyway they can. We may need to use them to block the al-Qaida fighters who are massing in western Morocco. I have a feeling they will be involved in the transfer of the material. Stay in touch with Sid back in Niger, and with us. Gloria and I will be taking a Black Hawk into Snipply on the Western Sahara coast to try and be as close to where the boat may land as possibly."

For Josh the two-hour flight seemed to take forever. As the Lockheed jet cruised along at 575 mph the only thing on his mind was the frustration of being a step behind the al-Qaida fighters with the bomb and biomaterial. Just the thought of the carnage left behind after the hydrogen sulfide attack on the village had him walking up to the cockpit.

Josh stuck his head in the cockpit and asked Dan Snivels, the pilot, "Don, we're on a time frame that could blow up in our faces any minute. Can you boost the speed and arrival time?"

"Yeah we can, Josh, but it'll jump fuel consumption."

"I'll stand for it; Uncle has more money than god."

"You're the boss."

As Josh walked back to the back of the plane, Dan slowly increased the jet's speed until the engines were whining at full pitch, and the jet was approaching Rabat at over 600 MPH.

As they approached Rabat Josh contacted the lead AWAC's.

"Tail 234, this is L-7. Do you read me?—over."

"Loud and clear, L-7. What can I do for you?"

"Assign one of your group to fly the African coast from the Straits of Gibraltar to a coordinate approximately four-hundred miles south, and then reverse and repeat until further notice. Have the coast monitored to detect any vessels that are indicated to be making landfall. Got it?"

"Yeah, but get ready for a lot of chatter. There are at least a hundred boats that are indicated to be in a position to make landfall."

"I'm aware of that, but we've got to try and pinpoint the boat before they pass off the material. Make a special note of any boat that is over fifty miles out that has a coast landing trajectory.—over and out."

"Copy."

"Captain, what's your ETA, Rabat?"

"Well, let's see***make that twenty-one minutes and fourteen seconds."

"Okay, don't taxi to the terminal. Pull off on the tarmac. A Black Hawk will be moving out to pick two of us up. After the pickup, you can pull up to the terminal and let Bob off."

"Roger."

The switch went quickly, and soon Josh and Gloria were flying across the western Moroccan desert heading for the Western Sahara and the African coast. Two-hours into the flight Josh received a briefing from the lead AWAC.

"Josh, we're hitting one dead end after another. I've made ten contacts with boats along the coast, and they have all turned up clear. We'll keep working, but the only boats moving along the coast are a couple of rusty freighters and commercial fishing trawlers."

"Okay, just keep me posted—over and out."

15

Deception

A heavily bearded man rushed to the bridge and shouted, "Shivigna run the motors at maximum power, and turn the ship due west." He was dressed in ragged fatigues and seemed to be ill at ease as he tried to maintain his balance on the rolling ship deck. However, his demeanor suggested he was in charge.

Rasandi el-Wahlie slapped his hands together to emphasize his authority. He was an especially tall man for someone of Middle East decent, and his lanky body seemed to hang on his boney frame. A jagged scar ran from the back of his left earlobe down the side of his neck terminating at the top of the shoulder in a deep angled scar. It was from a wound he received while attacking a Northern Alliance outpost in Afghanistan. He was stripping the body of a seemingly dead Alliance soldier, when the mortally wounded man made one last desperate swing with a machete. If the blade had hit him another 2 inches to the left, it would have split his skull. As it turned out, it was an especially grievous wound, and he nearly died from loss of blood and an infection. His slow recovery and daily indoctrination by an al-Qaida mullah strengthen his resolve to fight the infidels who supplied the Northern Alliance with the weapons that nearly killed him. He believed he was on a holy mission to protect Islam—and to exact revenge upon the Western nations who were trying to destroy it.

"Sir, we will miss the rendezvous with team Tiger if we don't stay on course."

"Of course we will! Do you think I am an idiot?"

"No sir, but…"

"Do it! Our man operating the detection console reports the infidel's surveillance patterns will intersect us by late afternoon if we maintain our current course."

The Captain quickly turned the wheel, pushed the throttle forward and put the ship, on a due west course.

"Maintain the due west course for the next two hours, and order the deployment of the motorboat."

"Yes, it will be done as you have ordered."

"And place all of the highly radioactive material onboard in the stern of the boat. Leave only the boxed non-radioactive material here. Be sure you have left nothing onboard that could be picked up by the American surveillance planes. Dump the containers overboard and clean the area where they were stored. If we can get the radioactive material into the hands of our al-Qaida forces there, it will give them a great weapon to use against the infidels. All they would have to do is explode a small bomb and they would contaminate a large area. Just think of what damage it would do if they could get it to a major Western city. And they have connections that may allow the material to get it into a city in Italy."

"Sir, if we remove the radioactive material from their containers and the boat is manned whoever is aboard will receive a lethal dose of radiation."

"Will the men be incapacitated?"

"No, but if whoever has the material around them for several days it will have damaged their health severely."

"It is a risk we must take. If we leave any of the radioactive material onboard, eventually the American planes will pick up the signals, and we will have their Special Forces soldiers attacking the ship. By doing this transfer, we can evade the surveillance and get the other biological material to the mission site."

"But sir, surely you aren't considering sending the material with the crew. They will be in close proximity to the enriched uranium, and it will surely have a detrimental effect on their health?"

"Captain, your job is to navigate this ship, not to question my authority. These men are expendable. They have volunteered for this mission, and they are willingly doing this. Now, have someone prepare the boat. I want it launch within the hour."

"Yes, if you insist…"

"Don't question my orders, Captain. It will not be tolerated."

"Yes, sorry. It will be done as you have ordered."

A whistle from the Captain brought a seaman to the bridge, and in less than an hour, the crew had moved a small motorboat into position near the bow of the converted fishing trawler.

El-Wahlie stood on the bow of the mother vessel and watched as the small boat was being readied, and as the three men prepared to board the boat, he called out to them, "Remember, when you come to the river, you are to proceed up the river. Be on the lookout for a group of our fighters who will be standing on the dock at the village of Zagosa. You are to turn the boat and material over to them and join with their forces. If you are captured by the Americans, you are to tell them nothing. Do not jeopardize this important mission."

"We will tell the Americans nothing!" The men shouted.

"Good; you will receive glory, and your families will be rewarded if anything goes wrong, and you are injured," said el-Wahlie.

"Allah Akbar!" The men shouted in unison.

"Allah Akbar!"

A few minutes later, the high-speed motorboat pulled away from the mother ship and headed due east for the African coast toward the mouth of the Sepojepig River.

16

The Woman

After the boat carrying the enriched uranium had been gone for an hour, el-Wahlie began to make preparations to send another decoy out to confuse the American planes he knew were searching for the ship. He stood on the bow of the ship and, as the minutes passed, he nervously paced back and forth on the deck knowing that if the motorboat carrying the enriched uranium was detected before it reached the coast, the AWAC surveillance planes would use a reverse vector to locate the mother ship. Even though his ship looked like a rusty, commercial fishing trawler and a large hoop net hung from one of the wrenches, it was sure to get inspected if the motorboat was spotted. The crew scrambled around the deck looking very much as if they were preparing nets to be dropped into the ocean. The ship had been cleverly outfitted to look exactly like one of the dozens of other trawlers that fished the west coast of Africa. However, the inside of the ship didn't resemble a commercial fishing vessel.

As he stood there, going over the preparations for the next launch, the ship suddenly reversed course and again headed due west away from the coast. It startled el-Wahlie, and he rushed into the ship's elaborate control room below deck where a sophisticated satellite imagining screen was being watched by a young man no older than 20. It was obviously innovative technology and the images it produced were from a combination of Russian satellite surveys, pirated AWAC signals, and heat seeking radar. With a touch of the screen, the man could locate the AWAC planes, and a second touch would flash up a detailed topo hydrophobic map of the African coast.

"Ahmed, why did you instruct the captain to reverse course and proceed westward? We must get closer to the coast if we are to launch our ultralight aircraft."

"The American AWAC flying the coastal grid would have picked us up if we had preceded any closer to the coast."

"What is the distance to the town of el-Shiriff, Ahmed?"

"From our present location it is one-hundred and seventy-five kilometers."

"And the range of the ultralight plane we have onboard?"

"Less than a hundred kilometers; however, I've plotted the grid of the American planes, and if we keep the west course for another hour and then wait thirty minutes, we can move the ship back to within seventy-five kilometers of the coast and launch the plane. I've plotted the grid the American planes are flying, and we will have twenty minutes to launch the plane. It would have to be refueled once it reaches the coast in order to carry out the rest of its mission, but we are in contact with our fighters on the coast, and they can refuel the plane when they pick up their part of the cargo. However, after twenty minutes in the launch location we must move due west again at our maximum speed, or the American planes will spot us."

"Excellent; instruct the captain to follow your instruction exactly, and notify Nerada that she must get ready to depart as soon as we arrive there. Once she is airborne instruct the captain to reverse his course and head due west until we are out of the American recon area."

"Sir, it will be done as you have instructed."

Thirty minutes later the ship suddenly picked up speed, turned, and headed directly for the African coast. On deck, a mechanic was putting the final wing connection bolts on an ultralight aircraft as a young woman stood by.

"Nerada, you are to be commended for volunteering for this mission. Your family will be well paid, and today you will be in paradise."

"I will gladly do anything to protect the faith, Rasandi. May my life that I will give help you to drive the infidels from our land."

"You are a brave woman, Nerada, but remember, if something happens and you fail to complete your mission, and you are captured by the Americans, take the pill you have been given. They would rape and torture you."

"Yes, I understand."

"Good; now get ready; the ship cannot stay in such a near shore position, but for a few minutes. As soon as the ship stops, get in the plane, and fly direct east toward the GPS signal on the plane. When you land, our fighters will be there to help you and to take part of your cargo, which they will put in a truck to deliver to our Moroccan fighters. They will give you an AK .47 for the last part of the trip, and program the plane where the automatic pilot will fly you directly to the target. The Americans survliance planes may spot you when you fly over the open desert, and if they do, respond with your weapon. Then you are to finish your mission. Do you understand everything?"

"Yes, Allah Akbar! I am ready!"

As Nerada eased into the small cockpit, one of the crew packed two small bundles into the space behind the seat, and another man secured a detonator attached to an explosive device, and placed it under the plane's seat. A nod from el-Wahlie, and a crew-member started the engine of the ultralight plane. The deck of the ship was long enough to give the small craft enough room to become airborne and el-Wahlie and his second in command, Omar Hamid, watched as the plane disappeared from sight.

"It seems we are going to a lot of trouble to evade the Americans, Rasandi," said Hamid. "Why would we send both the motorboat and the ultralight?"

"The Leadership Council knows best, Omar. This multi-prong attack will do several things. The biological material that the ultralight will deliver to our fighters will be passed on to the Moroccan al-Qaida cell. They will be able to easily get it across the

Mediterranean to a European city. The radioactive material will be put in the hands of a very determined group of our men, and they will be given a free hand to use it anyway they choose.

Of course, Nerada will fly the ultralight directly into the Moroccan base the American are using, and the result will be to divert all the American resources away from us. Of course, the material the ultralight carries will kill the Americans at the base and their Moroccan allies. But that is only a part of Nerada's mission. While the Americans are occupied with Nerada and the ultralight aircraft, that distraction will help us to move the most critical part of our cargo onto the African continent. We have taken extra precautions because what we still have onboard is the most important part of our mission, and if we succeed in this part, we will have a great advantage over the Americans who are trying to find us."

"But won't it harm our mission? We will have reduced the material down to one box."

"Not in the least. The two trucks that came from Libya had enough enriched uranium and biological material onboard for us to do ten strikes if necessary. We have never planned to use the enriched uranium, but to pass it on to our associates and let them have it. Even the nuclear scientist from Iran was a decoy. The Leadership Council convinced him to come into the jungle and arm what he thought were weapons. They were fakes. We don't have the expertise to explode a nuclear device. We knew the American would capture him, and one way or another they would get him to talk. Then they would be frantically looking for armed nuclear bombs, and not what we are really trying to use. Every time we send out a boat or anything with enriched uranium onboard the Americans will pick it up immediately and respond. Then we will be able to move this small twenty kilo package a little closer to its destination."

"You mean everything we are doing is just to move the seventy kilo package to Europe?"

"That is exactly right. All of the other things we are doing could turn out great, but our most deadly attack will come from the material in that box. We must divide the material we acquired from the Libyans in order to increase the likelihood that we will be successful. We have done this because of who the Americans have leading the team that has been given the mission to intercept us—a former Special Forces soldier named Josh Martin. He is the one responsible for killing so many of the former Leadership Council. The new Council wants to be sure that our mission is accomplished, and avenge the death of so many of our Muslim brothers. By doing everything we have, it greatly increases the chances of success."

"But how does the Council know his name and everything else you have told me?"

"The Council has one of our people working in a very high level of the U. S. Government. This person is privy to all of the communications that go between the American CIA and the Special Forces team that is hunting us. With this person's help, we will not fail this time. Our mission has been perfectly planned, and we will have continuous detail information about how the Americans are reacting as we move the material toward Europe. And the new Leadership Council is using a very large number of our fighters to make sure the attacks are successful."

***

Two hours later:

"Josh, this is rabbit 082. We have a strong signal coming from a speeding motorboat. The boat is only about a twenty-four foot outboard. And get this; this signal is so strong that the crew must be taking some radiation."

"Rabbit 082, this is Josh. Give me the vector and position of the boat."

"Coordinates, 1209 south and 1482 west of the 14th meridian. At the speed of the boat, their vector will put the boat at the African coast within an hour.—Copy?"

"Roger, 082. Give me an update every fifteen minutes, and run a reverse vector of the motorboat. It had to come from a much larger ship… over and out."

"Roger… over and out."

Josh turned to Gloria: "Gloria, the bastards have the radioactive material in a speedboat heading for the African coast. Take these coordinates and bring up a Google map of the coast and let's see if we can figure out where they may be heading."

In a few minutes, Gloria and Josh were peering at the screen as the position of the boat popped up with the arrow vector indicating the direction the boat was traveling.

"They've kept the exact course since the AWAC's picked them up. Is there a port or town on the coast that they will intersect?"

"Nothing, the coast doesn't have even a village on it for miles from where they will intersect," said Gloria.

"Just a minute; look there's a small river exactly at the end of their vector. A large ship couldn't navigate it, but a low–draft speedboat could get up there for several miles. Hey, look: About thirty miles up that river is a town of some sort. Could they be heading there? Bring up a Google detail of that village, and let's see if there's a dock or some boats that might show us if the river's navigable."

Seconds later, a closeup shot of the river and the village appeared. "Damn right, a speedboat can make it up the river! Look at the boats around that dock. Get me Tail 082."

Gloria handed Josh the phone as the AWAC's pilot voice boomed out. "What can I do for you, Josh?"

"Captain, I'm going to give you the coordinates of a village about thirty miles from the coast. Circle and give me a continuous image and analysis of the situation, and especially note any trucks or armed men. Also check out the dock on the river."

"Got it, Josh. I'll keep you posted."

"Well, it'll take 082 about an hour to get over the village. How long will it take the speedboat to reach the coast of Africa?" Josh asked.

"According to the last AWAC's spotting, and the estimated speed of the boat, they'll be at the mouth of the Sepojepig River in less than hour. That is, if that's where they're heading," answered Gloria.

"There's no place else for them to go. I'm going to get the two Black Hawks and SF guys heading that way. By the time the boat arrives at the village dock, our people will be there to greet them."

Minutes later, Josh was on the radio talking to Colonel Dowson, and the Black Hawks were on the way.

Josh was still concerned about the mother ship that launched the small speedboat, but his focus was now on the impending arrival of that boat with radioactive material onboard. His thoughts were interrupted by a call from Tail 082.

"Josh, Tail 082 here. I'm circling the village. I have a high-resolution camera on the dock and the area around it—hey, just a minute! There are two trucks driving into the village, and they're heading straight for the boat dock."

"What's in the trucks? Can you make out people?" questioned Josh.

"Not yet, the backs are covered—wait a minute—they're unloading now, and I'm not believing what I'm seeing. There must be ten to fifteen armed men in each truck. I estimate around thirty armed men have arrived at the dock."

"082 I've got to cut you off. Come back in five minutes; I have to alert Colonel Dowson and the SFs who are heading for the village."

"Got it... over and out."

"Gloria get me Colonel Dowson on the radio ASAP."

Seconds later, Gloria handed Josh the headset.

"Colonel, Josh Martin here. Listen up. Don't enter the airspace or land at the village I gave you earlier. There are at least thirty fighters there, and they are well armed. Call in the modified C-130 gunship from the carrier standing by off the coast, and have them contact me direct for orders. We need to even the odds before you come in."

"Okay, Josh, I'll get the gunship on the way. It should be there in about forty-five minutes. Is that too late?"

"No, I don't think so. The boat with the stuff won't make it there for at least two hours."

As soon as Josh hung up the phone, Tail 082 beeped him.

"Josh, I did a reverse vector on the motorboat, and it led straight to what looks like a fishing trawler. I think is the mother ship we've been chasing. There's not another boat within twenty-five miles. On a low pass, we're getting a very weak, low-grade signal. Looks like radioactive material has been onboard. The ship's heading due west at high speed."

"Roger 082, mark it on your GPS. We'll want to come back and intercept it, but right now we have our hands full. Swing back over the river and give us a progress report on the speedboat heading up the river—over and out."

"Roger, we'll get on it and keep you informed—over and out."

Josh nervously checked his watch every five minutes, waiting for a call from the C-130 gunship. His thoughts were interrupted by another call from Tail 082.

"Josh I'm back over the village on the river, and it looks like the fighters are congregating around the dock. They've got a truck backed up to the dock with its back open ready to take cargo. Oh, something else happened when the trucks unloaded some of the fighters: They herded the villagers out and away from anywhere close to the dock. I think the only ones in the village now are the fighters who came in the trucks."

"Roger. That's good news because when that C-130 gunship gets there, it's going to decimate the area around the docks—keep me posted—over and out."

"Roger—over and out."

"Gloria, get me the pilot of the C-130 on the radio if he's in range."

After a couple of tries, she was able to raise the C-130.

"This is Tail 03345, code horse, come in, Josh."

"Roger, horse, Josh, weasel, here. Listen up: This is going to be like a turkey shoot, but you need to confine your sweep to an area of one-hundred yards from the coordinates I'm going to send you. Your visual will be a boat dock and two trucks near the dock. Give them all you've got, and after twenty minutes get back to me. But don't hit the boat that just arrived at the pier.—got it?"

"Roger, Josh, will do. We should have a visual in about fifteen minutes. I'll get back to you to confirm the target then—over and out."

"Gloria, get AWAC 082 on and tell them the C-130 will be taking out the target in around fifteen minutes. Give me a visual when the C-130's finished."

"I'm on it, Josh."

Josh punched his Breitling Oceania Chorography II stopwatch and nervously paced back and forth. It was 22 minutes later when the pilot of the C-130 contacted him again.

"This is 03345 here, weasel. Do you read me, Josh? Over."

"Loud and clear. Go ahead. Over."

"We've raked the dock, village, and the area around where the trucks are parked. I don't see any signs of life except on the boat at the dock. It looks like three men are still on the boat... over."

"Good work; we'll have an intercept team on the ground in less than fifteen minutes. You can return to base. Over."

"Gloria, put me in contact with the SF Captain on the Black Hawk that's approaching the village—and hurry—it's critical."

Gloria quickly dialed the coded frequency, and in seconds Captain Hoover Winslow, SF team captain was on the radio.

"This is Hawk, 036, Winslow here. What've you got for me, Josh?—read me?—over."

"Yeah, loud and clear.. Listen up—we may have run down the bad guys with the radioactive stuff. Gloria will give you the coordinates in a couple of minutes. You're probably only thirty minutes away right now. The C-130 has finished softening up the fighters who were meeting the boat, but they've left the boat alone. Three bad guys are on the boat, and I am sure they're well armed. You'll have to take them out in order to secure the boat.

"Our AWAC says the men are staying on the boat, so take them out with sniper fire and send the containment team in fully protected to check out the boat. I directed the gunship not to fire at the boat or try to take out the armed men on deck. You are to do the same. Get the al-Qaida fighters, but don't direct any fire into the hole of the boat... over."

"Gotcha, Josh. Put Gloria on and we'll head that way... over."

"Give me a full report ASAP. Over and out."

"Roger... over and out."

"Gloria, get me AWAC Tail 082."

Gloria punched the coded frequency and in seconds Josh was on the line with the AWAC.

"This is Murphy, Tail 082. Do you read me L-7? Over."

"Loud and clear, Murphy. Note this: new pattern for all AWAC's. Go back to the coast and first recon the possible mother ship. The one you spotted before checking out the boat heading for the river town. I think the speedboat's carrying the material, but we still need to intercept the mother ship and check it out. Give Gloria the new coordinates when you get a visual... over."

"Roger, Josh. I'll get back with Gloria as soon as we locate it... over."

"Roger. When you make visual, contact this Black Hawk, and we'll head that way. Over and out."

"Roger. We'll start that way immediately. Over and out."

Gloria was on the phone seconds later spewing out a new grid for the AWAC's to fly, based on information she'd received from the AWAC. Josh was convinced that a slow-moving freighter would not be able to elude the new grid. Now they could only wait for the call and the confirmation. He would get the assault crew ready while he waited on the AWAC to give him the exact position. Then he thought of something that might save a little time.

"Lieutenant, do a reverse vector on that motorboat we tracked coming to the coast and fly it. That should save us some time."

"Roger, give me about three minutes to lock in on it, and we'll be off."

Lieutenant Jernigan was about to set his autopilot when Gloria handed him the radio mike.

"Hover Winslow with the SF assault team."

"Hover, this Josh. What have you got? Over."

"Josh, we took out the fighters on the boat with snipers and the containment team has just finished securing the material onboard. We're checking to see if any al-Qaida on the ground are wounded. It looks like they're all dead."

"Great job, Winslow. Continue to have the Control Team medics see if any of the al-Qaida fighters are still alive and need medical help. If they're all dead, leave them for the villagers to give them a proper Muslim burial—over."

"Gotcha. I'll get back with a detailed report as soon as the containment team finishes work—over and out."

"Roger—over and out."

Josh leaned back and, for the first time in a long time, he took a deep breath, cracked a slight smile, and nodded to Gloria.

"I think we got what we were after," he said, relieved.

"That's great, Josh. But why go after the mother ship if we have the material?"

"It's mostly to collect intelligence material. The ship's captain has a lot of intelligence about al-Qaida, and we'll get it out of him."

However, as Josh thought about radioactive material being on a boat with only three men to protect it, something worried him. Did they do that as the ultimate decoy? Surely, they knew we'd pick up something that hot with the AWAC's. Does the mother ship have more material onboard?

Suddenly, finding and boarding the mother ship took on a new urgency. Josh leaned over to where only Gloria could hear him, "Gloria, I'll feel a lot better when we find the mother ship. I've got a bad feeling that we're not out of the woods yet."

"What d'ya mean? We've *got* the material."

"Maybe." Josh leaned back and tried to relax as he waited on Tail 082's call.

17

Contact

Gloria was listening to a transmission from Bob Myers, who was operating the listening post in Rabat. She handed Josh the radio mike.

"Josh, I've got Bob on the radio. He just got a message from the CIA. Bob's ready to read it."

"Bob? Josh here. What've you got?"

"Our listening post picked up a coded message. They broke the code, of course. The message says: **Moving material on land—be ready.**"

"Oh, my god! They've split up the stuff, and are heading to meet the al-Qaida fighters in western Morocco! Get back to me as soon as you have anything new—I've got to move on this immediately—over and out."

"Gloria, contact Colonel Dowson on the carrier and tell him to get his Seals in the air and head toward the Western Sahara. I'll give him more details when he reaches land. I've got to contact one of our AWAC's and get a visual of them flying over land."

Soon, Josh had AWAC's combing the area from the coast to the Moroccan border with Western Sahara. Then he thought of something: *They won't travel on the highways—they'll move directly across the desert!* Josh grabbed the radio mike and in seconds he we talking to the lead AWAC plane. "Tail 082, come in; this is L -7."

"Read you loud and clear, Josh. What can I do for you?"

"Break off the search for the mother ship and do a high altitude visual over Western Sahara, and see if you can spot a plume of dust coming from vehicles that are traveling across open desert. Work from the coast directly east toward Morocco."

"Okay, will do. I'll get back to you if I see anything."

"Gloria, get Colonel Dowson on the radio and tell him to proceed due east toward the Moroccan border until he receives further instructions."

While Gloria was talking to Dowson, Josh contacted Bob at the CIA base in Rabat.

"Bob have the Moroccan troops move at full speed toward the Western Sahara Province, and proceed until they are within ten kilometers of the main Moroccan border. Then have them hold their positions until I give notice to move."

Josh pulled up a series of Google maps covering the North African coast and began to plot various vectors based on his estimate of where the mother ship was located when they launched the small speedboat.

"Gloria, we can assume the mother vessel was heading in a westerly direction from a launching location far enough out to sea to be out of our AWAC grid, probably focusing on a Western European target. However, I'm certain they know we are trying to intercept them. But we may be wasting our time. They could have put all the stuff on the motorboat and the trucks moving across the desert. We can't be sure of anything at this point. For all we know the mother ship may still has some of the material onboard, and it's moving toward a European target."

"Josh, just look at the range of possible targets using the vectors, and estimating the boat speed; in twelve hours, they could be approaching Europe, and the number of targets will mushroom. Why don't we focus on a corridor seventy-five miles out from the coast? That's the highest probable route for them to take."

"That *is* why we can't focus on the most direct route."

"I don't understand."

"Look, if you were trying to keep from being detected and killed, how would you proceed? You would take the most evasive route, not the most direct—get it?"

Gloria gave Josh a sheepish shake of the head as she realized how simplistic her recommendation had been. Her thoughts were interrupted by AWAC 082.

"AWAC Tail 082 calling Josh Martin—come in, Josh—over."

Josh grabbed the mic and clicked transmit. "Josh here, 082."

"We've spotted an ultralight aircraft flying inland away the coast. I think it probably came from the little town of al-Sharif a few miles down the coast. Of course an ultralight doesn't have a radio or any way to communicate—it's probably nothing—over."

"Give me some coordinates and a vector. We may be close enough to check it out—over."

As the AWAC pilot spit out the ultralight's position Gloria spotted them on her map and handed them to the pilot. A nod and he looked back at Josh.

"We can intercept in less than twenty minutes."

"Okay, but don't get too close. I don't want our rotor wash to flip the ultralight and kill some innocent, amateur pilot."

"Roger; I'll just get you close enough for a visual I. D.

Josh pulled out his binoculars and scanned the sky in front of the Black Hawk. Soon he spotted a speck in front of the chopper, just as the pilot confirmed the visual.

"Close in to about fifty meters, and proceed parallel to his trajectory."

"Got it; get ready, we should be in position in less than two minutes."

Josh snapped on a safety belt, opened the side door of the chopper, and focused his binoculars on the man piloting the plane.

"Yeah, looks like a local the way he's dressed—no—damn, it's a woman—hey! Wait a minute! She has a weapon! Everybody down! Get out of range, Tom!"

The words were no sooner out of Josh's mouth than hammering sounds from rounds striking the chopper announced that they were taking hits. Tom had already sent the helicopter into a steep dive as the bullets hit the side of the chopper, and seconds later, he was out of range.

"That bitch is an al-Qaida fighter! How in the hell did one of their women end up in an ultralight flying from the coast of Africa?" Josh raged.

"Hell if I know, Josh. Want our gunner to take her out?"

"Yeah, I sure do—hold it; she's dropping down—may be about to land—no—she seems to be heading for that group of buildings. Any I.D. on the buildings?"

"Hold it—yeah it is a Moroccan Army base that we use as a North African listening post."

"Oh my god! Shoot her down! Now! Hurry! We have men there!"

Tom whipped the Black Hawk around and sited in. "I'm going to use our Hellfire Missiles. I don't want to take any more hits. Locking in, ready… missiles launched."

Josh watched as two missiles streaked by the ultralight aircraft, and exploded harmlessly.

"Damn; you missed!" yelled Josh.

"Hell, I know it! It's like trying to hit a fly."

"Pull around and I'll try to take her out before she can get any more rounds off."

"Okay, Josh, but if she hits a rotor blade we're history."

Tom moved the chopper around behind the aircraft and began to move in position for Josh to fire. As he squinted through his sniper scope, he saw the barrel of her weapon swing around. Just as Josh squeezed off his first burst, and watched the woman slump over, the chopper was rocked by several direct hits.

"Problem, Josh! We're hit! High-octane gasoline is spewing out everywhere! We're going to be on fire unless I can get this baby on the ground!"

As Tom cut power on all but the main rotor and guided the chopper down into a controlled crash landing, Josh watched the ultralight continue to approach the army base.

"Flatten out! We'll hit the ground in three seconds—get out as quickly as you can!"

The words were no more than out of Tom's mouth than the Black Hawk hit the ground with a jarring thud. The forward fuel tank split open and a millisecond later the chopper was sitting in a lake of fire. Josh kicked a jammed side door open and the three-man chopper crew jumped into the fire and managed to make it out.

Josh was about to follow when he looked back and spotted Gloria, whose head had bounced against the chopper's inside wall; she was dazed from the controlled crash, unable to move. With one swift move, he threw her over his shoulder.

"Cover your face and close your eyes!" Josh barked, as he jumped out the side door of the chopper, sprinted a few yards through the blaze, and eased Gloria down beside the other members of the crew.

"Everyone move away from this bird" the pilot yelled. "It's going to explode!" The crew, Josh, and with Josh helping Gloria they ran about 50 yards and stopped. Seconds later, the chopper's other gas tank exploded with a thundering flash.

It took a few seconds to realize everyone was out of the chopper and okay, and then the pilot let out a string of profanities.

"A brand-new Black Hawk shot down by a damn woman flying in an ultralight! I can't believe it!"

"Look; the ultralight's still in the air; it's about to crash into those buildings on the bluff!" yelled Josh.

He quickly pressed his radio to connect with Tail 082, and began to bark commands" "082—Josh here! This is an emergency call! Contact the CIA listening post L-45 and alert them to a probable bioattack—an ultralight is about to crash into their headquarters building!"

The words were no more than out of his mouth when the ultralight had hit the main HQ building and exploded.

"Tail 082—notify HQ and send emergency crews in immediately. Tell them to be masked and carry responder disaster equipment to counter a probable bioattack—over."

"Read you loud and clear. I'm on it."

Josh turned to Captain Davis. "Captain, have the backup chopper head this way, and instruct your men to engage their protective gear. I strongly suspect the ultralight was caring biomaterial. This may be another attempt to throw us off the trail of the nuclear material. We can't let these diversions take our mind off of the chase. That's exactly what the enemy's trying to do."

"I'll have it on the way in the next five minutes—should we check on the area the ultralight struck?"

"No, we managed to get out of the chopper, but we don't have the proper gear in case the ultralight was carrying material that is bare skin sensitive. AWAC 082 is in contact with HQ, and they'll have emergency personnel on the site soon.

"All we can do is wait. But I do need to get the AWAC's to grid offshore. We've got to find the mother ship. The next attack could be the enriched uranium if there's any left on the mother ship. The consequences will be horrible if that ship makes it into European waters."

Josh stayed on the radio for the next 15 minutes directing the AWAC's toward their new surveillance grid. They had fallen for the decoy for the second time, and the mother ship slipped farther away. And as they chased down the two decoys, Josh could feel the anxiety building. They had missed the chance in the jungle to capture and kill an entire group of al-Qaida, and now, after two misses, the primary target was farther from being intersected than ever.

Gloria interrupted his thoughts with another message from HQ.

"Josh, you need to take this call; It's urgent."

He grabbed the radio and identified himself.

"Josh, Colonel Dowson here. We've just confirmed the ultralight was carrying biomaterial, and we've sent an emergency team to clean it up. There have been heavy causalities, and I'm afraid the American crew manning the listening post has been involved. I understand this attack was not the main thrust of al-Qaida. However, I can confirm we have the radioactive material that was in the speedboat. Do we have all of it?"

"Negative, Major; I've deduced the mother ship is carrying additional material, since the ultralight was clearly a decoy. The ship must have been within a hundred-mile gird of the coast in order to launch the ultralight. I've given the AWAC's a new grid, and we should have contact within the next few hours."

"Josh, I know you're doing everything you can to intersect the main group, but in a few hours they could be very close to some major metropolitan areas. We've picked up chatter that there may be a strike in less than seventy-two hours."

"I wouldn't be surprised if they try to divert us again," Josh said. "After all, they know we have aircraft searching for them, and they've been successful in sending out decoys the take us off their trail. I expect them to continue to do that unless we can locate the mother ship. I'll keep you posted."

There was a mic buzz and Josh's call was interrupted by a call from one of the AWAC's.

"Josh here. Go ahead 082."

"Josh, I've been checking out cross-desert vehicles. When I got to twenty-eight thousand feet, I engaged the ***********(classified) and did a horizon scan. I picked up several individual plumes, but only one looks suspicious. I dropped down and checked them out. There are four covered trucks, and we can pick up cellphone chatter from all of them. Just from what I'm hearing, I would guess somewhere around fifty people are on those trucks."

"Good spotting, Dan! I think you've located them. Give me their exact coordinates and a vector reading. We're about to put a deadly squeeze on those bastards."

Minutes later Josh was on the radio to Bob at the CIA listening post, giving him directions about where to position the Moroccan troops. Then, after plotting the location, speed, and vector of the al-Qaida convoy, he radioed Colonel Dowson with the Seal assault team.

"Colonel, I think we've located the main al-Qaida group that's traveling across open desert. They have some of the material from the boat or mother ship, and are taking it in a four-truck convoy across the Western Sahara's open desert. I'll give your pilot the exact coordinates after we talk. According to the conversations picked up by our AWAC's, there may be more than fifty fighters in the convoy.

"Sir, I think we need the additional Seal team deployed immediately. We have Moroccan troops positioned about thirty kilometers in front of the convoy. I'm requesting that you make a visual, and then follow them until they approach the Moroccan position.

"When they begin taking fire from the dug-in Moroccan soldiers, make your assault," Josh continued. "Hopefully, the second Seal team will be right behind you. But we can't wait for them."

"Don't worry, Josh; we'll be able to handle them."

"One more thing, Colonel: You can't fire at any space that could be carrying cargo. Have one of your snipers shoot the motors and disable some of the trucks, and then nail the bastards as they scramble out. Oh, one more thing: Be sure your boys have some good masks with them. One of those trucks probably has biomaterial onboard."

"Copy: Hold and I'll patch you through to the pilot."

After Josh gave the chopper pilot the coordinates, he directed his Black Hawk toward the intercept area. In another 25 minutes, the pilot spotted the dust plumes of the convoy.

"Hang back, just out of their line of sight. We don't want to give them any notice that they've been spotted."

"Roger."

Josh went back to his map and plotted the position of the Moroccan ground troops, Colonel Dowson's Seal team, and his Black Hawk.

"Gloria, the lead truck is less than twenty minutes from the Moroccan blocking troops, and the Seals are closing in. In the open desert, this'll probably be a turkey shoot. Those guys don't have a prayer."

"Josh, I've been holding my breath ever since they managed to get the material smuggled out of the jungle. Thank, god, we've finally got them cornered."

"Yeah, I've been frantic since we let them get away. I don't think there's any way to get out of this trap.—Okay, only ten more minutes until they run into the Moroccans."

Josh looked out the window and watched as the Black Hawk carrying the Seal team moved into position.

"Any time now...yeah!" A series of explosions reverberated and the convoy rolled to a stop. Seconds later, Colonel Dowson's Black Hawk came alongside of the convoy and the two door gunners began to disable the trucks. The chopper landed, and three Seals jumped out and began to lay down covering fire as the rest of the team piled out. "Put her down right behind the Colonel's chopper!" yelled Josh to Gloria. "Keep tabs on the containment team***"

"Hell no, Josh!"

"I can handle any weapon you can! I'm going with *you*!"

"We don't have time to argue—come on, let's go!"

The Seal team, Josh, and Gloria dropped to a prone position, and began to pick off the disorganized al-Qaida fighters, who now were taking fire from both sides. As the enemy fighters dropped, Josh could sense a quick but deadly firefight that would end with all the al-Qaida fighters killed, and only minor causalities taken by the Seal team and the Moroccan Special Forces.

Josh estimated that fewer than 10 al-Qaida were still standing, when one of the fighters jumped into a truck in the center of the convoy that hadn't been hit. And as Josh and the others watched, the man drove the truck straight for the line of Moroccan Special Forces, who began pouring fire into the front of the truck.

There was only sporadic firing now from a remnant of the al-Qaida fighters. The firefight seemed to be over.

"Hell, he's as good as dead," Josh said to Gloria, pointing to the truck that was now roaring at top speed toward the Moroccan troops.

The driver was crouched down below the dashboard as the truck approached the dug-in troops. Suddenly, the vehicle seemed to hesitate as it reached the Moroccan lines, and then— as the stunned Seals, Josh, and Gloria watched—there was a massive explosion.

"My god! A suicide bomber!"

However, the blast was confined mostly to the truck and Josh could see most of the Moroccan Special Forces, unharmed by the blast, moving forward to examine the wreckage.

Josh grabbed the radio, and in seconds he had contact with a circling AWAC that was monitoring the firefight.

"Tail 082, do you read me... over."

"Loud and clear, go ahead, Josh... over."

"Do you detect any radioactive material released from the truck that just exploded?*** over."

"Negative; we've been receiving straight-line signals before and after the truck exploded... over."

"Okay, 082... over and out."

"That doesn't make any sense," muttered Josh—"Oh, my god! The biomaterial!" Josh was stunned for a few seconds, realizing that if the truck wasn't carrying the enriched uranium, it would be carrying the H2S biomaterial that killed the villagers in Niger. That shocking thought had him frantically calling the colonel in charge of Moroccan Special Forces.

"Colonel Hasmine, have your men put on their gas masks! Quickly! The truck may have been carrying deadly biomaterial! Do you read me, Colonel? Colonel—Colonel Hasmine, do you read me?" Josh put down the radio and grabbed his binoculars.

He quickly scanned the Moroccan position.

One glance and Josh dropped his binoculars and yelled as a light breeze carried a yellow mist wafting from the Moroccan's troop position. That sent a surge of panic through Josh that they were in grave danger. It was just what killed the Nigerian villagers—the deadly H2S gas.

"Masks on! Hurry! Now!"

There was a rush to deploy masks, and after Josh checked them, he picked up his binoculars and focused on the Moroccan Special Forces position. The only sign of life was one soldier trying to crawl away from the site. He collapsed as Josh watched.

"Gloria, get on the radio and order in the containment team. Tell them there's been a full-scale bioattack on Moroccan Special Forces, and there are heavy causalities."

"Captain, we'll check the other trucks, but I'm guessing this group had only part of the material we are trying to intercept. Our AWAC's did not pick up any radioactive signals. The radioactive material was on the motorboat. I think we have it wrapped up, but to be sure, have your men search all the equipment and bring us any possible intelligence you find on the men or in the trucks."

"Gloria get AWAC Tail 082 on the radio." A few seconds later Gloria handed Josh the mic.

"082, Josh here—listen up. We've got a full-blown emergency with a bio release and casualties. But I think we have major part of the material, including all of the enriched uranium, as well as the additional biomaterial. However, to be sure we need to find the mother ship. Put up a seven-hundred-and-fifty-mile grid and bring in all aircraft available to fly it. Report any contact directly to me—over."

"I', already working on the grid, and three more AWAC's are on the way, but the boat may slip through before we can get enough aircraft in the area—over."

"Acknowledge—do your best—over and out."

"Gloria, get the CIA station listening post in Rabat is on the radio."

"Josh, Phil was holding while you were talking to 082. Said they picked up some chatter about a possible target."

"Phil; Josh here. What've you got?"

"Josh, you know how those guys like to brag... well in one of the coded messages from the trucks your group destroyed, there was a comment about another attack, so I think you should expect something like what just happened with the Moroccan Special Forces to pop up again, or maybe they were talking about the final attack with the material.— over."

"Roger; anything else?—over."

"Yeah, but the transmission was bad and scrambled. We're still trying to get a good read on a couple of key words. The one word we linked to the ultimate target was the word 'station'. It might not be an English word—over."

"Roger... scan everything in Spanish, Italian, and English to see how many fits we have in north Africa and western Europe. My guess is that we will have hundreds.—over."

"I've notified the CIA listening post in Spain and Portugal, and filled them in on the details of the operation. I'm going to hand you off to them since everything indicates the target is advancing north—over."

"Roger. I'll check in with them shortly—over and out."

"Captain, head due north for approximately two-hundred miles following the coast. Notify me when you reach that position, and keep an open mic to 082."

"You got it; changing vectors to north twenty-eight degrees east."

"Gloria, contact Langley direct and ask them to work up a high probability curve using the word 'station,' and assign a maximum target value and proximity. Tell them to use as a high proximity a point that's three-hundred miles north of our present location."

18

Transfer

El-Wahlie pulled out a slip of paper from his pocket and handed it to the captain.

"Captain, proceed to the exact coordinates listed on this paper. You must be there within an hour. Increase the speed of this boat to its maximum."

"Yes, but I thought we were to meet the code named 'Tiger,' just off the coast."

"Captain, that information was given to you in case we were assaulted by the American dogs. You can forget the old coordinates. Proceed at full throttle to the new rendezvous point."

"Yes, sir." The captain entered the coordinates and as the ship turned around, he pushed the throttle forward to maximum speed.

"Captain, there's a crate below marked with a crescent moon. Have two of your men bring it to the upper deck, and prepare it to be hoisted overboard. Do you understand?"

"Sir, I thought the radioactive material was all that was onboard."

"Yes, I'm sure you did. This material was loaded before the crew came onboard. It's the key to our strike against the infidels. It is not for you to understand what the material is or how we plan to use it. Do you understand?"

"Yes, sir. I'll have some men began to move it immediately."

"Good, be extremely careful and don't shake or drop it. An accident would kill everyone on board."

An hour later, the boat crane lifted the small box from the hole of the ship and placed it on the open deck. As the crate was set in place, the captain heard a beep from the navigation system indicating the programmed coordinates had been reached.

"Sir, we've reached the spot where your coordinates took us, and there's no ship in sight. Are you sure we are where we *should* be?"

"Captain, you ask too many questions. Just idle your engines and stand by to make contact."

"Yes, sir." The captain kicked the motors into neutral, and the ship stopped and rocked in light swells. Minutes later he looked up as a seaplane circled the ship, and then turned and sat down within 50 yards of the ship.

"Move the ship to within ten yards of the plane, Captain, and hold it there. Have your men load the crate and prepare to transfer it to the plane."

Thirty minutes passed and as crate was slipped into the belly of the plane, el-Wahlie hooked a zip-line onto the rail of the boat and prepared to cross to the airplane, but before he did he turned to the captain.

"Captain, your part of the mission is over. We have transferred all of the material from your ship. You may proceed to your homeport, but I would not be surprised if the Americans stop your boat and question you. Since you have an empty boat, they will do nothing. Remember, you are not to tell them anything. Do not even acknowledge them when they question you. Your silence is critical for this mission to succeed."

"Yes, sir; they will not get any information from me."

"Good, Allah Akbar!"

"Allah Akbar!"

El-Wahlie stepped over the rail and seconds later, he boarded the seaplane. As he got onboard, he nodded to the pilot and said, "Fly on this course, and fly as close to the water as you can. Our radar scans and recon grid from the American planes tells us we will have a window of one hour and three minutes beginning in exactly twelve minutes—and we'll have sixty-three minutes to fly through it. That should put us well into the Sahara Desert, and out of their recon coverage area. Fly at maximum power and land in the desert at these coordinates."

"Yes, sir."

Twelve minutes later the plane took off heading away from the ship toward the African coast.

19

Intercept

Josh, was standing by the radio when an emergency call light flashed. It was from one of the AWAC's.

"Josh this is AWAC 082. Do you read me?—over."

"Loud and clear; whatcha got, Woodrow?—over."

"I think we have located the mother ship. Your course is right on target. Stand by for the exact coordinates. You are about thirty-eight minutes flying time from the ship.—over."

"Roger, 082. Read them to our pilot. I'll switch you direct.—Over"

Minutes later the chopper made a slight left turn and the pilot yelled back to Josh, "ETA in fifteen minutes! We should have visual in less than ten!"

Josh went about getting everyone ready to secure the mother ship.

His preparations were interrupted by a ding from his sat phone. Very few people had his encrypted number. He glanced down.

"Shit, I can't ignore this one! Hello."

"Josh?... General Davis here....Have you pressed your red encryption button?......Good, got your report on the ultralight attack. The on-the-ground containment team confirmed it was loaded with biomaterial—a bunch of causalities—update me."

"General, we think the radioactive material was sent off in a small motorboat from the mother ship. The AWAC's picked up the signal from the small boat, and we vectored a reverse course back to the mother ship. I'll give you an update with details in a few minutes. We are approaching the ship now and in less than ten minutes, we will be boarding it. I expect resistance—oh, one more thing—by now our second Black Hawk is on site, and has secured the motorboat and the radioactive material. I want board the mother ship just to be sure we have everything. I am confident that within an hour we will have recovered all material that left Nigeria—over and out."

"Great work, Josh; Over and out."

Josh clicked off the sat phone, changed clothes, put on his wetsuit, and began to go over the intercept.

"Okay, this is nothing sophisticated. We don't have time for anything cute. The Black Hawk gunner will disable the boat and stand back fifty meters hovering at thirty meters over the water with a sniper in the gangway. If there is no return fire, the chopper will drop down and put everyone in the water without a raft, and you'll approach the boat and seize it anyway you can. You guys know how to do that."

Josh finished dressing and started going over the plan.

"Okay, guys, just like we trained off San Diego, we'll split up and circle the boat with Sgt. Murphy leaving half the team to the left, and I'll lead the other half to the right. When you hear this whistle, throw your hooks over the side and pull yourself up, and make damn sure you have your weapon ready when your head clears the deck. Murphy, you carry the flash-bangs and be ready to toss them below when I give the word. Shoot everybody onboard, if they resist, and be sure they don't scuttle the ship. Got it?—oh, one more thing: try not to kill the captain. We need to find out all the hows and wheres from him."

A nod of heads and Josh leaned over and yelled at the pilot, "What's your ETA?"

The pilot raised five fingers and cut one.

"Okay, guys, the sniper should keep them pinned down, so when we get onboard Murphy will toss a couple of flash-bank grenades down below, and then we'll follow 'em down."

The pilot in the chopper held up his hand again, one finger and his gunner opened the side door and pulled the .50-caliber machine gun across the open door where he was sighting straight at the open water below. The pilot pointed to his eye, indicating he had a visual sighting as he dropped the chopper down to within eighteen meters of the water heading straight for the boat that was moving ahead at an estimated 15 knots. When the Black Hawk got to within twenty meters, the pilot banked to where the gunner had a clear shot.

The roar of the big .50-caliber was almost deafening to everyone inside the Black Hawk. As the first shots hit the boat's rear engine, a plume of black smoke rose indicating the engine was disabled. The Black Hawk pilot pointed down, and the chopper dropped like a rock to within five meters of the water. Suddenly a rattle of an AK-47 came from the boat and shattered the side window of the chopper.

"Hold it! Don't jump!" the pilot yelled as he pulled the chopper up and out of the deck gunner's sight.

"Shit! We've got to take that bastard out before I drop back down."

The chopper whipped around and the gunner spotted an al-Qaida fighter firing the AK-47, and the .50-caliber machine gun began to roar. In seconds, the whole side of the deck where the sniper had been firing from was in splinters. A couple of minutes passed with no sign of life from the boat and the pilot yelled, "Okay, we're going in!"

The chopper dropped down to within five meters of the water and Josh jumped out, followed by his team. A sniper moved into the open hatchway of the first Black Hawk, which had moved back up to fifty meters above the water. He sighted in on the entranceway to below deck. The Black Hawk hovered there while Josh and his team headed for the boat that was about 20 meters in front of them, listless in the water. Josh swam around the front of the boat to the opposite side while the remainder of the six-man team positioned themselves around the boat.

A high-pitched whistle from Josh signaled the assault, and almost simultaneously six hooks landed on the deck hooking the side rail. As the hooks hit the deck, two of the al-Qaida fighters ran on deck with AK's, and Josh heard the splat from the slug as the sniper got the first one. Josh pulled his M-9 out of the waterproof case and pulled himself up with one hand just as an al-Qaida with a Markov pistol appeared on the edge of the deck, looking down at him.

An instant before the al-Qaida fighter could pull the trigger, Josh's slug hit him in the left eye, splattering blood, brains, and parts of his skull all over the deck. Within a minute, the entire team was on deck, converging on the open hole below. A burst of AK fire roared from the bottom of the stairs as two al-Qaida fighters showed they were not going to be taken prisoner.

"Flash-bang, Murphy!" Josh yelled. Murphy stripped two flash-bang grenades off his vest and threw them down the stairs about two seconds apart. Immediately there was a series of blinding explosions and flashes.

"Now, go! Go! Go!" Josh yelled. He sprinted down the stairs, followed by two other team members. Standing at the bottom of the stairs were two men holding their eyes waving their AK's, and trying to defend themselves. Josh shot one, and the combat diver behind him nailed the other.

Josh rushed back on deck and signaled the chopper pilot that the boat was secure. Then he stepped over the body of the al-Qaida fighter who had taken the initial barrage of fire and headed for the wheelhouse. He kicked open the door and there, cowering on the floor, was the boat's captain.

"Murphy, bring a hood and some containment cuffs. I have the captain," Josh yelled. Soon the boat was completely under the control of the SF team, and the chopper hovered over the deck to drop a member of the assessment team onboard to assess what, if anything was still in the lower hold.

The assessment team leader took his equipment, and went below to see if the boat was in danger of sinking and if any of the radioactive cargo was still onboard. He was back up on deck in minutes.

"Hey, look at the reading on this baby," he exclaimed, holding up the Geiger counter, which was almost off the peg, reading a significant level of radiation.

"No doubt about it, this was the ship carrying the radioactive material. I'm going back below to see if anything's left on the boat. Looks like this old tub's not going to sink anytime soon. I'll be finished in about an hour. You guys can re-board the chopper."

Josh walked over to where Sgt. Murphy was standing with the boat's captain and waved the rest of his team up the rope ladder to the Black Hawk as they waited for the assessment to be finished.

"Take his hood off, Sergeant. I want to have a little talk with him," said Josh.

Murphy shoved the captain over to the edge of the boat and pushed him down so that the man was sitting on the edge of the rail. He pulled off the containment bag and nodded to Josh.

Josh moved to within a few inches of the man's face and began to question him.

Do you speak English? French? Italian?" As Josh continued it was obvious the man wasn't even going to nod to any questions. It was a typical al-Qaida interrogation.

"Well, just as I thought, he won't acknowledge us. Maybe a few months in Gitmo will soften him up. Sergeant, put him back in full containment and subdue him with a shot."

As Murphy put the hood back on the boat's captain, Josh leaned back and tried to relax. He mentally went over the events of the day. He was convinced that the ultralight was the last attempt to divert attention to the final deposition of the radioactive material. Now that the SF team had secured the motorboat, the material was probably being encased and removed by the containment team, and his men had just commandeered the mother ship. His is mission was over.

He leaned back and thought about calling Nafisa, to tell her that he'd be back home in less than 24 hours, but his thoughts were interrupted by the containment major in charge.

"Josh, we've got a problem."

"What? I thought you said you were sure this boat carried the radioactive material."

"Yeah, it did, and that's not the problem. We have a spectral analysis of the biomaterial from the two attempts to deliver it, and there are traces of that material in the hole of this boat."

"Sure, but didn't we intercept both of the diversions they tried to pull? We have all the biomaterial—don't we?"

"No."

"What?"

"I'm afraid we don't. I quickly spotted where the other material was stored, but I picked up a trace of something very different from the other materials. It was in a separate area, and I managed to isolate a trace that had leaked out on the floor. It registers extremely toxic, but with the equipment we have with us, I can't pinpoint exactly what it is. All I know is that it's not of the same family as the other biomaterial the ultralight was carrying or what was on the suicide truck that hit the Moroccans."

"How could they have possibly removed anything else from this ship without being noticed by the AWAC's? They've been girding this part of the Atlantic for the last forty-eight hours and nothing has moved through their grid."

"I don't know, Josh, but there are imprints along the wall where the stuff was stored that indicates a carton was jammed again that wall. I suspect it was encased in a protective shell to prevent any of the material from escaping. The small sample I recovered isn't much bigger than a pinhead. I have it secured, and we'll send it to a Swiss lab to get an exact reading, but if my suspicions are correct, it may be one of the most toxic materials on Earth. It looks like your job isn't over."

Josh was in shock for a few seconds. Then he thought about the consequences of having some unknown agent still in the hands of al-Qaida.

"My god! They've managed to get it off this ship somehow! First we have to figure out how they did it, and then where they're taking it!"

Gloria had stayed with Josh after the remainder of the team had roped back up to the hole of the Black Hawk, carrying the boat captain with them. She had listened to the assessment agent talking to Josh, and she looked at Josh expectantly.

"Gloria, we must get the boat captain to Egypt as soon as possible. Use your sat phone and tell HQ to send a jet that can land at one of the nearest airports. I'm going to send Murphy with the boat captain, and have them flown to Egypt where the Egyptian interrogation team can squeeze the info out of him."

"But Josh, there's a new Egyptian government..."

"Gloria, I have connections within the Egyptian military that will take care of the interrogation. Don't worry about it. Just tell HQ to fly the two men to al-Alamine Airfield near Alexandria. They know the routine. Tell them I'll have the Egyptian team waiting for them.

"The first thing we have to do is to find out how they got the material off this boat... and the captain knows. Give the Egyptians three hours, and we'll know. Get on your SAT phone and have that jet waiting for us when we get back to our base."

"I'll get right on it."

Josh made sure the mother ship was secure, and would be stationary, waiting for the rest of the assessment team to scour it. Then he and Gloria roped back up to the Black Hawk. Gloria had already made the call, and a jet was heading for a rendezvous with them before they left the ship. Gloria began her calls to the AWAC's as Josh tried to make sense of how they could have missed the transfer from the mother ship to another ship.

It took two hours and twelve minutes to reach the designated airport. The jet was waiting, and the transfer went quickly. As soon as they were airborne, Gloria whispered to Josh, "Do you know a Mohammad el-Safed?"

Josh smiled. It was a name he remembered from his active SF days. Josh was an integral part of the CIA and SF "catch, hold, and send" game, and his missions sometimes took him to Egypt.

"Yeah, I know him. Did you talk with him directly?"

"Yes—and when the man that answered the phone heard your name, he immediately put el-Safed on the line. You must go back a long way with him the way he talked."

"Well, longer than I want to admit. I was a green SF when we met, and we clicked after an incident in Mali. We were lucky to come out of that one alive. I saved his hide, and he saved mine."

"I figured you were pretty close the way he talked."

"I guess he's going to do the job for us?"

"Yes, he didn't hesitate. He said he would personally handle the interrogation."

"God, I'd hate to be that al-Qaida boat captain."

"Do they water board?

"No, Mohammad considers that too slow. He has a twelve-volt battery with clamp connectors, and he hooks the connectors to a person's genitals, and that's just to get their attention. The really tough al-Qaida can take that, but when he switches to a direct two-twenty AC, even the toughest will crack. The boat captain we seized is not that deep into al-Qaida. The twelve-volt battery will make him rattle like a Mexican cucaracha."

"Josh, you know State frowns on using those methods of interrogation, and has specifically forbid the methods you just described."

"Yeah, I know. That's why I sent the worthless bastard to Egypt. Actually, I wouldn't have a problem doing it, but the Egyptians have a lot more practice, and I don't have the proper equipment. Mohammad will have a detailed transcript of his confession by morning. Then maybe we'll have something to chase. I guarantee you, that boat captain will regret the day he let al-Qaida use him and his boat."

"Are we going to take him back and send him to Gitmo after the Egyptians get through with him?"

"No. It's a matter of national security that this investigation not be made public, and there will be lawyers there just waiting to represent him if we take him back to Cuba."

"Well, what are the Egyptians going to do with him?"

"They'll just take him out and shoot him."

"My god, Josh! You mean you sent a man to Egypt knowing you were sending him to a certain death?"

"Had to, Glorida. This is a war, and if we're to win it, we must eliminate as many al-Qaida as we can. And to do that we must forget about this being anything like a war under the Geneva Convention. We've got to kill them with drones, snipers, SF troops, and even methods using Egyptian interrogators.

"Let's get a few hours sleep. Maybe we'll have the captain's info and the analysis of the biomaterial when we wake up. Give yourself about three hours' rest and then report back to this station."

***

Three hours later, Josh and Gloria were back at the communication center they were using as a temporary command post, waiting for the two reports to come in. It was 52 minutes after they'd arrived when the fax buzzed, announcing an incoming fax from Egypt. Josh was reading it while it printed.

"Oh, my god, Gloria! They picked up the biomaterial using a seaplane. Just a minute: Mohammad managed to get the flight vectors, assuming the airplane pilot was going on a straight line. Here take this sheet and plot me a vector and extend it."

Gloria quickly arrowed in the vectors direction to the map from where the mother ship was located when the seaplane left it, and then projected it.

"Josh the vector projection extends straight toward the African coast, and if you extent it, to the heart of the Sahara Desert."

Josh felt a momentary shudder come over him as he thought of the vastness of the desert, but he quickly shook it and concentrated on the fax from Mohammad.

"Here's some more good info: From the Captain's description they think the plane is a modified de-Havilland DHC-3 Otter, but there were no identifiable markings on the plane's tail. Send this info to HQ and ask them to find out the range of that airplane. Then let's assume it started with a full tank. What would be the maximum distance it could travel before having to refuel? And get on the phone and contact the AWAC's and have them grid the area a one-hundred and fifty miles around the possible range of the plane. And while you're at it tell HQ I want a continuous satellite picture scan beginning twenty-four hours from yesterday covering the same area, and bring it up-to-date to show any truck or on the ground movement that could be a spot for refueling. They may have trucked in aviation fuel. But just to be sure we don't let them slip through our fingers again, locate all airports within the range of the plane, and have one of our assets go on the ground to see if that plane has been in or out of the airport. Be sure and tell them to be ready to repel a hostile bunch."

It was two hours later when Josh received an emergency message from HQ. **Range of plane: 925 miles.** Scanning the message, he took another deep breath. It was a report from the Swiss lab, and the results were underlined. The sample analyzed was Agent Gold 234 isotope L-9728. The HQ overview stated:

"This is one of the most toxic biomaterial known. One drop can contaminate thousands of gallons of water, and if vaporized it would be fatally toxic to hundreds of thousands of people."

The last sentence was especially severe: **"Use any assets available and any means at your disposal to intercept. The CIA has a message from the Beirut ground station via an intercepted message that a major strike against a Western city is eminent.**

Our assessment group says disbursement of this toxic bio agent in a major city could cause at least a 100,000 fatalities."

"My god, Gloria! We've got a plane with the most god-awful stuff known to man flying out in the middle of the Sahara Desert, and we don't have a clue as to where it's heading. We need to get our team on one of the Black Hawks and head straight east into the desert down the most likely vector. We'll fly into the center of the plane's possible range and wait for the AWAC's or the SAT images to give us something to go on.

"Go alert Colonel Dowson and have his team loaded in fifteen minutes. We don't have a second to waste. And give the probable course vector to the Black Hawk pilot. Tell him to fly to within seventy-five miles of the inner ring we identified as where the maximum range the plane could go without refueling. The range is over nine-hundred miles, and the plane's hours ahead of us. We have our work cut out for us if we're going to intercept it before it gets out of Africa."

20

Chase

The seaplane had been flying for nearly two hours when the pilot leaned over and started talking to el-Wahlie, "Rasandi we have only twenty minutes of fuel left. Are we close to the rendezvous site?"

"Yes, in ten minutes you will see the oasis of Yamuna. Land the plane where the oil drums mark the runway. You will be refueled, and one of my men will accompany you north to Shaba. I will take the cargo. Your part of the mission will be over as soon as we transfer the material to a waiting truck."

In a few minutes, the pilot spotted the makeshift runway and landed the plane. In less than a half-hour the plane was refueled, the cargo transferred to a desert-equipped truck, and the plane back in the air.

Just thirty minutes after the plane had left the village, the truck with the biomaterial roared away at top speed. The cadre of local al-Qaida fighters who had met the truck moved into the village to wait for the Americans, who, el-Wahlie said, were sure to come. His instructions were direct and to the point.

"Remember, if the Americans come, have one of the villagers' tell them the plane refueled and flew north. Do not tell them about the truck. Let them come into the village when they first arrive, and do not fire at them, but when they return kill as many of them as you can."

***

Josh hurriedly made arrangements for them to leave, and twelve minutes later the Black Hawk was loaded and the pilot was flying to intersect the vector that had been plotted out based on the interrogation of the al-Qaida's ship captain. The Americans had been flying for two hours when they approached the inner ring of the plane's range.

"Set it down, Captain. We've got to wait for more info before we can proceed."

Everyone piled out to stretch their legs, and Josh looked out over the vast, trackless desert. There wasn't a living thing in sight, just the remoteness. And the daunting thought of finding a needle—an airplane with a range of 925 miles—in the hundreds of miles of wasteland had him depressed. Hours slowly passed, and then a call.

"Josh, we've picked up what looks like the tail of a plane from one of our late sat photos. It was taken earlier today. You're only about one-hundred and seventy miles away. I'll give you exact coordinates and you can sit down and check it out."

"Okay, I'll alert the team, and have them ready by the time we arrive at the sighting."

Josh hooked up the pilot with HQ and soon the chopper was airborne. One hour and 29 minutes later, it angled sharply to the right and dropped down to 100 feet above ground. The team readied for deployment.

"Okay, guys, this looks like just another oasis village, but treat it just like you would if you knew it was full of al-Qaida—and it might be."

A few minutes later, the Black Hawk sat down near a cluster of date palms and the SF team deployed and moved forward.

"Josh, I don't see anything that resembles an airplane. Just a few mud-thatched huts and palm trees."

"No, I don't see anything either. That photo was shot early this morning. The plane may refueled and left. Spread the men out and let's see if we can find anything that would indicate a plane was here. Be alert."

Twenty-one minutes later, Sgt. Murphy whistled.

"Over here, Josh. Take a look at this pile of palm fronds and check out these tracks."

Josh rushed over to where Sgt. Murphy was standing, and shook his head. His worst fears were realized. The plane had been mostly covered with the palm fronds. The sat photo analysis had been sharp enough to spot an uncovered part of the tail, but Josh and his team was too late. The obvious tracks from the plane led to a flat stretch of hard-packed gravel where the plane had taken off.

"Damn it! We're hours too late! Gloria, get HQ on the sat phone and update them, and have the AWAC's start flying grid north and east of this spot. I don't think there's any way that plane would fly south into the jungle. It is undoubtedly heading north toward Europe, and has a destination as a major Western city. We have go to find that plane or the consequences will be too horrible to even think about. Those AWAC's have a horizon-scanning radar, and if that plane's in the air heading toward the coast, one of them will spot it."

"Josh, I'm trying to think like a terrorist, and if I was trying to evade a search team, I wouldn't fly, I'd use a truck."

"Maybe you're right, Gloria, but I'm guessing the plane refueled, and is trying to get to a major city before we manage to track it down."

Josh and Gloria were still discussing the matter when the SF team leader came up with a report.

"Josh our Arabic-speaking SF has been talking with several villagers and they told him the plane landed late yesterday afternoon and two trucks arrived in the village last night. He didn't know exactly what went on, but from what a couple of men told me, I'm certain they refueled the plane. The plane took off less than an hour ago and they said it was heading north."

"Okay, let's load up and fly due north waiting on a call from the AWAC's. That plane can't possibly get to the coast before it's spotted," said Josh.

A few minutes later, the SF team was back onboard and the chopper was in the air, heading on a course due north. They had been in the air less than an hour when Josh sat phone dinged.

"Josh, this is AWAC 082; I have a radar sighting from a small plane without a flight plan. I've tried radio contact but no answer. In about three minutes I'll have a visual. I have the description of the plane, so I should be able to make a positive identification shortly."

"Good job, Stuart. I'm going to patch you through to our pilot so you can give him a position. We'll be heading your way in a few minutes. As soon as you get a visual positive, buzz me back."

"Roger."

"Josh, do you think we lucked out?" said Gloria.

"No, if that's the plane, we found it because we did the best work with the info we have. We can't depend on luck."

Josh's sat phone buzzed five minutes later and Tail 082 was on the line.

"Josh, I can confirm the plane is the one you're after. It's heading on a northwest course at two-hundred and twenty knots. You aren't going to be able to catch it without some help."

"Roger, I'll alert HQ. This mission has top involvement of all resources. They can get an interceptor to help."

"Gloria get HQ on the line and give them the coordinates of the plane AWAC 082 sighted, and tell them we need to intercept it ASAP. Tell them to force it to land by disabling the motor. They'll be able to land anywhere in this desert. After they force it down, tell them to come back with exact coordinates for our pilot."

Fifteen minutes later, Gloria reported back to Josh. "You won't believe this, Josh. HQ has managed to get a Libyan aircraft from Sheba to intercept. It seems they were on a mission to put down some Tuareg mutineers, and they have the firepower and speed to intercept. They're talking directly to AWAC 082 for coordinates. HQ said the pilot has U.S. training, and he knows exactly how to disable a small plane without taking it down."

In a few minutes, the Black Hawk chopper pilot and the Libyan aircraft were heading for a barren strip of desert about 175 miles southwest of Kufra Oasis. According to the AWAC calculations, that was where the Libyan aircraft would intercept the small plane. Fifteen minutes later Gloria received a confirmation from HQ.

"Josh, the plane is on the ground. Tail 082 said the Libyan attack plane shot the prop off and the plane glided in for a landing. We're only forty-three minutes from where the plane landed. 082 is monitoring the plane to be sure whoever is onboard doesn't leave."

"Great! Tell the team to be ready to take incoming fire. I would imagine they have several fighters onboard."

Forty-two minutes later, the Black Hawk dropped down to 100 feet as it approached the spot where the plane had been forced down. As the chopper popped up from behind a low ridge, they could see the small plane directly ahead of them.

"Josh, Tail 082 just said there were only two people on the plane. One of them is standing behind the plane, but the other is out front, and it looks as if he's carrying a weapon."

"Okay, let's take out the front man, and see if we can take the other one alive. We have many questions for him. Colonel, have the door gunner ready. I'm going to have the chopper pilot swing around so the door gunner will have a clear shot at the fighters who is standing in front of the plane."

The Colonel nodded and signaled the door gunner as Josh talked to the chopper pilot. The fighter out in front of the plane was raising his gun when the Black Hawk suddenly swung broadside to him, and before he could fire his AK-47 a burst of .50-caliber machine-gunfire sent him spinning to the ground.

"Okay, set her down, and get ready—ETA in two seconds."

The 12-man SF team quickly jumped from the chopper and fanned out in a ready position. As they approached the downed plane, the man behind the plane stepped out with his hands in the air. Something seemed amiss and Josh waved a caution signal as they approached the aircraft. *Only one fighter—where's the rest of the security?* crossed Josh's mind. The man who was trying to surrender seemed to be the only other person at the plane. The other fighter was sprawled out, ripped apart by the .50-caliber rounds.

Josh was the first one to the downed aircraft, which was intact, but its landing gear had collapsed and the plane was on its belly. Both doors were open and as Josh glanced in, he was shocked to see a totally empty plane.

"My god, Gloria; the damned plane's empty! The bio stuff isn't onboard! Where on earth did they put it? Sergeant, get a couple of men and be sure this plane is completely empty, and there's no hidden compartments."

"All right, Josh, I'll get right on it."

As the men started to go over the plane, Josh turned his attention to the man who had surrendered. He was wearing a pilot's cap with wings on it. He was obviously the man who had been flying the plane.

"Sgt. Murphy, bring the man over here, and ask the translator to come over here with him."

In a few minutes, Josh was questioning the man through the translator. It was obvious he was al-Qaida, but certainly not a very high-ranking person. The interrogation was going nowhere when Josh tried another tact.

"Gloria go get me the bag with the payoff money," Josh said.

Gloria handed Josh the bag, and he reached in and took out as many hundred-dollar bills as he could hold in both hands. He nodded to the translator, "Tell him we'll give him five-hundred thousand American dollars, fly him to Beirut, and he won't be harmed, if he tells us everything he knows about who he was flying, what his cargo was, and where the boxes are that he left the ship with. If he refuses, tell him we will send him to Egypt, and they will attach wires to his genitals and his nuts will fry—and when the Egyptians are through with him, he'll be shipped off to Gitmo or shot."

Gloria, nudged Josh and whispered, "Josh we don't have anywhere near five-hundred thousand dollars."

"I know that, but he doesn't. Let's see if he will take the bait."

Josh and Gloria watched as the translator vividly described what the man was facing, and then he described the prospect of having a huge amount of money and being safe in Beirut. It took another threat from Josh, which was an order to have him transported, before he agreed. An hour later, after quizzing the man at length and in detail, Josh nodded to Gloria.

"He said there was a box loaded on a truck, and he left before the truck did, so he doesn't know the exact direction the truck headed. So we need to go back to the oasis and quiz some of the locals."

"Okay, but what are we going to do with him?"

"We've got every scrap of info out of him, so he is no use to us. Take him over behind the aircraft and shoot him."

"What, are you serious, Josh? You know it's strictly against all regulation to execute a prisoner."

"Yes, it is, but I have been given special permission to use all force necessary to accomplish this mission, and having to delay deployment because of this man is a threat to the mission. Of course, since he is a terrorist, we can shoot him under order two two three."

"This is not Egypt, Josh. I'm not about to kill someone we have captured."

"You'd never make SF, Gloria," said Josh. He calmly pulled out his .9 mm Glock, and quickly sent a bullet into the man's brain. Gloria gasped as the man flipped backward from the impact of the powerful slug. Even Colonel Dowson, who was in charge of the SF, muttered, "Damn," and shook his head.

Josh turned to him and said, "Colonel, if we'd taken the man as a POW it could have caused mission failure. I couldn't take a chance. Get your men together and board the Black Hawk.

"Search the man I shot, give me everything in his pockets, and then leave him where he is. Have your men board the aircraft, and we'll head back to the oasis were the plane was refueled."

The Colonel hurried to tell the chopper pilot as the 12-man SF team boarded the Black Hawk.

21

The Hunt Continues

It was a two-hour flight back to where the plane had landed to refuel. As they flew back, Josh fretted that each hour the al-Qaida fighters were closer to getting the biomaterial out of the country. They had acted with uncharacteristic skill in transferring the material from one decoy to another with the idea that the critical substance would be the last thing moved, and the Americans would be forced to follow all of the decoys, delaying them in their hunt for the missing biomaterial.

He was sure the material was headed to Europe in order to explode it and infect as many Westerners as possible. His mind clicked off the possible targets until he narrowed them down to the ones he considered the most likely destinations: Rome—and the Vatican—Paris, and Athens.

He felt relatively sure the al-Qaida team wouldn't try to hit a target any farther. It would give his SF Team more time to track them down, and it would increase the possibility of mission failure.

In order to come up with his short list of possible targets, Josh had simply used the closest major Western cities with the largest populations. However, when he analyzed the possible targets further, he began to consider Rome the most likely target. And as he mulled over where an al-Qaida strike would harm the most people, he began to think about where the largest crowds of tourists would be in that city. Several sites came into mind, but as he weighed the possibilities, everything pointed to the old city and, specifically, the Vatican as the most probable al-Qaida target.

He knew Rome would be packed with American tourists giving al-Qaida a tempting target, and the place where more tourists congregated was around the Vatican. Something occurred to him, and he quickly sent an encrypted text to HQ.

"Please advise the following: The date and exact time of the next publicly scheduled papal address." Twenty minutes later, he had his answerer: **"The Pope will make the next papal address on the 20th of July, exactly 11:00 A M."** Josh punched his Nokia 920 calendar and gasped, "My god, Gloria, that's less than a week away!"

"What are you talking about, Josh?"

"I have a hunch the al-Qaida bunch will try and hit Rome, and there's a public papal address only a week away. We need to nab this sorry bunch while they're still in Africa. If they ever make it to the Italian mainland, the odds of intercepting them will go off the chart."

"Contact the AWAC's surveillance team and have them fly a grid that will cover all cross-country routes to the Mediterranean coast using a one-hundred-and-fifty-mile coastal spread, and then vector it with the refueling spot where the plane landed. And go directly to HQ and ask for sat coverage. Tell them to back the sat photo coverage up for three days, and note any movement away from the refueling spot. Let us know if they pick up any trucks leaving that area heading in the direction of the coast."

Gloria began to make calls as Josh poured over topo maps that he had spread out on a flip-out table. He waved the Colonel over and pointed to the map.

"Colonel, we know the material was loaded on a truck at the refueling point, but we don't have a clue which direction they went in when we left the oasis. When we arrive at the oasis, have your translators work the village and see if anyone saw the direction the truck was heading in when it left. Tell your man to wave some money around, and see if that doesn't bring forth some info."

"I'll have it lined up as soon as we land, Josh. What do you think is the most likely direction?"

"I think they're rushing to get the stuff into Europe, and the shortest route is northeast to one of several fishing villages on the upper Libyan coast. They wouldn't try to cross the border into Egypt, and they probably have a cell of al-Qaida fighters left over from the Libyan Revolution, who will help them once they get to the coast. This bunch is very clever, and we'll probably end up in a firefight if we corner them."

"The AWAC's and sat coverage has begun to sweep the area right now. If we're lucky, and the truck didn't leave the refueling spot earlier in the day, the AWAC's should spot it within the next two hours. My only worry is that it left earlier than we think, and it's already made it to the coast. There are at least ten fishing villages along the fifty miles of coastline, and we'll have to search every one if we don't pick up something within the next hour."

Josh was interrupted by the pilot.

"Josh, we'll be at the refueling spot in twenty minutes. Do you think we need to land in close or take evasive action?"

Josh started to shake his head "no" and tell the pilot to land as close to the village as possible, but then it crossed his mind that if al-Qaida was able to land the plane and refuel, they must have had the cooperation of the village elders. *Yeah, they did, and the sorry bastards sent us off on another wild-goose chase, but are there still al-Qaida fighters in the village?* He decided not to take any chances.

"Burt, don't land within two-hundred yards of any building, and put down where we can exit the chopper without being exposed to fire from the village."

"Got it, Josh. Stand by for a landing in six minutes."

Colonel Dowson looked at Josh questioningly. "Do you think we need to be that cautious? We didn't see a soul with a weapon when we checked it out earlier."

"Colonel, if an al-Qaida fighter opened up with an AK just as we were leaving the plane, how many causalities do you think we'd take? We can't afford to take a chance."

"Yeah, you're probably right, Josh. I'll have the men spread out in a flanking maneuver, and we'll get converge on the area near the center of the village."

"Perfect, Colonel, and it would be a good idea to have your men interview people in houses nearest to the hidden plane. Give each man a handful of hundred-dollar bills. Tell them to wave the money around telling everyone they'll pay them if they'll give us the info we want."

"ETA, one-minute," yelled the pilot.

Josh nodded and moved with the other SF men to exit the chopper. In a few minutes, the 12-man SF team was spread out, moving slowly toward the first row of mud brick houses. As they approached the village, Josh sensed something was amiss. As he looked down toward the village water well, he was surprised. No one visible. It was a red flag.

"Hold up, men!" Josh suddenly commanded, as he signaled the team to halt.

"Colonel, have the three men on our right flank move forward to where they have a view of that first corner house near the well. Have them ready to repel an attack when they get to within fifty yards of the house. Something's going on in the village, and we don't want to walk into an al-Qaida ambush."

Colonel Dowson sent a text message to the three men, and they broke away from the main group of SF men, and continued to approach the village.

"Colonel, send four men around to the west end where the date palms border the road, and tell them to hold their position using the date palms for cover. Split the rest of the team into two-man advance groups, and move forward until we reach the first house.

"Murphy, move over to that rise, take your binoculars, and watch the back windows in those houses facing us."

There was a shake of the head from the Colonel, but Josh ignored him, and said to the team, "Shoulder your weapons, and expect incoming fire."

Members of the SF Team deployed just as Josh had instructed and moved toward their assigned positions. Murphy, who was stationed on a rise directly facing the line of low, mud-thatched buildings, was moving his binoculars back and forth—making a sweep of the back windows as the team slowly approached the village.

"Weapon in the window of house number two!" yelled Murphy suddenly. The Team flattened out in the sands as an AK-47 raked their position. Return fire was immediate, and in seconds SF fire obliterated the window, along with the frame and the fighter who had managed to get off a few rounds.

"Medic! Medic!" yelled an SF Team member, who was clutching his arm. The SF medic rushed over to take care of the wounded man, as Josh waved the rest of the men forward. A quick command to the soldiers who had circled from the front, and in seconds they had kicked opened the front door and tossed in a flash-bang stun grenade.

"Flip a flash-bang through the window!" Josh yelled, as his lead man approached the shattered window. A few second later, two thundering explosions with a blinding flash followed, and before the echo of the blast had faded, the SF soldiers in the front of the house rushed in. A rattle of automatic weapon fire came almost instantly, and in a few minutes, the the team's lead man come out and approached Josh.

"There were three fighters in the house. Your fire got the man in the window, and we hit two more who were blinded by the flash-bang."

"Okay, good work. Let's split up—three and three—and start going door to door. I think that's probably all the men al-Qaida left in the village. But if no one answers the door, blow it and secure the house."

Josh walked back to check on the wounded SF soldier as the men, along with the interpreter, started to check each house in the village. The SF wounded soldier only had a minor flesh wound; that wouldn't need to return to base to see a physician. Only 12 houses were in the small, oasis village and in less than an hour, the men reported to Josh.

"Whatcha got, Murphy?" asked Josh.

"Well, when we began passing out hundred-dollar bills, and after the villagers found out we had killed the al-Qaida fighters, we had almost everybody in the village lined up to rat on the al-Qaida's truck and plane. They said the men with the truck unloaded a small box from the plane and refueled the plane. Then, right after the plane took off, the truck headed northeast. I had that confirmed by at least ten people, and one man told me he was a couple of kilometers from the village, and the truck passed him still going northeast. From the times they told me, I estimate the truck left the village nearly six hours ago."

22

The Switch

"Omar, is this the fastest you can drive this truck?"

"No, Rasandi, but I was worried about the material in the back."

"Forget the material; it's packed in a secure container, and it won't leak even if we hit something and roll over. Drive as fast as this truck will go. I want to be in Dhahran within the next hour. The Americans won't be long before they start looking at all the towns along the Libyan coast. They would be stupid if they didn't."

"Look, Rasandi, straight ahead; you can see the mosques in Dhahran. We should be there in no more than twenty minutes."

"Very good, Omar. Drive directly to the dock where the fishermen unload their catch. It's called Siyanda Dock. Just drive straight through town, and you will find it easily. Have you alerted our people to meet us?"

"Yes, and they confirmed. They should be at the dock when we arrive."

"Excellent. When you approach the dock, back up to the walkway and wait for someone to come and unload the material. I must speak with the men in charge."

"Yes, Rasandi."

It took another 15 minutes to drive through town to the Siyanda Dock, where they met Hamza el-Zawahli, the leader of the Libyan al-Qaida cell.

"Rasandi, it is so good to see you. I had wondered if you were going to make it out of the jungle and across the desert before the Americans grabbed you."

"Don't worry about the Americans, Hamza. The Leadership Council has planned this mission for a long time and they have left nothing to chance. I'm here with the material just as they told you I would be. Do you have the boat ready?"

"Yes, Rasandi, and everything is just as my message said to have it. You will have three of my men to go with you right now, and then later more of our men will be there to help you finish the mission."

"Excellent, Hamza, but we can't waste any time. Have your men remove the box with the material from my truck and place it in the boat. I must leave in the next few minutes."

"Certainly, Rasandi, I understand. Everything will be ready for you to leave very soon."

"Hamza, are you familiar with the rest of the plan—after I leave?"

"Yes, but do you really think the Americans will come here looking for you?"

"Of course they will. Let me give you some additional information concerning the ones who will come looking for me. Our contact tells us it is a former American Special Forces soldier who is leading the team that is trying to intercept us. He is the one who managed to kill our friend Patto, The Knife, and arranged to have the former Leadership Council attacked. Nothing could please me and the new Leadership Council more than for your men to kill him."

"Yes, I would gladly kill him, but my orders from the Leadership Council are just to delay the Americans as long as possible. How will I have an opportunity to kill him?"

"I have been thinking about this ever since I found out that this man is the one who is trying to track down the material, and this is the plan I have come up with. Of course, it follows the Leadership Council's orders to delay the American team, but my plan will give you a way to delay the Americans and to possibly kill this low-life pig who is leading the team. Pay close attention because this is a very good plan, and I have only a few minutes before I must leave.

"After I leave with the material, you are to take the truck and park it a few blocks away from the dock. The Americans, or their Libyan lackeys, will surely find it; and then they will split up their forces and begin to search all the buildings around it. About two blocks away, set up an ambush. Only one or two men will approach the place where you have the ambush at first. Shoot the soldiers in their legs so they must call for help.

"I am sure this Josh Martin will respond. Then, when he arrives to help his wounded men, you are to use all of your men to kill him.

"This will be a wonderful delay, since they will have to put a new leader in place before they continue to search for the material. How many men can you count on to mount the ambush?"

"I have twenty-three fighters who are all well equipped with the very best weapons. If this Josh Martin comes to rescue the wounded, we will kill him."

"Excellent, Hamza—now I must go if I am to stay ahead of the swine."

23

Confrontation

Josh was frustrated. "Damn! I was hoping they didn't have that big of a head start. Colonel, get everyone back onboard and give the pilot a vector toward the largest town on the coast. We'll head northeast on the most likely vector hoping one of the AWAC's or the sat photos will pick up the truck. If we don't get any direct sighting, we will investigate every port town within this thirty-mile arc; starting with the largest town."

"Gloria, call HQ and tell them we need backup CIA and all of the ground assets available from every town on the northeast Libyan coast. Have at least twenty men start working the coastal villages looking for any trucks coming in from the desert during the last twenty-four hours. Advise them that I believe the truck with the biomaterial is heading for one of the fishing villages along the coast, and they'll try to cross the Mediterranean by boat. You can pass on the info about the plane and village. Tell them we had to use extreme force and five al-Qaida were killed."

In fewer than five minutes, the Black Hawk was back in the air flying toward Dharma, Libya.

"Josh, at this speed we should be on the outskirts of Dharma in three hours and thirty-six minutes. Where do you want me to sit down?" beeped the pilot.

"Stand by for a landing spot. We'll have a CIA asset on the ground in less than an hour; call in a secure landing site."

"Roger."

"Gloria, talk to HQ and tell them to have our CIA man on the ground have two sets of local clothes for you and me. Be sure and tell them you're a female."

Josh turned to Colonel Dowson. "Colonel, our CIA asset will give us a landing spot that will allow you to have some privacy while you wait on my call to secure the biomaterial. We can't risk letting your men try to sneak into town in local clothes. It'll be difficult enough for Gloria and me to go undetected.

"We will use our local assets on the ground, and we may be able to get help from the local militia to find the biomaterial. I don't think they could have put it on a boat—yet. They aren't that far ahead of us, and they've had to drive a truck nearly four-hundred miles across the desert. So just sit tight while we try to sniff them out."

"All right Josh; you're in charge, but I think we could infiltrate the town and be a lot closer to you when you find the guys."

"Colonel, I appreciate your offer, and I understand your willingness to help, but this team of SFs hasn't been deployed in a Muslim country. It would be too difficult for them to be undercover. HQ has been in touch with the commander of a local militia force, and apprised them that we are trying to stop an international act of terrorism. The commander was trained at one of our bases; actually, I trained him, and he's very pro-American. He has promised to help us in any way he can.

"Gloria and I will be meeting with him later today. We still don't know for sure what town the truck carrying the biomaterial is heading for. Right now, we're operating by the seat of our pants. God, I wish the AWAC's would come up with something definite."

"Okay, Josh. It's your call. I'll have my men ready to respond."

"Fine, Colonel. This Nokia 920 has the best GPS around, and I'll be able to give you an exact location if I need backup."

Josh pulled up Google Maps and started to focus on the towns lining the coast, and as he did the number of old warehouses and other structure near the ports overwhelmed him.

"Damn, Gloria; look at this shot near the docks at the little town of Rasure. You could hide a battleship in some of those warehouses. We need some definite info if we're going to find those guys. There's no way, even with the local militia helping us, that we could search all the possible hiding places."

It was nearly two hours later when Josh received a call from HQ.

"Josh, we have a probable sighting from our sat photos. We backed up to a day before the plane landed and went forward. There's a jump of several hours from shot to shot, but I think we have some good dope for you."

"Great; we're about an hour out of Tubruq, and we have a local asset who's spotting up a staging area. Are we heading to the right town?"

"No, I don't think so. This is what we have. We have a photo of the refueling spot with a truck parked off about a hundred yards. The next shot has the plane there and the truck backed up to it. They're obviously refueling. Then we have nothing until about seven hours later when we see a truck approaching the town of Dhahran. That's it. Nothing else shows up and the AWAC's didn't get started flying the grid until after the last shot of the truck.

"I think the truck was in the town before the AWAC's could spot it. I'm sending you a computer-enhanced shot of the truck. We can't read any marking on the truck, but the computer says the truck we spotted in the last photo near the town of Dhahran is the same truck that left the plane's landing site. That's all we have, Josh."

"Thanks, Leroy; that helps. We were about to start searching the wrong town. I'll make the changes. Continue to monitor the area and put as much sat coverage as you can on Dhahran. I'll pull the AWAC's off the old grid and move it to the coast, and have them cover the Mediterranean and Italy."

"Italy?"

"Yes; I'm guessing that's their destination—Rome in particular. I think you should go ahead and put our Italian sector on alert, and tell them they could be faced with an act of terrorism within the next week. Now, this is just a guess, but the papal address from the balcony of St. Peter's Basilica could be the place,"

"My god, Josh; there will be nearly a hundred and seventy-five thousand people in the Square that day!"

"I know it, Leroy, and we are doing everything we can to make sure that nothing happens during the Pope's address."

"I'll get our sector chief on the line as soon as we hang up. Do you need any additional backup?"

"Yes, if we could have some light naval presence in the area between the Libyan coast and Italy it might be helpful. Don't send a carrier. We don't want to have them hitting the mattresses waiting for us to pull back."

"Got it, Josh. I'll be in touch."

"Gloria, give the pilot a new course to Dhahran and get me our area asset on the phone. We're changing our landing spot."

As Gloria passed on the info to the pilot and Colonel Dowson, Josh's Nokia 920 dinged. It was a computer-enhanced picture of the truck. Josh immediately sent the photo to the onsite chopper printer and in seconds had several copies.

"Josh, I've got the local asset on the phone. She goes by the code name 'T'."

Josh took the phone, and spent 10 minutes detailing the plan to locate the truck. And then sent her a copy of the truck photo from the sat computer-enhanced photo.

"T, have the local militia leader from Dhahran meet me at our new landing site in an hour and ten minutes. I'm sure you know him. He controls everything within seventy-five miles of Benghazi."

"Yes, I know him well. He is very cooperative, and I have already been in contact with him. He'll be waiting for you when you land."

"Fine. And one more thing: Our local man in Tubruq was to meet us with local clothes, but since we aren't going to be landing there, you'll have to come up with one set local medium female and one set of large male clothing."

"I'll have them, Josh."

"Good. I'll ETA you when we get within ten minutes of Dhahran. As soon as you find a good staging site for the chopper, contact the chopper pilot direct. I'll see you at the site in less than an hour."

"I know the place. I'll have the GPS coordinates to the chopper pilot in a few minutes."

As the chopper approached the landing site, Josh poured over the enhanced Google map printout of Dhahran. Just as he had suspected, the harbor was dotted with large and small buildings. Some were obviously warehouses, but others were smaller buildings with assorted retail stores on the ground floors and apartments on the second. The task of finding the truck and them the biomaterial looked daunting.

"Gloria, make a grid taking in every house within a quarter mile of the coast. We'll assign each CIA asset and agent a grid square to search. We can't depend on the local militia to check out individual houses and storage areas along the harbor. We'll use them to search for the truck. I don't think al-Qaida is stupid enough to park the truck beside the warehouse where they're hiding the biomaterial, but if we find the truck it might narrow down the search area."

"I'll have the grid ready by the time we land," said Gloria.

Josh continued to pour over the Google printout of Dhahran, especially the harbor. The blowup was detailed enough that he was able to count the number of fishing and pleasure boats docked. He made a mental note to have several agents and local assets search every boat docked. As he looked at the map, he had a feeling of uneasiness. *How long would it take to unload the biomaterial from the truck and put it on a boat?* crossed his mind. *One or several boxes—damn—thirty minutes at the most.* It was a sobering thought that as they approached the Dhahran staging site, the biomaterial could already be on its way to Italy.

His thoughts were interrupted by the chopper pilot who called out an ETA: "Six minutes, Josh!"

As the chopper sat down, Josh peered out the window and noted they were landing inside a walled compound. He could see the center of town, which looked approximately a half-mile away as the chopper sat down. The Black Hawk and the SF teams would be concealed until they were needed. The hatch opened and Josh, Gloria, and the SF team jumped out of the chopper and headed for a group of people standing by a low, mud brick building. A woman in full Muslim burka and Saudi headscarf stepped out to meet him.

"Josh, I'm 'T,'" she said in English with an obvious American accent.

Josh smiled, knowing how the CIA selected their operatives. This woman obviously had a Middle Eastern or, even more likely, a Libyan background. And as she talked with the men around her, she rattled off a brand of Libyan Arabic that could pass for native.

"T, I'm Josh. This is Gloria and Colonel Dowson. Do you have the leader of the local militia with you?"

"Yes, he's over by the building with his lieutenants. I think you will find him very cooperative."

As Josh and the others approached the men standing by the low, mud-brick building, one man stepped out from the group and rushed over excitedly to meet them.

"Commander Josh! Commander Josh! It is so good to see you again!" he yelled, as he approached them. "It is *Abdul*! Remember the Libyan Special Forces team who trained at Camp Thunder?"

Josh immediately recalled members of the team of Libyan Special forces who he had trained as a special request from the State Department. It was a bonus given to Colonel Gaddafi for normalizing diplomatic relations with the United States. He remembered how inept the unit was, but then he nodded, recalling Abdul. He was no better than the other members of the team, but he was always ready to learn, and by the time the two-week course was over he was excelling as a trainee.

"My god, Abdul; is it really you? Are you in charge of the local militia?"

"Yes, Commander Josh; I am in charge of all the coastal area from Tubruq to Benghazi. I have four-hundred and thirty-five men in my command. They are at your service."

"Abdul, you are very kind, and I wouldn't ask you to help me if it wasn't of the highest priority. We've been after some al-Qaida fighters who are trying to smuggle something into Europe that will cause many casualties, if we can't stop them. We have evidence that they have driven a truck into Dhahran carrying the material. Your men could be a great help in finding the truck."

"Commander Josh, my men would be honored to join with you to find the al-Qaida swine, but I must warn you, new al-Qaida fighters have come to Dhahran recently because there was already a very strong group of their men here. When we fought against Gaddafi, these men came from Morocco to help, and we were happy to have them. They helped stop the Gaddafi dogs from taking Benghazi.

"But there were problems after the fighting stopped. They wanted to have Shariah Law for the country, but most Libyans did not want that, so the al-Qaida fighters quit the militia. They are still here, and I think they are probably with the others who came across the desert. Beware when you find them because these men are trained fighters, and you may encounter as many as thirty of them."

"As you can see, I have a strong force to counter them, Abdul. But we need to pinpoint where the men who came with the truck are staying. If you and your men are willing, we need you to go down every street in Dhahran looking for the truck. When you find it, come and tell me. Don't try to confront the fighters with your men. We must capture the material they are carrying in the truck without damaging it. Do you understand?"

"Yes, Commander Josh; we will find the truck before the day is out. My men know every street in Dhahran."

Gloria stepped forward and handed Abdul a grid map of the city. "Abdul, organize your men to cover every square that's marked on the map. Do you understand?"

"Commander Josh is that your wish?"

"Yes, Abdul; the map is just to help you, and be sure we don't miss any streets."

Abdul nodded, motioned to his second in command, and soon they were roaring off in a cloud of dust. As they left the compound, T approached Josh and Gloria. "Josh we have ten local assets we can count on, plus five regular CIA agents. They all speak Libyan Arabic."

"Good, T. I guess we have almost every agent and asset in northern Libya."

"Yes, and several from Egypt and Morocco. How do you want to use them?"

"I think the bad guys headed for Dhahran to put the biomaterial on a boat, and probably transport it to Italy. If they tried to fly it in they'd be spotted by the AWAC's. I want you to use all the local assets and regular agents to comb the harbor and docks. Methodically check off every boat that you know is a fishing boat or some other type of commercial boat. That should help a lot. When you get that done, discretely begin to collect info that will further narrow down the search.

"Keep me posted, and if you see anything that raises a red flag, notify me immediately. Do you understand? Gloria will get you several color-coded harbor and dock maps."

"Yes, Josh; I'll text a report back hourly."

"Good, let's get started. I have a feeling that Abdul and his men will find the truck by late today. If they do, then we might have more on our hands than we can handle. Gloria, call HQ and see if we can get another SF team to fly in here. After what Abdul told us we may need more than one SF team to get the job done."

"I'll call them right now. Do you want them here in the compound?"

"No, tell HQ to put them on ready alert, and have them on one of the naval vessels in the Mediterranean. If the al-Qaida fighters manage to get the biomaterial on one of the boats, or if—God forbid—they've already left the harbor, we might need them intercept the boat. We need to do everything we can it keep the material from reaching Europe."

Gloria nodded, but as Josh acknowledged the possibility of the material already heading for Europe, he felt his breath quicken. Just the idea that the material was on its way to a city of several million people made him shudder.

Josh tried to get a few hours of sleep, but after lying awake for an hour, he got up and began to sketch out a plan to implement when Abdul and his men found the truck. He had a nagging suspicion, however, that the material had already been loaded onto a boat and that as he fidgeted, it was heading for Italy. Finally, when Josh couldn't get that thought out of his mind, he began to plan how he would intercept the boat or possibly another truck on the Italian mainland.

It was a daunting task, and as Josh considered all the possibilities, he knew al-Qaida was a jump ahead of him. He had to catch up some way.

His thoughts were interrupted by a ding from his Nokia 920. A quick glance at the phone, a quick text to Gloria, and Josh was hurrying to put on the local clothes T had brought. Ten minutes later, he was speeding into town with her.

A Google map with GPS sent him careening deftly through the dark streets. The truck had been located, and Abdul had pulled his men away from the site, just as Josh had ordered.

"Gloria, when we get within a quarter of a mile, we'll split up and approach the truck from separate directions. Walk past it and then circle back. I'll do the same. If we see any sign of the fighters who drove the truck, we'll call for backup. However, I don't expect anyone to be there.

"Be sure not to touch it. Those bastards probably have it wired to blow as soon as anyone opens a door. I'll check it out while you watch from the end of the block." Gloria nodded as Josh whipped the Land Rover around the dark, twisted streets.

"Okay, Gloria, take a quick look at this map, and memorize the streets for at least a block in every direction. Be sure you can exit the area quickly in case we stumble on some guards. Double check your weapon and grenades."

Gloria took a hard look at the Google map, nodded, and fingered her .9 mm Beretta BU9 Nano as she checked the clip.

"Okay," said Josh. "We're close enough. Circle to your left, and I'll go to the right. Remember, don't touch the vehicle, and when you see me approaching, walk on up the street. I'll text you when I want you to return."

Gloria took a deep breath. This was out of her element, and the thought of encountering al-Qaida fighters who might be guarding the truck made her apprehensive. *Damn, going from a CIA operative to an SF is a big step*, crossed her mind

"Josh, what if there're guards at the truck?"

"I'll assess the situation as I walk. Just follow my lead, and whatever you do, don't show recognition."

"Follow your lead? What's that supposed to mean?"

"If I stop. You stop. If I pull out my weapon, do the same, and be ready to repel an attack, or give me cover. If you see me stop and start looking under and around the truck, walk fifty paces, stop in a doorway, and cover me. Got it?"

"Yeah, I guess so."

"Hell, don't get so uptight; most of the time nothing will happen. We'll just end up looking at an empty truck. These precautions are for that one time in a hundred that all hell will break loose as soon as we approach that fuckin' truck."

Josh's words did little to assuage Gloria's nervousness as she hopped out of the Land Rover and started slowly walking down the narrow street. The sun was peeking over the low harbor clouds, as Josh headed in the opposite direction. As he walked, he managed to find a broken tree limb that he used as a cane, and he slowly limped along, he sometimes stopped to forage in the gutter for scraps of food.

"As he turned the corner of the block where the truck was parked, Josh noted a beggar curled up asleep in a doorway. He approached the sleeping beggar, slipped his hand under the loose shirt that T had given him, and thumbed off the safety of his .9 mm Glock. When he got even with the man sleeping in the door-well, he bent over to look through a pile of moldy papers. Josh acted as if he'd found something of interest, and he dropped to one knee to fumble through the pile of trash. As he did, he quickly glanced at the beggar, and noted an eye peering out from under a ragged blanket.

Josh stood up and turned, seemingly to continue down the sidewalk, but as he took the first step, his hand flashed out and there was a dull, very faint pop as he shot the man in the face with his Glock. The ultra-silencer worked perfectly and Gloria, who was only 10 yards away when Josh shot the man, barely heard the shot.

As the man slumped forward, a cellphone slid out of his hand onto the sidewalk. Josh picked it up and slipped it in his pocket, as Gloria walked up, shocked.

"Josh, why did you shoot a sleeping beggar?"

"How many beggars have you seen who carry a cheap iPhone? He's a low-ranking door watcher, but this cellphone may have some contact info that could be extremely valuable. I've checked the area and the rooftops to be sure there isn't another watcher around. Let's examine the truck, but I suspect, with only a single fighter watching it, it'll be empty.

"Have your weapon ready, and if you see anyone coming, don't hesitate to use it. Go sit where you can see the tops of the buildings on this side of the street," Josh whispered hoarsley. "And for god's sake, whatever you do, don't touch the truck."

Josh approached the truck, circled it once, and then got on his knees to peer under the rear of the vehicle. He slowly moved his pin light around until he spotted something. Then he nodded, reached in his pocket, and pulled out a custom-designed tool with several attachments. A couple of minutes later, Josh stood up and motioned for Gloria to join him.

"My god; these fuckin' people are so stupid, I can't believe it. Connecting the explosive detonator to a nine-volt battery, and then just leaving it sitting on a tire. If we'd opened the back or one of the doors, we would have been blown straight to hell. Have your weapon ready. We may have company when we open it up."

Gloria's hands were shaking as Josh reached open the tailgate of the large truck. *What if Josh didn't find all the bombs,* crossed her mind as he dropped the tailgate down and shined his pin light into the shadowy bay.

"Damn it. I was afraid of this. The truck's empty, except for a pile of explosives in the back. Shit, that's enough stuff to knock down most of the buildings around here. It looks like they took everything. We need to get back to base and send the assessment team and a detonation specialist to really check things out."

Josh was quiet during the 20-minute ride back. He was mentally organizing what would be a very detailed assessment and search of the buildings within a half-mile of where the truck was parked. The sun was just peeking through the Eucalyptus trees, and you could barely make out the shape of the mud-brick buildings when Josh and Gloria drove through the compound gate. A few minutes later, Colonel Jeffries, Josh, and Gloria were discussing the area where Abdul's men had discovered the truck.

"Colonel, we can't risk using Abdul's men. There may be al-Qaida sympathizers in the group. We must use the local assets and CIA team members we called in. Gloria, T, and I will have a search schedule ready by seven. Colonel, have your team on ready alert. I have a feeling, when we start searching, we're going to run into a nest of the sorry bastards, and if it's as many as Abdul says, I'll need your help when the shit starts flying."

"Josh, I think you're making a big mistake by not using all the force you have available. Are you sure you don't want us to set up checkpoints and cordon off the area?"

"I'm sure, Colonel. The Libyan government will turn a blind eye if we keep this undercover, but American troops on the ground would create an international incident."

"All right, Josh. I'll wait for your call. I just hope I won't get there too late to help you."

"So do I, Colonel. Oh, I do have one more thing I need you to do. Take this cellphone I took from the al-Qaida fighter, get HQ to send a jet to the Benghazi airport to pick it up, and fly it non-stop to CIA HQ in Langley, Virginia."

"Josh, are you kidding? Use a jet to fly a damn cellphone halfway around the world? Surely, a day or two won't make a difference."

"Colonel, if you're willing to risk a hundred and seventy-five thousand lives to save a few thousand dollars, tell that to General Davis."

A shocked Colonel Dowson shook his head as Josh continued, "And tell HQ to put an analyst on it pronto. I want a call and e-mail from him with every scrap of info off that phone, and I want it as fast a humanly possible. Have you got that, Colonel?"

Josh cracked a small smile. A former SF sergeant giving a full bird orders. That must be a first, he thought.

A nod from Colonel Dowson and Josh ended the meeting. "Colonel, pardon us but we need to get our assessment and search planned. Gloria, call T and ask her to set up a meeting at seven-thirity with the CIA agents and local assets."

Gloria began her encrypted text as Josh sent the enlarged Google map of where the truck was parked to the onboard printer.

"T acknowledged, Josh. The meeting's set."

"Good, let's grab a bite of breakfast. We may not get anything else today." Josh and Gloria hurriedly picked up a hard roll and a cup of yougurt for breakfast, and Josh started looking at the map of the area around where the truck was located. He'd have the CIA men and local assets spread out and do a house-to-house scan, looking for anything out of the ordinary. They would discreetly ask about seeing any newcomers or hearing anything unusual in the neighborhood.

It was a quick way to hi-grade the area around where the truck was found. Once they picked up clues pointing to unusual activity, they could focus on a few buildings, and have a better chance of locating the biomaterial.

By 9 o'clock, the agents and local assets were combing the area around where the truck was found, as well as the immediate dock area. The demolition control man from SF rendered the explosives neutral, and the bio-assessment team confirmed traces of biomaterial in the back of the truck. That added a new urgency to their mission.

Gloria and Josh were keeping in touch via their Nokia 920s, as they moved along the back streets; they were making notes about possible places that would likely be used by al-Qaida.

Josh's men had been in the area for nearly three hours when there was the sound of automatic weapon fire broke the silence from a street a few blocks away.

"Follow about thirty steps behind me and give me backup and cover." Josh sprinted down the street and around the corner, and then stepped in a doorway. Crouched behind a car were two of his men, and leaning over a balcony rail across the street was a bearded fighter, firing an automatic weapon. His men were both wounded and weren't returning fire. They were just trying to keep out of the line of fire. Josh pulled his Glock out from under his coat, and lined up the fighter in his sights. Two quick rounds sent the man tumbling down from his perch. Josh ran over and began to assist the men who were seriously wounded. Gloria rushed up and Josh turned to her and barked: "Call Colonel Dowson and get the SF Team coming. All hell is about to break loose—run to the next block and wait on them!"

24

Firefight

Josh spent the next few seconds moving the wounded men across the street to where a concrete barrier had been set up for utility work. He wasn't about to leave them, knowing the al-Qaida fighters would summarily execute them when they came out of the building that the door-watcher was guarding.

He crouched behind the concrete barrier, just waiting. In seconds, three men rushed out of the building looking around to see where the shots had come from. They spotted the dead door-watcher Josh had shot and began to warily search the area. It was inevitable that they would sooner or later cross the street and see Josh and the other two CIA agents hiding behind the barrier. Josh decided to use the element of surprise.

He peeked over the top of the barrier, and as the lead man moved toward the street, Josh shot him in the face. Then he moved his gun to take out the other man behind him. The second and third bullets disabled the man, and Josh sent another bullet into his head to kill-check him.

Josh wasn't fast enough to take out the third man, however, and a burst of AK fire rattled into the concrete barrier, just missing him. Josh ducked down as the man turned and ran back into the building. Then he reloaded and pulled his backup Glock out to have it ready in case he ran out of ammunition with his primary weapon.

He dashed off a text to Gloria on his Nokia 920, "Have SF Team land and focus on block where I am. Be sure the door gunner has view of street."

He had just punched "send" when he spotted two fighters sneaking around the back corner of the building—one of them kneeling to fire an AK-.47. Josh's Glock spit out several rounds of automatic fire and the man flipped back. The other fighter then slipped back around the edge of the building.

There was a pause in the action and Josh warily checked the street and building, spotting glimpses of armed men moving from behind cars that were lining the street where he and the two wounded agents were hunkered down. There was a volley of shots from them, and then four other men ran out the door from the building across the street. Then six more suddenly rushed out from where they had been crouched behind cars, and another five joined the first fighters who were now running toward Josh, firing their AK's.

Josh ducked behind the concrete barrier as AK slugs ripped the concrete top of where he was crouched. The six men who came from around the corner of the building were the closest to him, and he decided to fire on them. He eased down to the end of the concrete barrier, quickly looked, and fired a burst of .9-mm bullets into the group of men who were rushing across the street to where he was hiding.

There were screams as two of the men were flipped back from the force of the .9-mm slug. The others hesitated and ducked behind a parked car.

Josh jerked around just in time to see two bearded men with pistols rush at him from the doorway across the street. There was a hail of fire from Josh at the two men, but Josh had only his hand and gun above the barrier. He was looking into the glass reflection behind him as he fired. It took the entire magazine of bullets to stop the two men. Josh dropped his empty weapon and grabbed his backup pistol.

The six men who had been hiding behind a row of cars were now taking advantage of Josh's focus on the other fighters, and were rushing up the street wildly firing in his direction. A burst of automatic .9 mm fire from Josh's backup Glock sent the first two to the pavement screaming. The other four ran, trying to get behind a parked car, but Josh nailed one of them before he could take cover.

Josh had been in numerous firefights, and if he had only been thinking about his safety, he would have never stayed in a stationary position. But he knew that if he ran to another position and left the two CIA agents, they would be shot as soon as the al-Qaida fighters overran their position. He wasn't going to leave them, but as he glanced down the street, he saw at least a dozen more men circling down the narrow street in order to fire on his exposed back position.

Several shots into the group of fighters knocked two men down and forced the others to momentarily take cover. But Josh knew that it was only a matter of time until the men reached a point on the street where they could fire at his exposed position. However, that was only part of the problem. There were still three men not 20 yards away behind cars, and they were firing bursts of AK slugs into the concrete to keep him from firing on the advancing fighters coming from down the street.

A glance in the opposite direction shocked him. Four al-Qaida fighters had somehow circled around and were rushing toward him. He quickly fired several rounds, knocking down two of the fighters, but his backup Glock needed a new magazine. And as he rushed to reload the remaining two men suddenly were almost to his position.

Just as Josh glanced up to see the two fighters raise their weapons to fire, several shots rang out, and the men tumbled down falling almost at Josh's feet. Josh looked up to see Gloria running toward him, firing at the men coming up the side street with her .9 mm weapon. She jumped the concrete barrier and ducked down behind it just as a burst of AK fire riddled the ground where she had just been.

"My god, Gloria… I told you to stay and direct the SF Team."

"Yeah, you did, Josh, but I'm disobeying orders. They won't have any trouble finding us with all the firing that's going on. I'm going to get the weapons from our two wounded agents so we'll have loaded backup, when we have to repel the next attack. Colonel

Dowson sent me a text and said the SF Team'll be here in fifteen minutes. We're going to have our hands full till he arrives."

"Yeah, we are. I can't believe we're being hit by so many fighters. Usually, in these ambushes there are just a couple. It's like they were waiting on us."

The words were no more than out of Josh's mouth when he spotted movement on their right side.

"To your right—three o'clock!" Josh yelled.

Three fighters were trying to circle Josh and Gloria by going around the block, and coming down the alleyway from the same direction Gloria had come. Josh had already opened fire by the time Gloria spotted the three fighters, who were now raising their AK's. Josh's first three rounds hit the lead man in the chest and the next round struck his head where he fell.

Josh's finger kept squeezing the trigger as he methodically shot the other man, and then made a dead-check with another shot to the head. Gloria was still trying to get off her first shot as the third man fell to the pavement. Before Josh could reload, another fighter dashed out from the building across the street.

"Get him, Gloria!" Josh yelled, as he struggled to jam another magazine into his fully automatic .9 mm Glock. Gloria sent a barrage of slugs toward the running fighter, managing to connect with a couple, which sent the man to the ground, wounded.

Josh yelled, "Dead-check him, Gloria!"

"What?"

"Shoot him in the head!"

Gloria hesitated and a second later, the wounded man began to raise his hand. It dropped as Josh sent slug into his head. A pistol fell from his hand as he slumped to the ground.

"Damn it, Gloria, for god's sake don't question my orders again!"

There wasn't time for Gloria to even nod because a hail of fire rattled off the top of the concrete barrier, narrowly missing them.

"Damn, there are two of the sons-of-bitches on the roof across the street shooting over that parapet. Wave your burqa and give them something to shoot at. We can't hold out here with them pinning us down."

Gloria yanked off her black head covering and held it up above the barrier as Josh squinted around the corner of the concrete slab. Seconds later, he watched as the top of a head appeared, and then a pair of eyes. A flash from the barrel of Josh's gun was the last thing on Earth the man saw.

Like shooting turtle heads down at Lambert's Lake. crossed Josh mind. He returned to his position, knowing human curiosity would make the other fighter peek over the wall to see where the shot had come from. He did, and another flash and the threat from the top of the building was eliminated.

Josh turned to find Gloria blasting away at as many as 10 fighters who were dodging from behind cars and lampposts, rushing up the street toward them. Josh entered the fray and his Glock spewed fire, which sent two of the closest fighters spinning back with multiple slugs in their chests.

"Damn, Gloria, I'm down to my last mag. How are you doing?"

"I just put in a new one but that's it. This weapon eats shells like nothing I've ever seen, and I've already emptied the other agent's weapons."

"Switch to semi-automatic, and pull the last shell out of your mag and hold it."

"What?—What for?"

"I don't know what you going to do, but if we run out of ammo, I'm going to use the last shell I have on me. You can't imagine the death we'd face, captured."

"You're serious, aren't you?"

"Damn right, I'm serious. You do what you want, but remember, they are going to rape you more times than you can count, then cut off your breasts before they tie you to the back of a truck and drag you across the desert until you're dead."

"Okay, I understand—to your left!" Gloria screamed. Four fighters had managed to get behind a truck right across the street, and as Gloria yelled, two dashed out from one side and two from the other side.

"Take the left!" yelled Josh. His Glock was spitting .9-mm slugs as Gloria screamed. A shot opened a flesh wound on her cheek. She ducked down behind the barrier, but, realizing it was just a scratch, raised up in time to take out one of the fighters with a blaze of shots from her Beretta. Josh sent the third fighter spinning back with a rattle of shots to the head.

In the next few minutes, the incoming fire was almost continuous, punctuated by an occasional blast from an RPG, which blew pieces of concrete out like shrapnel. Josh and Gloria could only manage to get off occasional shots, but with Josh's marksmanship, nothing was random. He was making every shot in his dwindling ammo clip count.

"Josh, my mag is empty! I only have the one shell I saved for myself!"

"Don't use it yet! I've got three more rounds, and that'll give us a little more time. I'll make them count, and that'll keep them back for another five minutes or so—Damn, where is Dowson!

"Stay low, and put your last shell in the chamber, but don't use it until I holler "now". Then be sure it's a shot to your head—behind the ear."

"Okay." Gloria slipped her last shell in the chamber of her Beretta and pulled herself up against the concrete barrier as Josh peeked around the corner to access the situation. From his vantage point, he could see the legs of several fighters, who were hiding behind the truck across the street. *I'll give them something to distract them*, he thought. He squeezed off a shot aiming at a point about halfway down from the top of the man's kneecap to his ankle.

There was a scream as the .9-mm slug tore a jagged hole through muscle and shinbone. It did exactly what Josh hoped it would. Fighters scattered, knowing they were vulnerable. And as they dropped back, they dragged the screaming fighter with them. Josh knew the wounded man would only distract them for a few minutes, and it would make them even more determined to kill or capture the Americans. He was down to two shells now, and he knew one of them was going to be used to prevent him from experiencing a horrible end.

It was deathly quiet for nearly a minute, and from Josh position against the pavement, peeking around the edge of the barrier, he could see as many as 15 fighters grouping and then separating out to flank Gloria and Josh's position. He knew with only one shell left to defend themselves, it would all be over in minutes. Josh decided to take the offensive with his last shell. He carefully aimed at the head of the man who seemed to be giving instructions to the fighters. It was going to be a shot of at least 50 yards, but the man was standing still, which made the shot doable. He steadied himself with his Glock resting on his right hand, held his breath, and slowly squeezed the trigger. He was taking all the pressure off the trigger mechanism, so when he actually fired, the weapon would be motionless, and the shot would have the best chance of hitting the target.

Josh waited until the man turned to point out firing positions to his men. And when he turned to face Josh and Gloria, Josh took the last bit of tension off the trigger and a muffled shot discharged. When the .9 mmslug hit the fighter, he was gesturing toward Josh and Gloria. The impact of the bullet, right below his left eye tore off the top of his head and sent a spray of blood and human debris flying. The men, who were gathered around the fighter, screamed as their leader was knocked backward. They ran, wiping the spray of blood and brains from their faces.

However, it only a momentary distraction from their attack on Josh and Gloria. In a few minutes, Josh noted them regrouping, getting ready to start the flanking movement their dead leader had given them.

"This is it, Gloria. Be ready. There's no way we can hold out any longer," Josh said. He slipped the last bullet into his Glock and leaned back against the concrete barrier, waiting for the fighters to appear.

When they were in sight, he was going to say "Now" to Gloria and fire that last bullet into his brain.

As the al-Qaida fighters moved up the street, a hail of fire pelting the concrete barrier kept Josh and Gloria pinned down. Josh looked over at the young woman, who had placed the nose of her Beretta behind her left ear. Josh had his mouth open to say, "Now" and his finger was squeezing the trigger of his Glock against the back of his left ear—when he heard something. He recognized it immediately.

25

Salvation

"Black Hawk, Gloria!—Dowson's here! Shoot one of the bastards with your last round!" Josh yelled.

He raised his weapon and put a bullet in the head of the nearest assailant as the Black Hawk suddenly appeared just 30 yards down the street. It sat down and out the back exit jumped the SF Team—with the door gunner putting the .50 caliber door gun into action.

The sight of the Black Hawk caused the al-Qaida fighters to stop, and before they could open fire, the big gun was raking the area. Most of the fighters ran behind the trucks parked across the street, or one of the cars on the other side. As the .50 caliber slugs tore into trucks and cars, the force of the shells ripped through the thin metal as if it wasn't even there and offered no protection for the fighters.

It soon became a rout. The crack SF soldiers spread out and quickly ended any resistance. In less than 10 minutes, hundreds of rounds had been fired, and the narrow street was littered with the bodies of some 20 al-Qaida soldiers. Josh and Gloria stood up and Josh waved to Colonel Dowson: "Colonel, we need a medic over here. Two of our men have been seriously wounded—Damn, we're glad to see you guys!"

"Well, it looks as if we didn't arrive any too soon."

"That's an understatement," Josh said. He looked at Gloria, who had blood streaming down one cheek trying to compose herself. A medic rushed up to her, but Gloria shook her head.

"This is just a scratch. Take care of the two men behind the concrete barrier." The medics rushed over to help the two CIA Agents, who were leaning against the barriers. They had been hit, one in the left leg and the other in his upper right leg—seriously wounded, but not fatally.

"Colonel, as soon as the men finish with the mop-up of wounded al-Qaida, we need to set up an entry to the warehouse across the street. You don't have some twenty-plus fighters guarding something for nothing. I think we might be lucky and find what we're looking for inside. But we need to enter as you would to seize a secure enemy position, expecting to take fire."

In less than 20 minutes, the SF Team had secured the wounded al-Qaida fighters and were ready to move into the warehouse. Josh was on his Nokia 920 talking with Abdul the local militia leader, and, as he told Abdul what had happened, he smiled. Josh clicked of his sat phone and turned to Colonel Dowson:

"Colonel, Abdul knew all about the firefight, and he's glad we cleaned out this nest of al-Qaida fighters. They've been a pain in the ass for him. His men will be by to pick up the wounded in a few minutes."

"What will he do with the wounded, Josh?"

"You don't want to know, Colonel—is your team ready to assault the warehouse?"

"They're ready, Josh. Do you want to go in with them?"

"No, Colonel, they're a close-knit team, and I'd only be in the way. As soon as they secure the premises, I want to see anything that might have something to do with the biomaterial. Oh, yes: They're probably going to find the cell leader inside, and if they can take him alive, it would be very helpful. I am sure there'll be several bodyguards with him so take precautions."

"Don't worry about the team, Josh. They're one of the best in the world. I'll have them in the building in less than ten minutes."

"That's great, sir; we don't have a minute to lose."

Colonel Dowson waved to the team captain, and soon the 12-man SF Team moved to secure the warehouse. They first circled the building, posting men at every possible exit, and then, with a signal from the team leader, the doors were simultaneously breached, flash-bang grenades were tossed in, and the team dashed into the building with weapons ready.

There was scattered AK fire as they entered, but the flash-bang grenades had done their job and al-Qaida fighters were just blindly firing in the direction of where they thought the SF soldiers might be. A quick burst of fire sent the four guards down, and after checking out the open space in the warehouse they focused on an office at the end of the building.

Josh had followed the team into the warehouse, and as they closed in on the shuttered office, he motioned for a breacher to blow the shuttered windows and door simultaneously. After the charges had been planted, Josh waved for the team leader to come and talk with him.

"Put you masks on and throw in the *******classified, that should knock them out long enough to secure them. We want them alive if possible."

The team captain nodded, talked with the crew, and seconds later, everyone in the building had masks on. They were ready to blow the windows and doors.

The team captain dropped his hand and the charges blew out windows and doors. One SF soldier dashed up and tossed in a flash-bang grenade followed by two *******classified. There was some movement in the room for a few seconds, and then nothing.

"Give the *******classified some time to be sure," said the team leader. Later after minutes he nodded and two SF soldiers entered the room. Soon they came out carrying two bearded men.

"Great job, guys. Colonel. Gloria and I will work with our CIA contact and arrange to have these two men sent to Egypt. We'll accompany them where we can get the info and react immediately. Have your men go with Abdul and transport them to the Benghazi International Airport, where you will hand them over to an interdiction transfer team. They will have instructions on how to deal with these two. Gloria and I will meet you there."

"Will do, Josh."

"And now, let's go over everything in this office: Remove all papers, cellphones, and any correspondence on the bodies of the fighters outside and on these men. Put everything in a diplomatic pouch and take it to the airport with you. A separate plane will be there to receive it."

26

Directions and Deceptions

As Josh and Gloria drove down the coast road toward Benghazi, he briefed Gloria on why they were going with the men to Egypt and what to expect.

"Gloria, as you know, this mission has the highest approval to stop the al-Qaida fighters from causing a horrible mass killing that would dwarf even nine-eleven. We can't afford to waste a second. That's why we are going to Egypt—just an hour flight time away.

"And one more thing, don't be shocked at the interrogation methods the Egyptians will use on the two captured fighters. I've been cleared to use extreme force on any person I believe would have information useful to us."

"Oh, Josh, the CIA has been into extreme interrogation for years, and only recently did we stop."

"Gloria, you have no idea what extreme really is till you see the masters in Egypt at work. I suggest you use the earplugs in your kit, during the interrogation."

"Josh, you can't be serious."

"Okay, suit yourself. But remember I'm not one to give unnecessary instructions."

Gloria, was mildly amused, but nodded as if she appreciated Josh's concern for her sensibilities. *I may be a woman, but there's nothing I can't listen to or watch for our cause*, crossed her mind.

The drive down the coast road went slowly as they dodged the occasional camel and goatherds that found the road easier to walk on that the rough ground beside the road. A couple of hours driving put them at the Benghazi airport, where Abdul and a contingent of his militia were waiting with the two, hooded al-Qaida prisoners. Colonel Dowson had sent the request for two jets to HQ, and they were waiting on the taxiway when Josh drove up. The Colonel was talking to Abdul as he and Gloria walked up.

"Abdul, did you take care of the al-Qaida fighters—the dead and wounded?" Josh questioned.

"Commander, you and your men must have been excellent shots. There were no wounded, but we have arranged for all the dead to receive a proper Muslim burial."

Josh, cocked his eyebrow slightly, as he looked at Gloria. *No wounded? Yeah, there weren't any after Abdul got through.* Gloria rolled her eyes, but said nothing.

"Well, good work, Abdul. I'm sure Gloria here will make sure her people reward you for your service, and pay you well for the expenses you incurred."

"You are very kind, Commander, but we require nothing—well, maybe just some small funds for gasoline and ammunition—and of course food and other small items. We want to be ready to help if you ever need us again."

"Certainly, Abdul. You will have the funds within the week."

Josh turned to Gloria as they walked away and said, "Tell, HQ to send your man in Benghazi $500,000 in used $100 bills for Abdul."

Gloria looked shocked. "Josh don't you think that's a little over the top?" she whispered.

"Sure, it's over the top, but it will buy us an unbelievable amount of goodwill. But what it will really do is to put a price on any al-Qaida that we didn't kill in the firefight. Tell your man in Benghazi when Abdul brings him a report about his militia killing another ten or so fighters, he is to reward him just like we are doing now.

"Hell, Gloria, if we used old Uncle's money in the right way, we could clean out more of those lowlife nuts than an airborne division. Come on, let's get these guys to Egypt. My god, I've got the worst feeling that bio stuff is already heading for Italy."

Abdul handed the two al-Qaida fighters over to the interdiction transfer team onboard and Josh and Gloria settled in for the short flight to Alexandria. As Josh glanced back out the window, he nodded to Gloria: "There goes the pouch back to Langley. By the time we get these birds to sing, we should have everything code-broken and translated. Maybe we'll be able to locate where they're going to hand off the biomaterial when they hit the Italian coast."

He had just nodded off when he felt the wheels hit the runway at the el-Alcimene Military Airport west of Alexandria. The jet taxied to the end of the runway and the interdiction team moved the two al-Qaida men out of the jet, followed by Josh and Gloria. Seconds later, a military van-like vehicle pulled up; six men in uniform got out and thrust the two, hooded men into the back of the vehicle. Not a word was spoken and the interdiction transfer team boarded the jet, which moved onto an active runway and prepared to take off.

"Commander, Josh!" yelled a man who came from around the side of the van.

"Kassim! How are you? Still slinking around like a dog?"

"Ah, what else must one of us do? We all slink, but we also bite."

"Yes, I know quite a few that have felt your bite. But enough; I have a couple of higher level al-Qaida that we must have some answers from immediately. It's a matter of very great importance. Can you help us?"

"Commander, it will be my pleasure. We have always managed to get the information you wanted."

"Yes, Kassim, but these men are much more important than just regular fighters. I think we need to stabilize their heads before you start the interrogation."

"You mean the electronic probe? I rarely have to use that."

"I think you might have to on these two. They're hardened fighters, and they will be able to stand a lot of pain before they break."

"Very well. You and your associate will follow my van to the interrogation substation. Someone will serve you chai while we make the men ready. I understand you want to hear their confessions for yourself to save time. Is that right?"

"Yes, Kassim, and if you would have your best translator with me at all times, I would certainly appreciate it."

"It will be done. I'll have some dates and sweets brought to you while you are waiting."

"You are very kind, Kassim."

"Yes, and you are very generous," Kassim said as he laughed. "But of course, I would gladly do the interrogation for nothing—just as a favor. But of course, I do have men I must pay and a large family to support, so any way you can help is always appreciated."

"You will have the usual."

"Uh, but there are two to be interrogated."

Josh cracked a wiry smile and nudged Gloria, "Text HQ and tell them to double the money."

"Double how much?"

"Five-hundred."

"Five-hundred, uh…"

"Thousand."

"Oh."

"Commander, please tell your people to put in some twenties, and be sure no new hundreds."

"Got it—Okay, let's get on with what we are here for."

Soon Gloria and Josh were seated in the base's Officer's Club having chai, dates, and sweets. In about 30 minutes, an aide approached and beckoned them to follow him. They hopped in a Jeep-like vehicle and roared off to the edge of the base's complex to an austere building with only an entrance door. Gloria noted the padded door and the absence of windows as they walked in. There was a rectangular room inside the building, again with only a padded door.

As they walked in, Gloria was shocked to see the two al-Qaida men naked and strapped to chairs, with their heads in a vise-like contraction. Electrodes were attached to the men's nipples and genitals.

"We are ready to begin the interrogation, Commander. Do you have the questions you want answered?"

"Yes, Kassim." Josh said, handing Kassim the list of questions. "I'm sure you will make sure them answer correctly."

"Of course. Remember the monitor. If the red line is passed by the reaction from the answer, it will mean there is no answer or that the answer is incorrect. Shall we get started?"

Kassim started the questions very slowly, pausing after each question, as he gave the men an opportunity to answer. The first questions were very simple, like where they lived. The men refused to even acknowledge that they were being questioned. After 10 minutes of silence, Kassim began to talk softly to the men, explaining to them that they must answer or he would have no choice but to inflict pain until they complied. Still no answer.

Kassim was holding a palm-size piece of electronic equipment that controlled the attachments fastened to the men. He pressed one of the buttons, and there was a muffled scream from one of the prisoners as sparks flashed from the electrode attached to his left nipple. The smell of burning flesh filtered through the room. The simple questioning began again and this time the man who had received the shock answered a couple of basic questions.

Then Kassim turned to the other captive and pressed two buttons at once. There was a jerk, scream, and spark from electric shocks to both of the man's nipples. The questions were asked again, but there wasn't even a nod of recognition. Kissim pressed his hand down on the control gadget and then jerked it back. A surge of electricity went into both of the man's nipples, and this time into his genitals. The man stiffened, screamed, and jerked as the electricity surged into his body.

Now the smell of burning flesh was so strong that Gloria put a handkerchief over her mouth and nose. The last shock, however, produced only an acknowledgment of the man's name and the fact that he was a Muslim.

"Good," Kassim whispered to Josh. "Now we have a base line."

It was an hour into the questioning when Josh stopped Kassim. The questioning had produced some information but not anything vital. The destination of the boat was still a mystery as was the operative and place of docking on the Italian coast.

"Kassim, we must use the head electrodes. They have built up a tolerance for the other. More shocks won't do any good."

"Yes, Commander, I was about to suggest it myself." Kassim walked over and pulled out a long sliver of a wire with a small, toothpick-sized ending. The wire was split, with one end attached to an electrical circuit, and the other to the control box.

"Insert the electrode," said Kassim. The aide proceeded to one of the men and began to shove the wire with the electrode attached up the nostril of the man on the left.

"Put an extra strap on his head," Kassim ordered. The aide wrapped another leather strap around the captive's head and tightened it until it was biting into his skin. Gloria, who had been on the verge of throwing up as the interrogation continued, moved toward the door as Kissim asked the man a question about where the boat with the biomaterial was going. No answer. Again he asked, and this time he flicked the switch on the electrode that had been inserted into the man nostril. There was an ear-piercing shriek and a convulsive jerk, as the man vomited blood. Gloria grabbed her mouth and ran out of the room.

"We will give this one some time to think, Commander," said Kassim. His aide had wired the other fighter with the electrode inserted into his nostril while Kissim was questioning the other man. As he turned to the captive, he tapped a control button attached to the electrode that has been inserted into the man's nostril. There was another scream and a jerk that almost turned the chair over.

"Commander, we learned this trick from a Tibetan man who worked for the Chinese government. We rarely use it because it is so deadly. I think we can hit them both two more times, and then if they don't answer properly, we may have to give up. After that much treatment they are usually useless anyway. Two more hits and they probably couldn't tell you their mother's name.

"As you know, this electrode is placed very close to the junction of the spinal cord and the brain, and it produces unbelievable pain. However, after a few treatments the nerve damage is so great it is useless to proceed. Let's see if this first man is ready to talk.

"Listen to me! You have one last chance to answer the question I asked you before. Do you understand?"

"Yes, just don't do that again! Please!"

Kassim nodded to Josh, and asked the question about the destination of the boat. Josh listened as the man answered, "Sicily." The machine quickly jumped over the red line. Kassim yelled, "Liar!" and pressed the control button attached to the nostril electrode. The man went into convulsions, coughing up phlegm and blood, and became almost incoherent.

Then he blurted out again, "Sicily!"

"What did he say?" asked Josh.

"He said 'Sicily' but the machine indicates it was not a completely truthful answer."

A few minutes later, after the man stopped convulsing, Kassim questioned him again.

"Your answer was correct, but it was not complete. This is your last chance. What is the final destination of the boat carrying the material? Tell me now or I will press this button," said Kassim as he moved to where the control panel was in the man face.

"Tell me!" Kassim shouted.

"Italy!" the quivering man replied.

"Commander, he has answered truthfully."

The questions continued for another hour until Kassim was satisfied that both men had told Josh all they knew. It was fairly certain that as far as these men knew, the boat carrying the biomaterial was heading for the coast of Italy. In the later part of the questioning, one of the men had given Kassim a detailed description of the boat.

"Thanks, Kassim; you may dispose of them," said Josh.

"Yes, I am growing weary of this job. This was the hardest one yet. I think a little bonus from your friends would help."

"You shall have it, Kassim. Your work has been exceptional. You may take the men and put them away. They are no use to anyone anymore."

"They will be removed and taken care of immediately," replied Kassim.

Josh left the room and met Gloria who was standing outside by the door. She had put in her earplugs.

"My god, Josh, I have never seen anything so horrible. How can you be a part of something like that?"

"Gloria, when I was on active duty in Afghanistan, the Taliban captured one of our SF point men. We did everything we could to find where they were hiding him, but we found out later they had taken him across the border into Pakistan. It was about two weeks later when his body was dumped out in front of Bagram Air Force Base. He was mutilated beyond recognition. It was obvious he had been tortured for hours before they he died from the wounds inflicted.

"That's when I decided to play by their rules. And, by the way, because this is such an important mission and the lives of thousands depend upon being able to stop the placement of the biomaterial, I have full authorization for what just happened. It will be on my report to HQ in detail.

"Now, that's all I have to say about this matter. When you call HQ, tell them to double the amount they normally pay Kassim."

Gloria nodded and as they walked back to the waiting jet she sent an encrypted text to HQ.

"Josh, since these men are higher-ranking al-Qaida, will the Egyptians send them to Gitmo?"

"No, they're already dead—Come on let's get out of here. We have what we need."

"But..."

"Don't sweat it, Gloria. I'll have it in my report, and I'll take full responsibility. You won't have to worry."

"Damn it, Josh! Stop treating me like a woman!"

"What? Uh, how..."

"I'm an integral part of this mission, and I have concurred with everything that has happened; so include me in every report, and evaluate my actions as if I were one of your damn 'men'! Understand?"

Damn, I only wish my men were as good as that woman, crossed Josh's mind.

"Sure, Gloria. I didn't mean to imply you weren't doing a good job. Let's get on the plane and finish this mission together."

Gloria nodded as she walked ahead of Josh to board the jet.

As they boarded the plane, the pilot looked back and asked, "Where can we drop you off, Josh?"

"Palermo, Sicily."

Gloria looked at Josh and asked, "I thought the man they questioned said, Italy. Don't you think we should go to Rome and work back from there?"

"No, I don't. During the questioning one of the men blurted out 'Sicily' and Kassim said that was partially correct. Later he said the final destination was Italy. If we are going to do a thorough job of tracking down these guys, we can't jump around and not follow up on every clue. By the time we reach Sicily, the code-breakers and analyst at Langley will have a report on all the info we sent them from the firefight. Maybe then we can piece together why the man said 'Sicily'. Oh, yeah, and have the local CIA agent meet the plane with an extra car for us. Tell him..."

"It's a her."

"Okay, tell her to have a list of every possible port along the east coast of Sicily, and assign both an agent and a local asset to check each port. Give her a description of the boat and tell her that it may have docked for some reason before proceeding on to its final destination. Got it?"

"Yeah, Josh, I'll get this to her shortly, but you may be stretching things. There must be dozens, maybe more, places a boat could dock on that expanse of coast."

"Well, which ones do you want to skip?"

"Uh, uh ***forget it, Josh."—*You smart-ass SF son-of-a-bitch!* crossed her mind.

27

Palermo

The flight to Palermo took less than an hour, and as they approached Sicily, Josh dictated a message for Gloria to send HQ.

"Believe boat carrying biomaterial is heading to Sicily on the way to mainland Italy. Please have all local assets and CIA agents in southern Italy focus on the harbors along the east coast of Sicily. The boat description is..."

After Josh finished his e-mail, he began to review the answers that the two al-Qaida operatives had divulged. He calculated the approximate speed of the boat and decided that it would be logical for the boat to make the trip to the Italian mainland by stopping overnight in a port. The most likely place of them to stop would be in a large harbor on the east coast of Sicily, where they could blend in with several hundred boats. That narrowed it down to Catania and three other comparable ports. They would be on the top of his list to check out.

As the jet landed and pulled off the active runway to a vacant taxiway, a blue sedan pulled up beside the back exit of the plane.

"That's the CIA bureau chief. Her name's Sybil Derain. She's been in charge of the local CIA office for less than a year. About the only thing I have heard about her is she strictly goes by the book: a no-nonsense agent."

"Well, I won't hold that against her—oh, yeah, tell the pilot to hang around. He can leave the plane, but he should keep his cell with him. We may be flying out on short notice."

"Okay."

Gloria and Josh exited the jet and climbed into the sedan, and quickly headed off the taxiway to a back service gate. A uniformed guard opened the gate, and it sped into a maze of traffic. There would be no customs or immigration procedures to precede their arrival.

"Josh, this is Sybil Derain. She's the CIA bureau chief for southern Italy, which includes Sicily." Gloria had hopped in the backseat and Josh was riding beside Sybil in the front.

"Hello Sybil, I'm Josh. Please brief me on the status of the operation instructions you received from Gloria."

"Well, Josh, from the info I received, and after I waited for the confirmation from HQ, I still have quite a bit to do..."

"How much have you done?"

"Well, I've only had direct orders from HQ..."

"Forget HQ, my orders were direct, and you have had them for over an hour. Why didn't you proceed instead of double-checking? Damn it, minutes may mean the death of thousands!"

"I'm sorry, Josh, but I didn't know the urgency of the matter."

"Sybil, I'm sorry I yelled, but Gloria and I have chased these bastards halfway across Africa, and now they are probable either on their way to Italy, or they are here in Sicily. They have enough bio-crap that will wipe out everybody within five blocks after they detonate it. We've got to stop them, and minutes *do* count in this mission."

"Josh, I'll do everything I can, but we have only six men in this local office, and we have nine local assets to help. What you're asking is nearly impossible without another twenty CIA people and at least fifty local assets."

Josh, sat thinking, and then he pulled out his Nokia 920.

"Humm, I remember a man who helped us nail a suicide bomber who had slipped into Sicily on a tramp steamer... Yeah, here's his name. I'm going to give him a call. I'll bet he remembers me, but not from nailing the suicide bomber."

"Who is it, Josh. Maybe we know him."

"Don Pastori; ever heard the name?"

"Hell, yes; practically everybody in this business knows him. He's one of the kingpins of the Sicilian Mafia—don't call him. He'll offer to help, but he will only shake you down."

Josh ignored Sybil, and punched in Don Pastori's cell number.

"We'll see if he has the same cell number. I hope he will recognize my name. Hell, with the money we paid the bastard, he should. And I'm the godfather of one of his grandchildren—It's ringing…"

"Godfather? You're kidding! Josh, don't get involved. State sent us a directive that under no circumstance are we to use Mafia personnel for intelligence."

"Hold on," Josh said as he began to speak Italian. "He's answering—Don Pastori? This is Josh Martin… yes, I'm in Sicily. How did you know… oh, I forgot about your contacts at the airport… yeah, I'm here on business, and I need your help*** yes, if possible I would like to meet with you later today… M-28, we just got on from the airport… yes, I see the red car behind me… what? Since the airport… why… oh, yes, we'll follow him. Thank you Don Pastori, it will be a pleasure to do business with you."

Josh clicked off his cell and turned to Sybil, "That's one of Don Pastori's men in the red car behind us. He'll pass us and we are to follow him to a restaurant where we will meet Don Pastori himself."

"Josh, your reputation has preceded you, but I think working with Don Pastori is a big mistake. We can get help from Rome, and cover those extra ports by tomorrow…"

"Tomorrow might be too late, Sybil. I don't like dealing with bottom dwellers any more than you do, but I've found out that if that type has anything we can use it's worth it to get our hands dirty. Just play it laid back and friendly, and let me do the talking."

"I…I'll have to put it in my report about meeting with Don Pastori," Sybil said hesitantly.

"Sure, and it will be in mine too. Oh, by the way, how much cash can you lay your hands on in the next hour?"

"What?"

"You heard me: Cash is the only thing that works with the Don Pastori types. Can you come up with a hundred thousand?"

"Yeah, I can."

"I need it as bait for another four-hundred thousand in case his men find the boat. So get ready to do a little schmoozing with a real lowlife, and act as if you're having a great time—and, hell, order everything on the menu and act like it's the best stuff you ever put in your mouth.—Got it?"

"Yeah, I've got it," Sybil replied. "But how in hell did you get to know Don Pastori, and why is he willing to help us? It can't be just for the money."

"No, it's not, but he'll want a good slug of it—even though I did him a big favor a couple of years back. We've got about an hour's ride in this traffic to Don Pastori's restaurant, so lean back, and I'll tell you why Don Pastori will help us.

Sybil and Gloria were still shaking their heads in shock.

"Godfather of a Mafia don's grandchild?" Gloria muttered as Josh started his story.

"I guess it was about two years ago. I was at Camp Thunder right in the middle of a training session with a bunch of egomaniacs we call 'Rangers,' when one of my men came up and said there was a man at our gate who was asking for me, and he had a heavy foreign accent. Of course, he told the man to get lost, but the guy refused to go, and after we let him stand at our gate for three hours, I decided I had better talk with him just to get him to leave. So I drove down to the gate and started telling him what my guard had already told him ten times—that we were a private facility, and he couldn't come in."

"But Mr. Martin," he said in very broken English, "it is a matter of someone's life." And then he added in almost a whisper, "and involves a great deal of money for you."

"Well, that got my attention, and, of course, I asked him whose life and how much money. He wanted to come into a secure office to talk, but I don't ever let anyone penetrate my security unless we know them, so we just stood there at the gate and talked. After he told me his story I know my mouth must have dropped open."

"This is what he said:" "Mr. Martin, your reputation is very well known among our associates, especially since the incident with the man who was known as Patto, The Knife."

"That got my attention because outside of a few SFs, the CIA, and some al-Qaida folks, no one knows about that little situation. Patto was a hired assassin used by the Mafia and al-Qaida all across the Middle East. Al-Qaida hired him to kill me, and he came very close to doing just that including my new wife.

"I managed to kill him, but it was never made public. I immediately knew the man I was talking to was either Mafia or al-Qaida. He soon made it clear that he wasn't al-Qaida, and as you know the Mafia guys won't ever actually *say* Mafia. They talk of associates or partnerships or families. I finally managed to get him to at least admit it was the Mafia in Sicily he worked for. He never said the word, but he did nod when I finally pressed him. Then he proceeded to tell me a lot more than I needed to know.

"Finally, he got down to why he was at Camp Thunder. He wanted to hire me to rescue a Mafia don who had been kidnapped by a competing Mafia bunch. Of course, I told him no, but he wouldn't leave. Then we started talking money. He first offered a million dollars for me to bring a team to Sicily, storm a fortified villa in the central mountains of the country, and bring this man, Don Pastori, out alive.

"I began to walk away, but he was unbelievably persistent," Josh remembered. "The money went up to three million, and then it occurred to me that for the Sicilian Mafia to know about my killing Patto, they would have to be working with the Moroccan and Spanish al-Qaida. That's when I started thinking about doing the job. If this Don Pastori could finger all the al-Qaida plants in Morocco, Spain, and Sicily, it would be worth it to do the job, and I could sure use an extra three or four million to fix up Camp Thunder. This is what I said."

'I might be interested, but here is what I want if I do the job.' "Then I told him that this Don Pastori would have to give me the exact names, addresses, and phones contacts of every al-Qaida in Sicily, Spain, and Morocco. He almost choked when I said that, and after he finished stuttering he said, "I must contact my superiors before I can answer. You have offered a very difficult bargain. It may not be possible to accomplish that. I will be back here at the same time tomorrow to tell you what my superior says."

"Well, I walked away thinking I wouldn't see the guy again. You know ratting on fellow mob members, even if they're scum like al-Qaida is something those folks never do, but I thought I should brief my CIA contact in Washington, so I gave Bill Paxton, the CIA Agent in charge of southern Europe, a call.

"I said, 'Bill, Josh Martin here… yes, I'm fine. How are the wife and kids?*** Good… Listen I had a very interesting visit…' "and then I told him the story. But instead of being surprised, he filled me in on exactly what was going on in Sicily."

"He said," 'Josh, there are two major families in Sicily, and there's bad blood there to put it mildly. Up to recently they'd just been knocking off each other runners and other lowlife, but last week things really got out of hand. After a bloody confrontation in Palermo, where six men were gunned down, the rival gang captured Don Pastori and hustled him away to some place in the center of the county. We don't know exactly where, but according to our sources they are threatening to slowly kill him if he doesn't authorize his lieutenants to give them a shitpot full of money, and give this Rizzio Amizana complete control of the island.'

"Bill Paxton continued," 'Josh, you know we would love to have all the al-Qaida info Don Pastori has squirreled away. Hell, we could cripple a dozen al-Qaida cells if we had that. Those bastards are the one who pulled of the Spanish train job. But, hell, you know I can't tell you to do the job.'

"I said," 'I know that Bill, but I can't pull it off without some assistance, even though I have the manpower. If you could have certain weapons and chest armor plate available in the CIA's Palermo bureau office, and if you don't mind us using it for a few days, I might be able to get you some valuable information. God, ever since what those scummy creeps did to my wife, I've been looking for a way to pay them back. Are you interested?'

"He said," 'I'm more than interested, Josh, but you know I'll have to clear it with the Joint Chiefs. I'll see if I can get a meeting set up later today. What time is the man returning to meet with you?'

"I said," 'At about two P. M. eastern, tomorrow, and he said he'd try to have an answer the next day by noon.'

"I got a call from Bill about ten the next morning.

"He said, 'Josh, the Joint Chiefs turned me down, but they did give me an opening to get the deal working through another country—Spain.'

"I asked why Spain and he said that according to one of our listening posts in Madrid, al-Qaida was trying to set up another attack somewhere in Spain. He said, 'We have passed on the info, and their people are frantic to find out as much as they can where they can stop all hell from breaking loose. All it took was one call, and they agree to do anything we want if we can get some info about implanted al-Qaida in Spain. We think the Mafia in Sicily has connections in both Spain and Morocco. If the man you're meeting with today can assure you this Don Pastori will co-operate if you spring him, we are ready to go.'

"I said I'd quiz him, and see if his boss would co-operate. But I told him," 'Bill, you know I can't travel with the weaponry and body armor we need. Can you help me there?'

"And he said," 'Yeah, Josh, I have it cleared to move whatever you need into the Spanish consulate in Palermo. Just give me a detailed list, and it will be waiting for you. Oh, and you and your men will have some new body armor that we're trying out. Hell, our initial tests look damn good. It will take a fifty caliber bullet to penetrate it.'

"Of course, I said something like," 'Thanks, Bill; I'll get back to you later today and let you know if it's a go.'

"I walked back to the Camp gate at two, and the Mafia guy was already there waiting for me. I could tell by his demeanor something had happened. Even before I could say hello he was telling me that the money and information I asked for was available."

Yeah, I was shocked and then he said, 'Mr. Martin, it is of the greatest urgency that you act as soon as possible. The men holding Don Pastori have given us a deadline to meet their demands, and in the message, they sent part of a finger they said was Don Pastori's. I am afraid if something is not done very soon, they will kill Don Pastori.'

"I still didn't go for the deal so I said," 'I understand, but before I agree to do the rescue, we must discuss the details of the payment. Unless I must be assured the information you will provide about al-Qaida is correct, and the money will be transferred.' " I figured that would kill it, but I was wrong."

"Don Pastori understands, and he has made arrangements. There is a worker in the house that is part of our family, and she can pass messages to and from Don Pastori. This is what Don Pastori has done to assure you the payment we agree to will happen as agreed. Here is the name, address, phone number of an al-Qaida operative who lives in Madrid. It will be an easy task to have your CIA locate him and search his apartment."

"Wow, I couldn't believe that, but I took the piece of paper and at a glance, I recognized the name; it was on the 'terminate on sight list' that every agent and SF operative has. Then before I could say anything else, he handed me a deposit slip with my name on it. It was for five-hundred and fifty thousand deposited in my local U.S. account. I couldn't believe it. Hell, I knew the Mafia had connections, but being able to deposit directly into my U. S. account was shocking. When I got over my surprise I said, "If this name checks out, I will agree to lead a rescue team to Sicily. Come back tomorrow and bring the details of where Don Pastori is being held."

Hell, I couldn't wait to call Bill Paxton, and I had him on his cell while I was walking back to the office. Naturally, he was a little hesitant, but the al-Qaida name sure lit up his lights. He was just ecstatic.

"For god's sake, Josh; this isn't a small fish. We've had him on our hit list for three years! I'll put this on a top priority to our Central European Office, and by tonight we'll know if this info is legit."

"Well, Sybil, sometimes the old CIA can move faster than a snail's pace, and the next morning Bill called me with the news that al-Sakie ben-Mohammad had been killed while resisting arrest. Uh, yeah, you know like how Ben Laden was 'resisting.'"

"That afternoon, the Sicilian Mafia guy showed up right on time, and I cut a deal with him. He produced a packet of material, complete with closeup Google photos and a layout of the interior of the house where Don Pastori was being held. I walked away with the packet under my arm realizing I had a mission I'd agreed to that needed six top men to pull off, and I hadn't even mentioned it to any of my team. I had a selling job to do.

"That afternoon I took six of my best trainers aside and started talking about the job. Initially they looked at me as if I were crazy as I talked about a rescue mission for a Mafia chief. But I got their attention when I said," 'You will each receive two-hundred and fifty thousand whether the mission is successful or not.'

"Of course these guys are professionals, and even with big bucks being waved at them they weren't about to commit until they knew everything about the operation. We spent the next four hours taking the mission apart, and then we analyzed the house and the setting. There was one element that made the job a lot more difficult, but we figured it actually might work to our advantage. The little village of Coretta is very similar to one of the hilltop towns of Spain. The village church sits on the highest point on the hill, and the villa where Don Pastori was being held sat directly beside the church on the edge of a seventy-foot, nearly vertical bluff. The villa had a walled courtyard and a very substantial gate blocking any entry from the street. It was apparent that whoever was defending the villa would consider only the front as being vulnerable That was going to be our advantage. So this is what I told my guys:

"I said, 'Okay, guys, this is where that Ranger training is going to come in handy. Bruce, I know you can handle the repelling and climbing, so you and I are going to scale the seventy-foot cliff and come in from the back of the house. Davis, you will head up the frontal assault team. This is not going to be anything fancy. After Bruce and I scale the back wall, we'll set a demo device on this back door right here.'

"Then I pointed to the obvious main back entrance of the villa. Well, you might guess Bruce and Davis are two of my top men, and if I was going to do the job they would be the key. This is what I told them:

'Davis, while Bruce and I are scaling the cliff and wall you will plant a demo on the front gate. Make sure it's enough to blow it all to hell. When you see the villa lights go off, detonate the gate charge, throw in a couple of flash-bang grenades to blind anyone in the courtyard and then the four of you rush into the courtyard and take out the couple of guards the guy said are posted in front of the house. Quickly set up a defensive perimeter because when you blow that gate the rest of the security is going to come running. Two seconds after you blow the gate, I'll fire my charge, which will destroy the back door. Then Bruce and I will enter the house following a flash-bang, take out any resistance, and free Don Pastori. We will exit the front door, and I will hold my weapon up to signal you. Got it?'

"Heck, I can tell you I thought this was going to be a quick in and out, but just to be sure I needed those guys to be gung ho and they were. Yeah, they were really jumping to go, and it did seem like a lunch run. But it didn't turn out that way; not by a long shot."

28

Coretta, Sicily

"The next day we flew AA flight sixty-four direct to Rome, and then Alitalia on down to Palermo," Josh continued. "Since the job was on such a tight time frame, we went straight to the Spanish consulate, where we were given the VIP treatment, wined and dined before they would let us leave. After we got our weapons, ammo, and vests, we loaded everything into a touristy looking minibus and headed across town to meet with the Mafia guy, who came to see me at Camp Thunder.

"I really didn't know what to expect, but when we pulled up to the decrepit dump of a restaurant, it was a lot less than I'd hoped. However, we hadn't even exited the vehicle when everybody from busboys on up ran out to greet us. I really didn't want to hand the keys to a sixteen-year-old kid with all the armament we had inside, but a more senior guy who spoke good English welcomed us and assured me that my minibus was in good hands.

"The place might have looked like a dump on the outside, but the inside was a beautifully laid-out restaurant complete with a waterfall, fish tanks, and gobs of tropical plants. The man who welcomed us led us to a long side table separated from other tables by the waterfall. Three men were already seated, and one of them was the man who had come to Camp Thunder.

"He said," 'Ahaa, Mr. Martin, welcome! Welcome!'

"And then bussed me on both cheeks. Immediately, the table was surrounded by waiters and busboys who catered to us, getting us everything we could imagine to eat or drink. The matter might have been a life and death situation, but Italians are going to eat, drink, and socialize before anything serious is going to be discussed.

"About two hours later, the restaurant was empty—in fact, actually, I found out while we were eating and drinking that the fairly large crowd had been slowly removed from the restaurant to give us privacy. Then this Mafia guy, who called himself, Renaldo, started talking business.

"He handed me some pictures of a villa that he said had been taken just that morning."

"Notice, our man was able to get a good picture of the gate open, and you can see four armed men there in the courtyard," he told me. "You must be ready to engage these men, as well as others, when you enter the courtyard."

"He then told me that they had a woman house-cleaner reporting to them who saw at least ten guards in the house and courtyard.

"She couldn't tell how they were armed, but I assume they have semi-automatic weapons," the man told us. "Do you think this villa can be controlled with the six men you have here?"

"I said I was sure we would have the advantage of surprise, and even though the guards were heavily armed, our firepower would neutralize them. Then I asked him if he was sure Don Pastori was still locked in the basement?"

"He replied, "Yes, our woman carried him lunch at one o'clock today."

"So I told him our plan was to rest that day, and then the next day drive to Coretta and rescue Don Pastori. But our Mafia contact was not pleased, and he got right to the point."

"Mr. Martin, as I told you earlier, Don Pastori's life is in danger, and from what our person in the villa has over heard, we think tomorrow may be too late. Can you not do it tonight?"

"I said that it was late and that we wouldn't even dream of starting an operation like that until after midnight. Then I asked him how far it was to the village of Coretta."

"It is a trip no longer than one and a half-hours—an easy drive," he replied.

"I asked him if he was sure this couldn't wait until the next night, explaining that we were tired from traveling, and consuming a large meal, with wine.

"But he insisted that if we waited, "Don Pastori won't be alive to rescue tomorrow night," he said.

"I nodded and leaned back glancing at my men who were leaning forward to catch every word the man was saying. They were nods of affirmation.

"I told him we'd go that night and asked that our minivan be brought around so we could get started."

"Thank, you Mr. Martin," he said. "Don Pastori will consider it a great favor that you are willing to do the operation as tired as you are. And don't worry about the police in the village. I will have one of my men at the police station to assure them the noise they hear is nothing to worry about. They won't bother you."

"I was reluctant to do the mission, considering the shape we were in, but I thought the job was simple enough that we could handle it. It took less than a half-hour to get our armor on, weapons loaded, and the plastic demo charges packed in the van. We left town driving south on A-14, and as soon as we got within a few miles of Coretta we started looking for the markers that we had noted from the Google Maps and sat photos.

"As we drove into town, it was obvious where the center of town was located. The church we had spotted on the pics and sat photos was easy to find.

"I spent the next 10 minutes setting things up, noting an alleyway beside the church, where we would park the minivan. We would circle around the villa until we were directly behind it, and at the foot of the bluff.

"Yeah, we were pretty cocky, and I'm sure we were still feeling the effects of the wine and jet lag as we surveyed the town. It was about two a.m. and the town was totally vacant. It was a quiet as a mouse pissing on cotton..."

"Damn, Josh, can't you spare us that Arkansas drivel?" Sybil said suddenly.

"Hell, Sybil, don't you like a little color in a story?"

"Oh, go ahead; I do want to hear how you managed to get Don Pastori out of that villa."

"Well, as simple as the job looked, I couldn't imagine anything that could go wrong. After one more checkoff, we headed back out of town, and when we were far enough from the villa to not be seen, Bruce and I hopped out.

"I told Davis to let the rest of the guys out a few blocks away from the church, park the minivan, place a plastic charge on the gate, and then stay concealed until the lights went off. I also said to remember that when the lights went off in the villa, they would know that it would be two seconds until the demo charge went off.

"The team said they were good to go, so I said, "good, let's do the job.

"Bruce and I put on night visions goggles (NVG's) and started walking across a vineyard making a circle around the edge of town. The church steeple was well lighted so we didn't have any trouble keeping our bearings. However, the terrain around the edge of the steep bluff was rocky, and even with NVG's we were stumbling and moving slowly. It took a lot longer than I had figured. When we got to the bluff face we managed to move up the first twenty or so feet fairly easily, but finding cracks to put our pegs in was becoming harder and harder. I began to think we might have to call off the mission. However, Bruce is a climbing whiz and with his rubber hammer tamping in pegs, we steadily moved up. It took at least an hour until we made it to the top of the courtyard wall.

"I whispered for him to stop where he was and let me look over the edge of the wall. Then I was just about to pull myself up to could see over the wall when I heard the crunch of someone walking on gravel. The footsteps were coming directly toward where I was hanging right below the wall. I held on with one hand and pulled out my Glock .9 mm, with silencer.

"Finally, the sounds of walking stopped and a man's head appeared over the top of the wall. He was no more than three feet away. I shot him in the face before he could move, and pulled myself upon the top of the wall, just as another man with a flashlight came running around the corner.

"I shot him twice before he fell. And then I knew we had to move quickly because, even with a silencer, the Glock made a distinctly pistol-like sound. We would have others coming to check things out in a few seconds. Our lunch run [quick and easy job] was beginning to have problems."

"I whispered hoarsley for Bruce to hurry and cut the electricity on the house while I took care of the demo on the door!

"Hell, I could hear voices, and it sounded like several men excitedly talking. We were too deep into the rescue to back off now so as Bruce ran to cut the electricity, I headed for the back door with the plastic charge. Just as I wired the charge to the door, the lights went out.

"Then I knew all hell was going to break loose in the front, and we'd be right in the middle of it a few seconds later when we entered the house. As I listened to the chatter from the house and courtyard, for the first time I thought we might have been misled about the number of Mafia guards there, but before I could even think, there was a tremendous explosion. It was the charge Davis had placed on the front gate.

"I had a moment of regret that I had told him to be sure and place a charge big enough to blow that gate to hell. Pieces of that gate were blown over the house, and not only was the gate taken out, but about ten feet of wall with it.

"Bruce ran over to where I had retreated, which was back against the wall about twenty yards from the back door, and we crouched down. I slowly counted the seconds, and then touched the wires together. A millisecond later, there was a hole in the villa where the door had been, and we sprinted toward it, pulling out flash-bang grenades.

"I threw one just inside the open hole where there had been a door and Bruce chucked his as far down the hall as he could. We turned and ducked our heads down and waited for the thunderous explosion and flash. About that time, some automatic weapon fire began coming from the front courtyard, and I figured our team out front was in a firefight with the Mafia guards. Our two flash-bangs went off about a half-second apart, and we dashed into the villa after the blinding light dimished.

"Two men in the hallway were trying to make their way toward the door when we shot them, and as we stepped over their bodies, two other men fired from another room off to one side. Having NVG's with everyone else in the house in the dark or blinded by the flash-bangs was the only reason we weren't killed. We eliminated the other two men and turned down the hallway where the door to the basement was located. It was locked.

"We shot the lock off, threw a flash-bang down the stairwell, and followed it down to where a man was standing, blinded by the light. We shot him, and I slapped a plastic charge on the bolted door. In seconds, the charge blew the lock off—along with most of the door—and I stepped in."

"I said, "Don Pastori? Are you in there?" And he simply answered, "Yes, Mr. Martin.""

"Of course, it crossed my mind, *How in the hell did he know my name*. But I just told him to hurry and come with me before the police came to check out the explosives.

"But he told me, "They won't come. We have taken care of that, but we need to leave because Amizana may have other guards nearby who might try to stop us.""

"As we rushed up the stairwell with Don Pastori, we heard another blast of automatic weapon fire. And when I got to the open hallway and looked out, I could see my team members kneeling, ready, in a firing position—and about a half-dozen dead Mafia guys sprawled out on the courtyard. I waved my weapon over my head, and we dashed out what was left of the front door toward a big hole in the villa wall where a gate had been, with the rest of the team following us.

"We got to the minivan in about five seconds, but before we could get in a car rounded the corner a block up from the church heading our way as fast as it could go. I've been in enough stuff all over the world to know that means one thing. They're coming after your ass!

"I yelled for Don Pastori to get in the backseat of the car and lie on the floorboard. Then I yelled as my team got ready to fire on a car full of men who had just pulled more than thirty meters up the road from us, and were piling out like the Keystone Cops.

"Take 'em out!" I yelled. A hail of fire from us knocked down the three on the driver's side of the car. But, before we could get all the shooters, two managed to get behind the car. Hell, we poured enough fire into that car to sink a battleship, but didn't get either one of them. We couldn't just drive off and have the bastards shoot the hell out of our minivan.

"Bruce," I yelled. "Do you have any flash-bangs left?"

"Yeah, a couple." he said.

"I asked him if he could throw them far enough to land behind the car. But before Bruce could answer, Davis said, "Give me the flash-bangs. I was a quarterback in college, and I can damn sure throw them that far"—And he could. After two booms, I ran around the car and, sure enough, the guys had turned to see what landed on the other side of the car, and when they did the flash blinded them. I shot both of them in the face and ran back to the minivan.

"By then, we just wanted to get out before something else happened. I asked, "Anybody got anything serious?" But we were basically okay.

"Then I asked Don Pastori if he had any problems."

"No, Mr. Martin,' he said, "My ears are still ringing from the bomb you threw down the stairs, but other than that I'm okay. If you

don't mind, please drive me to my villa in Palermo. I'm sure your
men could use a little rest, and I can have a doctor come by and check
on your wounds. Of course, we have business to attend to."

"I told him that was very kind of him. We were tired, and I told
him that if he could find us accommodations where we could rest up,
it would be appreciated."

"Of course, my villa has plenty of extra bedrooms and you and
your men will be my guests for as long as you care to stay," he
answered.

"So that's the story of why Don Pastori is willing to work with
us."

"That's a hell of a story, Josh," said Sybil, thoughtfully. "How
many of the Mafia did your team kill, but why did Don Pastori make
you the godfather of one of his grandchildren? Was it because you
rescued him?"

"The Italian police said ten men were killed in a Mafia shootout,
and since it was Mafia shooting Mafia—we weren't mentioned. And
Don Pastori made sure we weren't bothered by any police
investigation. You would not believe how tight the Mafia controls
things. Of course, they do it all from a web of hundreds of low-
ranking people, and nothing is ever out in the open.

"And I'll get to the godfather story in a bit, but it wasn't because
of the rescue.

"Well, back to the story: We arrived at Don Pastori's villa,
which, by the way, appeared to be just a nondescript, secluded house
off a side street in Palermo. However, once you walked into the big,
walled courtyard, you had a feeling that the villa might be rather nice.
And rather nice was the understatement of the year! It was huge and
lavish to the point of being mouth-dropping.

"After we had time to clean up and meet Don Pastori in the one
of his many large sitting rooms, he praised us for about ten minutes to
his wife, sons, and others. And then he told me he would be eternally
grateful since I had saved his life—and any service he could provide
would be gladly done. Of course, he added that since he had such a

large number of men working in his organization, he would expect some financial help with expenses, if we called on him for help later.

"Okay, I understand, but what about the godfather bit?"

"Well, you know we had some minor injuries so we need to get them tended to, and, of course, we were dead tired from jet lag and everything that had happened to us during the rescue. Don Pastori was the ultimate host, and he insisted that we stay until everyone was in shape to travel. Of course, we could have left the next day, but after lounging around the swimming pool, drinking Sangria, and eating pasta for a few days, it became difficult to leave."

"Yeah, I'll bet," quipped Sybil.

"Then another incident happened that really surprised me. One of Don Pastori's daughters was expecting her first child, and after we were there a few days, we were made aware that her pregnancy had been difficult up to that point, and her doctor had told her she could expect to have a breach birth, if the baby didn't turn. Two days after we were there, she went into labor and her regular doctor was out of town. He had gone to Rome and wasn't available. Don Pastori was frantic, and I tried to be helpful by calling the American Consulate.

"Then just blind luck. Someone at the consulate told me that a team of American doctors were in town at the University of Palermo Medical Center doing a seminar on prenatal surgery. It just so happened that one of the doctors was a childbirth specialist. To make a long story short, he came to the hospital and assisted one of the Italian doctors in the birth.

"The American doctor told me later that the Italian doctor was very capable, and he handled everything perfectly, but Don Pastori was convinced I had pulled off a major miracle, and he named me the baby's godfather—And there is a three-year-old kid around here somewhere named 'Josh.'

"That is the most over-the-top story I have ever heard," Gloria asserted. "So, did did you work with Don Pastori after that?"

"Yeah, and after a few other encounters with him, I began to know the routine. He is gracious, and he will do almost anything he can to help me, but he wants expense money, which, of course, is a lot more than his expenses could ever be. He's sure Uncle has deep pockets, and he won't do anything without being paid off.—Say, I think we're nearly there. Slow down and let the red car pass, and follow it."

Sybil was clearly out of her element since she was the Sicily CIA bureau chief, and she was having to follow a Mafia underling through town, but as the red car passed them and flashed his lights, she dutifully went along. They snaked around through the back streets Palermo for another 20 minutes, finally stopping in front of a nondescript store that sold religious items.

The driver of the red car, which had stopped in front of them, hopped out and rushed around to open Sybil's door for her. In perfect English, he said, "Please follow me, and watch your step; the stones are loose around the door stop."

Sybil, nodded and Josh began to converse with the man in Italian as they made their way into the store, with Gloria and Sybil following them. The man led them straight through the store where they weaved through racks of religious wear, wall icons, and shelves of books.

"Just a minute," the man said. He pressed his thumb down on a thumbprint reader and nodded as the door lock clicked.

"Follow me, and please use the handrail. This is a very old staircase and the steps are narrow."

The group climbed the stairs, and as they exited the stairwell, they walked into a second -floor restaurant.

After walking through the first floor, with its religious artifacts, candles, and robes, it was a shock to the senses to walk into a lavishly appointed restaurant occupying the entire second floor of the large building. Josh surveyed the room and sitting at a back table, with his back to the wall, was a bear of a man.

Don "The Bear" Pastori rose as Josh walked toward him, and soon they were embracing with the customary Italian style buss on each cheek—and then the extra buss, which is only given to someone of extraordinary stature. Don Pastori was as his nickname indicates, a stocky man, about 5-foot-6 inches tall, with salt-and-pepper black hair.

His complexion was a much darker shade than the average Sicilian, and his bushy eyebrows set off a sharp, stern face. Don Pastori's whole demeanor indicated that he was a man to be reckoned with. His pinky finger was bandaged, and Josh remembered the man who contacted him saying that Don Pastori's captors had cut off part of his little finger to put pressure on his associates.

"My friend, The Bear, so good to see you again!" enthused Josh. "I would like for you to meet Gloria and Sybil. They are American CIA Agents."

Sybil looked as if Josh had slapped her when he revealed her identity, but Don Pastori merely smiled and said, "Oh, yes, Senoia Sybil; we have never met, but I am well aware of your position, and I must say you run a very responsible office. My men tell me you work nearly ten hours a day."

Sybil tried to regain her composure as Josh laughed. "No secrets in Sicily, Sybil. At least not from The Bear."

"Ladies, you and Josh please join me. This is the best food in Sicily."

"I'm starving, Don Pastori. We'll be happy to join you," said Josh.

"Ah, very good, and don't bother to look at the menu. The staff will serve you only the best available. I am sure you will be pleased.

"But first we must have some good, red wine. Ladies, I know American women always ask for something like Chardonnay but, alas, Italians don't make a decent white wine. Ah, but we do make the best red wines in the world, and this afternoon we will enjoy them."

He waved his hand and a waiter delivered two bottles of what Josh recognized as a great Super Tuscan Red from an area north of Florence, wines that would rate a high three-figure price in a restaurant.

"You are spoiling us, Don Pastori," quipped Josh.

"Oh, don't worry my friend; wine is of no use unless it is shared with good friends, but maybe we can do some business that will help me pay for this modest wine."

"I hope we can, Don Pastori. But first it would be a sin against God if we did not enjoy your hospitality, and your wonderful food and wine."

"Yes, my friend it would, and coming from an American, it is an especially considered compliment. Too many Americans are in such a big rush to do something that they miss out on some of the finer parts of life. Here in Sicily, we believe in enjoying life, and I am glad to see that you are a Sicilian at heart. A toast to our friendship: May it endure and prosper."

Josh smiled, raised his glass and nodded for Gloria and Sybil to join in the toast, and so began a lengthy lunch stretching into mid-afternoon. It was during the first after-lunch glass of Grappa that Don Pastori mentioned business.

"Josh, I would be a foolish man if I believed you and your friends just happened by to join me for lunch. If there is any way I can assist you on your mysterious quest, please tell me."

"Don Pastori, for such a wonderful lunch a trip to your wonderful county would certainly be worth it, but, yes, you are right. We are here on business, and, as you know, my business is to go after those who threaten the United States."

"You think there are some in Sicily who are a threat to your country?"

"Yes, but not Sicilians. We have been tracking certain men from central Africa who we have reason to believe will try to use something terrible to kill many people—maybe not in Sicily, but possibly in Rome."

"You think these people may be in Sicily?"

"Maybe. But Sicily is probably not their final destination. If possible, we would like to apprehend them before they reach the mainland."

"Tell me more. Maybe some of the people who work for me have seen them."

"All right, this is what I think these people are doing…"

"Josh, I know you mean, al-Qaida, just say it. We are very familiar with them. Of course, our connections are strictly business. As you know, we ask no questions about the transfer of funds from one place to another, but we do not participate if violence is to be committed. These are just sometimes business partners—nothing more."

"I understand, Don Pastori—and, yes, I am talking about al-Qaida. They are transporting some very dangerous material from central Africa, and we know they left Libya in a fishing boat headed toward the Italian coast. One of their men, when questioned, mentioned Sicily. That's why we are here.

"Here is a description of the boat that may have docked at some eastern coastal port in your country during the past twenty-four hours. We have local Sicilians and our people trying to check every port in eastern Sicily, but we are very short-handed. We could use your assistance."

"Let me have the description of the boat you are looking for, and I will send it out to some of my associates along the coast," said Don Pastori. "By the time we finish our second glass of Grappa we may have an answer for you."

"You are very kind, Don Pastori."

"Thank you, Josh, but we are not a charity. It is a very expensive operation that I run here in Sicily, and my people are constantly asking for more and more operating funds."

Josh knew Don Pastori would never come out and ask for money, but he also knew that if his men found the location of the boat, it would require a hefty payment.

"Well, finding the boat would be a great favor, and our country would look upon it as one of genuine friendship."

"Yes, friendship is very nice, but let's see what my people can come up with before we talk 'friendship.' Friendship does not pay the bills."

Don Pastori nodded and one of his assistants came over. In minutes, the boat description was scanned, sent to Don Pastori's Nokia 920, and then forwarded to a long list of men, with an urgent message to respond as soon as possible.

"Now, let's put business behind us for a few minutes. Enjoy another glass of Grappa, and tell me about you new wife, Josh. Nafisa is her name, I believe. Is she becoming an American? One of my associates in Cordoba told me that the assassin Patto almost killed her. What happened to him? I heard they found him killed with his own knife."

"Yes, Don Pastori, Nafisa is becoming an American after nearly being killed. It was a horrible time for her in captivity. She was tied to a chair for days, but she's doing well now."

"Do you know what happened to Patto? You know he was hired by some who might be even in Italy—of course I would never hire him to do anything."

Josh, knew better because Patto, working as an assassin, had, as his clients, almost all of the Mafia dons in southern Italy, but he only smiled as Don Pastori cocked his eyebrows, knowing Josh had the answer to his question.

Josh knew that revealing classified CIA information to someone like Don Pastori, a noted Mafia don, was strictly forbidden, but he also knew that if Don Pastori could provide him with information about the boat with the biomaterial, then revealing classified information would be worth it.

Josh motioned for Don Pastori to lean toward him and whispered, "Send the servers away."

One wave of his hand and only Josh, Gloria, Sybil, and Don Pastori remained in the room. It was a shocking display of power and control.

"I killed Patto." Josh stated.

"Ha! Yes! That is what I told my consigliere! I knew it had to be you; of course, the Spanish police would not cooperate and tell me. For some reason they don't trust us."

Don Pastori leaned back in his chair smiling broadly. He knew Josh had given him classified information, and it pleased him greatly. He was about to finish his third glass of Grappa when the soft ding of his Nokia 920 alerted him to incoming text.

"Must be important to interrupt lunch," he mused, glancing at the message. "Humm, well, Josh, we do have some information that may be useful to you." Don Pastori stopped in mid-sentence as Josh instinctively leaned forward, anticipating information.

"My people didn't give me all the details, but, of course they are available from my man in charge of the area." Don Pastori hesitated a few seconds, and then finished the sentence… "and he will tell us where they found the boat."

"It will take him about a half-hour to drive here. We can wait on him in my downtown office. I am sure you need to make arrangements before we meet. I'll have one of my men escort your car through town to the CIA office, and then–let's say in an hour—he will be there to drive you to my downtown office."

"That is very kind of you Don Pastori. Yes, we do need to make arrangements before we meet."

Don Pastori rose and after Josh and his team did, also, they were escorted back out of the restaurant and to their car, which was double-parked on a very narrow street. A police officer was in the process of writing a ticket when they walked up. However, before Josh could protest, Don Pastori's man stepped forward and spoke only a couple of words. Josh couldn't hear what he said, but the policemen stopped writing the ticket and stopped traffic so they could get into the car and drive off.

As they weaved through traffic, Josh, pulled out a notepad, and wrote, "Don't talk! Car bugged!" Sybil and Gloria nodded and they proceeded to the Palermo office of the CIA. When the escort driver pulled up in front of a nondescript building—a building with absolutely no indication that any governmental agency of any kind occupied space there—Josh eyed Sybil.

"Yeah," she admitted, obviously chagrined. "This is my office."

As they walked to the front door, Josh quipped, "Well, so much for keeping secrets in Sicily." Sybil didn't particularly like the comment, and said, "Well, they may know where I work, but not much more."

"Oh, don't you think this walkway to the door is bugged?" asked Josh.

"What?"

"Yeah, that's an old trick. Sometimes things are so hot the agents start talking before they reach a safe room. I would be willing to bet there's a bug or two along this walkway."

That prompted an abrupt silence as Sybil used retina detection to gain entry. When they were in her office Josh began to review the situation, but Sybil stopped him.

"Josh, your actions and conversations with a Mafia don violate almost all CIA procedures. I can't believe you told him classified information. I'm afraid I will have to report it in my daily briefing."

"Listen up, Sybil, because I'm only going to say this one time: I'm in charge of this operation, and I am responsible for every action. If I decide to cozy up to a Mafia don, that is my decision, and for god's sake, don't you think Don Pastori already knew about me killing that assassin Patto? Hell, the Mafia and al-Qaida work hand-in-glove, and al-Qaida sure knew I killed the sorry bastard.

"Look, we have got to get every scrap of info from Don Pastori we can, and to do that, we have to get him to double-cross some of his al-Qaida business partners. Now go ahead and report every word I said to Don Pastori, but be sure to copy General Davis."

The comment about copying Gen. Davis set Sybil back, but not for long.

"Josh, the CIA hasn't been able to confirm that there is a direct working arrangement with al-Qaida and the Mafia…"

"Shit, Sybil, you must be deaf. Didn't you hear Don Pastori mention business connections with them? Hell, forget protocol, and let's talk about what we need to do. First off, we're going to have to come up with some serious money to get exactly what we want, and it's not just where the boat is parked.

"I will be willing to bet al-Qaida has switched boats, and all we we'll have is an empty boat. We need to find out the who and where, and that's going to cost an arm and a leg—How much cash do you have on hand?"

"I have *some*, but…"

"No buts, Sybil… how much?"

"Two-hundred and fifty thousand but…"

"Put it in a bag, with the hundred thousand I have, and request another seven-hundred thousand from HQ. Gloria will patch you through."

"Josh, I will have to get authorization…"

"HQ will okay it when you ask for the seven-hundred I need. Just tell them you are acting on the direct orders from Josh Martin and General Davis will confirm."

Sybil walked back to her inner office and minutes later returned.

"Damn, Josh, you have enough clout for all of us. They're flying in the bucks you wanted later today."

"Thanks, Sybil. Now let's get down to business. In a few minutes, a car from Don Pastori will be by to pick us up. It is bugged, of course, and the driver will profess not to speak English. This is what we need to do—discuss the information we need, but mention satellite pics that we are tracking and anything else that sounds as if we have other sources of information. We want him to have the feeling he is not the only source we have.

Of course, he *is*, and we'll pay almost anything to find out who rented the boat that is heading toward the Italian coast, and where it will land. But if Don Pastori thinks he has critical information that we can only get from him, he'll up the price so much you won't believe it. So posture as if we're going to have it, like tomorrow. Everybody got it?"

Josh walked over to the office computer and checked the security cameras that covered the driveway in front of the office.

"Okay, let's go; he just pulled up. Hand me the money bag, and, Sybil, I know you are wired; every agent is. Record every word Don Pastori says."

"I will, Josh."

Josh led the agents out to the waiting car, and this time a motorcycle policeman escorted their car through the maze of traffic. As they approached the center of town, Josh leaned over to speak to Sybil.

"By the time we're done with this meeting we should have satellite blowups of every port in western Sicily. I don't think we'll have much trouble picking out the boat with the description we have. But finding out where the boat docked is not going to be worth much to us. We need a lot more information than that."

There was a slight smile from Gloria, who knew Josh was speaking loudly and clearly, hoping that Don Pastori would be picking up the conversation. As they reached a new glass-and-steel office building on the corner of one of the busier streets in town, the police officer stopped the oncoming lanes of traffic, and their car made a U-turn into an underground garage. The steel, underground door opened and their car continued to the elevators. In a few seconds, they were standing in an outer office being ask if they would like coffee.

"Yes, we would all like cappuccino, and please bring a small amount of extra cream, please," said Josh in perfect Italian. A few minutes later, they were sipping a rather strong cup of coffee that Josh had doctored with extra cream to make it fit an American palate. And then Don Pastori walked out from his office.

"Welcome to my modest office," Don Pastori enthused, as Josh shook his hand and then received the customary buss. "Modest office" was an understatement. The office was demure, but stylishly decorated in elegant but extremely expensive taste.

"Put your coffee down and follow me into our conference room," Don Pastori instructed. "Someone will bring your cappuccinos to our meeting."

They walked down a dimly lit hallway, and, at the end, stepped into a large, open room featuring a 20-foot-long, ornate, walnut table with 12 heavy chairs. One man sat near the end of the table with a beat-up folder in front of him. Don Pastori took a place near him at the head of the table, and motioned for the others to join him. After their drinks arrived, Don Pastori began to discuss finding the boat.

"Josh, as you know, we have a very large organization here in Sicily. Very little comes or goes that we don't know about. I have found out that information is good for business. Now, let's talk about the boat you were looking for. My man has pictures he took just an hour ago of the boat. From the description you gave me, I am sure it is the right one.

According to one of our people who lives nearby, the men who came in the boat arrived late yesterday." Don Pastori pushed the folder toward Josh, but Josh made no move to look at it.

"Don Pastori, you continue to amaze me at how efficient your organization operates. However, the boat is just a boat unless it comes with the men who brought it here. And from what I gather, they are gone. That is what we need to discuss."

There was an uncomfortable silence around the table until Josh lifted his briefcase and placed it on the table.

"Don Pastori, I understand how delicate your relationships are with your business associates, but I need to know more than where the boat is located."

"Josh, I wish I could tell you where the men went, and what they are doing now, but I have only so much information."

"That is regrettable, because I will have find out this information in the usual manner."

Don Pastori looked puzzled.

"In the usual manner? What do you mean?"

"By five o'clock we will have another twenty agents on the ground and with our satellite blowup, we will pinpoint the boat and begin questioning everyone who lives around the port. I know you are aware of how we get information. It's right here in this briefcase."

"Josh, it might be easier for me to find out some of these things for you, but if I use my men it will be very costly. Just exactly what do you want to know?"

"Don Pastori, I actually need very little information, but I need it in a hurry. I want to know where the men from this boat went. I think they bought or rented another boat and left in that one. And I need to know their destination and an exact description of the boat."

"Humm, you are asking for very little, but it will be difficult to come by. I have found out these men are connected to some loyal clients, and it is impossible for me to release any private information."

"I understand, Don Pastori, but the information I seek is so critical that I must ask you to betray your confidence with your clients in order to save thousands of lives."

"Josh, you are forever telling me that what you are doing will save thousands. Surely you don't expect me to believe that."

Josh snapped open the briefcase and opened it wide enough for Don Pastori to see inside. Then he said, "I will leave this briefcase on the table and walk away for the information I requested. It is a million American dollars in cash."

"Josh, I am a man of modest means, and certainly this is a great temptation, but money sometimes cannot buy the betrayal of an associate."

There was silence around the table as Josh considered the situation. Then as he surveyed the room, adorned with an Old Master painting of Christ with Mary, he thought of something.

"If your actions in some way protected the Pope from harm, would you reconsider?"

"The Pope? You cannot be serious! How could my betrayal of a confidence have anything to do with the Pope?"

Josh leaned back and slowly went over the mission he was on, and as he wove the pattern that the al-Qaida fighters were taking, he told Don Pastori how he believed these men were going to use the biomaterial to poison the crowd that assembled to hear the Pope.

Don Pastori was shaking his head as Josh finished.

"They always told me it was the Americans they were after, and that the help I gave them would never be used for terrorism. They were usually just laundering money. But I must take what you have told me very seriously. If I didn't, and something terrible happened, I could never forgive myself.

"Yes, you shall have the information you requested by dark. I'll call you on your cell—have you changed the number?"

"No, Don Pastori, you have the correct number. But how will you extract the information?"

"The man who rented the boat has*** family."

Josh nodded and got up to leave, and as he did so he closed the briefcase.

"Josh, leave the briefcase."

As Josh turned to leave the room, he looked back at Don Pastori.

"This is an urgent matter, Don Pastori. These men may already be on their way to Rome. Time is not on our side."

"I will have my best men on it within the hour. Expect a call before five o'clock."

It was a silent ride back to Sybil's office, but as soon as they were inside, Sybil began to question Josh.

"Do you think we'll get the info we need?"

"Yes, but it probably won't be everything. The bastards we are after would not leave a very good trail. However, Don Pastori will get something even if he has to make it up. There's nothing to do now, but to wait on his call. But while we're waiting lets coordinate the search for the boat, if we assume it's heading for the Italian mainland. Even if it left when Don Pastori thought it did, they couldn't have made it to any port close to Rome.

"Gloria, have the AWAC's work off a grid that encompasses the Italian coastline all the way up to the old port of Rome: Lido di Ostia. And Sybil, get your CIA agents to stand by for deployment along the Italian coast and on all entry roads into Rome. Gloria, call HQ and ask them to inform the Italian Government that we believe the material is headed to Rome. Tell them we will probably need Italian cooperation, and their men on the ground between the west coast of Italy and Rome. Details will follow as soon as we have new information."

For the next two hours, the three plotted grids for the AWAC's, as well as road, and waterway checkpoints for the CIA agents. It was almost 5 when Josh received a text message from Don Pastori: **Josh, could not question the right person, but we do have some information. The person who rented the boat lives at 545 Tviilie near the port of Catania. We could not locate him, but his neighbors told us he would be back later. He is an Egyptian guest worker. We do have a description of the boat he rented, and a picture. I will forward it to you shortly.**

29

Deception

Josh didn't want to think they had wasted precious hours being solicitous to Don Pastori, but he felt frustrated having to wait on anybody or anything. His thoughts were interrupted by a ding on Sybil's encrypted fax, announcing an incoming document.

"It's probably nothing," she commented walking over to the printer and releasing the print by fingerprint I. D.

"Josh, it's from HQ! It's a report on all the cellphone calls and other information from the stuff you retrieved from the fighters you and your men killed in Libya."

"Clear off your conference room table and the three of us will go over everything," Josh said as he viewed the flood of papers being spit out by the fax printer. There were volumes, and at a glance, he knew 99 percent of what was on the various cellphones and other papers would be worthless, but he knew from experience that one kernel of critical information might be in the stack of translated data.

Hours later, they had managed to high-grade the volume of papers into several piles.

"Sybil, go over to the European wall map, and put a location pin in every country or city we call out. Gloria, help me work through these two stacks. Every time you see a call to a European city, shout it out, and I'll do the same as I work through this other bunch.""Rome," yelled Gloria as she turned over the first sheet on the 6-inch pile of paper. It was after midnight when they finished.

"My god, Josh, we've got to get some rest. I can't even think any more."

"You're right, Sybil. You and Gloria go into the safe room and get a little rest. I've been trained to concentrate when I'm exhausted."

Sybil and Gloria were too tired to object, and they left Josh staring at the map of Europe covered with pins. They had placed aside all the translated calls with European destinations.

Josh, methodically eliminated each call that was to a relative or a business, using ******classified. Then he pulled all the pins that were calls to women. As he worked through the night, he looked for a pattern of calls. Gloria and Sybil walked back in the room just as he finished the last high-grade of the data.

"Okay, you're fresh. Take a look at the remaining pins. What's your impression?"

In a couple of minutes both women nodded, and Gloria spoke first, "Italy and Rome; it looks pretty clear to me."

"Yes, I agree," said Sybil.

"Well, don't you think it's a little too clear?"

"Huh?" said Sybil.

"Hell, a junior agent right out of college, just hired, would jump all over Italy. I think we're being lured off the trail—again! Whoever is heading up the al-Qaida group pulling off this thing has been feeding us crap for days to slow down the chase. I think they knew we would have this stuff after we found out where they had offloaded the biomaterial. Let's skip Italy for now and see if there are any clues, even the slightest hint of where that boat is heading. Now, forget Italy and let's look deeper."

It was two hours later when they had finished high-grading the remaining material.

"Okay, what have we got left?" asked Josh.

"Several cities in France seem to be the second choice," said Gloria.

"Forget France,'" Josh countered. "Too far. They would never expose themselves in that much open water, and the calls I've checked out from France are all to either women or family. What's next?"

"Well, there's Malta and Crete," offered Sybil.

"Yeah, I spotted Crete, too, but it's only one call and it could be nothing. The Malta call looks like it's to a business, so that leaves Crete. We can't act on a scrap of info. We don't have much choice but to go with Italy and put everyone on full alert. Gloria alert HQ."

Josh had walked over to review the pins in the map one more time when his cellphone dinged. A glance. "It's Don Pastori," Josh whispered as he answered. "Hello," he said, pushing the phone's speaker button so that everyone in the room could hear the conversation.

"Josh, I have some information for you, but I'm sorry it is not complete. As you know, we have located the boat that came from Libya. It is at dock three along the pier at Catania, and my men have been able to confirm what you were thinking.

"When the boat arrived a man everyone there knows as The Egyptian met it. He is a known smuggler, usually dealing with small stuff like cigarettes. My men were watching as he helped unload the boat. We monitor people like him to be sure they pay us our tax. I have a picture of three men and the Egyptian unloading the boat that just arrived, and then loading something onto a nearby boat."

"Have your men talked with The Egyptian?" asked Josh.

"No, he has disappeared. We have asked everyone that knows him, and they all said they haven't seen him since yesterday. The boat they loaded left about mid-morning yesterday, and no one has seen him since. However, we do know where he lives. The address is number three Traduce Street. It is only a few steps from the dock. I will send you a picture of the house and, of course, the new boat."

"Don Pastori, did anyone overhear where the boat might be going, or in what direction it was heading?"

"No, when someone attempted to speak to the three-man crew, the Egyptian would step between them and talk. He didn't mention any destination, but a fisherman told one of my men the boat headed up the coast toward the mainland. I'm sorry, Josh, but that's all I have. Maybe I should send the money back."

"You have been a great help, Don Pastori. May God bless you for what you have done. Please send the photos as soon as possible—and you may keep all of the money."

Josh hung up the phone and walked over to where a large map of Sicily and the southern Italian coast was hanging. Sybil and Gloria followed him, and then Sybil smiled and said, "What's this 'may God bless you' to a Mafia don?"

"Didn't you see how his office and restaurant were covered with religious icons, paintings, and pictures of church festivals were everywhere?"

"But a Mafia don can't be a Christian, can he?"

"Only God can answer that, Sybil, but remember he only consented to betray al-Qaida after I told him the attack might be directed toward the Pope. Anyway, I want to keep on his good side, and that's why I told him to keep the money. Hell, the Mafia isn't just a Sicilian organization; it's all over Italy, and that money and 'may God bless you' might help get cooperation from hundreds of Mafia underlings in Rome. But enough about Don Pastori. Let's see if the information he gave us is any help."

Josh traced his finger up the coast of Sicily from Catania then, as he started toward the Italian mainland, he stopped.

"Josh, if the boat keeps going north, then any small port on the coast opposite Rome would be an ideal offloading spot and a short drive to Rome. Don't you think we should alert HQ and send some agents into every city on the western Italian coast, and have the docks covered?" Gloria asked.

"If?"

"Well, that's the logical route of the boat, that is if you use the vector approach."

"What if you don't?"

"I don't understand... oh, I see; the boat could turn and go east into the Aegean Sea."

"That's right, Gloria, but the odds of it doing that are what?"

"Nil," said Sybil.

"That's exactly right," said Josh, "but it's important to not overlook any possibility, even one that slim. I think that's about all we can get from the info Don Pastori gave us so there is just one thing left for us to do. We need to search the house where The Egyptian lives."

"Do you want me to get a search warrant?" asked Sybil. "I can have one in a couple of hours."

"No, we won't waste any time getting a search warrant. They already have a ten-hour head start, and we can't afford to give them any more time. Let's take the jet and fly to Catania. From the info Don Pastori gave us we shouldn't have any trouble finding the house. Sybil have a car waiting for us at the Catania airport when we arrive. We don't need a driver."

"It will be waiting for us, Josh."

The flight to Catania took less than an hour, and the search for The Egyptian's house, even less time.

"Sybil, park the car where it shields the door. I'm going to use a couple of tools I have since we don't have a key."

Sybil pulled the sedan up so that the car blocked the view of the front door from the street, and Josh hopped out. As he pulled out his lock jammer and pick, he stopped. *Was that noise coming from inside the house?* crossed his mind. He then spotted a young boy coming around the side of the house next door pushing a bicycle. *Yeah, that's what I heard.* Seconds later, he twisted the lock jammer and the door opened.

Josh pulled his Glock .9 mm, waved the two women to follow him, and shoved the door open with his foot. He stepped back, the peeked in, and finally walked inside the house. The room was almost bare with only a beat-up couch, a TV and two chairs. The kitchen was just part of the larger room and he could see an empty bedroom off to his right.

"Sybil, take the bedroom, Gloria you check the kitchen, and I'll check out this room."

Josh kept his Glock ready with the safety off as he slowly and methodically went over everything in the room. He was surprised at how little he was finding. By the time Gloria and Sybil had finished searching the kitchen and bedroom, Josh was down to thumbing through a stack of magazines that had been left on a coffee table. He dropped the last magazine back in the stack as the women returned to where Josh was standing. They were shaking their heads as they walked up.

"Absolutely nothing, Josh," Sybil said. Gloria nodded the same.

"Well, I'm not surprised. The guys we're following have been very careful not to leave anything behind. It looks like we'll have to try and intercept them somewhere along the upper Italian coast—hey, wait a minute. Did anyone check that small closet in the corner? I'd better check it out just to be sure we didn't miss anything."

Josh stepped over, grasped the knob on the door, and pulled it. The door began to open, but as it opened there was a thud against the door and the force of someone's shoulder sent the door slamming back against Josh, who was knocked back against the wall. A fraction of a second later a man burst out of the closet with a revolver in his hand, firing at Sybil and Gloria. Sybil clutched her arm and fell back over the couch as Gloria ducked for cover behind one of the overstuffed chairs.

As she ducked out of sight, the man turned to shoot Josh, but he was too slow. Josh's first shot hit him above his right eye and the second hit him 2 inches lower. It was all over in less than two seconds.

"Sybil, are you okay?"

"Yeah, it's just a bad scratch. Hell, I'm glad these bastards are such bad shots."

"Well, that one won't be taking any more shots. I'm guessing he's The Egyptian, by the way he looks. Let me check to see if he left anything in the broom-closet while Gloria checks his pockets."

Five minutes later, Josh shook his head as he walked out of the closet. "Nothing here. What did he have on him, Gloria?"

"Just a wallet and cellphone. Nothing else. The wallet's about as empty as anything I have ever seen, and it looks as if he's deleted everything on his cellphone. Here take a look."

Josh, glanced at the phone just as a call-back number popped up. It was an interrupted call. "He must have been on the phone when we pulled up in front of the house."

"Gloria, I just got a call-back number. Check out the country and area code. It's thirty for country and two-hundred and eighty-one area."

Gloria pulled out her Nokia 920, went to the Bing search engine, and typed in the number. "Just a second, Josh; the info's coming up—oh my god, it's Crete!"

30

The Trail

Josh was stunned. He had noted Malta and Crete as possible destinations, but it was only because he didn't want to discard any clues. He was speechless for a few seconds.

"My god!" he exclaimed. "It all makes sense now. Even the Pope's speaking to thousands—the perfect target—the text messages and cell calls, all pointing to Italy and Rome. They knew we'd put that all together and focus on Italy."

"Josh, are they really heading to Crete?" asked Gloria.

"No, it won't be Crete. They would never bother with such a small target, but, yes, a staging area to attack... where? Gloria, what's the largest city in proximity to Crete?"

"How big, Josh?"

"What's the biggest, one that would have a large square where thousands congregate?"

"Well, that's easy; there's only one, unless you go all the way to Istanbul. It's Athens, and with all the demonstrations in Constitution Square because of the opposition to the austerity measures mandated by the European Union, you can be sure they will have a square full of people at least once a week."

"Yes, Athens—where the world's the first democracy was founded. They hate our system of government and hitting Greece would be a perfect place for them to strike a blow against democracy. It must be Athens, but I feel sure the boat they rented here in Sicily won't be the one they take there. They will undoubtedly spend some time on Crete before they try to make it to Athens. We may have a couple of days to track them down on Crete."

"But Josh, everything else points to Italy. Are we going to use all our resources to focus on Crete and Athens when the attack may be on Rome?" questioned Sybil.

"No, we can't take the risk that we're wrong, so keep the high alert on Italy, but we must shift some of our resources to check out Crete. Take this phone number and have the CIA agent on Crete check it out. Tell him to go directly to the address associated with this phone and interview the person who owns it. Tell him exactly what we're looking for, give him the boat description, and have him use his local assets to comb every port on the western and northwestern coast of Crete—Got it?"

"Gloria, keep the AWAC's working the Italian west coast grid, but ask HQ to assign extra surveillance from Sicily to Crete and then continue to fly a grid to the Greek mainland. One other thing, Sybil; be sure your man on Crete has some support when he goes to that cellphone address. These people are ruthless, and we don't want a lone agent walking into an ambush."

"I'll get right on it, Josh. This little grazed shoulder from the bullet doesn't need treatment. I'll just put a little antibiotic on it and a Band-Aid. That will take care of it," said Sybil.

"Josh, I'll contact the local police about the man you killed. We can claim diplomatic immunity, and, of course, it was in self-defense…"

"Forget calling the police. I'll take care of the body and the investigation."

"What. How? Josh, we have very good connections here in Sicily…"

"I said, I would take care of it," said Josh. He pulled out his Nokia 920 and speed-dialed a number.

"Don Pastori, I hope you are feeling well. Yes, I'm fine, but we have a small problem. The man known as The Egyptian was in the house when we went to check it out, and there was a confrontation… yes, he's dead… no of course we haven't called the police... I would certainly appreciate your help... fine. We will wait until your man arrives.

"Thank you Don Pastori, you are a true friend. May God bless you."

Josh slipped the Nokia 920 back into his shoulder holster and turned the two women, who were looking at him inquisitively.

"Someone will be by in a few minutes to pick up the body and dispose of it," said Josh succinctly.

"Josh, you know I'll have to include this in my report," said Sybil.

"Of course, Sybil. Just tell them I authorized it over your objections due to time constraints," Josh said. "Now, while we're waiting on someone to come by and dispose of The Egyptian, let's formulate our plans on how to approach Crete while continuing to monitor the Italian coast."

"Josh, I still think Crete is a long shot. I'm not comfortable with weakening our surveillance along the Italian coast."

"Neither am I, Sybil, but we can solve some of that problem by having your man on Crete track down that phone number on The Egyptian's phone."

"Yes, I agree, and I've already contacted him to trace the call. We should have something from him within the next four hours."

"Very good. Okay, then we'll keep the surveillance of the Italian coast as a top priority until we get some definite clues that point elsewhere. Wait a minute—someone's outside; it must be the man Don Pastori sent to pick up The Egyptian."

Josh opened the door and a man holding a body bag was standing there with two women behind him, carrying cleaning equipment.

"Good evening, sir; my name is Leonardo and these women are Maria and Sofia, my assistants. I understand someone here has been in a tragic accident."

"Yes, Leonardo, you are at the correct house. I'm Josh; Gloria and Sybil, my associates, are inside. Follow me, and I'll show you the body."

Leonardo and the two women followed Josh inside, spoke to Gloria and Sybil, and went straight to where The Egyptian was lying. Leonardo quickly slipped the man into the body bag, zipped it up, and carried it to a van parked outside.

As soon as he was out of the way, the two women began to clean up the blood and other material on the floor where The Egyptian had fallen. Josh's Glock .9 mm had done its work rather well and it took more than a few minutes for the women to clean things up. They had just finished when Leonardo walked back in.

"Sir, Don Pastori said to give you his best, and to tell you that this matter has been taken care of."

"Thank you, and tell Don Pastori I said, 'May God bless him for his generosity.' I will not forget his kindness."

"Yes, thank you sir. Don Pastori is a very devout man, and he will certainly appreciate your thoughts." And with that comment, Leonardo and the two women left.

Sybil shook her head, and said to Josh, "I've been posted here for nearly a year, and I am still shocked at how the Mafia controls so much of this country. I thought the Government had cleaned things up, but evidently that didn't pertain to Sicily."

"The Government only made the Mafia keep their heads down by grabbing a few of the more visible Dons. The majority of the Mafia's operations are still active, especially in Sicily. We need to be very solicitous to Don Pastori. We may need his help in Rome and even in Crete."

"The Mafia is in Crete?" asked Sybil.

"Of course, and if the biomaterial gets out of Crete, and makes it to Athens somehow, we can really use his help there. The Greek Mafia, or whatever they are called, is alive and well in Athens, and these guys do favors for each other."

"Josh it still looks as if there's a good chance that al-Qaida is heading for Rome. Are we going to set up a command post in Rome?" asked Sybil.

"Not right now. We can't leave here until we get more info on which country the bastards are going to target."

"Gloria, what I want you to do is to review every scrap of information, and see if we have overlooked anything. Then you need to high-grade every possible port on the Italian coast. Be sure to review the roads leading to Rome—places where we can set up checkpoints between the port and Rome if we get an I. D. from AWAC's or other info.

"And Sybil, you do the same thing with Crete. I'll take Malta, and I'll get back in touch with Don Pastori and have him give his counterparts in Italy and Crete a heads-up."

Josh stayed in touch with HQ for the rest of the day and night as the AWAC's began to comb the seas off the Italian coast from the air, and the Italian security units working with the CIA agents and local assets tried to check every boat in every port along the Italian coast. Every pass of AWAC's and every boat that was checked without any results increased the tension Josh felt.

Three hours passed and the team now had a list of ports in all three countries, as well as a plot of all available roads or trails that might allow al-Qaida to have access to either mainland Italy, Greece, or Malta.

"Sybil, how do most people get from Crete to mainland Greece?"

"I guess the hydrofoils carry more people, but there are car ferries that take a good number, and of course there are numerous flights."

"Okay, those are all the obvious. If you were trying to get into Greece and avoid detection, how would you do it?"

"Well, knowing we would have all the ones I mentioned covered... it would have to be either a small private plane or a boat."

"Yeah, a small plane is probably the most likely, but the AWAC's would spot it, and we might be able to track it and intercept it when it lands. I'm leaning toward a very fast boat. One that would leave in the wake of a hydrofoil, and use the hydrofoil for cover until they got close enough to the coast to make a run for it."

As they were reviewing the possibilities, Sybil's encrypted cell made an unusual beep. She jumped up from the table and rushed to her desk to answer the phone.

"Emergency call, Josh. I programmed it so when it's a very high-level call to beep—Hello? Yes, go ahead... Oh my god, are you sure?***Yes, it's extremely important... do you have any description of the gunmen?*** Okay, when you have more details, get back to me. Goodbye."

"Damn, our agent in Crete and two locals assets were gunned down in Akra Melissa, Crete. They were at the house where the phone number was registered, and were attempting to enter the house, when the door opened and four men rushed out shooting. One of the local assets managed to get away, and he said the men looked foreign, but that's all the info we have.

"The men left the house and drove off on a road leading to the central Crete town of Gortya. The police are on the way. We'll get more details later."

"Hold on, let me get the blowup of Crete and let's find the town of Akra Melissa."

The team poured over the map until they found a small fishing village on the country's southwest coast.

"Yeah, here it is. Right on the coast, and it's a direct line from Sicily. Sybil have someone go to the docks and see if the boat that left Sicily is there. I'd bet almost anything it is, but it will be empty. If I had to make a guess, I would say they have off-loaded the biomaterial, and have taken it into the interior in preparation to move it to mainland Greece.

"Forget the town of Gortya. They would stand out like a sore thumb. They must have a hideout somewhere in the mountains of central Crete. Their next move will be to cross the Aegean Sea to the Greek mainland."

"Why do you think that, Josh?" asked Gloria.

"Several reasons: First, the boat they left Sicily in is too slow to cross that much water without being noted by our AWAC's: second, they have decided to make the jump to the Greek mainland in two hops to evade detection. This is the first hop, and the next one will be directly toward the target they've selected. And finally, they sure aren't going to stay in that little village or any other town. People in a small villages know everyone in town, and they would stick out, especially since there has been shooting in a town not far away. So they would normally head for the largest city in the country where they will blend in and not be noticed. However, they're too far away to do that so going into the interior is their only option.

"Get the AWAC's and satellite working on central Crete and give us the location of anything suspicious."

"Are we putting Crete at the top of our list?" asked Gloria.

"There is no list: it is *Crete*—start packing and call HQ to send a jet to pick us up and drop up off at Heraklion International Airport. Tell them we want transportation to stand by. We may have to fly to Greece at a moment's notice. Alert HQ that we are certain the biomaterial has been offloaded in Crete in preparation to moving it to Athens.

"Request all available agents and local assets to rendezvous with us in Heraklion. We will assign them when we meet. Got it?—Oh, one more thing; have a small surveillance chopper available. We'll probably need it to survey the interior."

Minutes later the team was driving to the airport, and as they wove through heavy traffic, Josh was busy on the phone calling Don Pastori.

"Don Pastori, we have very good reasons to believe the material I mentioned to you has been transferred to Crete, and they will probably try to get it to Athens. We need your help in tracking down the men who have the dangerous material."

"All my resources are available, Josh. But you must know that I will have to hire additional men to work in Crete and around Athens. I have excellent connections in Athens, but not so much in Crete. Can you fund the operation, if I have to move men into Crete?"

"You shall have the extra funds, Don Pastori. I'll have details where to assign your men later."

Josh clicked off his cell and turned to Gloria and Sybil.

"Hell, no wonder we didn't spot them along the Italian coast. They were heading for Crete with at least a twenty-four hour head start, and now they have the biomaterial within one- hundred and fifty miles of a major European city—and they're getting ready to transport it to Athens!

"Gloria, have HQ send us a plane. We're going to Crete, and call off the Italian coast watch and switch it to the Peloponnese. Sybil get the station head in Athens to deploy every agent and local asset available. With the AWAC's and radar tracking everything that moves in the air. We have to assume they will try to get the material into Greece by boat or small private plane."

It was a hectic few minutes as Josh and Gloria redeployed AWAC's, agents, and SFs from the western Italian coast to the Peloponnese and Greek mainland.

Less than an hour later, Gloria and Josh boarded the jet at the Catania International Airport, and an hour later they landed at Heraklion.

"Sybil, I'm sure you can arrange a suitable place for us to use as a base while we're in Crete."

"It's already been taken care of Josh—-just a minute; I just received some additional info from our on-the-ground agent in Akra Melissa—that's where our men were killed trying to pin down the person who received the al-Qaida cell call."

"Yeah, anything new?"

"Just a minute… Uh, huh a couple of things. One of the local assets has found the boat. You might know, it was empty. And here's another bit of info; four men were seen leaving Akra Melissa, heading north toward the village of Gortya. He said the area is very rugged country with numerous trails and sideroads."

"Well, they probably have a safe house somewhere in those mountains. Get satellite and AWAC coverage as soon as possible and get a car description from someone on the ground to them as soon as possible."

"Are we going to Akra Melissa and try to track them down?" asked Gloria.

"No, if we get back in the sticks, away from transportation, and they somehow managed to get the biomaterial to the mainland, we'd be up Shit Creek without a paddle. We'll stay put until we get another break."

"Josh, give us a break from that Arkansas slang," spit Sybil.

"You got it, bitch," said Josh, as he winked.

"Now let's see if we can narrow it down to exactly how they are going to try and get the stuff to Athens. And let's don't overlook anything, no matter how lame or obvious it might sound. Okay, our best info has four men with the biomaterial hiding out in the mountains of central Crete. I think that's to our advantage. After all, how many roads are in and out of that area? The first thing we need to do in to set up roadblocks on every road within twenty miles of where they were first spotted. Can you handle that, Sybil?"

"Yeah, our bureau in Athens has already informed the Greek Government that we have an emergency terrorist situation, and we need extra personnel to apprehend the suspects."

"Good, now first thing in the morning Gloria and I will take the stripped-down Black Hawk Chopper and survey the spots we've high-graded on the topo map. Sybil, you coordinate the surveillance along the northern coast."

"Okay, is everybody onboard? Good. It's late, so let's get a little rest and pick up where we left off at daylight."

31

A Missing Man

"Sonsin, our plans have changed. The Americans have somehow tracked us to Crete, and we must expedite the material to the mainland. Do you have the transportation ready to use?"

"Yes, Rasandi, everything is prepared just as you ordered."

"Good, contact Hasanni Abdula in Athens and alert him that the transfer will take place immediately. Tell him I will give him a pickup time and place, as soon as I am sure of where it will be."

"Yes, Rasandi, I will text him immediately."

"Very good, and tell him to get the other material as soon as possible."

***

Josh and the rest of the team spent another two hours reviewing the topo map of Crete. It was late and the team was about to leave for their quarters when Sybil got an emergency text from the Athens bureau chief.

"Josh, listen to this, Greek security forces just reported a break-in of a munitions depot near Corinth. Approximately fifty pounds of high-grade plastic explosives and cords were the only things stolen. This may not be connected to your mission, but I thought it was something you should be aware of.

"It's signed by the CIA Athens bureau chief. Do you think that has anything to do with the al-Qaida bunch we're chasing?"

"Damn right, I do! That much plastic explosive will blow up half a city block, and if the biomaterial is attached, it would contaminate thousands. We've got to nab those bastards within the next forty-eight hours or it'll be too late! But we can't accomplish anything else tonight. Get a little rest and report back here at daylight."

***

It was 5:50 the next morning when the team started to work again. Josh went to the large topographic wall map of central Crete that they had worked on the night before, and as he combed over the terrain again, he began to block off areas that could hide a possible safe house for the al-Qaida fighters. Sybil had satellite shots of Crete e-mailed to her from HQ, and with all the data, which now included satellite images and new AWAC pictures of central Crete, Josh was able to eliminate a large portion of the area.

However, he was concerned that even after eliminating that much of the central Crete highlands, there was still a large amount of uncharted territory that could conceal hundreds of men. The work continued all day and well into the night. Josh turned in to get his usual four hours of rest still unsure that they would locate their hideout the next day when they scanned the center of the country with the small chopper. But is was their only hope to intersect the al-Qaida terrorists before they reached the Greek mainland.

At daylight the next morning—while Sybil coordinated the roadblocks and checked the entry and exit points that would allow the material to leave the island—Josh and Gloria boarded the chopper, and by 10 o'clock they had eliminated five of the top possible sites. As place after place was checked off, Josh was getting concerned that they wouldn't be able to locate the house.

As they checked out mountain cabin after mountain cabin, the topographic map looked as if red ink had been spilled on it. Spot after spot was scratched off, and as they approach the most rugged areas of the central mountains, the terrain made it more difficult to discern whether the cabins they were checking out had places where someone could conceal a car.

It was well after lunch when Josh noted something suspicious. It was a rather simple cabin, but there was a shed in the back and a dim trail of a driveway leading from the front of the house around it to the back. It was hard to see what was in the shed, but Josh could make out a gray tarp covering something.

"Gloria, we've got to check this one out on the ground. That may be a junked car that's covered in the shed out back, but we've got to find out for sure. I think we can land about a mile away on this flat" cleared area," Josh said, pointing to a cleared spot on the topographic map.

"Ted, put us down at this clearing on the topographic map," Josh instructed He handed the pilot the topographic map and began checking his gear. "Gloria, we need to expect resistance if those guys are in that cabin. Get ready."

Josh took out his M-1 with a Dawson sipper scope and Gilles silencer, checked his ammo clip, and prepared to disembark. Ten minutes later, the chopper landed and Josh and Gloria started hiking cross-country toward the mountain cabin. They were about 200 yards from the cabin when Josh, after watching for movement at the cabin with his binoculars, waved Gloria down.

"There's a man just off the edge of the front porch," Josh said. He peered through his binoculars, and nodded, " he's armed. We can't get any closer unless we take him out."

"Josh, what if he's just a Greek hunter?"

"It's hunting season, Gloria, and even at this distance, I can tell that his weapon is not a hunting rifle."

"Well, just be sure. It would be a major international incident if you killed a Greek citizen just because he was carrying a weapon."

"Yeah, I know, and it sure as hell would be an international incident if these bastards managed to slip through our net and kill a hundred thousand people."

"Are you sure you can make the shot at this distance?"

"Yeah."

Josh sighted in, and a few seconds later there was a soft pop, and the man's head jerked as he flipped backward. He was motionless on the ground.

"Head shot," he whispered to Gloria.

"Come on, Gloria; follow me and don't make a sound. We're going to circle around to the back of the cabin. We may have just lucked out." Josh and Gloria slipped around to where he could get a view of the attached shed. "Now I can see the car, and it's the one described by the local police."

It took about an hour more to approach the back of the cabin, and as they did, Josh became very deliberate. His movement was so slow it was almost imperceptible. They had just entered an open area when Josh grabbed Gloria suddenly and pushed her down.

"Stay low; there's a gun barrel in that open window," he hissed. Those words were no more than out of his mouth when several rounds rattled from the window, kicking up pieces of the log they were hiding behind.

"Stay completely below the log and don't move," he whispered. Josh slowly crawled down to the end of the log and eased around so that he could see the window where the gun had been. He poked the barrel of his gun through some weeds, thumbed off the safety, and waited. Ten minutes passed and then 15. Finally 20 minutes slipped by, as Josh remained motionless.

It had almost been 30 minutes since the first shots were fired at them when the green top of a military-style cap became visible in the window. Josh's finger tightened on the trigger, and he waited. Soon the eyes of the fighter appeared, and Josh squeezed a little tighter. The man's nose came into view and then his chin, and his head began to turn to survey the area around the cabin. That was the last thing he saw, as Josh's round hit him in his left temple.

"Come on Gloria, we need to get to the road that leads down the mountain. I've got a feeling that the two men still there will try to leave before we nail them."

Josh and Gloria hurried around to the front so they could block the road leading from the house, but before they were in position, the terrorists' car, which had been concealed under the shed in the back, suddenly roared to life and headed down the road.

"Start firing, Gloria!" Josh yelled as the car sped down the road.

Gloria began to shoot at the driver, breaking the windshield and the side windows. But Josh leveled his M-1 and sent round after round into the vehicle's motor.

"Come on, Gloria. I sent enough lead into that motor to stop a tank. They'll try to make a run for it when the car stalls. I'll take the lead fighter and you take the one behind him. Got it?"

Josh and Gloria charged down the road after the speeding car, which was slowing down perceptibly.

"Get ready! The car's about to stop!"

No sooner than the words were out of his mouth, than the driver's side door flew open and an armed fighter exited, firing wildly in their direction. Gloria, who had an open shot, emptied her Beretta at the man hitting him with several rounds, none of which were enough to stop him, while Josh dropped to one knee and took aim, slightly leading the man, who was staggering down the road.

Just like deer hunting back in Arkansas crossed his mind as he squeezed off three quick rounds. They connected and sent the man spinning and rolling down the rocky road. However, because of the fighter's evasive running, Josh's rounds weren't fatal. And as Josh prepared to finish him off, his rifle jammed.

"Damn, take him out, Gloria!"

The fighter struggled to rise and manage to raise himself up on one knee as Gloria emptied the second magazine of her Beretta at him. She managed to hit him in the shoulder, but instead of falling, he turned and the AK-47 he was carrying sent a burst of fire toward Gloria and Josh. Bullets rattled through the surrounding trees and kicked up dirt beside them, just as Josh cleared his weapon of the jam, and his M-1's answering volley sent the fighter sprawling back into the ditch beside the road..

"Damn, I really wanted to capture at least one of them, but I'm not going to get much out of that one. Counting the two I shot, we've killed three, but the witnesses at Akra Meissa said there were four who drove off in that car over there."

"Do you think the other one's in the house?" asked Gloria.

"Maybe, but I'll be surprised after the shooting that he didn't show himself. Let's check out the house and see. Stay about twenty yards behind me and cover me, while I circle the house and look in the windows."

Josh carefully approached the cabin and crept along beside it peering into the windows as he passed them. He could see inside the large, one-room structure with a table and several chairs. It looked empty. *Damn, where did the other guy go?* kept crossing his mind. Finally, he finished an exterior check of the house and walked over to Gloria. "Looks like an empty house."

"Do you think the guy's hiding somewhere inside or in the woods?"

"No, I don't think so. I don't think anyone could have left the cabin and not be seen by us, and the room doesn't seem to have any closets or places to hide. But don't step on the porch or open a door until I give you an okay. Let's check out the one we shot before we go in."

Josh walked over to where the fighter's body and quickly checked to be sure he was dead.

"Yeah, he's with the forty virgins. Let's go check out the house; we'll come back and go over the car and body after we search. Keep your fingers crossed. We may have nipped this plot before they could get the stuff out."

Josh warily approached the porch, slowly walked up to the front door, and looked in each window beside the door. From these front windows, he could see almost the entire room, and there was no sign of anyone or anything of interest there.

Josh nodded to Gloria as he approached the door. He pulled out his knife, flipped it open, and ran it around the edge of the door.

"Don't touch the door! It's wired!*** Yeah, here's the lead and ground wires ***cut the ground first," he mumbled, pulling an all-purpose tool from his backpack. "Now the lead wire*** okay, it's disarmed. We can open it, but whatever you do don't open anything in the house. Just look until I check it out."

For the next hour, Josh and Gloria combed the cabin looking for the biomaterial. When nothing was found, they went to the car that had been used, and although it seemed the trunk had recently carried a heavy box—from indentions in the trunk mat—there was nothing in the car.

"Three men; and we have several witnesses who all said there were four men—two of them in the backseat and two in the front. I've got to believe four men came up here, and we're relatively certain that they had the bio stuff when they left Akra Melissa. Where in hell is the other man and all that deadly material? Come on let's go back to the house and see if we can find any clues about where he went."

It was two hours later when Josh retrieved a scrap of paper from a trashcan. The trash had been emptied, but stuck to the bottom of the trashcan was a piece of paper 3 inches long and 2 inches wide.

"Gloria, take a look at this. It looks like like it might be instructions on assembling something. Hell, I wonder why it's in English. Scan it, send it to HQ, and request an immediate run through every database available. This is the only clue we've got. It's probably nothing. Tell them it's an emergency, and run it immediately; then text us back within the hour. While we're waiting let's comb the outside and see if we can find anything else."

Josh and Gloria were outside looking at some scuffmarks on a rock plateau that dropped off abruptly when Gloria's cellphone dinged with a text.

"HQ is answering the scan, Josh—oh my god! The scrap of paper is from an instruction manual for a motorized hang glider!"

"A motorized hang glider? surely not!"

32

Athens

The shock that an al-Qaida fighter had managed not only to elude them, but toprobably launch a motorized hang glider had Josh almost in shock. He was either in the process of flying to the Greek mainland, or possibly had already landed, Josh thought. He had never even considered the possibility of using something of that nature. However, after taking a few minutes for the enormity of the situation to sink in, he went into action.

"Gloria, get HQ to check out the range of the motorized hang glider, assuming a light west-northwest wind of twelve to fifteen knots. Then notify our team in Athens and have them secure all roads leading into the city. I have a feeling that even with the hang glider motorized, it won't be able to make it all the way to Athens. He'll probably land somewhere on the Peloponnesian Peninsular since that's the nearest Greek mainland. Tell the team to immediately secure the Corinth main highway from the Peloponnesian to Athens. Got it?"

"Yeah, Josh, I'll get right on it."

Gloria grabbed her encrypted cell and in seconds was talking to HQ.

"Josh, they figured you would want to know the range of the hang glider when they found out what was on the scrap of paper. It's one-hundred and sixty miles, which would put it somewhere in the middle of the Peloponnesian peninsula. They already have AWAC's flying over the area, and satellite pics will be forthcoming. The Greek Government is being appraised as we speak, and they'll be asked to help intercept the fighter with the biomaterial."

"Gloria, I've been calculating how much time the al-Qaida carrier had to put the hang glider together, and about what time he could have flown out of here. He should be landing somewhere in the Peloponnesus right now. I don't think he would have had time to assemble the hang glider and fly to the mainland much before we arrived. We probably only missed him but by a few hours."

"Josh, what if the hang glider was already here and assembled, and all the man had to do was transfer the biomaterial into a backpack and fly toward the Peloponnesian coast?"

"Damn, you're right! If that's the case he could already be in Athens. Get our pilot on the phone and tell him we need to fly to Athens ASAP."

A shiver went up Josh's spine as he thought about trying to find a man who would be intent on hiding in a city of almost four million people. It seemed to Josh that he could eliminate certain parts of Athens and concentrate the search on the highest probability areas of the city, but he'd need all the help he could get. Josh's thoughts were interpreted by the thump-thump of the chopper, and, seconds later, they were flying to the airport. As the chopper headed for the airport at Heraklion, Josh quickly punched in a number on his Nokia 920.

"Don Pastori, this is Josh Martin. How are you today?

"I'm so glad to hear that*** "Good, yes you're right, I need your help. We've been unable to intercept the goods I told you about.

"How did you know we killed three of the al-Qaida fighters?...

"Yes, but...

"Are you sure?...

"As always, you are correct, and yes, your information is astounding...

"If your man is correct, the al-Qaida fighter should have landed somewhere on the Peloponnesian peninsula by now...."

"Yes, of course..."

"You believe the man and the material may already be in Athens? Are you sure?

"Could you have your contact in Athens help find the man we are looking for?

"Very good, and there is one other matter. A Greek government arsenal was robbed a day ago, and I think it may have something to do with spreading the biomaterial with explosives. The men got fifty kilos of plastic AZ explosives. I need any information about this robbery that you or your men in Athens can provide.

"Yes, I will confirm one million for your work and another million for the men working for you in Athens."

"Good, we will be in Athens in about two hours, and I will confirm that to your man there."

"The lobby of the Grande Bretagne Hotel? Yes, I know it well—eight-thirty will be fine."

"Oh, one more thing. I'll pay a bonus of one million Euros to the man who delivers any of the men we are looking for to me—alive."

"Thank you, Don Pastori, and may God bless you."

The jet, along with Sybil, was waiting for them when the chopper landed, and 41 minutes later, they landed at Athens International Airport. They skipped customs and had their driver take them directly to the Grande Bretagne Hotel where they were met by Ponder Sinuie, the Athens CIA bureau chief.

"Let's go to my room and review everything," said Josh, after a hurried introduction. As soon as they were in their suite, Sinuie pulled out a folded map of Greece and started pointing out roadblocks and other checkpoints leading into the city."

"Ponder, according to my sources, the al-Qaida fighter and the biomaterial may already be in the city."

"I think it might take days for the man to reach the city," Ponder said. "After all, he probably flew into a very remote part of the Peloponnese, and some of the roads down there are only passable with an off–road vehicles. By the way, who's your source?"

"Don Pastori. Do you know him?"

"Know him? Hell yes! He has his tentacles into Sicily, most of southern Italy, and even has connections in Greece. We've been helping the local authorities to accumulate enough evidence to indict him. But, shit, we know the Italians won't extradite him, so we're spinning our wheels. How did you get involved with that scumbag?"

"I'm the godfather of one of his kids." Josh smiled slightly, knowing that this comment to a CIA professional was going to be hard to swallow. There was a stunned silence from Sinuie, who finally was able to mumble a "But... but..."

Josh interrupted: "And I had the opportunity to do him a rather large favor. I saved his life. Listen, Ponder, I know it's strictly against standard protocol to deal with Mafia dons, but our situation is becoming more desperate by the minute. We've got to use every tool available or the sorry bastards are going to pull off something that will make nine-eleven look like a birthday party."

"I have his Athens connections already working for us, and I'm going to meet with the head of the Athens Mafia—or whatever they're called—in about an hour."

"You're going to be meeting with Alibis Dupoplious? My god, Josh, he's the most ruthless, corrupt mobster in the country. Hell, I wouldn't meet him without some support."

"I'll have Gloria with me."

"Shit*** Uh, no offense, Gloria... but whatever you do I wouldn't meet with him without enough firepower to control any situation that might occur. By the way, where's this meeting to take place?"

"Downstairs in the hotel lobby."

"You're not serious!"

"Damn right, I'm serious, Ponder. Now let's get a few things straight. First off, I'm in charge of this operation, and my orders are to do anything—and I mean anything on the face of the earth—to keep a horrific tragedy from occurring. And if I have to use the devil himself to accomplish that, I will."

"Now, let's set serious about using every potential resource to accomplish our mission. I want you, Sybil, and Gloria to work very closely with Dupoplious so we don't have any duplication of efforts. I'll set up a meeting for you when I meet with him later."

Josh was interrupted by a vibration of his Nokia 920. It was an emergency signal that ended with a low hum. He yanked out the cell from his black leather carrying pouch and glanced at the text message.

"Yeah, just as we suspected," he commented to Gloria and Sinuie. "The lab results confirm the material was in the trunk of the get-a-way car. Now, we know it's probably in Athens."

"Just a minute, Josh. I still think the stuff hasn't made it out of the Peloponnese."

"Well, that's always a possibility, Ponder, but Don Pastori thinks the stuff is already in Athens. Maybe we'll know after our meeting with Dupoplious, or maybe the AWAC's or satellite pics will tell us. Gloria and I need to head down to the lobby. You and Sybil review both situations, and develop the best interdiction methods you can. When Gloria and I return from our meeting with Dupoplious, we can see if they mesh with what his men are going to do. Let's go, Gloria. We don't want to keep the gentleman waiting."

Sinuie grimaced at "Gentleman" as Josh and Gloria headed downstairs to the lobby.

The two walked into the lavishly appointed lobby and slowly strolled onto the white marble floors, seemingly headed to the front door as they weaved through groups of Japanese tourists. They were almost to the front door when a young boy, who looked to be no older than 12, started to walk beside Josh.

"Mr. Martin?"

Josh stopped and nodded in the affirmative.

"Please follow me."

The boy quickly turned and began to move through the Japanese tourists. Gloria and Josh followed and at the end of a lobby corridor they came to a mahogany door with "PRIVATE: Hotel Manager" in bold black lettering on the door front. A mature, imposing man stood beside the door. He never glanced at Josh and

Gloria, but watched down the hallway. The young boy opened the door and motioned for them to enter. And as they walked in, he closed the door behind them.

An elderly Greek man sat behind the desk, seemingly working on some papers. Gloria and Josh stood in the doorway for a moment and as they looked at the dignified man sitting behind the mahogany desk, Josh was sure they had intruded on the hotel manager's private office.

"I'm sorry, sir. We're in the wrong office," Josh said. They started to back out the door when the man got up and came around the desk.

"No you are in the right office. I am Alibis Dupoplious," he stated.

"But..."

"I mentioned our meeting to the hotel manager, and he insisted we use his office. Please sit down, and tell me how I can help you."

Josh and Gloria sat down in a couple of ornate, brown leather chairs, and Josh began to talk about the al-Qaida threat when Dupoplious interpreted him.

"Mr. Martin, pardon me for interrupting you, but our mutual friend, Don Pastori, has informed me of these matters, and I assume you would like me to help you find the man who flew into the Peloponnesus in this." He handed Josh an 8-by-10 color photo.

"Oh my gosh—the motorized hang glider. Where is it?"

"Here are the directions to the plane, but of course the man and the material have left."

"Mr. Dupoplious, we must get our people there as soon possible, before they move the material to Athens."

"It is too late for that, Mr. Martin. The material is already in Athens."

33

The Search

"Are you sure?"

"Of course, I'm sure. Do you think I would give you incorrect information?"

"No, but how can you be so positive?"

"When one of our men was notified by someone that a strange plane had landed, he rode to the place on a motorbike. About the time he reached the site, two men drove up in a gray Fiat 600, loaded a small box from the glider into the trunk of the car, and drove off. The car was last seen on S-23—the direct route to Athens. They've had plenty of time to make the three-hour drive into the city."

Josh took a few seconds to let it sink in that the biomaterial was almost certainly somewhere in Athens, a city of several million. It seemed as if this were it were a hopeless cause, but after a deep breath he asked:

"Mr. Dupoplious, where do you think the material might be?"

"Mr. Martin let's not be so formal. Please call me 'Alibis,' and I will call you Josh. Is that satisfactory?"

"Yes, of course."

"Well, the material could be in a thousand places, but if it were me, I would eliminate some local places such as small communities on the outskirts of the city. In Greece, everyone knows everybody, and it would be hard for three bearded men not be noticed. And then, within the center of the city, in the more upscale neighborhoods, security guards are everywhere. So that only leaves two possible areas where the men could hide out: the commercial warehouse area and the Pakla.

"I would lean toward the Pakla because of the number of foreign tourists. It would be much easier to blend in with such a mix of people."

"How big is the Pakla area?"

"About five-square miles, and more than a million people live there."

"Alibis, it's extremely important that we find the men," Josh said. "If we don't, they could easily kill thousands. Tell me, are there any big demonstrations scheduled for Constitution Square in the next week or so?"

"Yes, three days from today all the trade unions in Greece will hold a big rally. There will be one-hundred and fifty thousand people there, protesting the new austerity measures."

"Oh, my god! Al-Qaida will certainly target the demonstration," Josh exclaimed. "Can it be canceled?"

"I'm afraid not. Even if the government and the unions believed that there was danger, the people, who don't trust the government, would show up anyway, and some activists would say the government was just trying to stop the rally—and more people would come. The rally will happen."

"Then we've got three days to stop what could be a great tragedy. Will you help us to stop this massacre?"

"Certainly Josh, but I am a businessman like yourself, and I have expenses***"

"How much?"

"What?"

"How much money do you want?"

"Josh, I dislike you referring to me as a hired security service. What I can do, or I might do for you is a favor and not a purchase."

"Yes, I understand, but as you know my superiors won't agree to an open-ended payment."

"All right, but if I use fifty of my men or twenty-five, it will make a great deal of difference."

"How many men would be the maximum available?"

"I can easily provide fifty-three men to search in the Pakla. The cost would be one- million, seven-hundred and fifty thousand dollars."

"My government would be willing to pay that, and give you, personally, a one-million-dollar bonus, if you deliver one of the three men to me. However, the man must be alive. Do we have an agreement?"

"Yes, most certainly. I will have my men working the Pakla within the hour."

"That's excellent Alibis. Here is my cellphone number. If you capture one of the men, call me, and I will tell you where to deliver him."

"If they are in the Pakla, we will find them," Alibis assured him. "My men know the area and every alleyway. We also have hundreds of associates who give us information each day. I will find the men, but it may take a few days."

"I understand, but as you know, we may have only three days for you to do it."

"Yes, now if you will excuse me, I have work to do."

"Thank you, Alibis"

"You can thank me when I deliver one of the men to you." And as someone outside opened the door, he briskly left the room.

"Let's get back upstairs, Gloria We've a lot to do."

Josh held his finger to his lips and shook his head, knowing there were listening devices planted. They went back the lobby, which was still teeming with Japanese tourists, took the elevator, and walked briskly to their room. In a few minutes they were back in the safe room where Ponder and Sybil were waiting.

"Ponder, within the hour we'll have an additional fifty-three men scouring the Pakla, and if the al-Qaida operatives are in the Pakla, Alibis's men will find them."

"What, are you serious? Who are these men?"

"I guess you might call them Greek gangsters."

"You hired Alibis's low-rent hoods to work for us?"

"That's right—and, Gloria, get in touch with HQ and tell them to wire a million, seven-hundred and fifty thousand to Sybil, and have another million waiting."

"Now let's get something straight. Ponder, we need all the help we can get, and if hiring all the thugs in Athens can help us stop those bastards, we should do it. I don't give a damn if they are the scum of the earth. If they can find those lowlifes who are trying to kill thousands of innocent people, I'll pay a king's ransom.

"Okay, since that's settled, we need to grid the entire Pakla and see if we can coordinate our men with the Alibis group to find those guys. The big union trade rally is the obvious choice for al-Qaida to hit. Let's get to work and see what we can come up with."

The next few hours consisted of integrating the 53 men working for Alibis and the CIA's 16 men and 12 special operations personnel into a cohesive unit to comb the Pakla. As the operation started, Josh had the nagging feeling that by concentrating on just the Pakla they might be overlooking other sites where the al-Qaida men might be hiding. But he could do nothing but wait as the hours ticked by.

On the afternoon of the second day, Josh, Gloria, and Sybil met with Sinuie, the CIA bureau chief, to assess the situation. The news was disturbing.

"Josh, we're picking up chatter about an upcoming terrorist attack, and it sounds very much like it's the one we're trying to stop. My men and the special operations guys haven't picked up a clue that would help us. How about the bunch we're paying an arm and a leg to work for us?"

"Nothing… absolutely nothing. The only thing that comes to mind is that we're looking in the wrong part of town. Let's look at the blowup of the city again and focus on where the Corinth highway enters the city. After all, it makes since to think they would want to go undercover as quickly as possible."

After pouring over city maps for an hour, Josh highlighted a warehouse district near the industrial section of the city. It would be the first major concentration of buildings on the Corinth Highway before entering the metropolitan part of Athens.

"It's becoming obvious the men we're looking for are not in the Pakla. The only other logical place to search is the warehouse area west of town. After all that would be where they entered the city. It seems to me they might want to seek cover as quickly as possible," said Josh. "What does everyone think about shifting our search to that area?

"What about it, Ponder?"

"Josh, with nearly seventy-five men searching the Pakla, I can't believe we haven't come up with even a clue."

"Okay, let's pull everyone off the Pakla and reassign them to this area," Josh decided, highlighting an area in the warehouse district. Sybil and Gloria immediately objected.

"Josh, I think we shouldn't give up on the Pakla. After all, our men have not really covered all the possible buildings," said Sybil. She was backed up by Gloria, and for the next few minutes they discussed the pros and cons of changing the search areas. Finally, Josh made the call.

"We've got to try something different. Every report we've received is a big nothing. No car—not even a sighting of the men. I just have a gut feeling those guys aren't in the Pakla. After all, they've done just the opposite of what we thought they would do at every turn.

"Put every man we have in the industrial zone."

"Josh, I want to go on record as opposing your decision," Sybil said formally.

"Noted; put that in our report, Gloria—Now let's get moving. We have less than twenty-four hours to stop what will be one of the most horrendous public acts every committed. We've got to do everything possible to stop it from happening."

Sybil was shaking her head as they left the room.

Josh immediately called Dupoplious. "Alibis, we're calling off the Pakla search. Two days with nearly seventy-five men searching hasn't turned up clue one."

"That's right, Josh, and I can assure you that if those men were in the Pakla we would have some clues at the very least. They are not there."

"That's exactly what I have concluded. So let's pull off all our men from the Pakla and have them work the industrial warehouse district in the western area of town."

"Good idea; that's really the only area left where they could hide. I bet we'll come up with something by morning. I have a rotating squad of men who will work through the night."

Josh felt a little relief from the pressure that had steadily increased since the biomaterial had made it to Athens. He was realistic in assessing his chances of stopping the attack, and as he turned to Gloria he spit out, "Damn it!—ten percent at best!"

"What?" Gloria answered in shock.

"We have less than a ten percent chance of stopping the attack," Josh answered. "The bastards have every advantage. We'll just have to be damned lucky to stop it. Tomorrow, when we are in the center of town anywhere near Constitution Square, have your gas masks with you at all times.

"Now let's assume you were going to plant the material as close to the Square as possible. I want us to grid the Square and have some of our men in every building. Sybil, have Sinuie contact the Greek Government and close all entrances to the Square four hours before the rally starts. Got it?"

"Yeah, Josh, but the Greek Government is trying to keep a low profile. They're considered the bad guys by the demonstrators. They can't be in force or in uniform or they'll be attacked. The Greek police or the army won't be any help. We can't close off the Square. It would cause a major riot, and attract even more people to that area."

"Damn!"

Josh, Gloria, and Sybil worked to position Alibis's men and the CIA agents in the most likely spots where they could stop someone trying to enter one of the surrounding buildings with anything like a bomb. After posting the men, the three went to their rooms and tried to get a few hours of sleep. Josh was awakened at 4 a. m., however, by incessant dinging—an emergency ring.

"Martin here*** you found the car! That's great. I'll be there in ten minutes. Don't touch anything, and focus all of your men within a six block circle of the car."

Josh alerted Gloria and Sybil, and they raced across town to an industrial area where they found Alibis standing beside a gray Peugeot.

"This is the car, Josh. My men are certain, and we've found a man who lives in an upstairs apartment who saw the men arrive."

"Did he give you any description?"

"Yes, he said three men rushed into the building, and he only noticed them because they had full beards. You know Greeks almost never have beards. Mustaches, yes, but rarely beards. He said the men looked foreign, and two of them carried a box into the building."

"Have you searched the building?"

"My men are searching the building as we speak, but we may be too late. The man said late yesterday afternoon that a man driving a minivan stopped on the street, and as soon as he stopped, two men came out carrying the box. They jumped in the minivan and drove away. I guess we're too late."

The words "too late" sent a shiver down Josh's spine, and he involuntarily shook as he considered the situation. It would be daylight soon and people would be coming to the Square for the rally in less than four hours. He was about to call off the search when he thought about what the neighbor had told Alias, …*Yeah, he said three men arrived…and only two left in the van. They have the material in the van, but maybe there's one man still here somewhere. If we can find him maybe he'lll talk… by god, he'll talk or I'll kill him,* Josh thought.

"Alias, bring all your men to this area and search this building and the adjacent buildings. Go over every nook and corner. I believe there is one of the men still here."

In minutes, Alias had his men spread out in search groups. They started with the ground floor of the four-story warehouse, fanning out as they checked every room, closet, and even the ductwork. It was very though, but time-consuming. Josh, Gloria, and Sybil watched as the search continued. As the hours passed, Josh became more and more agitated. It was nearly 10:30 in the morning when the search crews finished checking out the warehouse where the car was parked, and now the men were working on adjoining buildings that had doorways opening into a joint hallway between the buildings.

The search teams had just finished the first floor when Josh noticed something. A third-story window was being slowly raised.

Josh exchanged glances with Gloria and Sybil, and then pointed to the open window where just a man's bearded head appeared.

"Don't move," Josh whispered. "I'll take him when he gets down."

The man in the window began to climb out, but stopped when he was almost out the window, and looked in their direction. An instant later, he jumped back inside and slammed the window down.

"Gloria, go tell Alibis that the man's on the third floor! Tell him to double-cover all exits, and proceed with his best team up the stairwell to the third floor. We want him alive. Tell Alibis there'll be no reward if the man is killed. I'm going to go up the fire escape and climb in the window where we saw him—Damn, how could he have spotted us?"

Josh ran for the fire escape while Gloria hurried to tell Alibis the man had been spotted. It took Josh about 10 minutes to climb the fire escape to the third floor. When he got to the window he tried to raise it, but it was bolted down.

"Damn!" he muttered, but, seconds later, two rounds from his Glock shattered the bolt and Josh raised the window. Josh had several flash-bang grenades tethered to his vest. He tossed one into the room before he tried to enter. There was a thunderous, blinding explosion and seconds later Josh slipped through the open window and surveyed the room. It was empty. And now it would be a cat-and-mouse game to hunt down the al-Qaida fighter who was somewhere in the huge, four-floor warehouse building.

Josh moved to the doorway and slipped into the hall outside the room. Then he stopped and listened. He wouldn't be the one to move around and give away his position. The flash-bang had alerted the fighter that Josh was in the building, and the sounds from below—where Alibis's men were moving about searching the building—were sure to move the man upward to the top floor.

Josh remained motionless for nearly 10 minutes, listening intently for any sound that might come from the floor he was on, or from the floor above. While he was waiting, he removed his shoes so that he could move silently around without being heard. He could hear Alibis's men slowly moving through the first floor, opening every door and looking in any possible hiding place. He decided to let Alibis's men to get to the second floor before he moved.

It was just as one of Alibis's men began to come up the stairs to the second floor when Josh heard a board creak. The sound was from almost directly above him. Quickly and quietly, Josh moved down the hallway to the stairwell, and in a few more seconds, he had climbed the stairs and was on the third floor—where the al-Qaida fighter was. Josh continued climbing the next set of stairs, however, and stood quietly behind an open door that led from the staircase. He'd noticed that this was the only staircase in the building, and as the search groups from the lower floors slowly moved up, the fighter was sure to try and get to a higher level.

Josh would be waiting for him when he did.

Josh's thoughts were interrupted by several rapidly fired shots coming from the floor below, followed by a scream from someone who obviously had been hit.

"Damn, I hope they didn't kill the bastard. He's the only hope we've got to catch the others," Josh thought. Seconds later, he was relieved

when he heard footsteps coming up the stairs. *Here he comes—get ready*, Josh told himself as he pulled his weapon and got ready to crack the fighter's head with the barrel of his Glock.

The man made it to the top of the stairs, and Josh anticipated that he would walk through the open doorway in seconds—when he heard the man start up the stairs to the top floor.

Damn, I've got to follow him—maybe a flash-bang will stun him, Josh thought. He yanked a flash-bang grenade from his vest, tossed it up the stairwell, and turned his head.

"Hey!" he screamed hoping to make the man look down the stairwell into a blinding flash of light. A second later, another explosion shook the building. Josh quickly ran into the stairwell hoping the al-Qaida fighter would be standing there blinded so he could capture him unharmed.

Josh had just started up the flight of stairs, however, when several shots hit the banister. He looked up to see the al-Qaida fighter pointing his gun straight at him. Josh jerked aside just in time as several rounds shattered the old plaster wall.

Shit, that bastard almost got me, he thought frantically as he crouched behind the door facing. Now he knew the odds of capturing the man alive were decreasing and the likely end to the chase would be a gunfight with the fighter being killed. Alibis's men would be rushing up the stairwell after hearing a flash-bang and shots, and the overwhelming force that would be after the man would almost surely end in his death.

We've got to take him alive. It's our only hope. Josh positioned himself at a landing on the stairwell, and in seconds the first wave of Alibis's men arrived. Josh waved them down.

"A thousand-dollar-per-man bonus, if we can take him alive!" Josh yelled at the first group of men who reached him. In seconds, one of the men who understood English yelled the reward offer back to the rest of the men. There were some puzzled looks and then some nods.

"Try to make him use up his ammunition," Josh whispered to the man who was translating from English to Greek. He nodded and began to tell the other men behind him. As they reached the next floor, Josh waved for the men to stop moving, and they stood silently while Josh listened for the al-Qaida fighter to take a step.

There wasn't a sound for 10 minutes, and then the telltale sound of a creaking board gave the man away. Suddenly there was a metal clanking sound, as if someone were climbing an iron ladder. Josh recognized it immediately.

"He's going for the roof! Let's go!"

Josh waved for the men to follow him as he rushed to the end of the building where a metal ladder was hanging down under a trapdoor that opened to the room. He was almost to the ladder when he caught a glimpse of the man exiting onto the roof. As Josh rushed to the bottom of the ladder, he could hear sounds of the man running, above.

Then it occurred to Josh that the man wasn't going to be captured. He was going to commit suicide by jumping from the roof.

"I've got to stop him," Josh muttered as he raced up the metal ladder. Josh looked out on the roof just as the man made it to the 3-foot parapet wall.

"Shit! He's going to jump!" Josh pulled his Glock and started to fire, instinctively aiming for his head. *No, his feet! Shoot his feet!* he thought. The man's hands were on the top of the parapet wall and he was about to pull himself up when Josh begin to shoot. There was a hail of .9 mm fire that began to rattle, first hitting the roof in front of the man. Then as Josh raised his gun, several rounds hit his lower legs. The man flipped backward, screaming in pain and trying to pull himself up to climb the wall. Before he could think to turn his weapon toward Josh, however, Josh yanked him off the top of the parapet and subdued him. Alibis's men were there in seconds and quickly tied the man's hands behind him.

"Wrap his feet tight enough to stop the bleeding and take him down to one of the office rooms in the warehouse," Josh instructed the men.

Alibis' men roughly yanked the man down the stairs, and by the time they got him to the office on the first floor, he was gasping for breath from screaming about his wounded legs.

"Okay, you can leave him with us. Go outside and wait. I'll take care of him."

Josh sat him in one of the office chairs, and secured him with some restraining tape. He tightened the wrapping on the prisoner's feet, noting that his wounds were flesh wounds and the man wasn't seriously injured.

Alibis walked up as Josh finished restraining the man.

"Josh, I'm sure you agree, that my men are responsible for capturing this man, and we deserve the extra reward money."

"Of course, Alibis. Gloria you're instructed to direct HQ to wire the funds agreed upon to Mr. Dupoplious's account. He'll give you the details."

"Josh, you're a man of your word. Thank you so much."

"You're welcome, Alibis, but please excuse us because it's critical that we interrogate this man, and we must hurry."

"Of course; I will leave that to you, but if you need one of my men to apply a little extra pressure, just give me a call. You have my cell."

"Thanks, Alibis, but I think I can convince this man to give us the information we need."

As Alibis left the office, Josh locked the door behind him, and started to approach the man he had strapped to the chair. However, before he could question him, Sybil began to protest.

"Josh, you know this matter must be handled by the CIA. I insist we take him—first to the hospital to have his wounds taken care of, and then to our downtown headquarters where we have trained personnel who'll question him."

"Sybil, we don't have time to do that. If we have figured it correctly, the bomb with the biomaterial will explode at somewhere around noon. By the time we do what you're suggesting it would be well after that."

"Josh, it will look extremely bad on your record, and you know I'll have to report that you ignored a direct request from a bureau chief."

"Well, Sybil, I suggest you go ahead and start the write-up because I'm going to get some information out of this bastard, or I'm going to kill him. Gloria, strap this monitor on the man's left arm, about three inches below the bend in his elbow."

"Josh, before you do anything, I want you to know that you cannot torture this man. You could spend fifteen years in the stockade if you do," said Sybil.

"I'll risk it, Sybil—that looks good, Gloria. Hold this gauge and give me the reading and marking each time I ask for it."

"I demand you take me to the hospital! I am in pain!" the man screamed.

"Well, we're in luck. He speaks English."

"We're going to take you to the hospital after you answer a few questions."

"I'm not answering anything. You heard the woman. You cannot torture me, and even if you do, I will not even tell you my name."

"We'll see."

Josh turned to the man and yanked his pants and shorts down, exposing his genitals.

"What are you doing?" he screamed.

"Josh, you can't do those things the Egyptians do with the electrodes. You'd be courtmartialed and, without a doubt, convicted. If you touch that man's genitals, I will personally see that my report goes to the Joint Chiefs."

"Shut up, Sybil, and don't bother me again. I'm not going to use electrodes. I don't have any, and I don't have time to bring them here. I'll have to do it a little more direct."

"Don't you touch me!" screamed the man.

"Listen, I don't know your name, but I assume you are a Muslim. Is that right?" There was a slight perceptible nod, Gloria said, "He's telling the truth. He is a Muslim."

"Well, when I shot you in the leg you were trying to climb the parapet wall and commit suicide. Is that right?"

Another slight movement of the head, and Gloria commented, "Yes, he's agreeing with you."

"Good, well if I remember my Muslim studies correctly, if you had committed suicide you would have been considered a martyr. Is that right?"

"He is in agreement with you, Josh," said Gloria.

"And you would have had forty virgins when you arrived in paradise. Is that right?"

"He is agreeing."

"Now, I want you to listen very carefully to what I am going to say, because your life depends on your answer."

"I have no fear of death! Allah Akbar!"

"I'm sure you don't, but before I kill you, I am going to make your time in the afterlife a living hell, and your final minutes on Earth will be unbelievably painful."

"You are forbidden to torture me. That is a direct order from your president."

"I am overriding the authority of my president because you are a threat to thousands of innocent people. If you don't answer my questions truthfully, what I am going to do to you will be worse than death."

There was a smirk from the man, and he spit in Josh's face. Josh calmly wiped the spittle from his face and nodded to Gloria. "Gloria, each time I ask a question, shake your head 'yes' or 'no' after he answers."

"All right, Josh. I'm ready."

"Answer this question or face the consequences," Josh said to the prisoner. "Where will the bomb be placed and at what time will it explode?"

There was no answer as the man looked at Josh with contempt. "You know where the bomb is to be planted. Is that right?"

There was a nod of 'yes' from Gloria.

"All right, since you have the information we are requesting, I will give you one last chance to give me the where and when."

There was no answer.

"Okay, you give me no choice. Listen very carefully because what I am about to do is going to be critical to your time in paradise."

There was a questioning look from not only the bound man, but from Gloria and Sybil.

"Unless you give me the information I am requesting, I will do the following: Each incorrect answer will result in the loss of part of your penis."

Josh pulled out his knife, and made a sweeping close movement across his arm. The knife easily cut the hair on his arm. He stuck the knife in the wooden arm of the chair and continued to talk. However, before Josh could speak there was a clamor of protest from the prisoner, Gloria, and Sybil.

"My god, Josh! Surely you aren't serious!" yelled Sybil.

"Josh, I agree with Sybil. You can't do that. It's barbaric," said Gloria.

"Barbaric? Who's barbaric? Am I barbaric trying to prevent the deaths of thousands, or is this piece of slime the really barbaric one? He's determined to kill thousands of innocent people, and I'm only going to kill one criminal."

"Josh, I'm commanding you as a CIA bureau chief to not torture this man!" Sybil yelled.

"I'm in charge here, Sybil, and if I have to cut the asshole up in little pieces to get him to talk, I will."

The bound man just laughed. "Do you think your threats will make me tell you anything? I know you are prevented from doing this. You are only using that threat to intimidate me. I will tell you nothing, even to the point of death."

Josh, obviously irritated, grabbed the man's full beard and wrenched it until most of it had been pulled from his face. After the screams died down, Josh bent over until he was right in the man's face.

"Now that I have you attention, listen very closely, because I'm not through talking," said Josh. "If you absolutely refuse to answerer my questions, I will slowly cut off a piece of you penis each time you answer incorrectly, and then I will feed your penis to the hogs—that is after I kill you and bury you head first wrapped in a hog's skin."

There were looks of disbelief from everyone in the room, but Josh, who calmly continued to speak. "Think about being buried as a non-Muslim with your head pointed straight to hell—wrapped in a pig skin. And even you do ascend to paradise, you will be with forty virgins—without your penis! Now, let's start the questions. Tell me the exact location where the bomb and biomaterial will be planted."

There was a dead silence from everyone in the room as the bound man gave Josh a look of contempt, and then again spit in Josh's face.

Josh calmly wiped the spittle from his face, pulled his knife out of the chair arm, and reached down between the bound man's legs.

"You are going to regret that," Josh said.

He grabbed the man's uncircumcised penis and proceeded to slice the foreskin. Josh was circumcising his prisoner.

"*Ahaaaa! Stop! Ahaaaaa!*" His screams continued, and then there was a protest from Gloria and Sybil.

"Stop, Josh; you have got to stop!" Sybil screamed.

"Shut up, Sybil. Leave the room, if this bothers you."

"I can't be a part of this— you have gone too far," protested Gloria.

Josh ignored them both, and with a few more strokes of the razor sharp knife, he finished the circumcision. At first the man jerked and screamed, but as Josh continued to cut, he gritted his teeth and absorbed the pain without another sound. Josh finished, knowing the fighter would be extremely hard to break. To get the answers he wanted, it would take much more pain.

"You can now pass as a Jew," said Josh, as he dangled the man's bloody foreskin in his face. "Now, before I go any farther, are you ready to answer my question? Where's the bomb and biomaterial being planted?"

No answer.

"Okay, but you're sure going to disappoint a lot of virgins if you don't come up with some answers." Josh wiped the blood from his knife and got ready to make the next cut. "Gloria hand me that book on the table."

Gloria hesitated, but finally handed Josh a 2-inch thick book.

"This is your last chance before you lose part of your penis," Josh said. He looked at the man, and for the first time, there was a hint of fear in his eyes. It was just exactly what Josh was looking for. He had seen that look many times and it always was followed by a suspect's breakdown. Josh paused for a second, and then grasped the man bloody penis and stretched it out on the book that he'd placed between the man's legs.

"Wait, stop! I beg you! I do not know anything!"

Josh glanced at Gloria. Her head was shaking "no".

"You're lying!"

"No, I'm not! They didn't tell me anything! I only know them as associates!"

Gloria glanced at the gauge and shook her head "no".

"You don't understand do you? If you don't stop lying, you're going to lose your penis. The only way you can keep your penis is to tell the truth. Now, I'm giving you one more chance to tell the truth. Where is the bomb and biomaterial going to be put?"

"I promise on Allah's name that I do not know!"

Another shake of the head by Gloria, and Josh placed the edge of his knife on the tip of the man's penis.

"Josh, that's enough!" screamed Sybil. "You have got to stop!"

Josh ignored her and began to slowly draw the razor sharp knife across the tip of the man's penis. The al-Qaida fighter was silent for a few seconds, but then his screams reached a new intensity. Then just as suddenly, he quit screaming and yelled, "Stop! I will tell you what you want!"

Josh wiped the blood from his knife and slipped it in his holster. "All right, but I'm warning you; if you lie to me again, I'll slit your penis all the way up to your nuts. Do you understand me?"

"Yes, but you must believe me, they only said in Athens. I don't know exactly where. That is the truth."

"He's lying, Josh," reported Gloria.

Josh shook his head, got his knife back out, and began to cut deeper into the man's penis.

"Ahaaaaaaaa! No! No! Stop! Please stop!" his screams were deafening and even Josh drew back and hesitated.

He looked up at the man and asked, "Are you ready to answer the question?"

There was no answer and Josh pulled the knife across the tip of the man's penis again, cutting a little deeper. Another series of pleas and screams followed as Josh push the blade down and about a half-inch of the man's penis dropped off. The man was in uncontrollable sobs and screams now as Josh calmly picked up the piece of his penis and held it in front of the man's eyes.

"The next cut'll be bigger, and the next after that will be even bigger until I've cut off your entire organ—and then I'm going to kill you. Do you understand?"

The man's chest heaved as he threw up, gagging on vomit. Josh paid no attention to his misery, knowing he was close to having the man break down, and tell him what he wanted to know.

"Where will the bomb and biomaterial be planted? If you answer incorrectly, you will lose a full inch of your penis. Do you understand?" There was a look a fear and panic in the eyes of the bound man. Josh knew he was very close to breaking.

"You have five seconds to tell me the correct answer...one...two...three...four...five. You are a fool to lose your penis, but it is your choice," Josh said. He lowered his knife again and began a slow slice across the man's penis. The man stiffened, vomited again, and then screamed, "No! No! Stop! I will tell you."

Josh raised his knife, which was dripping blood, and held it in front of the man's eyes. He knew unless he showed complete willingness to continue and to dominate the man, he might still not tell him where the weapons were located.

"Tell me right now, or I'll cut your entire penis off!" Josh yelled. "Speak to me! Or it will be too late! Tell me right now!"

"Yes... the bomb will go off at twelve. It is being placed in the subway tunnel very near the hotel..." Suddenly, a shot rang out and the man's head snapped back.

Josh turned around to see Sybil standing there with her gun outstretched.

"What in god's name are you doing?"

Before Sybil could answer, Gloria yelled, "He was telling the truth, Josh!"

"Sybil, why on earth did you shoot him? He was about to tell us exactly where the bomb was located!"

"I couldn't stand to see you torture him, and then kill him. I thought it would be better for him to just die."

"Well, that was just plain stupid, but I know the area around Constitution Square, and there's only one subway station. And it's right across the street from the Grande Bretagne Hotel. That's got to be where the bomb is to be placed. The fifty pounds of plastic explosives they have will breach the subway ceiling and contaminate the entire Square."

Josh glanced at his watch, and beckoned to Gloria as he turned to leave the room.

"My god! It's twenty minutes till twelve. Let's get out of here. It's going to be hard to get to there that fast."

Josh was hurrying across the room toward the office door when Sybil stepped in front of him. It seemed an unnatural move and he hesitated. Then he stopped in shock as Sybil pointed her Beretta at him.

"You're not going anywhere, Josh. And neither are you, Gloria."

"Sybil are you crazy? If we waste another minute, it might be too late! For god's sake, woman—if you're so upset because I tortured the man let a courtmartial decide my punishment. Get out of the way!"

"If you take one morestep toward me, I'll kill you. I'm not going to let you stop our strike against you infidels."

"Our? Oh, my god, Sybil, surely not."

"Yes, and there's nothing you can do about it," she countered.

Josh faltered, considering the situation, but before he could do anything Gloria jumped behind the office desk, drawing her weapon as she hit the floor. Sybil fired at her, shattering the top of the desk. Then, as Gloria rolled on the floor behind the desk trying to dodge Sybil's shots, Josh lunged to try and grab the woman's outstretched arm.

He was a half-second slow, however, and Sybil whipped her Beretta around and sent a slug into Josh's chest. The force of the slug sent Josh staggering back, but he regained his footing and charged forward again. The Beretta coughed out two more shots into Josh, but his momentum carried him forward.

Josh grabbed Sybil's outstretched gun hand an instant before she could fire again, and he slowly pushed her hand down to deflect the next shot. There was an instant when Sybil seemed to be subdued, but her left hand caught Josh by surprise, cracking him across the neck and nearly making him lose his grip. An upward kick and a crushing karate lick across his neck made Josh lose his grip on Sybil's gun.

He hit the wall and slid down as Sybil lowered her weapon and pointed it at his head.

34

Desperation

A single shot rang out, and Sybil shook from the bullet that sliced into her temple splattering blood and brains. Gloria had recovered and got a clear shot. Sybil fell dead.

Josh slowly stood up, and Gloria rushed over to him.

"Come on, Gloria! We need to hurry or it'll be too late!"

"Josh, she shot you in the chest three times! You've got to go to the hospital!"

"No, I don't! This new body armor stopped that little Beretta's slug. I'll just have a couple of bruises, and three holes in my shirt, but that's about it. Now, let's go!"

Josh stepped over Sybil's body as he and Gloria rushed outside. Gloria started for the car they'd driven from the hotel, but Josh yelled for her to stop.

"We can't try to take a car! The traffic will be stacked up for miles around the Square. We need to find a motor scooter or motorcycle to buy or rent. But before we do, I need to call Alibis."

"Why?"

"I've got a feeling al-Qaida's going to send some of their Athens sleeper cell fighters to act as security and make sure the mission goes off without a hitch. If they do, then we're going to need some help, and there's no way Greek policemen will be able to move through that anti-government crowd and assist us." Josh quickly punched his cellphone.

"Alibis, Josh here. We've got the information, but we need your help***" "Yes, we know where the bomb is to be planted—I need at least six armed men who will take orders from me, and won't

305

hesitate to use their weapons. Do you have men in the crowd at Constitution Square who can meet me on the corner by the Grande Bretagne Hotel across from the subway station? Yes—have them there in fifteen minutes.

"Of course, there will be an additional bonus... five-hundred thousand... good, yes, I'll have Gloria make the transfer. Remember, the men must be armed and willing to use their weapons... Fine. Thank you, Alibis."

"Come on, Gloria; let's find a scooter." Josh and Gloria ran up the side street to where the main thoroughfare connected, and Josh began to wave down boys riding Mopeds. Finally, after Josh waved a handful of money, one stopped, and Josh rushed up to him.

"We need to buy your scooter! I've got a thousand dollars, American. Will you sell it or let me use the scooter for an hour? You can pick it up later a Syntagma Square this afternoon." Josh quickly yanked out a zipped-up liner to his backpack and waved a handful of $100 bills at the young boy.

"Uh, no, no sale—but you said I could have it back?"

"Yes, we need it only to get to the Square, and then you can come pick it up."

"Do you promise you will leave it there?"

"Yes, here, take the money! We have got to get there in fifteen minutes!"

In seconds, Josh and Gloria were on the scooter roaring down the street with Josh's finger beeping the horn. As traffic picked up, Josh turned and started driving on the sidewalk; then, as he turned back into traffic, he passed between lanes, sometimes clipping the side mirrors on cars.

Since almost all the traffic was heading toward the Square, he maneuvered out into the oncoming traffic lane and drove against the sparse traffic.

"Josh, for god's sake, you're going to kill us!—Watch out for that truck!"

"I see it. Don't worry, I grew up riding a scooter like this—hold on!" Josh abruptly whipped back into the line of slow-moving traffic headed in his direction, and he zig-zaged through the two lanes of traffic until he spotted an open sidewalk. However, the sidewalk was open only because a police barricade was across it.

"Damn! Duck and hold on tight!" Josh yelled. The scooter knocked down an aluminum railing, sending pedestrians scrambling, and a whistle blew from policemen standing in the intersection. He chased after them yelling for them to halt, but Josh never slowed down.

The closer they got to the Square, the more crowded the streets became, and soon Josh gave up trying to proceed with the flow of cars and pedestrians, and drove out again into the oncoming rush of traffic. For the next several blocks, Gloria ducked down and closed her eyes, expecting a collision any second.

Josh calmly guided the scooter directly toward a space between the two lanes of traffic as cab drivers and others screamed at him. However, Josh knew if he held his course the cars and trucks would move over enough for the scooter to slip by. And as they did, he picked up speed and careened through the maze of vehicles.

Josh was just a few blocks from the Square when he misjudged the space available between two trucks. The scooter roared into the space, with its handlebars bouncing off both trucks, until it became wedged between them. The trucks began to slow down—with Josh and Gloria still hanging onto the scooter. As the truck driver braked more, thinking they had run over the scooter, Josh yelled to Gloria.

"Get off, and run!"

"I'm going to die!" screamed Gloria, as the scooter continued to be pulled along by the two trucks. Josh pulled her off the scooter just as the rear tire of a transport truck clipped the front of the vehicle and sent it underneath the truck beside it. There was a crunch of metal as the truck's tire flattened the little scooter.

"Damn! We owe a kid a scooter!" yelled Josh. He grabbed Gloria and pulled her along, managing to squeeze out from between the slow-moving vehicles. The two finally popped out into the open, but they were on the inside lane of a five-lane roundabout. Now it became a race to get across four lanes of moving traffic to the sidewalk—without getting hit.

"Come on, get to the sidewalk! We're almost there!" yelled Josh. Gloria turned loose of Josh's hand and tried to run cross the lanes of moving traffic, but after a few steps, panicked and froze. Josh was almost to the sidewalk when he looked back and saw Gloria standing in the middle of four lanes of horn-honking, cursing, and fist-shaking drivers.

"Damn it! Move your ass, Gloria!" Josh yelled. But she just kept looking from side to side, trying to see a break in the traffic. There was none.

Josh dashed into the traffic lanes waving for the cars to stop, and in a few seconds he had her by the hand and was pulling her back into the traffic as he held his free hand up in a policeman like stop sign. When they reached the curb, Josh grabbed Gloria and shook her.

"Come on; we're nearly there! We can run the rest of the way!"

Gloria took a deep breath, and they started jogging through the throngs of people gathering for the rally. She kept up the best she could, but Josh, being in much better shape, had to wait for her when they were a block from the Square.

"Follow me. I know a shortcut that'll keep us from having to push through the crowd."

He sprinted down a back alleyway, turned, and ran to the back service entrance of the Grande Bretagne Hotel. He grabbed the door, but it was locked— but only for a second after Josh pulled his Glock and disabled it.

"Come on, Gloria, we can make better time going through the hotel than we can pushing through the crowd." A quick sprint through the kitchen and into the lobby, then through the revolving doors, put them within 20 yards of the subway entrance. Josh spotted Alibis's six men standing on the corner by the hotel across from the subway entrance. As he ran up to them, he shouted Alibis's name, and soon he had them huddled around him.

"English? Who speaks good English?" Josh said as they stood in a group waiting for Josh to give them orders.

"I do," said one of the younger men.

Josh quickly told the young man that a terrorist group was about to set off a bomb in the subway, and it would kill many people. It would be up to them to stop it from happening. He took a good look at the crowd before he led the men across the street to the subway entrance.

"Oh, my god," he mumbled. Josh gazed across the sea of people who had packed the large public Square. It not only filled the Square, but also spilled over into the side streets that led into the Square. Even the area from the hotel to the subway entrance was packed with humanity. Josh tried to put out of his mind the thought that he was too late to stop the explosion. But it was there. A glance at his Breitling Oceania Chronograph II watch made him gasp.

"My god, it's five minutes till twelve. Let's go! Follow me and have your weapons ready. Don't hesitate to shoot!" Josh shouted to Alibis's men. He waved them forward, and they plowed through the crowd.

The group crossed the street to the subway entrance and hurried down the steps toward the underground platform loading area. At the bottom of the first flight of steps was a level area before the second flight, which led to the gate that opened to the subway platform. However, before Josh and Gloria could descend the second flight, they were stopped by a uniformed Athens policeman. He raised his hand and ordered them to stop.

"I'm sorry, but this station is closed until the demonstration is over. Please use another entrance."

Gloria, who was right behind Josh, stopped and looked surprised. Josh studied the policeman closely, and then turned to leave. The six men behind him hesitated and slipped their weapons back into their jackets. However, as Josh turned he pulled his .9-mm

Glock, quickly whirled around, and shot the policeman in the face. There was a pop from his silenced weapon, and the bearded police officer fell to the ground.

"My god, Josh! You just killed a Greek policeman!"

The others looked at Josh in disbelief, but Josh just shook his head, and hurried over to the dead man. He quickly pointed to the body and said, "Al-Qaida—Greek policemen are not allowed to grow beards." He nudged the man's full beard as everyone nodded, and the young man who was translating, spewed out something in Greek. There was an understanding nod from everyone, and they moved to follow Josh who had already started down the lower flight of stairs, and was about to enter the station platform area.

Josh waved his weapon and shouted to Gloria and the men behind him, "Follow me, get your weapons out, and shoot anyone you see in this station! No one's here but al-Qaida—Let's go!" As the young man translated, weapons appeared and everyone started down the final flight of stairs that led to the entrance to the station platform.

They were rushing down the stairs, hurrying toward an open subway station door at the bottom of the stairs, when two armed men suddenly appeared in the subway station door. There was an instant shock of confrontation, as the two groups saw each other.

"Shoot them!" yelled Josh. He had approached the subway gate with his weapon drawn, the safety off, and was holding the Glock out in front of him ready to fire. Being ready to engage gave him the advantage, and he immediately sent several shots into the head of the first man, and then tried to shoot the other man before he dodged behind a concrete door pillar. Before Josh could shoot him, however, the al-Qaida fighter was able to send several rounds toward Josh's men.

"Ahaaa!"

There was a scream from one of the men beside Josh, as he took at slug in his shoulder. He limped back up the stairs, as Josh and the rest of the group continued to move forward toward the place where the second al-Qaida fighter was crouched.

"Come on, Gloria; hurry!" screamed Josh. He ran directly toward the other man with his weapon in a firing position. He was only a few steps away, when the man started to look out from behind the door pillar and tried to fire. Josh was squeezing the trigger as he detected movement—and when the man's head cleared the door, a bullet from Josh's Glock sent him tumbling back. Josh was in the doorway to the station in an instant.

"My god! They're here!" he yelled to Gloria. He recognized the heavily armed group of men in the platform area, and stepped back to where only his right eye and weapon were in their line of fire. Then, in a fraction of a second, Josh spotted a bulky package sitting on a rectangular wooden box. The package was strapped to the box, and a man seemed to be working on something attached to it. Josh could see wires scattered on the concrete floor.

Damn, he's wiring the detonator, crossed Josh's mind. They had surprised the men who had brought the biomaterial into the subway, and there was a moment of hesitation from the group of fighters. Josh quickly deduced, from his demolition training, that they were in the final process of wiring a plastic charge to the detonator. He had only a split second to react, and he did, getting off a shot at the man wiring the detonator— a shot that sheared off the top of the man's head.

Then he turned his gun and blazed away, sending several rounds into a group of al-Qaida fighters who by now had raised their weapons toward Josh and his men. The al-Qaida fighters quickly responded and unleashed a torrent of automatic weapon fire that ripped across the concrete entrance where Josh had been standing.

As Josh pulled back from the doorway, he heard screams from several of the al-Qaida fighters, indicating that some of his rounds had found a target. Then a continuous roar of automatic weapon shots came from the platform. Josh felt several rounds nick his outstretched arm, and he backed away from the open gate.

"Get back, Gloria!" Josh ordered. He shoved her back away from the door, just as a second burst of gunfire roared out the subway tunnel. Several slugs ripped though Josh's shirt, and two rounds slightly wounded him in the arm. Josh reached his arm into the doorway, and—remembering where the al-Qaida fighters were standing—emptied his Glock in that direction. There were more screams, as several of the rounds hit the fighters still standing with weapons raised ready to fire.

Josh quickly jammed another magazine into his Glock, stuck his hand around the concrete door pillar, and fired into the tunnel area. This time there were no causalities, and Josh knew they had backed away from the open platform. However, he also knew that the best he could hope for was to back them off and keep them from connecting the detonator. He had no doubt they would set off the charge in a suicide attack as soon as they could. It was imperative that they attack the fighters, and control the area with the plastic charge and biomaterial.

"Gloria get everybody ready to go into the tunnel. I'm going to throw a couple of antipersonnel grenades onto the platform. That will back them off, and might even take a few of them out of the fight. Then I'll throw two flash-bang grenades in about two seconds apart, and then right before we go in, another one. The third one should catch them with their eyes open. We can't afford to wait because if we do one of those guys will hook up the detonator and blow everything to hell and back. We've got to stop this thing right now, or one way or another they'll be able to set off the charge."

"Okay, now get ready and be sure everyone on the team is in position to charge into the subway platform area when I give the word. Fifteen to twenty al-Qaida fighters are in the tunnel."

Gloria quickly pulled the young man aside and told him what to tell the others. She nodded, and Josh threw the first of the live, anti-personal grenades onto the platform, and then seconds later began to toss the three flash-bangs into the subway tunnel.

"Close your eyes and turn your heads," Josh yelled. Seconds later, there was a blinding flash and a thunderous explosion.

"Number two is in!" Josh hollered, tossing the second flash-bang.

Another explosion, and Josh yanked the last flash-bang from his vest. As he did the timer began to tick, and Josh counted along with it until only one second was left. He threw and quickly turned his head knowing that it would explode before it hit.

"Get ready! Last one's in!"

The words were barely out of his mouth when a blinding flash of white light followed by another thunderous explosion belched from the subway entrance. The explosions from the grenades and three flash-bangs, followed by automatic weapon firing, had sent people crowded in the street around the subway entrance into the Square, fleeing in panic.

Before the echoes from the last explosion faded, Josh yelled, "Now! Go! Go! Go!" He sprinted through the doorway, and rolled across the floor. There was immediate automatic weapons fire from the back of the platform, and a burst of fire popped the white shirt of the man behind Josh, who had run into the station without any evasive action. It knocked him back into the arms of the man behind him. The bloody man with froth from his bullet riddled lungs set off a panic from the remainder of Alibis's men, and they dropped their weapons and dashed back up the stairs toward the street.

"Damn!" Josh screamed. "Come back!" But as the last of Dupoplious' men disappeared up the stairwell, leaving Josh and Gloria on the platform, he realized it would just be Gloria and him to stop the fighters from detonating the bomb. Gloria, who had followed Josh onto the subway platform, yelled to him, "Josh, should we go for help? There are at least a dozen al-Qaida fighters on the platform that I can see, and more behind the support beams!"

"No, they would rush up and detonate the bomb if we leave. We've got to stop them at all costs."

As Josh finished the sentence, he made another evasive roll toward the wall and, ended up with his left arm outstretched, pointing his Glock in the direction of where the gunfire came from. He looked in that direction as an al-Qaida fighter moved to try and get a clear shot at Josh. Josh was a fraction of a second quicker, and before the man could sight in on him, Josh squeezed off another shot. The top of the fighters head exploded as the slug ripped out his left eye.

Gloria quickly moved to be beside Josh, and as they looked down the platform, what they saw was shocking. At least a dozen or the enemy were in various recesses of the subway tunnel, and all of them were advancing toward the dead al-Qaida fighter, who was lying beside the detonator and the bomb wiring attached to the box of biomaterial.

Josh and Gloria ducked behind one of the metal pilings that supported the subway roof, and Josh tried to access the situation. The men hadn't been blinded by the flash-bangs because there were so many nooks and impediments on and around the subway platform. This sure wasn't going to be a turkey shoot.

He and Gloria had only two extra magazines left, and the odds were heavily on the al-Qaida fighters' side since they had the numbers and firepower to eventually overcome the two. Josh knew he had to even the odds, and as he looked at the brightly lit platform he had an idea.

"Put on your NVG's!" Josh yelled. He began to shoot out the lights above them, and in seconds darkness shrouded the station and a deathly silence hung over the area, occasionally punctuated by the groans of wounded men. Josh peered into the darkness, and even though the NVG's amplified the available light, he could barely make out the fighters scurrying around on the far end of the darkened platform.

Josh calmly aimed and sent a slug onto the head of one of the more careless individuals.

"Move," whispered Josh, knowing that the flash from his gun barrel would draw an immediate response.

They quickly bolted across the narrow passageway and lay down against a concrete wall, as a rattle of automatic weapon fire kicked up concrete chips where they had just been crouched. Josh could see the bomb attached to the biomaterial; it was about 10 yards from where they were hunkered down.

He knew the fighters, who were somewhere in the dark recesses of the subway tunnel, would soon try to overpower them. And after he and Gloria were killed, the bomb would be armed. Then, seconds later a horrendous explosion would destroy the roof of the subway tunnel and send the toxic material spewing out to infect some 150,000 people gathered in the Square.

Josh was considering how to react to this imminent threat when he heard steps descending the stairwell into the station platform. It was a squad of Greek police officers, who had heard flash-bang explosions and the automatic weapons firing. The explosions and gunfire had been reported, and they were investigating.

Josh yelled a warning, "Stop! Don't enter!" But it was too late. There was heavy automatic weapon fire from the al-Qaida fighters in the darkened end of the tunnel, and the first two Greek policemen were sent sprawling on the platform. The rest scurried back up the steps.

As soon as the Greek policemen left the area, Josh noticed movement from where the vicinity of the al-Qaida fighters. The fighters had spread out, ducking behind support columns, getting closer and closer to where the bomb was. As Josh looked, he could make out NVG's on some of the fighters, indicating they were a well-trained group of al-Qaida soldiers, who had been equipped with the latest gear. He took some assurance that his armor and NVG's were the newest and best on the market. However, that would give the two of them only a slight advantage. As Josh assessed the situation, he began to understand why al-Qaida had sent such a large group of men assembled to detonate the bomb.

"Gloria," Josh whispered. "I think this team is a special suicide group. They sent so many fighters because of the importance of the mission. When they get closer, some of the team will engage us while the remainder of the team rushes for the bomb, and even though we'll be able to take out several of the fighters, some of them will surely be able to connect the last wires to the detonator. They're going to blow up this subway station no matter what the cost—and take us and them with it."

"What are we going to do? Should we stay or go for help?"

"We can't leave. They'll set off the bomb minutes after we leave the station. Just hunker down and make every shot count."

Josh was preparing for the attack when he felt a vibration in the floor.

"Oh my god, a train's coming into the station!" he hissed. "The transit people operating the train don't have a clue about what's happening, and as soon as the train comes to a stop, the doors will automatically open and the platform will be full of people."

"What are we going to do?"

"Follow my lead. When the engine light illuminates the fighters who are preparing to attack us, start shooting and take out as many as you can. Then, when the car doors open and the passengers spill out onto the platform, we'll crawl into the crowd and use them as a shield as we go for the bomb. I can disconnect everything if I have a couple of minutes with the detonator. You cover me while I work on it. If I can disable the bomb, we'll worry about the fighters later. The bomb must be deactivated. Get ready, here comes the train."

35

Resolution

Josh and Gloria had only an instant to react because in a few seconds the train engine rounded the last curve, and now the flashing running lights of the train and the beam of light from its engine could be seen as the train approached the station. It would be passing them in less than a second, and as it approached, the light from the engine began to illuminate the dark subway platform where they were crouched.

"Flatten out against the wall, Gloria. We're going to be sitting ducks when the engine light hits this section of the platform." Josh and Gloria moved behind one of the iron beams supporting the station ceiling, and they flattened out on the platform floor as the train approached. In a few seconds, the light from the engine lit the dark station platform, and as it passed Josh and Gloria, they hugged the floor and huddled down behind the iron beam trying not to be seen.

For a few seconds, however, they were in the bright light of the engine. A rattle of automatic weapons fire came from the group of men hunched down at the other end of the platform. The al-Qaida fighters had seen them, and were trying to take them out of the firefight. Josh felt one of their rounds rip through the sleeve of his shirt, grazing his upper arm.

Blood began to drip down as Josh tried to stay behind the iron support column. Then, in a few seconds, the engine passed them, and they were in the dark again. Josh felt a stabbing pain, and then looked at his right arm where the slug had opened a flesh wound that was oozing blood.

"Gloria, are you okay?" Josh asked.

"No, I took a hit on my left leg, but no broken bones. I can handle it."

"Okay, get ready to even the odds when the engine light hits those bastards."

Josh was already raising his Glock getting ready to fire when the engine light's beam illuminated the fighters at the other end of the platform.

"You shoot the men to your right, Glorida, and I'll take the ones on the left. Now!"

"Take 'em!" hollered Josh.

As the light flooded the darkened end of the tunnel where the al-Qaida fighters were huddled, the two began to try to take cover behind anything they could find. Josh's first shot took out one of the laggards, who wasn't quick enough to duck behind anything substantial.

In seconds, Josh and Gloria had poured a torrent of fire into the remaining fighters, taking down four more of the ones who didn't find cover. The engine was almost to the fighters when it slowly rolled to a stop. A whistle sounded announcing that all the door were about to open, and as Josh and Gloria watched, the automatic doors flashed, and the passengers got ready to step out onto the shadowy subway platform.

"Damn, four cars and they're all packed! They must be coming to take part in the demonstration. This is really going to be a shock when they step out onto a dark platform right in the middle of a firefight. My god, this is going to be horrible!" Josh whispered to Gloria.

"Listen up. This is the plan: When the subway riders get off, use them as a shield, and head for the detonator, but crawl; don't stand up and give those bastards an easy shot. When we reach the bomb, cover me while I disconnect all the wiring. Get ready!"

The doors on four subway cars opened, and nearly 200 riders—men, women, and children—stepped out. There was a moment of surprise from the puzzled passengers, who as they spilled out of the cars onto the dark platform, but in seconds, most of them figured it was just another failure of the Greek government to even do the ordinary and necessary: keep the lights on. As the crowd moved slowly toward the only light—the entrance to the subway platform—Josh and Gloria got ready to scamper on all fours toward the subway riders. The riders were moving slowly because of the darkness, but in a few seconds, they were between Josh and Gloria and the al-Qaida fighters.

"Now!" hissed Josh, and they started forward on all fours toward the bomb. It was only a few seconds later that the al-Qaida fighters realized Josh and Gloria were moving to take control of the bomb.

***

"Stop them! They are trying to reach the material!" yelled el-Wahlie to his men. "Shoot! Shoot them all!" he shouted.

As the train left the station, the al-Qaida fighters began to fire into the crowd trying to hit Josh and Gloria who were on their knees, weaving through the passengers moving toward the bomb.

The automatic weapon fire sent a half-dozen panicked passengers sprawling down, either severely wounded or killed. The remaining ones screamed as they rushed toward the only light at the entrance to the subway platform.

As the crowd rushed past them, Josh took one last shot to try and stop an al-Qaida fighter who was out in front of his comrades, and trying to use the crowd of people to reach the detonator. The sound of Josh's gun from within the crowd of people, the screams of wounded fighters, and the hail of automatic weapon fire into the helpless group of people intensified the terror as they rushed toward the exit, stumbling over the bodies of the slain passengers.

It was total chaos.

Josh and Gloria were almost through the throng of subway passengers, and were about to make their move toward the bomb and detonator when Josh saw the al-Qaida commander wave the rest of his men forward.

***

"Go, and kill them all!, For Allah! Allah Akbar! Do not let them reach the bomb!" screamed el-Wahlie. As he waved his fighters forward, he lowered his AK.47 and sent another hail of fire into the already panicked mob.

***

"Come on, Gloria, let's go! They're making a run toward the bomb!"

Josh and Gloria scrambled along, keeping as much of a low profile as possible and weaving through the last of the horrified subway passengers, who were trying to reach the platform entrance. Crawling on the darkened platform floor, trying to reach the light at the stairs leading out of the subway tunnel, Josh and Gloria made headway as they slowly crawled over bodies and across the bloody platform floor toward the bomb and the detonator.

Josh reached the edge of the crowd, and had just risen up to fire at the approaching terrorists, when he saw men pushing throughout the crowd at the subway entrance. Josh and Gloria were about five yards from the biomaterial when helmeted men with flashlights came running down the stairs pushing people aside as they hurried into the station area. Josh and Gloria flattened out on the floor as the men scanned the area with their lights.

Subway riders, who were panicked by the gunfire and screams of wounded fighters and injured passengers, continued to try to exit up the narrow stairway. And the al-Qaida fighters were seemingly confused by the new group of armed men who were thrust into the scene. They had started for the bomb and biomaterial, but now they were unsure about what was happening. They hesitated.

***

"Shoot them! All of them!" al-Wahlie screamed! An instant later the fighters opened fire again indiscriminately, unleashing a torrent of automatic weapon fire at anyone standing. The result was devastating as dozens of innocent people were mowed down.

***

"Oh, my god; it's a Greek SWAT team!" whispered Josh. "Stay flat on the floor, and keep inching toward the bomb. They must have been called out after the two policemen were shot trying to check out the flash-bang explosions!"

At first, al-Qaida fighters were firing into the crowd of subway passengers, sending dozens of them reeling from automatic weapon fire. But as the SWAT team began to return fire, the fighters turned their fire on the SWAT team members. The two lead members of the SWAT team were sent tumbling backward, hit by multiple rounds of automatic weapon fire. And as the gunfire swept the platform, subway passengers continued to fall.

As the Greek SWAT team came under fire, they tried to take cover, and soon it became a pitched firefight between the al-Qaida terrorists and the SWAT team. As the roar of gunfire and screams of the subway passengers echoed off the concrete walls, Josh and Gloria continued to slowly crawl through the crowd over bodies and through puddles of blood. They were almost to the bomb when Josh saw two al-Qaida fighters, who they had not noticed before, crouched over it, and one of the men had wires in his hand.

"Damn, they beat us to the bomb—shoot them!" yelled Josh. His first shot hit the man holding the wires in the side of the head killing him instantly. The fighter fell beside the bomb still holding the two detonator wires. But before Josh or Gloria could shoot the other fighter, he ducked down behind the dead man and jerked the two wires from his comade's dead hands.

"If if he put those wires together the detonator is armed and one push will explode the bomb!" yelled Josh. He leaped from his crouched position and tackled the al-Qaida fighter as the man began to connect the wires. The force of Josh's body knocked the man away from the bomb, and he dropped one of the wires. Josh then pinned him against the floor, quickly pulled his knife, and thrust it toward the man's throat.

Suddenly, a rifle butt smacked the side of Josh's head, and he fell off the al-Qaida fighter stunned and disoriented. A member of the

Greek SWAT team stood over him and kicked the knife from Josh's hand.

The fighter quickly rolled over, got to his knees, and grabbed the detonator wires. He was putting them together when Gloria screamed, "My god! Stop him!"

The SWAT team member gave Gloria a puzzled look, and did nothing to stop the fighter from connecting the wires. Gloria was still holding her Beretta, but the Greek SWAT team member was pointing his weapon at her, putting her under arrest. The fighter quickly finished connecting the wires, dropped them, and reached toward the detonator.

"Stop him! You have got to stop him!" yelled Gloria. The SWAT team didn't understand Gloria, however, and he still didn't move. But before the fighter could press the detonator, automatic weapon fire came from the remaining al-Qaida fighters, and a burst of slugs rippled across the SWAT team man's chest sending him sprawling backward. Gloria was squeezing the trigger of her Beretta before the SWAT team officer guarding her hit the ground, and this time she remembered what Josh had told her: Three quick shots to the head of the man about to press the detonator stopped the fighter's hand right above the plunger.

Gloria didn't have time to even react, however, because now a full-fledged fire fight at close quarters was in full swing between the remaining al-Qaida fighters, who were rushing toward where she was crouched, and three Greek SWAT team members who were still able to fight. The al-Qaida fighters were using some of the subway passengers for cover, and as they ran through the crowd of people, they fired toward the Greek SWAT team members who were trying to return fire without hitting the passengers. However, with hundreds of shots being fired, innocent people were being hit by direct fire and from rounds glancing off the concrete walls and floor. The platform floor was covered with bodies and pools of blood.

Josh was still lying on the floor—addled from the blow to the head, but trying to raise up—as Gloria screamed at him. "Josh! Help! The fighters are coming, and we can't hold them off much longer!"

The words were barely out of her mouth than a shot hit her in the shoulder sending her back against the concrete wall. Her Beretta fell from her hand and slid across the floor falling off the platform onto the train tracks.

"Josh, get up! Help me! They're coming!"

Automatic weapon fire was almost continuous, coming from the two remaining Greek SWAT team members who were flattened out on the floor trying to hold off a group of six al-Qaida fighters who were advancing through the panicked passengers. Two of the fighters jumped out of the crowd and sent a spray of AK fire at the two Greek SWAT team members, rolling one of them over. However, the other SWAT team member managed to return fire and both of the fighters were hit.

Josh had managed to rise to his knees and begin to search for his weapon, when the remaining four al-Qaida members turned fire on the Greek SWAT team member. He was killed in a blaze of fire, but took one of the fighters with him.

The remaining three fighters continued to rush toward Josh and the detonator, jumping over the bodies of fallen subway passengers, SWAT team men, and some their own dead and wounded men. Gloria had pulled herself up to a sitting position, and was frantically searching for a weapon. There was nothing around her. Then she thought of the knife Josh had given her when they were in Africa. It only had a 4-inch blade, but it was something. She opened it and got ready to throw.

Josh seemed to regained consciousness, and began scrambling to dodge the incoming al-Qaida rounds while he frantically trying to find his gun. A burst of AK fire narrowly missed him, but before the terrorist could fire again at point-blank range, he stumbled over the body of a Greek SWAT team member.

That hesitation was all Josh needed; he grasped his Glock and sent several rounds into the head of the lead fighter. The other two were almost on him, however, and one jerked his weapon up to fire at Josh. It would be a point-blank shot to the head from less than six feet.

Gloria threw the knife as hard as she could, and it hit the fighter right under the chin, and lodged in the fleshly part of his neck.

"*Ahaaaaa!*" A scream and then as he tried to pull the knife out, Josh emptied his Glock in his face. The other fighter, al-Wahlie, ignored Josh and rushed toward the detonator. Josh was on his feet immediately and tackled him just as his hand was about to press the plunger down. The two men were locked in a deadly struggle, but Josh had the upper hand with a strangle hold around the man's neck. As Josh applied the pressure, it looked as if the struggle would be over in seconds. Then there was a flash as the man's free hand pulled a knife from his pants and he began to slash randomly at the American.

Josh applied a tightening throat choke, but the fighter's knife slashed Josh's arm cutting a tendon. His arm, which was choking al-Wahlie, became useless, and as they struggled, the two men tumbled off the edge of the platform onto the subway rails.

With one arm useless and the al-Wahlie coming at him with a knife, Josh was in a terrible position. Al-Wahlie lunged at Josh, who managed to grab the man's knife-wielding arm, but as he did, they fell off the platform onto the subway tracks. Al Wahlie was on top of Josh, and he was thrusting his knife toward Josh's throat. Josh's strength was not enough to keep the knife, which al-Wahlie was gripping with both hands, from slowly approaching his throat. It was inches away when Josh felt a vibration. A train was rapidly approaching the station and both men were lying prone on the tracks—with al-Wahlie on top of Josh.

Josh figured he could keep the fighter's knife at bay for a few more seconds, but the fast-moving train would kill both of them. And then, when the Greek police moved the bomb and biomaterial, the booby-trapped bomb was sure to go off. He was the only one who could disarm it safely. He had one chance before the train ran over them.

Josh's physical fitness was beyond that of even the instructors at most gyms, especially his lower body strength. He tensed his lower body, and then with an upward thrust, flipped the man off as he rolled over against the wall of the platform. The train passed immediately over al-Wahlie, as the wheels brushed against Josh's leg.

"Ahaaaaa…"

The train came to a stop as Josh pulled himself back upon the platform and crawled toward the detonator.

"Gloria, help me disarm this thing—grab one of the flashlights and shine it on the detonator cap."

Josh managed to pull himself up to a sitting position as he got to the bomb, and Gloria dragged herself over to where a flashlight from one of the SWAT team members had fallen.

"I can't reach any further, Josh. Is this enough light?" Gloria said. She raised the flashlight over her head with her good arm so it would shine down on the booby-trapped trigger.

"Yeah; hold it right there," Josh replied. With his one good hand, he slowly removed the ground wire and booby-trapped trigger, and minutes later, he had completely removed the detonator device and had thrown it as far as he could down the platform. He examined the explosive device to be sure it didn't have a second booby-trap attached to the plastic explosive material, and when he was sure the bomb was completely disarmed, he crawled over to check on Gloria, who was a few feet away, leaning back against the concrete wall of the station and still holding the flashlight.

Then, for the first time, a sense of relief flooded over him. Josh slumped back against the concrete wall beside his compatriot, took a deep breath, and looked at her. She was applying a compress to her shoulder wound.

"We did it—thank God! We need to call Sinuie and get the containment team over here. Can you help me put a compress on my arm, too?"

"I can't Josh," she gasped, in pain. That last shot I took put my right arm out of commission."

"It's okay, just rest easy. I'll take care of it."

Josh ripped his shirt into shreds and tightly wrapped a strip of cloth around the knife wound to stop the bleeding. Then he helped wrap Gloria's shoulder wound.

"There, that should hold you until we get to the hospital—oh, yeah, remind me, we owe that Greek kid a new scooter, and one more thing: I've changed my mind. You could make SF."

A flood of lights filled the platform area as another Greek SWAT team, backed up by Greek Special Forces soldiers, rushed in.

The mission was over. It was time to call Nafisa.

www.ingramcontent.com/pod-product-compliance
Lightning Source LLC
Chambersburg PA
CBHW071204020726
47502CB00002B/535